Congressional Suicide

A Kenna Hannigan Mystery

Dan Winkle

DISCLAIMER

This is a work of fiction. Unless otherwise indicated, all the names, characters, businesses, places, events, and incidents in this book are either the product of the author's imagination or used in a fictitious manner. Any resemblance to actual persons, living or dead, or actual events is purely coincidental.

DEDICATED TO AND REMEMBRANCE OF

My sister ... a lover of a great mystery. Taken from us too soon, she now knows the answer to the greatest mystery of all.

SPECIAL THANKS TO

The trio that offered constructive criticism and, often times, brutal honesty: Lynn, Skip, and Trisha

PROLOGUE

"If there is any larceny in a man,
golf will bring it out."
Paul Gallico (1897-1976)
New York Times, 6 March, 1977

JUNE 2016—OUTSIDE MANASSAS, VIRGINIA

Hot, humid wind blew across a broad grassy hilltop. Lightning streaked the night sky and illuminated the sweat-beaded faces of two determined women. They may have appeared to be an unlikely duo, but this moment was meant to be. Concentration outside the aged, abandoned shack, Gran Lockwood was a polished Irish lady, now a naturalized American citizen by virtue of her late husband, who died far too young. She was forty years senior to her granddaughter, whose stare outside matched her own.

Kenna Hannigan followed Gran Lockwood's every move, as would any student with a penchant for learning from their teacher. The Irish good looks and inner drive of the elder had filtered down to bless the younger. The eyes, the expressions, the subtle movements, the concentration, and even speech patterns were all virtually identical, as was their calling card, the fiery red hair of a woman born of fire.

In the lightning, matching gray mackintoshes shimmered with rain that fell from a jagged hole in the roof and shed over a dead tree branch dangling through it. Wind howled through decayed walls with missing boards. Hanging from the swayback roof by a single length of bailing twine, a broken weathervane rattled against the rotten siding.

"Nervous?" Gran Lockwood asked.

"Of course," Kenna didn't add *because this is the first time you've allowed me to accompany you on an arrest.*

Gran Lockwood lifted her cell phone and typed in a text, *"In position."*

Her phone chirped, *"On the way."* She turned to Kenna, assessing her state of being.

As a young girl, Gran Fiadh Dougherty-Lockwood had followed in her father's footsteps. Fascinated by crime solving, she knew every Arthur Conan Doyle and Agatha Christie mystery by heart. Her specialty quickly evolved when her insight helped her father capture a high-end art thief. Blossoming in her twenties, she had been instrumental in locating Vermeer's *Lady Writing a Letter with her Maid,* stolen from Russborough House in Ireland.

Today, she was after an elusive thief involved in a three-million-dollar jewelry heist in Boynton Beach, Florida.

Following the money trail brought her north. Further leads and some undercover sleuthing brought them to this abandoned farm.

"Jeremy will be here shortly. Relax but remain alert. Anson Beck is an elusive man; some would say nothing more than a shadow."

"Shadows don't steal jewels," Kenna said, nerves on edge. "You're positive he'll show?"

"If he took Jeremy's bait of being a fence. Like all thieves, Beck wants to get rid of the evidence."

"Always thought it was about the money," Kenna added.

"For a professional thief, it's more, my dear. Oh, so much more."

Gran Lockwood checked the chamber of a Glock G26 subcompact pistol. Kenna lifted one from a shoulder holster and did the same.

"Ever had to use it?" Kenna asked.

"More than once, which is why I insisted you learn. With what you want to do … well, killers don't like to be caught."

"Apparently, neither do thieves, Gran," Kenna countered.

The clicks of Kenna's slide action filled a brief silence an instant before another roll of thunder. A shell was chambered. Her thumb pushed off the safety, then on. She slid the weapon back into the shoulder holster.

Vehicle lights out the window turned them. Kenna wiped a trickle of rain from an eyebrow to conceal a trembling hand. She pulled up the sleeve of her rain gear and cleaned her watch face. If violence came, it would be a first for her. Organization was her strong suit. *Then, why are you here?* She asked herself.

Kenna studied Gran Lockwood, whose eyes were fixed outside, "Without emotion, and at all times, it's all business," she remembered Gran saying before they left.

In his mid-30s and behind the wheel of a Ford Expedition, Jeremy "Wiggy" Heffernan didn't glance in their direction when he drove past the shack. He stopped in front of an aged, leaning wooden barn 50 yards away. He jumped out into the rain, opened the swinging doors, and drove inside.

Kenna leaned against the wall to stare out a broken window. A gust of wind loosened a large shard of glass that nearly slapped her face. She reached for it. A streak of lightning crisscrossed the hillside, followed instantly by a crack of thunder that rattled the entire shack. The weathervane slapped the window. She jumped. The glass sliced down the middle of her index finger. The weathervane broke free, shattering the remaining glass. She jerked it back, only to have a second shard lay open a deeper cut that extended the lifeline up her palm. Blood spread rapidly across her hand.

"Dammit!" she yelled and spun against the wall.

Gran Lockwood grabbed her hand and tugged a kerchief tight around the wound. Blood soaked it quickly. Kenna tried to flex her fingers but couldn't.

"Got a nerve," she said near a scream. "I can't move my fingers."

"There's a first aid kit in the Expedition," Gran Lockwood said.

Gran Lockwood turned for the door just as car headlights flashed across the room from a fold in the land 300 yards to the east … the throaty growl of an engine filtered through the rain.

"No time now," Kenna said, "our guest has arrived."

The elder's attention was no longer on the cut; they squatted. Rain peppered the roof like hail. Heavy breathing filled the air. Large, nervous eyes looked out the wall cracks. A new Jeep Rubicon passed. Its headlights crept up the wall, turning from white to the vehicle's red taillights that brightened them in a demonic hue.

Gran Lockwood patted Kenna's shoulder, "Sit this one out, leanbh."

"You aren't going in alone, Gran," Kenna said in a raised whisper. "I have two hands."

The Jeep bounded over uneven ground, around an abandoned stone water well, and stopped at the barn doors. While surveying the area, Anson Beck, a tall, muscular man with glaring eyes, stepped into the rain and opened the 15-foot-tall double barn doors. Inside, Wiggy leaned against the Expedition, unarmed and calm. Once back inside the Jeep, Beck hesitated, eyes continually scanning the area.

"What a sly one, Mr. Beck," Gran Lockwood said to herself and turned to the door.

"Gran, aren't we waiting for backup?"

"Stop watching cop shows, Kenna. There is none, and I'm not letting him escape again. Wiggy's inside," Gran Lockwood hardened, something Kenna had never seen, and shoved a finger against her shoulder. "Stay out front in case the bastard makes a break."

The kerchiefs around Kenna's hand were soaked red. Regardless, she made her way to the door behind Gran Lockwood. Gran turned when Kenna grabbed her arm. Their eyes locked in a silent battle of wills: Kenna wanted her to wait; Gran insisted that they go.

Inside the barn, Beck stopped the Jeep behind the Expedition. He stepped out, hand firmly on a pistol in his back, and swung the doors closed.

As they stepped out, a bolt of lightning illuminated the barn like a black-and-white photo. A second later, the still was broken by the crack of thunder. Kenna knew Gran was right; the opportunity … Beck … had presented itself. Now was the time. She leaned against the wall. Her elder hurried through the wind-swept night until a silhouette against nature's backdrop. Kenna swallowed hard and lifted the Glock with her left, non-shooting hand. Trembling, a curse pierced her lips.

"Rather be having a single malt," she whispered to herself and …

She moved into the driving rain. Dizzy, she grabbed the shack doorframe. Horizontal rain beat against her face. Unable to focus, she walked towards the barn. When she was 100 feet from the large double doors, the first gunshot preceded a man's scream. The Jeep's engine roared to life.

As best she could, Kenna ran. The Jeep smashed backward through the barn doors. The aged hinges snapped like a pencil. Decayed wood disintegrated as if hit by a bomb. The Jeep's windshield shattered when Wiggy fired from inside. Gran Lockwood fired from the side as the door hit her, knocking her aside. The Jeep passed; Beck fired an Uzi while passing her. Gran Lockwood was thrown back by the impact. Beck fired into her again while she was on the ground.

Kenna screamed, "No, Gran! No!"

Hurrying forward, Kenna fired, blowing holes through the Jeep's windshield and rearview mirror, slicing open Beck's cheek. Beck fired at Wiggy and accelerated the Jeep backward towards Kenna. She lunged to the side too late. The Jeep's rear bumper slammed into her leg, throwing her across the ground. She slammed against the stone water well, landed face down in the mud, and rolled over as the Jeep slid to a stop a few inches from her head. Anson Beck stared down on her and shifted. She reached for her fractured leg, then her gun a yard away in the mud.

"Incompetent buffoons," he snarled.

Their eyes locked in an eternal moment for Kenna. She tried to focus on his face but couldn't. She grappled for the pistol, only to pull back a handful of rain, mud, and grass.

Illuminated by the headlights, blood covering his face, Wiggy staggered from the barn with a small satchel. He stumbled towards the Jeep, firing. Beck lifted the Uzi to Kenna's narrowed eyes, but she collapsed once again.

Wiggy's bullets blew out the Jeep's windshield; one hit Beck in the arm. With a scream, he floored the accelerator, spinning the Jeep away and spraying Kenna with mud. Beck fired a burst at Wiggy; he grabbed a thigh, then a shoulder.

Gunfire stopped; taillights darted into the driving rain. The roar of the engine subsided as the Jeep reached the distant fold in the land and disappeared. Mud and rain filled Kenna's eyes. It was then she felt the burning of a bullet in her upper chest. She turned back to the barn. With a great roar of internal pain and loss, Wiggy collapsed to his knees alongside Gran Lockwood.

With gritted teeth, Kenna pulled herself alongside Wiggy and Gran Lockwood. Wiggy opened the satchel; Gran Lockwood looked at the jewels inside with a satisfied grimace of finality. She reached for Kenna and Wiggy; she went limp, and her eyes closed for eternity.

Great emotion filled Kenna as she touched her grandmother's dead face. She turned to where the taillights disappeared with an immortal scream. Energy spent, she collapsed alongside Gran Lockwood. Lightning lit the sky, and thunder cracked as Wiggy lifted his cell phone.

I

JUNE 2019—CONGRESSIONAL COUNTRY CLUB—
BETHESDA, MARYLAND

Heavy rain inundated the golf course. Lightning and thunder provided the special effects. A bit tipsy, Kenna had become a seasoned sports reporter, though reporting was the furthest thing from her mind that night. She walked along the cart path near the 18th green, sipping on a wine bottle. Her grandmother's beauty remained with her, even in the rain-soaked clothes and stringy wet hair. Uncharacteristically, she seemed a bit lost … and sad. That happens when you mix too many wines and whiskeys with memories of losing the most important person in your life.

Kenna was, as her father said, "A gnat's ass taller than five-six" and athletically muscular at 140. She didn't work out to maintain her figure. She was one of the blessed few to be born with it. She had what her mother called "tomboyish good looks." But by the present condition of her love life … non-existent … Kenna often doubted if her mother knew what she was talking about. But the real reason behind her situation was simple: she was far too busy for a relationship.

Much to her father's chagrin, Kenna came out of the

womb the wrong sex, at least for him. He wanted a son to mold into the next Heisman Trophy winner and then to take a position at his side, a serious journalist to direct the family television business into the future. Making things worse, Kenna wasn't very good at sports, "mediocre at best," in her words. She loved the competitiveness and determination of the players, but that's where the similarities ended. Kenna was driven by her work and enjoyed a good party, oftentimes much to her own chagrin.

She had no interest in joining the family television business. The corporate environment was juxtaposed with her free spirit. Father pounded it into her that she would go nowhere as an independent. At first, it seemed he was right, but she survived that bleak, dark year. Then, at her grandmother's insistence from the grave and Wiggy's insistence above ground, she joined her father in a loose arrangement, allowing her freedom. From then on, she and Wiggy had done what they swore to do that night in Virginia.

She toasted the storm and took a drink, her words buried in the thunder, "We'll find him, Gran."

As the thunder faded, a distant, muffled, angry, and demanding voice turned her. In the dim Clubhouse lights and rain, two male silhouettes stood near the 18th green. Aggressive and angry, a small, thin man grabbed a larger but docile man's coat lapel, jerking him forward. The thin man continued with muffled, angry instructions.

Kenna squinted to see more clearly; it didn't help. She took a big drink, "Friday night at the fights … Congressional style … roll the camera, Wiggy."

The argument continued, as did her interest in it, then yelled, "Don't you know it's raining?"

The silhouettes spun in her direction. She anticipated a sharp rebut about minding her own business, but none came. The two men shared a brief verbal exchange masked by the storm. The thin man released the docile man's lapels and hurried away. Broken, the docile man walked slowly, dejectedly in the opposite direction.

Kenna shrugged and stumbled from the cart path into the trees. She leaned against a tree, lowered her pants, and squatted to pee. Finished, she tried to stand, lost her balance, and fell. "Ah, not in the …"

Disgusted at her hands and clothes, she tried to stand but lost her balance. With a laugh, she lost her balance and threw the bottle, trying to break the fall. It smashed against a tree. She slid down a short slope and came to rest against the tree. She lifted the broken bottle; it pricked her finger. She watched the blood mix with the rain and trail down her extended lifeline. Emotion overcame her.

"Three years today, Gran," she said. "I miss our cocktail sessions, your guidance, but mostly, your wisdom."

She rolled onto her back, allowing the rain to wash her hands and face. A flash of lightning close, immediate thunder. She raised a hand defensively to a light in her eyes, realizing it was a flashlight.

"Always talkin' ta yerself," Wiggy said. "Could hear ya from the Clubhouse."

Wiggy's a highly irritated, muscular, and barrel-chested Bostonian of Irish descent. The Irish blood, though, was just background. To Wiggy, the blood that ran through his veins was distinctly American. A human fireplug, he was four inches taller than Kenna, 70 pounds heavier, and carried their camera and equipment with little effort. He was Kenna's sidekick, her righthand man, the one behind the camera she smiled into. But, oh, so much more. Tonight, his expression hid the disappointment behind his eyes.

"What the hell you doin' out here, Fiery? Are ye fuckin' thick, as they say in the old country?" He motioned to the rain, pulled her from the ground, and steadied her.

"Remembering the night," she said.

"So, ya got yerself totally sloshed. Don't ya have any sense, bein' out in this rain?"

"Had to piss," she offered.

"There's a perfectly good jacks in the room."

"Got lost tryin' to find it … musta been the third Jameson."

"Three? Ya was on that when I paid the tab, lass."

She remembered the argument, "About saw a fight on the 18th green."

He examined her hand, "Looks like ya been in one."

"Brought back the night … with Beck …"

"Get yer head out. Don't want you slidin' into that dark place ya did back then, lass."

"Never happen, Wiggy. I owe it to Gran to find that bastard if it takes the rest of my life."

"We both do," Wiggy reassured her. "Until then, you can't wander off on yer own."

"I won't hide in fear, Wiggy. I still carry the Glock Gran gave me," she patted her back belt, realizing it wasn't there, "Well, in spirit."

"Ya left it in the room again," he said. "For this cover to work, we hafta follow your father's idea. That means …"

"I know … we still gotta pay the bills."

"These late nights are killin' me." He playfully slapped her butt. "If ye get sick over this, I'm gonna kick this pretty butt-a yours."

Kenna laughed, wobbling along the cart path towards the Clubhouse, "You know I like the rough stuff, Wiggy."

They both knew her words were in jest and knew why. She turned a serious expression, "I saw him again … Beck … that night at the barn. It was … so real."

Lightning and thunder gave her pause. Kenna turned to the 18th green across the pond and asked herself, *had the silhouettes been a vision, as well … or real?*

II

SATURDAY—DAY 1

On the veranda of the Clubhouse bar, important and powerful people lingered with coffee or tea, depending on their self-proclaimed status, as measured by the elevated angle of the nose. Using all the primary colors, plain knit blouses to prints, they arrived to impress the impressionable. In a futile attempt to maintain youth, middle-aged men sported casual pants, Lacoste's and Polo's, with the arms of sweaters seemingly ironed over their shoulders, tied in a single loop on their chest. It didn't seem to matter that it would soon be 90 degrees. Yet, fashion couldn't camouflage the aging evidence of colored hair, toupees and comb-overs, expanded waistlines, liver-spotted hands, and crow's-feet eyes. Women of too many years, children, and slices of cake at afternoon teas festooned the event with short skirts or Spandex that implied a lack of consciousness or ignorance of the view that followed them.

There were a few, the stuffy tea-sippers with elevated noses, festooned in thousand-dollar suits, dresses, or pant suits from the world's most expensive tailors. They stood out, even in this elite crowd. But that, after all, was the point.

"Here, look at me," it said silently but profoundly.

One of the latter during normal times, Senator Harvey Chamberlain, had been a senior member of Congress for over 20 years. These were, however, far from *normal times*. With the eyes of a nervous man, he wiped his mouth with a cloth napkin and tossed it to the center of the table. This morning, he had foregone coffee; whiskey was his drink of choice. His eyes danced through the crowd, half ignoring constituents who called his name and shook his hand. Out of character, none of it registered. Everything and everyone were irrelevant.

Harvey Chamberlain wasn't only nervous; fear consumed him. Disheveled, hair mussed, face unshaven, his linen suit was wrinkled as if slept in the night before. Indeed, it had been. A brilliant red power tie hung loose over the rumpled, whiskey-stained white shirt. He glanced at his watch repeatedly as if time would change for his benefit.

Clearly waiting for someone, he looked to the 18th green and remembered what had been said the night before. He finished the drink and waved at the waiter for another.

III

Kenna was anxious when she stepped from the golfcart at the 18th tee box. Thankfully, she had burned off the hangover on the front nine. No, she wasn't any good at golf and freely admitted it. This was her penance, spending a casual morning with her father's old family friend. She waited at the golfcart while Senator Malcolm Bridgewater and two other Senators teed off. Exhausted by dutifully paying homage to the *great man*, she wanted it to be over.

Malcolm Bridgewater was in his late 60s and still very active physically. Kenna had known him since childhood. Her father was a senior member of the Party in Texas, and they had attended many fund-raising events and conventions together. Photos in the family album attested that the senator had attended her first birthday and baptism.

Malcolm played a decent game of golf and preferred lesser clubs, which resulted in him nearly always being in the middle of the fairway. No one had ever accused the Tennessee senator of being in the middle politically. Off the course, he was an arrogant, professional politician who'd been in Washington more years than home. He remained guarded around Kenna. She was, after all, a journalist. They could be your greatest ally or your worst enemy. Malcolm teed off, driving the ball into the center of the fairway.

"Nice, Malcolm, right down the middle," a junior Senator said with a laugh.

Ignoring the banter, Malcolm moved to the cart as the others teed off. He noted the boredom in Kenna's gaze and dropped his 3-wood into the bag.

"Been meaning to ask," Kenna said to break the ice, "how is the great State of Tennessee?"

"Still making whiskey."

"When's the last time you were home?" Kenna continued, taking a jab at him. "You know, to relax on the porch, put your feet up, sip whiskey, and pat the bloodhound."

"Don't have a bloodhound. Whiskey tastes the same here as in Tennessee."

"There are other capable men to take the gavel … you've spoken of Senator Chamberlain, for example."

With Kenna's Cheshire grin, Bridgewater didn't like the inference he should retire. Yet, like the game of golf, he would also play her game. No one could out-debate him.

"And leave government in the hands of the young rabble? Never."

"You've slain enough dragons in your lifetime,

Malcolm."

"More lurking in the next cave. You, for example."

Kenna found humor in that, wondering if she had gone too far. She ignored his annoyance and walked to the women's tee. She jokingly checked the wind and drove the ball 150 yards down the center of the fairway.

"Fortunate for you, Kenna, you are a better reporter than golfer," Bridgewater offered.

"It's in the fairway … first time today."

"They say there's always one shot that brings you back," Bridgewater said.

Pleased with her effort, Kenna slid into the golfcart. Driving, Bridgewater followed the senators in the other cart. Kenna wiped the sweat from her brow.

"Is it always this hot in June?"

"Thought you were half Texan?" Malcolm got his dig in, knowing Kenna hadn't been to Texas in years.

"It's a dry heat in Dallas."

"Last hole, your suffering's almost over."

"Thank God. I need a drink."

"From what I heard, you had your fill last night."

"Just keeping the great state of Tennessee in business, senator."

"Which we appreciate, my girl. I spoke with your father this morning—"

"And we were having such a good day. Let's not ruin it until we reach the nineteenth."

"Then, I'll ply you with drinks. I need to find out what you're really doing here," he said. She allowed her lips to curl up; Bridgewater was not amused. "And if it has anything to do with finding your grandmother's killer."

After playing their approach shots, they joined the other two senators on the 18th green. With the pond and Clubhouse as backdrop, a slight breeze rustled the trees. Bridgewater lined a 30-foot putt, then struck it. The ball lipped into the cup but spun out; he groaned with a curse.

Kenna snickered, placed her ball for a 20-foot putt, and lifted a Gold Lion coin ball marker. A sharp edge on the marker pricked her finger; she recoiled with a chirp.

"Warned your father about that old ball marker when he carried it," Bridgewater said. "He never learned, either."

Kenna ignored her finger. She looked up with intensity. She wanted this … and struck the ball …

IV

The hot summer sun settled over the Clubhouse. Sweat beading on his face, Chamberlain stared at the 18th green, not seeing the group playing, not caring. He had never felt so weak, been so out of control. Indeed, strength of conviction had always been his calling card. Today, had to reverse the downfall; it just had to. There was no going forward if it didn't. It would be the end.

Laughter roared from the end of the veranda. Golf aficionados boasted of their knowledge and expertise in the game. To the casual listener, one might think these weekend hackers were professionals. Chamberlain ignored them; none could shoot under 100.

Chamberlain stared solemnly at his whiskey glass. Dangerously low, he raised it for another; the waiter acknowledged. Chamberlain couldn't remember how many he'd drunk. Today, it didn't really matter; only one thing did.

It took little more than a month for his perfect world to be turned upside down. Any moment now, a man was going to walk from the cloud of a very old nightmare to reintroduce the senator's past, something he believed had been buried decades ago.

Fresh from the course and glistening with sweat, a group of golfers gathered near the senator's table. Champagne was poured into tall crystal glasses, a toast lifted to sunburned skin and an escape from the weekly grind. Without clubs, they practiced the air guitar of golf with overemphasized back swings and follow-throughs.

Chamberlain turned away; this group couldn't shoot under 100, either. Any other day, he might have joined in the revelry. But today, there was nothing to laugh about. He stiffened. A broad man in a cheap, plain brown suit and pencil knit tie shouldered through the crowd. The senator's attention narrowed; his brow furrowed. There's no need to look at the watch now.

"Senator Chamberlain," the stranger said with a heavy German accent. "Beautiful sun today, no?"

Chamberlain's answer was questioned in silence, *Should I know you?* The German stood over six feet tall, in his mid-50s, with a defined muscular body, bright blue eyes, blond hair, and stout Teutonic nose. *The byproduct of German racial purification programs,* Chamberlain thought. There were no pleasantries when the German took the chair beside him. The senator swallowed the last mouthful of whiskey, soured by it. The waiter brought the senator's refill and a pint of beer for the unwelcome guest.

The German continued, "But, too warm for me. I prefer cooler climates."

Chamberlain frowned, "You wanted to meet; I'm here."

"Very well. To some, the document in my possession is priceless, no?" Again, Chamberlain was silent. The German took a drink, then lifted the glass against the sun. "Not German, but it has a robust flavor."

"You didn't cross the Atlantic to critique the beer," the senator grumbled, feinting confidence where there was none.

"Answer my question," The German smiled against the lip of his glass … a slow drink and swallowed. "Unlike these golfers, I play no games, senator. Your assistant didn't tell me—"

"Avery Gowen doesn't know everything about me," Chamberlain insisted, though weakening. "I say again, get to the point, Herr Altmann. What I think about the document's value has no relevance."

"Americans … always in a hurry. You should learn to enjoy the surroundings." Altmann's brilliant eyes followed a middle-aged woman as she strolled past with a smile. "For instance."

"I don't have time for this ridiculous—"

"Why else would we be here, senator?" Altmann asked

with a wry smile. He set the glass down, eyes narrowing. "Very well. Today, your nightmares become reality."

"A terrorist's creed," Chamberlain interrupted, "if I understand your past as Gowen painted it."

The senator's eyes flicked to the crowd. *Where's the damn whiskey when I need it*, he wondered, then realized it was in his hand. Altmann leaned forward and slid the pint glass to the center of the table with both hands, clinking against Chamberlain's whiskey glass.

"So, it appears that Mr. Gowen told you more about me than I was led to believe."

"Yes, for instance, your name—"

"Is unimportant," the German snapped. "What I possess is the discussion topic."

"You couldn't know the document's significance; you weren't there."

"Whether I was there or not has no relevance. That I possess it does," Altmann said with a crisp whisper, followed by a full drink. "I planned this mission long before the Taliban fell. I predicted they would, you know, and escaped before being executed."

Chamberlain couldn't hide the shaking hand that lifted the whiskey, "I could call the U.S. Marshals and tell them of our visit."

The German took a drink of beer, annoyed by the game. He slid his cell phone across the table, motioning for Chamberlain to use it. Chamberlain cringed, refusing.

"Save your hollow threats, senator," Altmann demanded with satisfaction. "If you believe the document isn't authentic, then I understand there are journalists in the Clubhouse waiting for the big announcement tomorrow. No doubt, at least one would be interested."

The senator's face flushed; shadows deepened beneath sleep-deprived eyes. The German remained impassive and reached into his coat. The sun bounced off a single sheet of white paper he handed to the senator. The politician opened it and froze. In an instant, Chamberlain was alone within himself, oblivious to the surroundings. He lifted the blank stare of a man a few feet from the top of Everest the instant before his frozen, oxygen-deprived body collapsed.

"I didn't think you really … how did you come across this?" Chamberlain hesitated when a hush befell the veranda. He folded the document and lifted it to a breast jacket pocket.

Altmann continued, "Show the others. It is, as I saw in a Western movie last night, *my bona fides*. "

Chamberlain's lower lip trembled. The glass slipped and

fell, spilling whiskey on the glass-topped table. Yet, he did not react. The waiter wiped away the mess and offered to clean his trousers. The senator didn't feel the cold on his legs and pushed him away.

"A long … time ago," Chamberlain mumbled when the waiter had gone. "All copies were destroyed many years ago."

"Obviously not. I retrieved this from Taliban Intelligence and kept the original for my private collection. I knew it would be valuable someday. I do apologize. I don't believe I told your man Gowen I knew the Taliban's Intelligence Chief."

"So, this is about … blackmail?"

"Such a nasty word. In today's political and social climate, I prefer … business."

"And how much will this business transaction cost me?"

"Five million dollars."

"That's ridiculous!" Chamberlain bawled with a heavy breath.

"I am happy to make it ten."

"No!" Chamberlain yelled. The crowd spun to them; he calmed. "Between my divorce and this … I might as well kill myself."

"Which leaves you with an obvious decision to make," Altmann offered. "Pay or contact the others. They have no choice but to help."

Chamberlain lowered his stare, "It was a study group. I was just an observer."

Altmann chuckled, "Come now, senator, we both know the opposite to be true."

"I'm not lying!" Weakened, revealing he was, indeed, lying, the senator shifted his weight. "But … it has no bearing on today."

"The traitor's credo," Altmann whispered and leaned forward on muscular arms. All emotion left his face; it was no longer a game. "My demand is not negotiable. You have twenty-four hours."

"Dammit, I need more time!"

"Which I do not have," Altmann retorted. "We both know the Party coffers are more than adequate to cover this … investment."

"What do you mean, we both know?"

"I've been dealing with the Chinese, the Afghanis, and the Iraqis for a long time, senator. They have been very cooperative in telling me about payments made to your political action committees," the German finished his beer.

"What does that have to do with this?" Chamberlain snapped out the paper. "Nothing, nothing at all!"

"It's all linked, senator. PAC money. One of the great faults of the American system, but also its brilliance. Do you think the pubic realize you keep the PAC money you don't spend … after leaving office?" Altmann snickered with confidence. "The millions … contact the Party! See who among them is your friend."

Chamberlain paused at the German's demand. His entire life's work flashed before his mind's eye, "The Party? You can't involve the—"

"I don't intend to. I'll leave that up to you."

"My God—"

"The Party or your God make no difference, senator."

"There are people who will lose a lot if this is made public."

"Dare we say … everything," the German said with a wry grin. "But that's something they will live with, not me."

The German stood but froze in anger when the senator grabbed his arm, "I am prepared to deal, Altmann."

"Then, organize the payment."

"I swear to you I can't get that much. I … I could give you something else."

"There is nothing else I want."

"There might be … hear me out," Chamberlain pleaded.

"I don't care … your friends in the Party, your personal PAC savings, you have my demand. Bring it tonight, or I will paper this city with the truth."

"But you said twenty—"

"Your weakness sickens me," Altmann drank Chamberlain's whiskey and walked away.

Neither man saw that, across the pond, Malcolm Bridgewater and the Senators walked from the 18th green, congratulating Kenna, who was holding up her index finger, the *one shot*.

V

The round had been the best golf of Kenna's life, but that didn't mean a lot. Taking handicap into account, though, she had beaten all three of the senators. That did mean something … to her.

Coming off the 18th green, Wiggy spoiled her celebration. He met her with a golfcart and reminded her they were at the Country Club to work. He was that way, you know. Work always took precedence. Drinks at the 19th hole had to wait. After a quick clean-up in the room, Kenna held on for dear life while Wiggy sped the golfcart in the direction of the practice tees.

"It's not the Indy five hundred, Wiggy, they'll wait," she said.

Her words had no bearing on his driving. He sped along the path without slowing for other carts and golfers. It did, however, attract the glares of Country Club employees. Wiggy ignored them. This day was no different than any other. He was always a man on a mission.

"Professionals don't like waitin', Fiery," he said. "They're busy, too, and like even less bein' disrespected."

It was that honesty Kenna admired in Wiggy. He was as

much her teacher and confidante as anyone had been, save Gran Lockwood. But then the Grand Ole Dame, as he called her, had taught them both the art of story and their greater passion, solving crimes.

'Jeremy is like a child in a candy shop while also being the bull in the China shop,' Gran Lockwood had said. *'But, above all else, he is honorable and trustworthy. He will never abandon you or lie to you.'*

It was Wiggy that got Kenna's head into the reporting game, but it hadn't been easy. He bucked the formative years of her father's strict guidance, telling her to *forget that rubbish'* and be herself. Derick Hannigan went out of his way to undermine Wiggy and the Grand Ole Dame. If Kenna was to be a reporter, she would be one in the family-owned business, not as a freelance.

After Gran Lockwood's death, that changed. Kenna's inheritance gave her a cushion to afford what she wanted, not what her father wanted, and to be what she, not others, wanted her to be. She lived simply, except for the Manor House in Boston, which Gran left her. It was where she met Wiggy so many years ago and where she went to reflect.

Wiggy slid the cart to a stop behind the roped-off practice tees. Reporters formed a half-circle in front of professional golfers Ko Jin-young, Jessica Korda, and Lexi

Thompson. Wiggy jumped out and grabbed the shoulder-held camera, tossing a cordless microphone to Kenna.

"You'll be at the back, so let 'em know yer there."

"When you ever known me to be shy, Wiggy?"

Kenna put on her reporter's face and made her way to the crowd. Wiggy slapped her on the back for encouragement, working the crowd for the best angle to include Kenna and the women professionals. She began into the microphone as if it had been rehearsed:

"Our travels this week bring us to the famed Congressional Country Club in Bethesda, Maryland, just outside the Nation's Capital. We've been invited as part of a two-fold visit. The first is to get a sneak preview of the planned improvements to the Blue Course. Perhaps most important, though, is the announcement of future events. Rumors are circulating that the Women's PGA will be at Congressional in a few years. Hopefully, the professionals behind me can shed some light on that."

Kenna shouldered into Randal Duncan, a tall, handsome reporter roughly her age, "Randy, this is the ladies' announcement. Did you have a recent sex change operation?"

Randal blushed, but it was short-lived with the crowd's

chuckle, "Golf Magazine reports on the entire game, Kenna, regardless of the sex."

With the crowd's full attention on her, Kenna went in for the kill, "I find that interesting. Everyone here, including our lovely and very talented lady professionals, would like to know why, over the past six months, there has been only one woman on the cover. Could you shed some light on that for us?"

The crowd, Ko, Jessica, and Lexi looked to Randal for an answer. Scrambling for self-control, Randal stiffened. He didn't like confrontation and didn't have an answer.

"I'm just a reporter, Kenna. I don't do layout design or approve the issue."

"Maybe you should report to the editor that female golfers of the world are watching … and reading."

By now, Kenna stood in front of the reporters with Ko, Jessica, and Lexi's full attention. While recording, Wiggy worked his way to the side for the best angle. He gave Kenna a thumbs up.

"Ladies, what can you tell us of the upcoming announcement?"

An LPGA official walked onto the practice tee, waving her arms, interrupting the gathering, "That will be done at the announcement tomorrow. So, I suggest you all attend. Right now, these ladies have a meeting to attend."

The reporters followed, shouting last-second questions at Ko, Jessica, and Lexi. Kenna did not. For her, it was over when it was over. She wasn't and never would be a paparazzi. Wiggy joined her with a bottle of water, which she guzzled eagerly.

"Nice job getting their attention, Fiery. I'll see if I can arrange a one-on-three with the lassies."

"You might want to address them another way."

"Aye, Dame Hannigan. I'll be on me best behavior," he replied and turned away. "Been tryin' me whole life to get the Gaeilge outta me mouth."

As they walked from the roped enclosure, a young girl shoved a cap to her. Kenna looked up, somewhat taken aback, "My first autograph. Thank you."

"I want to be a reporter like you when I grow up."

Autograph in hand, the girl smiled and hurried away to her mother. Kenna and Wiggy loaded into the cart and eased it into motion towards the Clubhouse.

"Any good angles?" she asked.

"Nah, horrible material, probably trash it in the room," he said sarcastically. He steered around the girl and her mother. Kenna and the girl exchanged waves. "I'll only say it once …"

"I know, we should've been on time," Wiggy started to object; she stopped him. "I should have been."

They followed the professionals' and reporters' carts and peeled off near the practice green. Wiggy stopped at the side of the Clubhouse. Stepping out, Kenna turned to a commotion behind.

Wiggy jumped out, demanding, "I'll not have ya interrupting her work."

The words were directed at Senator Bridgewater, now in full battle gear … meaning tailored suit and tie, polished wingtips. Kenna tensed at his presence. Malcolm had something up his sleeve. She saw it behind those devious, aged, but oh-so-intense eyes.

"I don't mean to interrupt …"

"Ye already have," Wiggy spat out with anger.

"If I had called, Jeremy, you would have forbidden my seeing the girl. I just want a word about something important."

"That couldn't have been said over eighteen holes this morning?" Wiggy objected.

"It just came up, I'm afraid. It won't take long."

"It's never that simple with ya, senator."

"Twice in one day, Malcolm. To what do I owe this honor?" Kenna asked, separating the bull and the matador.

"A politician's work is never done," Bridgewater boasted.

Wiggy snarled, "I'll tend to the equipment and material, lass. Don't get yerself into somethin' outside the work."

Kenna patted Wiggy on the shoulder, "No chance."

"That not be what he thinks," Wiggy said. "Watch the slight-a hand."

"Go off and let me speak to the girl alone, you old potato farmer," Bridgewater insisted.

The pupil frowned at the teacher. Mumbling his discontent, Wiggy gathered the equipment and strode off towards the Clubhouse.

"You and father have a lot in common, Malcom. One is that neither of you realize I'm no longer a girl."

"Always will be to us."

Kenna saw something in Malcolm's eyes she didn't like. He expected her to still be the snot-nosed kid of 20 years ago, starry-eyed in the presence of the nation's political elite. She wasn't now and doubted the senator understood that.

With more than three decades on The Hill, Bridgewater

wielded power only a few equalled. As the oldest sitting member of Congress, his commanding presence was revealed in eyes that pierced others like a Judas cradle. His power and control were not lost on his constituents, who paid homage when they strolled along the path towards the Clubhouse.

Brief conversations seemed genuine. Yet, Kenna knew the opposite to be true. She had heard and seen it many times. The smile was as much a smokescreen as the warm grip. Both were lethal. Malcolm Bridgewater was, first and foremost, a politician who chewed up friend and foe alike and left nothing for regurgitation. When alone …

"I need your help on something, my girl."

Kenna leaned against a tree and lifted a palm, "You needn't go any further, Malcolm. I sensed you were up to something. Before …"

Ignoring her, Bridgewater continued, "Harvey Chamberlain … something's not right with him. He and Gloria are divorcing."

"Send 'em to a marriage counselor."

"He hasn't been on the floor for more than two weeks," Bridgewater grabbed Kenna's arm; she didn't like it. "We were supposed to meet and talk about it, but he'd already left. The waiter said he talked to another man and left with a blank stare.”

“Have Jimmy take care of it,” Kenna said, annoyed with this exchange. “That’s his specialty, isn’t it?”

“Too close to home. I want it kept quiet until I know what he’s doing.”

“And you think I’ll keep it quiet?” the not-so-snot-nosed kid asked, put out.

“As a favor to me, yes.”

A political favor was akin to a political noose tightening around her neck. There was little in life she detested more. She had seen it too many times with Bridgewater and her father, had watched the two titans manipulate and cajole their way to the top. It didn’t matter who stepped in their way; they were swept aside like the regurgitated refuse. She never wanted any part of their life or their game and wanted even less of Bridgewater’s now.

“When Wiggy finds out you’ve asked me to do this, he may turn into that old terrorist you always talk about.”

“There’s no need for him to know.”

“I don’t keep anything from Wiggy,” Kenna insisted, indignant.

Anger filled Bridgewater. He understood loyalty only to

him. He glanced at his watch, "A civil servant's work is never done, you know."

You mean leach on society, Kenna thought. She'd heard it all before, hundreds of times. Soon, ingratiating platitudes would be showered on her to lower her over the Judas cradle with a smile, to have the obedient *snot-nosed kid* bow her head and accept the torture. He was the political disease, in a constant search for an executioner to perform the dirty work.

"Like I said, have your caged leopard Jimmy do it."

Malcolm and her father spoke of Kenna's narrow view of life, while they believed everyone should pay homage to theirs. What everyone else did or wanted was inconsequential, if not on their behalf and to their benefit.

"Thanks to Gran Lockwood," Kenna continued. "I'm different from you and father, always have been. I won't give up what's important to me for what's important to you."

"Even for your country?"

She found humor in that, "Sell it on the campaign trail, Malcolm."

"Then, you won't help?" Bridgewater asked, grabbing Kenna's arm.

"Your strongarm tactics disgust me, always have."

Kenna removed the aged hand from her arm, surprised at the strength in his grip. "We'll talk after the announcement."

"That may be too late."

The politician's trademark: the world was going to end if she didn't bend to his way. Kenna squinted at a distant reflection of sunlight and turned away from Judas' cradle.

"Then, it'll be too late."

VI

The longest-sitting member of Congress was also one of the oldest-standing members of Congressional Country Club. Senator Bridgewater had arranged for Kenna to stay in the Premier Residence on the course, Suite No. 40 in the Clubhouse. Being from the old school, where sacrifices and cheap hotel rooms in fleabag hotels built character, Wiggy had disapproved. It was one issue on which they disagreed. His stance reminded her too much of her troubled year after Gran Lockwood's murder.

Suite No. 40 was on the top floor of the Clubhouse, on a wing away from the hustle and bustle of everyday activity. The multiple-room apartment was immaculate, with expensive furniture from various corners of the world. Paintings were originals by renowned artists, with hand-carved sculptures and vases. Each day, fresh bouquets of flowers were placed on the entry table in the living room and in the bedrooms. Fresh fruits were left in a basket on the bar. The sheets were turned down in the evening. A Ghirardelli chocolate was placed on each pillow. The mahogany wet bar was fully stocked; specialty items were complimentary.

Kenna now awaited the call to vacate the room. Relaxed from a massage in the spa, Kenna drank a beer on the balcony, taking in the evening sun. Leaning on the balustrade, she smiled down at the activity around the club's two swimming pools. Golfers played on the 10th, 15th, and 18th greens. Ground crews drove carts across the course. A knock at the door. She looked at her phone for the time and strolled through the room of overstuffed chairs and posh throw rugs.

"Wiggy's in a hurry for a whiskey," she said to herself. She pulled open the door to the adjoining rooms.

Wiggy looked up from slipping on his trousers, "What's the hurry, lass?"

"I thought …" A knock at the main door into the suite interrupted her.

She turned for the door. Wiggy followed, deck shoes in-hand, hopping into trousers. Kenna opened the door.

Agent Miriam Edelman and Agent Vinny Salvatori brandished wallets with U.S. Marshal credentials. Serious, they weren't there to shoot the breeze. Edelman's eyes had long ago lost their youthful innocence. She had spent a career fighting evil men without once thinking of gender, theirs or hers. She was 38, tall for her family at 5'8", and a fit 145 pounds.

Salvatori was tall and fit, the opposite in appearance, less caring about clothes, but with the same serious gaze. He was junior to Edelman in service but no rookie to the work. Over 20 years in military intelligence honed his abilities. His service in Europe ended when the Taliban collapsed and U.S. forces took control. The U.S. Marshals Service became his new home.

"Ms. Hannigan?" Edelman asked.

"One of several, I'm told," she said.

"My name is Miriam Edelman, U.S. Marshals."

"You forgot to say, trust me, I'm with the government." Her attempt at humor fell on deaf ears. Kenna pointed at Wiggy. "This is Jeremy Heffernan, my partner, a Bostonian in an American's clothes."

Edelman aimed a crooked scowl, all business, no levity. Many years of high pressure and long nights left deep marks of premature age across her face. She wore a baggy pair of plain brown polyester pants that matched her jacket. She snapped the wallet shut. Kenna had no doubt that with a better presentation, Agent Edelman would have been attractive.

"I'd like to see that long enough verify it's real, lass," Wiggy said. "And that ya are who ya say ya are?"

"It is, and I am," Edelman said, annoyed by the request.

Kenna looked at it anyway, "Thanks."

"This is Agent Vinny Salvatori," Edelman said. "May we come in?"

"For what reason?"

"I'd like to ask you a few questions."

"You obviously know who I am and that I have a press conference tomorrow."

"Tomorrow being the operative word, Ms. Hannigan," Salvatori interrupted.

"With your cooperation, this won't take long," Edelman leaned forward but nearly lost her balance when Kenna didn't move.

"Mind yer manors, Fiery."

Eyes not leaving Edelman, Wiggy opened the door. Where Kenna sometimes saw annoyance, Wiggy saw opportunity. As the agents entered the room, Kenna thought of Malcolm with a curse under her breath.

"A better approach would have been to tell me what you want of us," Kenna said.

"You met with Senator Bridgewater today," Edelman offered to the point. Kenna remained silent, waiting for the *and*—

Salvatori leaned forward, "Answer our question."

"I didn't realize one had been asked," Kenna said.

"We speak with a lot of people, agent," Wiggy said to Edelman.

"Yes, we spoke briefly. What else do you want?" Kenna insisted, curiosity growing.

"Witnesses say your conversation was more than a few sentences," Edelman insisted.

"I don't remember them joining us," Kenna countered.

"What was discussed?" Edelman asked.

"The senator's an old family friend. Boring stuff, the weather in Texas."

Edelman pressed, "Did he ask about Senator Harvey Chamberlain?"

Kenna paused, "Why?"

"That isn't your concern," Salvatori insisted.

"Until you knocked on my door."

"We simply want to ask him a few questions," Edelman replied.

Simply' meant the opposite in the bureaucratic world. Kenna didn't believe the thick, sweet innocence. It sounded like the first time Gran Lockwood told her it would be *a good exercise* to remove the snow from the hundred-yard-long drive into the Boston manor house. Hours later, exhausted after shoveling, Kenna had collapsed in front of the fire.

'A lesson, leanbh. I asked you to remove the snow, not shovel it. A phone call to a removal company would have saved you a lot of sore muscles.'

"Then, why are you talking to us?" Kenna insisted.

Chamberlain's problems, Kenna kept thinking. How Malcolm planned to get her involved was standing in front of her now. The Texan in Kenna said if Harvey Chamberlain had problems, they were his to work out. Apparently, everyone else thought otherwise.

Edelman turned to Wiggy, "Did you speak with Senator Bridgewater?"

"Aye, we've known each other a long time."

"Let's cut to the chase," Kenna insisted. "If you want to know what Senator Bridgewater wanted with Senator Chamberlain, go ask them!"

The two agents glanced at each other. There was an immediate change in both. Salvatori lifted a grainy picture from his inside jacket pocket and held it a few inches from Kenna's eyes. Their stares locked; she ignored the photo.

"We have reason to believe this man has returned to Washington," Salvatori said.

"Returned?" Kenna asked, pushing the photo away.

Edelman's cat-like glare at Salvatori, "That has no bearing on why we're here."

"The hell it doesn't!" Salvatori demanded. "It's the reason we're here!"

Edelman reached for the photo; Salvatori jerked it away. There was a long moment of silent conflict. He shoved it back to Kenna.

"He's free-lancing under the name Altmann," Salvatori continued, glare remaining on Edelman.

"None-a this has anything to do with us," Wiggy said with a smirk.

"I'm asking for your cooperation," Edelman offered.

"The cutesy shit doesn't work, Agent Edelman," Kenna insisted. "Stick to the bad bitch, I'll break your nose if you don't help routine."

"Everyone has a chance to come clean!" Salvatori said.

"Come clean from what?" Malcolm's face flashed before Kenna. "This is getting very boring, guys."

The old man hadn't gotten his way, so he ordered some government henchmen to apply the pressure. Any moment now, she expected her father to walk in.

"Perhaps you know more than you're implying," added Salvatori.

"Watch yer tongue, my man," Wiggy said with a half step forward.

Kenna's hatred of all things political intensified, "I resent your accusation if you're trying to make one, Agent Salvatori."

Salvatori stepped forward, only to be stopped by Edelman's level glare, "We aren't here to give you a hard time, Ms. Hannigan."

"I can't take a threat any other way," Kenna retorted and snapped a finger hard against the photo. "Why do you want this guy, anyway?"

Salvatori rattled the picture, "We broke up a terrorist plot six years ago. In the process, this guy killed one of our people and escaped."

Kenna insisted, "What does that have to do with us, and … or Senator Chamberlain?"

"In that operation, the senator's name was recovered from Altmann's apartment as a possible target," Edelman said.

"We want to make sure the senator isn't involved today," Salvatori included.

Involved was a strong and strange word. There was something else they weren't saying. It had to do with

Edelman's presence, not Salvatori's. Kenna had avoided reporting on sporting events around Washington, D.C., like the plague. She wondered *why now* but remembered … Anson Beck. She'd had enough.

"Then, ask him, not us!"

"If we could find him, we would."

"He's a U.S. Senator! How hard can he be to find?"

"I assure you, we are looking into it," Edelman offered without much conviction.

Salvatori bolstered his shoulders, "We know your background, Ms. Hannigan."

"Meaning?"

"You have a propensity for sticking your nose—"

"That's enough, Salvatori!" Edelman snapped.

Kenna and Wiggy looked at each other with like expressions. They had gotten themselves into something, but right now, it was clear as mud what it was. Wiggy opened the door for Edelman and Salvatori to leave. As he closed the door …

"My skin's crawlin' with the thought of Malcolm Bridgewater."

"What the hell's he up to?" she wondered aloud.

VII

Dorothy Baldwin circled the small reception desk and took the coat of the most knowledgeable person in government. It was not the first time she had done that on a Saturday night in the past 36 years. It would, as well, not be the last. She hung it on a wobbly wooden coat tree and brushed it down, just as she had the first time 36 years ago.

Washington insiders knew that Dorothy Baldwin was the second most knowledgeable person in Washington. Those insiders paid her the respect due an assistant to the most powerful man in Congress. Others, ignoring or ignorant of that fact, found out the hard way that Dorothy Baldwin had earned and not been given that respect. A bad word directed at her would receive equal scorn, if not worse, from the powerful senator as would one directed at him.

Now 37 years senior to her inaugural trip to Washington, D.C., when she was introduced to the young senator, Dorothy Baldwin still carried her thin frame erect and proper. Casual dress was not appropriate at any time in Malcolm Bridgewater's office. Accordingly, she wore a stiff blue dress with a red sash around her six-handed waist. Her short, graying brown hair was pulled tightly to her thin head, combed over small, pointed, un-pierced ears. A hint of youthful beauty sparkled from her aging, blue-shaded eyes. The powdery, wrinkled skin had once been smooth, without a blemish. Introduced as the senator's assistant 36 years ago, Dorothy Baldwin had turned many heads.

The combination of intelligence and beauty had caused more than one newspaper to spin romance yarns about her and the senator. During the *Terrorist Era*, as she and the senator openly referred to the nineties and turn of the century, the Post coined them the *Hill Top Duo* because of their late-night work sessions. To add fuel to many reporters' fiery presses, Dorothy had never married. To hear her tell it, saving the U.S. from terrorism was far more important and satisfying than *"any man could ever be."*

With the possible exception of one, all insiders believed.

She carried a cup of coffee … with caffeine, as the senator demanded in defiance of the medical profession … and placed it on his desk. The old man sat in the same old wooden office chair that had been in his great-grandfather's law firm. With steady hands and petite skill, Dorothy tilted a quarter inch of Tennessee Sour Mash into the center of the cup, which was the only difference between morning and evening coffee. She did not stir it. The senator did that while reading the paper; tonight, he did it half-staring out the window at the city.

"The committee on Un-American Activities called and would like for you—"

"Joe McCarthy died a long time ago, Mata Hari," the senator said in a political monotone. "But inference noted."

"I haven't heard from Devon Whyte. How bad is it?" she asked.

"I won't know until I talk to Chamberlain. His hiding doesn't give me a damn bit of comfort."

"And if Jimmy can't find him tonight?"

"I'll string him up by his balls."

"If he still has any," she said with a subtle smile and turned.

The phone rang. Dorothy lifted the receiver, unclipped a large turquoise earring, and pressed the phone against the side of her face.

"Senator—" she was interrupted. "Hold while I see if he's available," She placed the call on hold. "Your favorite son."

She stretched the receiver out to Bridgewater. He took the phone, for some reason, putting a hand over the mouthpiece, "Trace this."

Dorothy hurried to the outer room and closed the door. Bridgewater gave her time to contact security, then punched the line onto the speaker.

"Harvey, where in blazes are you?"

Chamberlain sat in the front seat of a Cadillac, a bottle of whiskey on the opposite seat. He stared at the dark Potomac River, "That doesn't really matter now, Malcolm."

"The hell it doesn't. We need to talk this out."

"It's too late. He knows about the Chinese connection."

"He—" Bridgewater fell into an uncomfortable silence. The ancient chair creaked as he leaned forward onto his elbows. "He … he can't have it."

"Can and does. Gowen involved someone else."

Bridgewater hesitated when the light for Dorothy Baldwin's line went out. She came to the door, peeked in, and nodded. He scribbled a quick note, *"Have Jimmy find that SOB,"* and she left.

"That little bastard … I'll crucify him," With a racing heart, Bridgewater gathered a breath. "What are you going to do?"

A yacht cruised along the river. Chamberlain wished he was aboard and took a drink, "I have no choice but to meet him again."

"Where? I'll have Jimmy go with you."

"No," Chamberlain insisted. "I'll do it alone."

"Don't make a deal unless someone else is there."

"I have to," Chamberlain said, faltering. "Remember what happened last time."

The oldest member of Congress hesitated, "No, dammit. Do you hear me?"

"He's come back, Malcolm, and this time he wants everything. That's who Gowen involved … the German."

"How the hell did that happen?"

"I don't know," Chamberlain said and took a swig of whiskey. "Bad luck or plan. Fuck, I just don't know. It's over. He wants me to involve the Party."

"We can't," Bridgewater stammered, "that's out of the question."

"What choice do we have? The bastard wants five million dollars for his silence."

"Good God!"

"I don't know what went wrong," Chamberlain mumbled. "It could have ended back then if only he'd shown for the meet."

"Get your ass in here."

There was a pause, "I don't believe it. They suckered us … me."

"Dammit!" Bridgewater screamed, only to have it fall on

a disconnected line. "Dorothy!"

She opened the door as he stood, "Get Jimmy back on the phone!"

"Line two," she said and pointed her red-colored nail at the phone.

"Jimmy, find that bastard and hold onto him until I get there! Hear me?"

VIII

Kenna stepped onto the shadowy veranda bar. The sun lay against the western horizon; it was beginning to cool. Some of the afternoon crowd remained, by now, full of alcohol. The last of the thousand-dollar suits passed, acknowledging her insignificance, and walked inside. Laughter and boisterous conversations bowled into her. She moved as far away as possible.

The concierge, a tuxedoed middle-aged man, stopped her, "Ms. Hannigan, this arrived at the front desk."

She accepted the private messenger envelope with curiosity and took a seat at the glass-topped table where, unbeknownst to her, Chamberlain met Altmann. When she opened the envelope, a hundred-dollar bill fell out. She read the typed message.

I trust you have enjoyed revisiting the area on the anniversary. Your efforts to find me, as always, are inept. Perhaps we shall meet again someday. I hear the Clubhouse Scotch inventory is legendary. Have one on me. Anson Beck.

Immediate anger furrowed her brow; she was relieved to be alone. She wanted to break something, to hit someone, no, to kill Anson Beck. She motioned a waiter over.

"Do you have a lighter?"

"Smoking is not allowed on the veranda, ma'am."

"Then, take this," Kenna said, handing him the hundred-dollar bill.

Not knowing how to react, the waiter hesitated. Wiggy slid two pints of beer onto the table.

"Thank you," the waiter said and left, happy but confused.

"What was that?" he asked.

She extended the note. While Wiggy read, Kenna turned her thoughts away from Anson Beck and back to her old family friend. Bridgewater often likened himself to an undercover operative. When she was a child, her father spun yarns about Bridgewater's grandfather's involvement at Congressional during World War II when it was transformed into an OSS training facility. Kenna was certain the story wasn't true. It was a Texas father's yarn to challenge a young, inquisitive mind.

What happened to that innocence, papa? she wondered.

As she looked out over the darkening course, though, she visualized Bridgewater at the pulpit of a clandestine secret society, preaching of sacrificing virgins, with Anson Beck behind him, casting them into giant pots of boiling oil, and eating the raw livers of baby sheep. She wiped away the thought with a chuckle when …

"So, another one-a-his smokescreens," Wiggy said and swallowed half his beer.

"It would appear so if he wasn't involved somehow. His day will come," Kenna said, for some reason calm. "There is a bit of comfort, though, knowing Beck isn't lurking in the trees."

"Somethin's on yer mind."

"I was recalling a very strange childhood image I had of Malcolm."

She chuckled, and they toasted. She took a sip; Wiggy swallowed the other half of his beer.

"The senator admires yer work and keeps returning because he needs yer help."

"Nah, he just wanted to say hi to an old family friend," Kenna's sarcasm was profound.

"Balderdash," he would say. "He's a ruthless politician and only does what's good for him. Wha'd he want?"

"Senator Chamberlain's gone AWOL."

"The name's familiar. How's a senator go AWOL?"

"Basically, what I asked," Kenna offered, changing the subject. "Malcolm's a lot older, more fragile than I remember. Those eyes were less demanding today."

"That doesn'a make him any less lethal, Fiery."

"I remember the first time I saw him in grade school, an imposing figure to a child."

"Apparently, still is," Wiggy added, eyes looking over the lip of his glass.

"As the years went on, I got to know his charged political side, as well as his logical one. He and Father used to debate until late in the night. I sat and listened, numb. For fun: that's what they did over whiskey and cigars."

"He got to ya, kid," Wiggy lowered the glass. "And that's not good for work."

"Since high school, they've been trying to get me into the family business or to run for political office … anything but allowing me independence."

"If not fer Gran Lockwood, they might'a succeeded," Wiggy paused for effect. "So, what'd ya tell him?"

"Only thing I could tell him … no."

Wiggy managed a rare smile, "Good, kid. So, let's go eat. We have a big day tomorrow and appear to have time on our hands."

"No," Kenna said. "We're going to have a few beers, a good dinner, turn in early, and after tomorrow, turn our efforts back to finding Anson Beck."

They toasted and stood to walk into the restaurant. In the distant dark shadows, the grounds crew mowed the 18th fairway.

IX

In his late 40s, James McDowell had been alongside Senator Malcolm Bridgewater in one capacity or another since his own father's death nearly 35 years ago. At an early age, he learned the senator preferred to do things for himself, no matter how arduous or trivial. Above all else, though, the senator demanded loyalty.

There was a story behind Jimmy, as only the senator and Dorothy called him on The Hill. His father was killed in a car crash on a Tennessee backwoods road. Or so the coroner's report read. The rumor mill had it different: While delivering the word to vote for Malcolm for the senate back in the '80s, Fred McDowell had been killed by a radical Republican challenger.

Bridgewater had never forgotten Fred McDowell's ultimate sacrifice. Or, apparently, the silence that accompanied it. In exchange, young Jimmy was folded under the senator's protective wing. After Jimmy's graduation from high school, an arrangement was made for a scholarship to Vanderbilt, where Bridgewater had graduated. When the time came, McDowell was *helped* into the U.S. Marshals training program. Graduation was all but guaranteed, regardless of grades. It hadn't mattered;

McDowell excelled.

It came as no surprise when the graduate was assigned to Bridgewater, at that time one of the very few senators to have 24-hour U.S. Marshals protection. McDowell had been at the old man's side since. With each movement, they were like gloves and hands. That is, every night but tonight.

McDowell walked into the Bull 'n Bear Tavern in Old Town. A sign as he entered boasted of a hundred different beers on tap. He wondered, *why haven't I been here before?*

Inside, the line of taps behind the bar indicated that the sign was not just a boast. His eyes scanned the dark room: A sanctuary for a mixed bag of patrons. In one corner, businessmen in thousand-dollar suits consummated deals, while three steps away, construction workers downed their after-work nectar of the Gods. It was here that one could sink into anonymity for as long as he or she wanted or a place where the crowd hid you if being alone was your preference. It was a place, if questioned, from which you never remembered a face, never heard a conversation. All of that was why Harvey Chamberlain sat at the bar with a hollow stare fixated on a half-full pint of beer and an empty shot glass.

McDowell pointed to a tap, "Dortmunder."

The bartender slapped a mug from a nearby shelf, spun

it in a palm, and propped it under the spigot the instant beer flowed. A heady lager was slid across the black counter without talk or eye contact. There was no exchange of money. The bartender marked a tab with a thick red pencil, slapped it down in front of McDowell, and took another order.

Twenty feet away at the opposite end of the bar, Chamberlain tumbled the shot glass between his index finger and thumb. The rumpled shirt, askew tie, and open jacket with pulled-up sleeves told McDowell their suspicions of his mental state were correct. When the senator took a drink, his eyes were closed, only to open again when he looked down.

The bartender raised an eyebrow when McDowell grabbed his arm. He raised the other eyebrow when a $20 bill was slid across the counter. McDowell nodded at Chamberlain.

"How long's he been here?"

"The senator? Hour, maybe two."

"One or two: which is it?"

"Closer to two; I don't pay much attention."

"Any visitors?" McDowell asked.

"Hey, man, I just pour the drinks."

"Don't make me ask again."

The bartender stared at the intensity of McDowell's glare and swallowed hard, "He comes in every few days. I don't ask questions and leave him alone. Just like I would you. He seems depressed lately but still tips well … what can I say?"

"I do, too," McDowell said. He slid another $20 onto the bar but kept a finger on this one.

The young man looked up, "One man. Heard 'em talking, a German."

"How do you know that?"

"Said so. Asked if we had anything that could compare to the beer in Dresden. I thought he was fuckin' with me, so I served him a Coors Light. He didn't catch the humor."

"Could get kneecapped serving that piss-water to a German," McDowell said. "What else?"

"They were talkin' a lotta money, man."

"When did the German leave?"

The bartender glanced at a clock over the taps, "Not more than a half hour ago."

"Anything else?" McDowell asked and lifted his hand from the money.

The bartender contemplated for a moment, "The senator told the guy he needed more time. That irritated the German. He said, *'he was taking it to the others.'*"

"Did they talk about the others?"

"Somethin' about a club," the bartender said, noticing McDowell's apprehension. "Yeah, I know, sounds like somethin' kids would say, but it wasn't. They were dead serious, man. A few moments later, the senator yelled that the *premise was simple,'* whatever that meant."

"Did the German say what the money was for?"

"Nope, but the senator offered an exchange."

"Of what?" McDowell asked.

"Figured it was time to put my nose where it belonged."

"That may have been a wise decision."

McDowell smiled as he swallowed his entire beer. He set the empty mug heavily on the bar and straightened his coat.

"Use a couple bucks of that to call your mom."

"She ran away with the milkman when I was five."

McDowell threw another $20 on the bar, "Then, buy a new shirt."

McDowell stared across the bar. Chamberlain's face was frozen as if in perpetuity. He knew Chamberlain's problems had nothing to do with his wife. A man held power over a society maybe once, and it was usually short-lived. With longevity, losing that grip was devastating, perhaps more devastating than anything else a politician experienced.

McDowell felt the bartender's eyes following as he moved around the highly polished black bar. The din of the crowd became one elongated noise, not recognizable in any single form. He concentrated on the senator's blank stare as if a surrealistic image. A large drunken man lost his balance, fell against the bar, and spilled his drink.

Chamberlain's head came up and to the right. Their eyes met. McDowell met the senator just as he stood. Chamberlain fell back onto the barstool. He ordered another shot with the flip of a finger. He didn't turn back until it was poured, and he downed it.

"Looks like I need to find a new watering hole."

"They're madder than hell, senator."

"Fuck 'em … Fuck all of 'em."

"Why didn't you tell them about this earlier?"

"It's my private watering hole," Chamberlain said.

"You know what I'm talking about. They want to talk."

"I don't have the time."

"Make time," McDowell insisted.

"Tell 'em to take a hike: Gloria's attorney, the subcommittee, the majority leader, Altmann, and you. All of ya, McDowell!"

"Get your act together, senator!"

Chamberlain laughed so hard he spit up through his nose. He blew it into a napkin, "You have your own troubles; forget about mine."

"The U.S. Marshals …"

"A bunch of patsies," Chamberlain snapped, knocking the shot glass from the bar. "Remember where the fuck you are!"

The bartender placed a clean glass on the bar and filled it, "On the house, senator."

Chamberlain acknowledged the gesture with one swallow, "You don't get it, do you, McDowell? All of this was avoidable. All of it! If only they'd listened six years ago."

"Listened to what?"

"Not what! Me, God dammit!" Chamberlain stood. McDowell tightened his grip on the senator's arm. "For Christ's sake, I have to piss."

"I can help you, senator."

"I can piss by myself, Jimmy."

McDowell was taken aback by the informal, "What happened six years ago?"

"If you knew that, you'd be in my shoes," the politician said, his moist, bloodshot eyes staring directly at McDowell.

He didn't say, *where you don't want to be.*

Chamberlain turned to the bathroom, walking through the crowd. McDowell realized his mistake too late. He pushed his way through the crowd and shouldered open the swinging door to the marbled, stainless-steel bathroom.

"Senator!"

He hesitated and caught the door on the backswing, greeted by several blank stares aligned at the urinals. Looking under, he saw the toilet stalls were empty. Spinning on his heels, McDowell turned into the hallway to the rear. A service door swung shut. He pushed it open, ignoring an employee's yell, and marched to the rear exit. It opened to an alley.

McDowell stepped out and hesitated at the edge of darkness near a streetlight. He lifted out his cell phone. Behind, another voice shouted over the din of voices inside. It drew his attention. In the corner of an eye, movement: he shrugged.

A dull impact to the back of McDowell's head sent brilliant flashes of light through his vision an instant before his legs buckled. Without pain or feeling, yet semiconscious, he dropped the cell phone and slumped to the pavement like a freshly butchered slab of beef. Shrieks filled his ears as his head hit the bricks. In slow motion, a bloody metal object fell alongside his head.

He couldn't lift an arm to the pulsating blurry face that faded in and out above him. A worn loafer crushed McDowell's cell phone. A doubled fistful of hair lifted his head.

The face, "Stay away!"

McDowell's head was dropped. Colorless trousers hurried into the shadows. His face rolled to the side, cheek against the wet pavement. Car lights flicked on, then faded as his eyes closed to darkness.

X

Inside the Clubhouse, Kenna and Wiggy walked from the restaurant pleasantly plump. They passed the maître d', a tuxedoed and smiling middle-aged man, at the reception podium.

"Enjoy the balance of your evening," he said.

"A nightcap, then off to bed," Kenna said with her best-pleasing voice.

"Perfect night for a Jameson," Wiggy agreed.

"When isn't it a perfect night for a Jameson?" Kenna asked with a chuckle.

As they walked onto the veranda, the night was warm. A yellow quarter moon reflected off the pond at the final hole. Walkway lights illuminated the spray of the green sprinkler system. Clubhouse lights added to the performance of a million silver tracers arching towards the elongated dark shadow of the 18th green. The sprinklers suddenly stopped.

Vehicle headlights approached the cart path, then another. Flashing blue and red emergency lights of other vehicles roared onto the course from several directions. Officers in uniforms jumped from vehicles, all converging on the 18th green. The first onto the green was Vinny

Salvatori. He shouted instructions out of earshot, pointing to delineate an area.

On the veranda balustrade, a woman pointed, "What's happening out there?"

Two tall and muscular agents wearing U.S. MARSHALS black waistcoats approached Kenna and Wiggy. The elder agent stepped forward. The younger gave the impression he was permanently poised for trouble.

"Agent Salvatori wants you to come with us, Ms. Hannigan," the elder said, then to Wiggy. "You, as well, Mr. Heffernan."

"What's this about, my man?" Wiggy asked.

"I don't ask questions, sir. Just do what I'm told."

The two agents escorted Kenna and Wiggy from the veranda just as their nightcaps were delivered. All eyes followed them down the steps and onto the cart path leading to the 18th green.

"So much for the nightcap, Fiery," Wiggy said and took hold of Kenna's arm. "Bridgewater's behind this."

Kenna's eyes took in the wild scene, "Whatever this is, Wiggy."

Tubes of white light interspersed with flashing red and blue beacons streak the darkness like rave party lights.

Officers rushed to secure the scene, yelling and pointing fingers. Salvatori shouted instructions; Kenna and Wiggy's expressions did not change as they entered the ring of flashlights surrounding the 18th green. Wiggy nudged Kenna's arm and pointed to …

"Agent Edelman. I'll have a chat with her."

"This doesn't appear to be her show," Kenna said with a glimmer of anticipation.

The younger agent grabbed Wiggy's arm, "You're to wait here, sir."

Wiggy glared at the hand on his arm. His angry, silent refusal said it all. Kenna reached out to him; he jerked away.

"Have you ever been in a fight to the death, my man?" Wiggy asked of the agent.

Salvatori wasn't amused, walking up from behind. "Several times. I've also been to hell," He loosened the agent's grip on Wiggy's arm. "It's Ms. Hannigan I want to speak with."

An army of plain-clothed men and women attacked the course like ants. Kenna followed Salvatori to the sand trap on the right side of the approach to the 18th green. A man's body lay face down. As Kenna moved around the trap, his face came into view.

"It appears, Ms. Hannigan, we found the elusive Senator Chamberlain."

"It does, indeed, Agent Salvatori."

"Don't go anywhere. We have to talk."

"You have my full attention," she said, as much to the dead body as Salvatori.

The trap was undisturbed, save the fallen politician. Rake marks in the sand outlined the body. A stream of blood originated at a single bullet hole in the senator's temple and then fanned out like an open palm into the sandy slope. The senator's arm lay down the slope of the trap and ended with his fingers touching an array of bloody sand.

Someone yelled from the trees, drawing Salvatori's attention. Kenna stepped forward. With an annoying monotonous beep and flashing lights, a Coroner's wagon reversed towards the green. A short, round man draped in a white smock with "CORONER" on the back stepped out and snapped on latex gloves. He was met by Salvatori at the rear door. They spoke without emotion while two assistants rolled a gurney from the back.

Thumping blades of a helicopter filled the valley and descended from the darkness. Its searchlight spread across the 18th green and fairway. Salvatori pressed a cell phone against an ear. Men scrambled as the helicopter sank out of the darkness to sit heavily on the fairway. Rain, dew, and sprinkler water swirled from the grass like a tornado and dissipated into the trees.

A tall, slender, bearded man stepped from the back. Several bodyguards joined him, eyes encompassing everything. Salvatori met him, both yelling above the rotors, words heard only by those in the immediate vicinity. Salvatori pointed to the sand trap and trees, then to his head, as if re-enacting the incident.

Kenna turned to the sand trap. With her cell phone, she took photos from as many angles as possible. When she turned …

Hands on hips, the bearded man remained straight-backed, scanned the scene, and then turned to Salvatori. The agent squinted against the rotor wash and cupped a hand over his ear for a brief, one-sided conversation. The bearded man entered the helicopter, closed the door, and within a few moments, the machine lifted into the night.

As the helicopter flew directly over, Salvatori ran towards the 18th green. Just then, Kenna noticed that the crime scene had not been taped off. Neither had the location of the deceased been clearly marked. The coroner had not taken the body's temperature. There had been no discussion about the cause of death or approximate time of death. She hadn't seen a camera or a flash other than her own.

Looking down, Kenna covered her eyes as the rotor wash disturbed the scene where Harvey Chamberlain had fallen. A quick glance across the green to Wiggy and Agent Edelman brought stares of disbelief from both. Something on the green, she took a final photo.

"Alright, everyone, let's wrap this up!" Salvatori yelled, running to the edge of the green.

Without hesitation, the U.S. Marshal gnomes flopped the late Senator Chamberlain onto his back and folded his hands over his chest. Two assistant coroners lifted his remains into a body bag. They didn't brush the sand from his face, from his hands, or from his clothes. They didn't close his eyes.

A gun remained in the sand where Chamberlain's feet had been. Salvatori folded the grip into his bare palm and ejected the clip. Another young agent handed him the single spent shell casing. Salvatori dropped everything into a plastic evidence bag without sealing it.

As he did, Senator Chamberlain's face was turned directly at Kenna. The eyes of the living met the hollow stare of the dead. Kenna hesitated.

'Life ... and death both come down to a few defining

moments,' Gran Lockwood had said many times. *'Always be prepared for the moment. Never show emotion.'*

Salvatori joined her, "Perhaps if you had cooperated, this wouldn't have happened."

"This isn't on me, Salvatori," Kenna insisted. "Could be that your search prompted it."

She looked across the green to where Wiggy and Edelman were talking. Wiggy had a way of convincing others to talk. Kenna trusted that the Bostonian would find something of value.

Salvatori turned, "That just about puts Edelman's case in the tank."

Case? Kenna wondered, "How so?"

"Her lead … sprawled out like a piece of shit in front of you."

Lead? "No respect for the dead, Agent Salvatori?"

"None for a fool. Now, the German's mine."

Wide white eyes contrasted his dark complexion as though Salvatori had found an ancient art object. Kenna understood Salvatori's reaction. Avenging the death of a comrade from six years ago now brought with it one more reason.

"How long ago?" Kenna asked.

"I've been here about a half hour."

Kenna masked her surprise, "No. I mean, how long has he been dead?"

Salvatori turned away without answering or interest. He directed several agents to the trap. A squad appeared. Across the green, Wiggy pulled Edelman to the side.

"Something's wrong here, lass," Wiggy said to her.

"There's been something wrong for some time, Mr. Heffernan," Edelman responded softly. "I got a call from the senator's assistant …"

An agent interrupted them, "Agent Salvatori would like you to supervise in the trees, Agent Edelman."

She and Wiggy made eye contact and touched each other … *there would be further discussion*. The Bostonian nodded, watching his colleague across the green.

Kenna followed Salvatori while the latter directed traffic like a cop. Framed in the red taillights of the coroner's wagon, Kenna reached out for his arm. He ignored her. Kenna grabbed him again. They paused on the grass at the low side of the bowl-shaped sand trap. Before she could speak, though, Salvatori turned to a young agent who escorted the club's superintendent to the green. Several agents pushed their way between Kenna and the two men.

All the while, agents with shovels filled large plastic bags with bloodstained white sand.

Kenna turned to Salvatori, "What are you doing?"

Roots Hobson, as he was known in the Clubhouse, stood 5'10" and was 165 pounds soaking wet. Yet, where the care of his domain was concerned, he was fearless. Congressional's superintendent of grounds moved to within two inches of Salvatori and bumped his chest against the agent's. For a brief time, neither spoke, sizing up their adversary.

"Young lad!" Hobson yelled and grabbed Salvatori's arm. Salvatori balled his fists. Hobson's stubby finger was thrown at several workers, then brought back firmly against the agent's chest. "I know ye have a job to do, but ye could do it without destroyin' everythin' I put me life into. The green … and kindly tell your goats to take it easy on the … and what are ye doin' in …"

"Footprints in the trees!" an agent yelled from the shadows.

Salvatori turned, "No shit, Philips. You're at a fucking golf course. Do you think everybody plays in the fairway? Do your job!"

Kenna followed Hobson's lifted a finger to the agents

shoveling sand. Behind them, at the edge of the trees, sod was stripped, rolled, and bagged. Edelman stood alongside them without emotion. The worker ants threw the full plastic bags into the canvas-covered back of a pickup … *feeding the queen bee,* Kenna thought.

"Back off," Salvatori snapped to Hobson.

"Unbelievable," Kenna said to herself more than to them.

Salvatori turned back to Hobson, "Fix what we tear up. Here's my card. Send me the bill after we've cleaned up this mess."

With narrow eyes, the aged superintendent hesitated for a long moment. He turned to Kenna, then back to Salvatori, "Wha' do ya mean?"

"I said, bill me!" Salvatori demanded.

Hobson blinked hard, not believing the havoc being wrought on his masterpiece, "You're a bloody damn wreckin' crew, tearin' up me work like this."

"You're going at this all wrong," Kenna insisted to Salvatori. "It's a crime scene! You aren't …"

"Crime?" Salvatori interrupted and pushed Kenna aside. "Since when's suicide a crime?"

"Bloody suicide? The senator? If that don't beat all," Hobson mumbled and stepped forward when Salvatori turned away. Their eyes locked again in a lengthy stare.

"I said get out of my way," Salvatori insisted.

"Why did ye ask me here, lad?"

"To give you my card."

Kenna froze at the corner of the green but caught Salvatori before he could leave. The agent stared at the grip on his arm until she removed it.

Hobson hobbled to the edge of the trees where the sod was stripped and bagged. Kenna and Salvatori turned when the superintendent yelled. The old man pushed workers into the fairway. Several large agents grabbed the older man and hauled him screaming towards the Clubhouse. Edelman shook her lowered head.

"Suicide?" Kenna objected. "You said this had something to do with a German."

"No, you did. If you're thinking about leaving the Clubhouse, don't. We aren't done talking. That's why I wanted you here."

Salvatori stomped away and yelled at the coroner as the doors to the death wagon were opened. He unzipped the body bag, dropped in the pistol and shell casing, and checked Chamberlain's body. He and the coroner exchanged a few words, then Salvatori waved his hand. The bag was zipped, and the body was pushed into the back of the wagon.

Workers continued their unrelenting treks from government vehicles to the scene of Chamberlain's death. More evidence ... *the mess* ... was carried away. The coroner's wagon, bearing the deceased, drove away without flashing lights without a siren.

The dead were in no hurry.

Kenna turned away. As the sickies say, *she didn't even get to smell the meat.* She took a step towards the sand trap but was stopped by the heavy hand of the young agent who brought her. Two more like-sized young men stepped forward to join their partner. The third contacted Salvatori via walkie-talkie.

"Only like this much muscle if I ask for it," Kenna said.

Salvatori hurried across the green, "Be a good girl ..."

Kenna calmed, "Amazingly cavalier about a senator's death."

"It's my job, Ms. Hannigan. Unlike you, I take orders. They say clean up the senator's mess, I clean it up," Salvatori turned to his henchmen. "Escort her into the Clubhouse. She looks like she could use a drink."

The two agents pulled Kenna across the green. She yelled over her shoulder:

"You owe the senator's family an accurate account of what happened here tonight!"

"That's what exactly what I'll do once you're out of the way."

A Maryland Sheriff met Salvatori while Kenna was ushered away.

"Which is what I want to discuss, agent," the sheriff said. "Jurisdiction on this case …"

The first of the press vehicles arrived at the Clubhouse, drowning out the sheriff and Salvatori. Teams of local police, U.S. Marshals, and club security met them. There was shouting. Men and women carrying bright lights and cameras swarmed down the hill to encircle the pond across from the green. A scuffle broke out at the edge of the pond. A light went out with a crash: another scuffle and screaming, angry people. A camerawoman hit the ground hard and tumbled down the hill. Reporters in front of spotlights and cameras shouted into cell phones and microphones.

The perimeter of enforcement officials widened around the 18th green. Mundane cars loaded with dark-suited, muscular young men and women arrived to confront the growing army of press. No one without authorization got within 100 feet.

Wiggy whispered into Agent Edelman's ear, and then yelled to Kenna, "Our nightcap's waitin'!"

To Kenna, it sounded like a great way to arrest the acid that suddenly burned a hole in her gut; *so much for a good night's sleep.*

XI

Kenna and Wiggy stood at the highly polished bar inside from the veranda. A handsome young bartender slid Wiggy a whiskey neat. Outside the open French doors, the crowd watched with fascination the activity around the 18th green.

"I told ya a thousand times, kid, I thinks better with a whiskey," Wiggy said. "Only been that way since the Grand Ole Dame poured 'em."

"No, you mean you talk more with one," Kenna rebutted. "This is hardly the time, Wiggy. You never know when to shut it off."

"Shut off the humor ya die, Fiery."

Wiggy pulled a bar napkin from his pocket and dropped it on the bar. On it was a rough sketch in pencil. Kenna did the same, though her sketch was in ink. It was a ritual they developed with Gran Lockwood when, as she put it, *'their involvement was inevitable'*. They sketched the scene of the crime independently and, over a drink, compared what they had seen.

"Ya think this was Anson Beck sendin' a message?" he asked.

"Beck's mayhem personified; this was cold and

calculated. And damn sure, no suicide. A blind man could see it."

"And one blind woman in the U.S. Marshals," he said of Miriam, surprising Kenna. "Aye, she said as much before goin' into the trees."

Kenna took the sketches and smiled. Gran Lockwood was a *'finder of things'* and had saved Wiggy from a life in prison. After one of Wiggy's failed robbery attempts as a youth, she took him under her tutelage. Some years later, she put him to work, helping her manage the information flow of the crimes she investigated. Wiggy was a fast learner and took an instant liking to both games. During this time, he took to the computer and rapidly became more prolific. Appreciating what she'd done, Wiggy juggled his time to where her needs always had priority.

'Though sometimes impetuous and energetic to the point of self-destruction,' Gran Lockwood had told Kenna. *'Jeremy is a tenacious bulldog at the leg work.'*

Kenna had found her to be on the mark.

"That seems to be our calling card, kid. Not many agree with us, fewer like our means, but they smile at the results."

"Almost everyone," Kenna said.

"Aye, but if they are behind bars, they deserve it. Just as

I did as a foolish pup."

After Gran Lockwood's murder and Wiggy's recovery, he *'rescued'* Kenna from the *'dark path'* and got her *'on proper track'*. After nearly three months of daily badgering, Kenna agreed to join him on a mission he and Gran Lockwood had not completed. Kenna's involvement lifted her from the quagmire of guilt and self-pity. Realizing how well they worked together, they agreed to go after Anson Beck and visited Kenna's father.

"Follow yer instincts, lass, or you will end up like Chamberlain. And the Grand Ole Dame'll never forgive me that." Wiggy paused. "Ya were close to losing it with Agent Salvatori."

"A bureaucratic idiot."

"I have eyes, lass. But ya need ta be on the outside ta find things."

"Another Wiggyism, to be sure," she countered.

"This is gonna get locked up tighter than a nun's privates before ya get anythin' out of the government lads. He's takin' orders. Ya saw that."

"I don't back away from anyone, Wiggy."

"Three hundred thousand at Dunkirk learned the value of livin' to fight another day, kid. You've got to feel these things," the Bostonian said, just like the Grand Ole Dame.

"Gran taught us to follow our own path to accomplish the task at hand. I've got my ways; you have yours. Together, we get results."

"Salvatori doesn't know what you know." Wiggy paused with the drink at his lips. "Aye, that's why Bridgewater came to ya."

"We're both thinking the same. He mistakenly believed we could be led around on a leash."

"While Salvatori and the feds scramble the pieces of the puzzle."

Wiggy motions to the 18th green. "At the moment, Agent Salvatori has his hands full."

Just off the 18th green, Charlie Sommer was handsome, fit, and angry as a hornet. He yells out of earshot and knocks Salvatori's hand away. Another agent grabs him, and Charlie struggles. A Third Agent helps take Charlie away, still struggling and yelling.

"The late senator's assistant, Charlie, something … ah, Sommer," Wiggy said.

"Bear trap memory, Wiggy," Kenna said as the Agents shoved Charlie outside the crime tape. She turned back to the veranda. "When Chamberlain met the German, someone had to see them.”

“Beyond that, kid.” Wiggy pointed to the young man carrying beers out to the veranda. “Someone waited on him.”

Kenna and Wiggy moved to a table on the veranda. The waiter brought two beers. A swipe of the table with a cloth said that he not only chose the service industry as a profession but also took pride in his work. Kenna introduced herself and shook the man’s hand.

“I admire what you do, Ms. Hannigan, on camera.”

She was appreciative. “Thank you. I understand you waited on Senator Chamberlain this afternoon.”

A bit taken aback, he hesitated. “Yes, ma’am. And when he returned this evening.”

“Did you see who he was with earlier today?” Wiggy asked.

“Yes, sir. This afternoon, a big man joined him; brown suit. Sounded like a European. A rather rude one, I might add.”

“How so?”

“The conversation was unfriendly, and the senator left quite upset. I’ve waited on him many times and never seen him like that.”

“Did you hear anything that was said?”

"Something the foreigner was selling."

"Did he say what?"

"No, but I heard the figure of five million."

"Dollars?" Wiggy asked, trying not to spit up a drink.

The young waiter shrugged, "Guess so."

"You said he was here this evening, my man?" Wiggy asked.

"Alone and feeling no pain. He seemed really down about something." The waiter turned away when a man two tables away called for him. "Please, excuse me."

"If you think of anything else, please let me know," Kenna said, then pulled money from her handbag.

The waiter lifted his hand, "No thanks. I liked the senator. I hope you find out what happened."

"I don't like it, Wiggy," Kenna said when the waiter was gone. "But it looks like we're in this. I'm trying to figure out where the groundskeeper plays in this. He found Chamberlain."

"But Bridgewater was to meet him." Wiggy took a drink. "I'll look into Hobson's background. All I know is he's half Brit and half Scottish, so that makes him half human and half a descendant of Robert the Bruce."

"No history lectures, Wiggy. I lived with you and Gran

so long, I know them better than you do. Let's talk to him if you think he'll lower himself."

"Ye mean, The Bruce or ole Hobson?"

"Not funny."

Wiggy pointed to the shadows, "I asked him to join us."

"I never had the pleasure of meetin' the Bruce, young lass. A few years before me time," Hobson said from the shadows, then stepped into the light.

The tart aroma of Scotch … *no, Irish*, Kenna thought … whiskey preceded him. *A touch of the bottle was a constant for the old superintendent,* Kenna believed. Like a roadmap, blood vessels streaked his nose and eyes. With a thick, scarred hand, Hobson pulled a pipe from his pocket, packed it with tobacco, and lit it with a stick match. He sat heavily and leaned on the table.

"Yer man here tells me ye do more than smile into the camera, young Kenna," Hobson said. "Says ye find things, as in answers."

"Some have said."

"So, what is it ye want from this ole Scotsman?" Hobson asked. He tapped Kenna on the shoulder, grasped her right biceps, and said matter-of-factly. "Need some meat on these bones to wrestle the government dragon, lass."

"She learned long ago to clip the dragon's wings!" Wiggy said.

"Ye don'a say?" Hobson without emotion. Kenna frowned, impatient. Hobson's stare fell over Kenna's shoulder to the confusion at the 18th green. "Aye, it's a bloody sin what they're doin' to me course."

"It is at that," Kenna agreed. "What did you tell Agent Salvatori?"

"I didn'a tell him anythin'. He didn'a ask, and saints behold wasn'a about to listen."

"What do you mean, *'He didn't ask'?*"

"Just that. I told him I found the senator. Asked if they wanted me help; he said no. Your man here was the only one who'd listen."

"How long ago did you find Chamberlain?"

Hobson checked his watch. "About two hours."

Kenna recalled what she had seen: the senator face down, blood in the sand. "How long since the sprinkler system had been on?"

"I'd hafta check, why?" Hobson asked.

"Just a theory I'm working on."

"When I found the senator, I put everything off and called the coppers."

"The police, not the U.S. Marshals?"

"The coppers, yeah."

"But the Marshals were first to arrive," Kenna said.

"It don'a matter what's in the movies," Hobson said. "When there's trouble out here, it usually involves a politician, and that's when the federal lads take over."

"I understand," Kenna said, though she didn't. It was a moot point.

"The obstinate bloke, the Italian's been pushin' everyone about," Hobson continued with the flip of his head. "He talked to the members about the senator and some bloody German earlier today. He talked to you, didn'a he?"

"Did you take them to the body?" Kenna asked, ignoring the question.

"Aye."

"Directly across the green?" Kenna asked to a blank stare. "Did you walk around the green, or did you walk across it?"

Hobson shook his head. "Nay. We walked down the cart path to the edge of the sand trap. Why all the questions, lass? Ye don'a think I had anythin' to do with it?"

"Just trying to put the pieces together."

Yelling from the 18th green turned them. Hobson sighed,

"And I had it perfect for the ladies tour."

Kenna hesitated, "Could I ask you something unrelated and personal?"

"I'll give ye me answer after ye ask it."

"Wiggy tells me that at one time, you were considered for full PGA recognition. The course was magnificent. Why didn't you get it?"

The old man frowned and drank the last of his whiskey. "They didn'a want a bloody Scotsman lookin' after their bloody greens, I suppose."

"Their loss."

"Thank ye, lass," Hobson said.

Kenna watched Hobson walk away, "What do you think, Wiggy?"

"I think yer up to somethin'. We didn't discuss Hobson's past, other than if I knew him."

"I do research, as well, Wiggy." She smiled at her mentor. "Just wanted to see if it was a sore subject."

"Appears ya got the answer, kid," Wiggy said.

"What did Agent Edelman have to say?" she asked.

"Some badges took her away before I got any details."

"This has been one hell of a day," Kenna said. "Why don't they give a damn about the obvious? Why would they—"

"In Hobson's words, Ms. Hannigan, they are destroyers," a man's voice from behind.

"Yer day's about to improve, kid."

XII

Kenna followed Wiggy's stare to the left. Air was sucked from her lungs. His masculine good looks were beyond belief. Charlie Sommer was roughly her age, tall and slender, with a natural athlete's posture. She was smitten, or was it weakened? It felt as though her jaw dropped to the lip of the beer glass. She blinked hard, trying to concentrate on the beer but incapable of doing so. He wore the tailored suit perfectly … as Bond wore a tuxedo. Kenna inhaled springtime.

"I have work, kid," Wiggy said and walked from the veranda towards Agent Edelman.

"A curious duo you make, Ms. Hannigan," Charlie said. "He calls you, kid?"

"Boston childhood, a term of endearment to a really good friend," she said. "Wiggy's harmless, really."

Charlie processed her words for a lengthy moment. "Wiggy?"

"Nickname from a time later in life. He doesn't talk about it."

"Given to him by a woman," he said with a smile, sipping from a glass of whiskey. "What he must have done to earn it.”

Kenna liked the way he said, *‘earn it’*. The motion of his throat as he swallowed warmed her. *He knows whiskey, this man,* she thought. *And knows how to play women.* She liked both aspects of his game.

“Next to my grandmother, the best teacher I’ve known,” she said.

“Teacher? But you are a professional. How could you possibly need a teacher?”

“Even Einstein had a teacher, Mr.—”

“Charlie Sommer.”

“Ah, yes, Senator Chamberlain’s pupil, as it were.”

“Teacher and pupil, an interesting dynamic,” he offered. “Logic would dictate that the teacher would be smarter than the pupil.”

“Teachers impart knowledge for the pupil to apply,” Kenna said. “A gifted student processes the teacher’s knowledge, resulting in a progression of intellect or skill.”

“Such as you, you did not say. Be it on or off camera,” Charlie offered.

“My ego is relatively small, Mr. Sommer.”

“I find that difficult to believe, Ms. Hannigan.”

Small talk troubled her, always had, “True … and

humble … but we've gotten off-track."

The hundred caret emerald eyes bore into Kenna like a laser. Flashing lights shimmered against his short, styled blond hair. Nature's pure skin, never damaged by an aging sun or tanning bed, shone like a delicate pearl in the veranda lights. Naturally red lips were pouty and wanting simultaneously. She shivered with imagination.

Charlie moved forward with the agility of a cat, sliding into the chair beside her with a rustle of fabric. Manicured nails on hands that had never lifted a hammer or changed a car's oil were perched atop the table. The expressionless yet demanding emeralds cut through her.

Inside Kenna, the investigator was curious; the professional calm; the woman shivered. She feared the impulse of female hormones and thought of baseball, of football, of being shot by Beck. No, she wiped that last thought out. Charlie had experienced immediate female attraction before and was not intimidated by it. With confidence, he liked it and was fueled by it.

"Are you an expert on the habits of politicians or a casual observer, Mr.—"

"Charlie, please," he said in a long drawl, extending a firm hand.

Kenna gathered it as if a priceless gem, "Georgia?"

Charlie lifted his chin with a smile that stretched his firm neck muscles. His face crystallized when he turned that stare to the swarming mob of governmental meddling on the course. As would an attorney about to cross-examine a witness, he snapped to point. The transformation nearly took Kenna's breath. *Gather yourself, kid,* she scolded herself.

"My goodness, no, Ms. Hannigan, Virginia native."

"I am at a disadvantage. You seem to know me," she retorted. "Have we met?"

"Only in my dreams," he said with a smile. Emeralds flashed at her for an instant.

Of that, you are correct, Kenna agreed without saying. He was what every woman wanted in her dreams. No, wanted to wake up next to. In reality, this type of man just didn't happen to the typical woman. And no matter how handsome, Charlie Sommer had pissed off more than one woman in his life. That's just how things worked in the real world.

"Why are you here, Mr. Sommer? Speaking to me, that is."

"Please. Charlie," he insisted politely.

Recognition hit her, and her all-business face appeared.

What a stir you are going to cause, she thought, *if you already haven't.*

"Some time ago, Harvey asked me to look into your background, *'as sorted as it may be'*, in his words. I didn't understand at the time why he wanted me to do that. Now …" He hesitated; glistening eyes held back emotion. "He wanted me to see if you would help."

"He wasn't alone."

"What does that mean?" Charlie asked. Kenna's silence answered. "Did you know Harvey was being blackmailed?"

The emerald darts struck her full-face. She blinked hard and nearly ducked. Strange warmth overwhelmed her. This man was hard, without emotion, serious. *God,* she thought, *how dangerous he would be if emotion cracked that cast-iron visage.* She couldn't respond.

"Of course, Senator Bridgewater," Charlie continued to himself. "And then … the Marshals paid you a visit."

With reservations, Kenna decided to open up, "Everyone wants to know about a German he met today. You worked with Harvey. What can you tell me about the meeting?"

"Nothing," he answered, shaking his head. "He's been aloof these past two months."

Kenna remembered Bridgewater's remarks about

Chamberlain's voting record of late. *The German and blackmail equal motive*, she thought.

A glimmer moistened the corner of his right eye. "Harvey said you knew each other. How well?"

"We met many years ago when I was young."

"How could this have happened," he said more than asked.

"The U.S. Marshals say suicide," Kenna snapped.

Charlie turned. "And what say you?"

The distant shouts of the wrecking crew at the green drew a contemptuous glare by both. Without showing it, she felt sorry for Roots Hobson, who stood alongside the green and watched.

Kenna realized that few men blossomed in anger. Charlie Sommer was one. He was a vision, stern, and self-confident. She was attracted by the strength inside as much as the physical. She almost shook herself to make sure she wasn't, indeed, in a dream.

They stared at each other across the golden hue of a single electric candle in the center of the table. He didn't smile, and she admired that. He was to the point but not abrupt. He knew what he wanted and likely fought until he got it. It was difficult, if not impossible, to find a flaw.

"Would the senator kill himself if being blackmailed?" Kenna snapped, to Charlie's surprise.

Charlie leaned back against the chair. "You were taken in so easily?"

"If you did your homework, you know I don't take things at face value."

Another small grin formed tiny lines at the corners of his mouth: a deeper, longer-lasting shiver.

"I always do my homework, Kenna," Charlie said with confidence. "After the call, they had found Harvey. I came out. By the time I arrived, they had already taken him away. I decided to get a drink. When I walked in—"

"There I was," Kenna said dubiously with outstretched hands. "How did you know me?"

Charlie spun toward the 18th green and spoke at the same time. "It isn't difficult to find the best-looking journalist in sports, Ms. Hannigan."

Kenna hesitated with the beer glass against her lips. She tried to remember how she looked, positive it was none too impressive. Perhaps Mother was right. She was of no mind to argue, given present company.

"A vast emotionless void envelopes this city." Charlie paused and gathered a healthy drink, not a sip. "All of us were too late to help him."

"But not too late to find out what happened."

"*Did* Harvey kill himself, Ms. Hannigan?" His body accentuated the question when he spun to face her.

She settled her glass onto the table and leaned forward. "Only the evidence knows … and that's what we're after."

She came to Congressional to find Anson Beck first, then to do the story on the Blue Course improvements and the upcoming LPGA schedule. Both had been more important than helping Harvey Chamberlain. Now, it was different. Any announcement would be hollow. She couldn't forget the *'higher duty'* Gran Lockwood drilled into her as a youth. She would never let Gran down and, as an extension now, Harvey Chamberlain.

She rolled the pint glass in her hands and formed a thinker's triangle of index fingers and thumbs over the rim. Charlie's brilliant eyes turned slowly. It was a Clark Gable glance that seduced Vivien Leigh. Neither were men who gave up easily.

"I'll rephrase," he offered. "Do you *believe* Harvey killed himself?"

"I don't offer opinions, Charlie. Evidence speaks the truth."

"I saw it coming. I could have prevented it."

"You can't blame yourself."

"Who else would you blame?"

"The one who pulled the trigger."

His eyes moistened, then his emotions flipped in an instant. He leaned close, serious, "I assure you it wasn't suicide."

Goosebumps stiffened the hair on the nape of Kenna's neck. "Which leads to my next question: How do you know so much about me?"

"While looking into your past, I came across your family relationship with Senator Bridgewater."

"My father's relationship with the senator, Mr. Sommer, not mine."

"Curiosity took me deeper. I asked if he thought you could help me find out what was wrong with Harvey. He said of you, *The girl finds things.* 'The next time I see him, I will correct him."

"Oh?"

He smiled, then sipped the single malt. "You are most definitely a woman."

"Thank you for noticing."

"Will you help me discover the truth, Ms. Hannigan?"

Helping had always been a relative term in this city and in her life. It was an education process with her father when she was younger: helping meant earning the things Mother gave her. Father hid them for her to find, even at Christmas. *Helping* meant learning how to find what she wanted. It got them off to a bad start in life. She was determined to beat her father at that game, and she eventually did. In a strange way, though, Kenna believed her father's *games* helped mold the woman sitting before Charlie Sommer.

With all his charming masculinity, Charlie was part of what was wrong with Washington, D.C., but so damn good at it. Channeled properly, he could become what should be right with this city. Without admitting it, Charlie was mesmerized by the Party and the invincibility of her father and Malcolm Bridgewater. He knew the power game and its players inside and out. Though brilliant, he didn't know that her father spit out Washington politicians like watermelon seeds. The one exception had always been Malcolm Bridgewater.

"Were you sleeping with Senator Chamberlain?"

Charlie smiled. "Then, you have spoken to his wife."

"An intuitive question, nothing more."

"One that says you will find out what happened here." Charlie set his empty glass on the table and lifted his brilliant eyes, "As to your question, it's none of your damn business."

"Perhaps not yesterday, but perhaps today. You made the first move, Charlie."

A brief pause. "I am guilty of many things, Ms. Hannigan, but not of that. In Washington, you answer to everyone and to no one. The right flavor is found in the lies, but it takes more than knowing someone's sex life to find the truth."

He is quick; quick, indeed, Kenna thought. "And what is your flavor?"

"To see if there is one person left in this God-forsaken city anyone can trust."

Instinctively, Kenna reached out and grabbed his hand. His skin was smooth, his palm callus-free. She enjoyed the strength of his grip when he pulled away.

"I worked for Senator Chamberlain over six years. I did not sleep with him, and I never approached him in any manner other than professional. We both demanded that. Yet, during those six years, we withstood the most horrid lies. It cost him his wife, the drunken—" Charlie's eyes said more than his words.

"What are you afraid of?" Kenna interrupted.

"This city, Ms. Hannigan," he chuckled to hide sadness.

"It killed Harvey Chamberlain."

"That won't help find the person who pulled the trigger, Charlie. Only facts will."

Charlie Sommer snapped his eyes across the entire veranda; urgency filled him. Or was it fear? He glared at her, stood, and, without hesitation, strode for the exit. He turned before reaching the door and half-heartedly smiled.

"I'll be in touch."

Literally, Kenna hoped and followed his strong gait until he disappeared into the Clubhouse. She blinked hard and wiped a single bead of sweat from her brow. She leaned back, breathless in a daydream, only to be awakened by the reality that she was involved in the death of a U.S. Senator, like it or not. *Fuck!*

Kenna turned back to the 18th green, where Salvatori was talking to Edelman. *Oh, to be the fly on the lapel in that conversation.*

'Every criminal is one dimensional, the thinker's triangle.' Gran Lockwood had said. *'But every crime is three dimensional, a pyramid, working from the bottom to the top.'*

Kenna formed a vertical thinker's triangle with her index fingers and thumbs, then dragged her connecting thumbs across the table to form an imaginary pyramid. She pointed to the corners of the imaginary base of the pyramid, whispering to herself:

"The victim, Harvey Chamberlain; the evidence, destroyed; the truth, in process; the lies, too many to count; leading to …" She placed her finger on the imaginary top of the pyramid. "The guilty."

She toasted the imaginary pyramid and emptied the glass. "I'm coming."

XIII

Devon Whyte was a four-sport high school letterman 35 years ago. It had been cross-country running that earned him a full-ride scholarship to Temple University in his hometown of Philadelphia. It hadn't taken long for him to realize he would never sign a million-dollar contract running. That's when education became his focus.

To keep his mind sharp, he still ran every morning through the streets of Washington, his routine since being chosen as Chairman of the National Democratic Party. This morning's ritual was different. He and his wife had taken an overnight trip to the beach on Saturday, had left their phones off, and did nothing but stare into each other's eyes for the day and a night. Without so much as listening to the radio or reading the paper, they had driven home before dawn. He ignored the messages on his office and cell phones and went out for the run.

Devon Whyte didn't know his friend Harvey Chamberlain was dead.

Whyte was a tall African American with long, sinewy legs that carried him fluidly through the winter cold and the sultry summer heat. He ran at least two marathons a year, as well as a handful of 10Ks. As he took to the streets, he toyed with the thought that this year might be the last for the marathons. Today was warm and sticky; sweat glistened on his brow by the end of the first few blocks. Though several decades older than other people who followed the same routine, he took pride in the fact that he ran as fluidly as any.

Like every day, his route took him through the heart of this decaying metropolis that he loved … but also loathed. Each day reminded him that much work remained to be done for his people. It also reminded him that his people needed to do more work for themselves.

Proud of the fact that he was raised in the streets of Philadelphia at the birth of civil liberties and governmental programs, Devon Whyte, in his own words, had lived through the *prejudices of which rich liberals knew nothing, but professed to be such champions'*. Yet, Devon aligned himself with the Party of the liberals. It seemed an incongruity to many political analysts but not to him. For here, he could do the most good.

Whyte's face bore the marks of a childhood fever that common medicines could have prevented but a poor ghetto family could ill afford. In his latest book, he questioned how any politician, liberal or conservative, could ride in a limousine through the heart of a dying city ... their city ... and never once stop to see the people. He had never seen an elected official bring food, medicine, or other necessities of life unless at election time.

Where his parents had coined his generation the *'Forgotten Society'*, a play on Lyndon Johnson's *'Great Society'*, Devon had not been so kind. He called the newest generation the *'Lost Souls'*.

Whyte had beaten all barriers placed before him and mastered a system created to keep him at the bottom. He had done so not by listening to the falsehoods of his inferiority but by believing in his superiority. It spoke of his inner strength, which he owed to his parents. Succinctly, that strength brought success and catapulted him into the Party hierarchy.

The Democratic Party Chairman believed he could improve the system and had taken action to do so. Two decades ago, Whyte's philosophy had inspired changes in Party policy and direction. They now welcomed the kiss of death from some Party members. He was losing control of what he wanted all along, moderates supporting a diverse middle class of all races.

'The legacy of the sixties American liberal policy,' Whyte had written years before, *'is not a birth, a*

rejuvenation, or even a living American spirit. It is the death of American ideals, the death of American dreams, the death of American society.'

He checked his heart rate on his watch; a smile of approval followed. His breathing deepened as he passed several men sleeping in an abandoned building stoop. He sealed the street corner in a memory bank. Several young boys were awake with the sun, as always, and coaxed the *'old man'* on with cheers of inspiration, running alongside. For their benefit, he pressed it hard the next block. When he slowed, his heart raced, lungs pounded in his ears.

The sun peaked through the rowhouses as he turned to run directly into it. V-shaped patches of sweat stained his gray tracksuit. He lifted a pair of sunglasses from a tummy pouch. The boys stopped, watching him. Up a slight incline, he groaned, feeling his age, hating it but also accepting the inevitability of it. With it came wisdom: *no marathons this year.*

A parked car sat at the alley between the brick row tenements; he angled to his left to avoid it. He didn't see another vehicle lung forward as he bounded down the curb onto the pavement. When the car appeared in the right corner of his eye, his reactions weren't quick enough to avoid contact.

The chairman slammed against the quarter panel and toppled over the hood. Tires squalled as the vehicle came to a stop. Face down on the pavement, Whyte turned over and cleared his head. A sharp pain knifed through his leg; sunglasses lay broken on the ground. He pulled back a hand from his face, somewhat relieved there was no blood. He didn't look up as a man leaned over him.

"Good morning, Devon."

The man's head was hooded; he wore large sunglasses. Backlit by the sun, he was unrecognizable. Whyte squinted for a brief instant, blinded by brightness. Uneasiness engulfed him when the driver placed a hand on his shoulder. The strength in the grip brought the chairman's hand up. Whyte leaned on an arm to stand; the man held him down.

"No need to get up just yet."

"What do you want?"

"So, you haven't seen the news this morning," the driver said. "No need. You will understand when you do. I'm here to collect, Devon: five million dollars. Have it by tonight. Talk to the Party, empty your PAC accounts, do what you must, just get it. I'll call with the details."

The hooded man straightened, got back into the car, and rapidly drove away. Whyte forced himself up, unable to concentrate on anything but the car driving away. His young admirers ran to him and tugged on his sweatshirt.

"We saw everythin', mister. You want we should call the cops?"

"No," he said and watched the car turn a distant corner. He didn't attempt to get the license plate; there was no need. "I'm … fine. I'm … fine." Knowing full well, he wasn't.

XIV

With a cup of coffee, mind racing, Malcolm Bridgewater looked out his office window. *How have we gotten to this point*, he wondered? A slight scuffle as his door opened.

"Good morning, senator," the deep voice came from behind.

A large square man in military uniform filled the door opening behind the dainty Dorothy Baldwin, her arms pressed against the doorjambs to block his entry. The general allowed a grin to crease his granite visage as his large hand engulfed her shoulder in a hug. She glared up at him, but he moved her aside as easily as pinning another medal on his much-decorated chest.

"You have an annoying knack for unannounced entries, general," Bridgewater replied.

"It's called a surprise attack, senator."

General Hunter Treadway was a rock-hard Army Ranger chiseled from a childhood in the Pacific Northwest, where lumberjacking was fun. While still in his mother's womb, his father had left that way of life to protect his country from Communism, as had so many other young men. In 1968, his father put his life on the line to protect Saigon during the Tet

Offensive. His bravery cost him that life. Hunter's only remembrances of his father were from his mother's scrapbooks.

A strong woman always stood behind a great man; Treadway was no exception. His mother pushed him hard to outperform everyone, whether in studies, in sports, or in work. He grew up early, and when other boys were just that, boys, he was his own man. His disciplined manner, attention to duty, and leadership qualities were combined with a youthful vigor for the daring. He was afraid of nothing … save his mother.

Hunter Treadway never received a grade below 'A' in his rural high school and graduated Valedictorian in a small class of 85. No one doubted the results would have been any different had his graduating class been 1,000. He lettered in every sport every year and was elected student body president … they didn't have individual class officers … his sophomore, junior, and senior years. The quintessential scholar-athlete, Hunter studied foreign languages outside the classroom and, at his mother's insistence, military history to honor his father. The latter became not just his passion but also his obsession and life's mission in his teens.

Sponsored by his local Representative, soon to be Governor … who favored Treadway's widowed mother and would eventually marry her … Hunter was accepted into West Point. Four years at the Academy sharpened an aggressive personality into a logical, thinking military machine. His self-discipline shaped a natural leader and brilliant strategist. Promotions and battle ribbons became frequent occurrences. He was part of the U.S. Military Assistance Command Saudi Arabia. His first Purple Heart was legendary.

Treadway led the Joint Special Operations Command into Iraq in 2002, the first American boots to enter. He coordinated negotiations with friendly Iraqi military leaders to stand down during the coming invasion. Unaware of a grenade sewn into her belly, a girl walked into the building, begging for food. The device detonated not more than 10 feet from Treadway's chair, killing everyone in the vicinity but him. The blast had ripped away most of his uniform and left him semi-naked, shrapnel in the shoulder, thigh, and hip. He was, however, only slowed. Using a broken table leg as a cane, he organized his men and fought off the Iraqi military.

Then, Hunter Treadway went on the offensive. His group outflanked the enemy, cornered nearly an entire battalion, and systematically eliminated all resistance. He remained in Baghdad until occupation, providing intelligence on the Iraqi army's strength and actions. These efforts earned

Hunter Treadway a Silver Star and a field promotion to major.

Surprised at Treadway's ability to withstand the pain and function with such vast wounds, an Army surgeon coined the only nickname that was to stick with him for the rest of his life. From that moment forward, his men no longer reported to Major Hunter Treadway.

In a recent interview with *Military History* magazine, he revealed that he had talked to or visited his mother weekly until she passed away a year before. They never discussed things such as the weather; these were not manageable events. How one coped with such events was discussed; reaction to them was manageable.

"Do you read the paper, general?"

"Every morning, senator. I'm aware of what happened to Chamberlain."

"Then, you should respect the dead and give us a chance to help the widow make arrangements. That's why we're here today."

"You work every day," Treadway said. "If you want me to quit annoying you, support my appropriations."

"I am not your only roadblock, general," Bridgewater retorted a heartbeat later.

"Your people in the press caricaturize me as the damned Gestapo. That's absurd, and you know it." Treadway planted a large fist on the desk. "You're avoiding the real issue, which is gangs and drugs on the streets while local governments weaken the police."

Bridgewater returned to his desk but lifted his stare, "Your solution isn't the answer."

"Then, what is? We must act before our inner cities become war zones!"

"I am well aware that our cities must be under the control of law-abiding citizenry but not supported by Army tanks."

"You Great Society Democrats can't see it. No, you refuse to see it."

"I've seen a lot over the years, general. Including several men just like you."

"Not with open eyes, apparently. A lot of good men … boys have died over the decades because you guys in these ivory towers don't have victory as your objective. Does the fight have to happen here for you bastards to wake up?"

The senator breathed hard, "I'll take my chances that the pile of shit tomorrow won't be as big as you're telling everyone it will be."

With a single step, the general approached Bridgewater;

wood creaked under his weight. Flared nostrils inhaled the fire that earned the fear and respect of the men under his command.

"Why we allow men like you a voice in military affairs is beyond rational thought."

Bridgewater, a clear head shorter, was unmoved, "Exactly why we're elected. Someone has to keep the Terror Treadway's of this country under lock and key."

"You supported the Iraq wars and Afghanistan. Now, you've become a dove? Perhaps in hawk's clothing?"

"With age comes wisdom, a character trait missing in youth. At least to some."

"Bull shit. Political winds from Congress are blowing your skirt up, senator," Treadway challenged. "Every modern strategist believes we will fight regional conflicts, and our greatest threat is still the Communists."

"Same old rhetoric, general, we'll be fighting the Chinese."

"I'm saying we can deal with the Chinese, terrorists, or any other splinter group with my appropriations. Even if they're American."

"Balderdash!" Bridgewater leaned against his desk and lifted the coffee cup to take a sip. "Are you implying an

American would terrorize other Americans?"

"Were you asleep when McVeigh blew down the federal building in Oklahoma City?" Treadway insisted. "He isn't the only nut-case out there!"

Bridgewater exhaled, "I won't allow you to curtail personal freedom."

"That's not what I'm proposing!"

Malcolm Bridgewater heard the door to the outer office open and close. There was a commotion. Dorothy spoke and laughed.

"Seems my appointment has arrived," the senator lied. "Excuse me, general."

Treadway remained firm, "Everyone with knowledge of my plan knows it's the right thing to do. Our nation will be safe from any adversary. Without it, we will be fighting to save hundreds of thousands of American lives in the not-too-distant future: on our streets."

Bridgewater stood beside the big man and crumpled his brow, "The military will never rule the streets of my America."

The general straightened, lips firm against his square jaw. Those dull hazel eyes, which his men swore turned red during the heat of battle, bore into the smaller man.

Bridgewater saw the twinkle of fire.

"Is that your final word, senator?"

"You will have that on the Senate floor or just before they plant me six feet under."

"Let's hope the latter isn't too soon. I'll enjoy this fight."

"As will I," Bridgewater said.

Dorothy Baldwin knocked and entered, smiling, "Kenna's here, Malcolm."

"Good God, I can't get anything done with all the interruptions." The old man moved for the door. "Show her in. She should meet this Neanderthal."

It had been twenty-some-odd years since Kenna stepped into Malcolm Bridgewater's *celestial chambers,* as a child thought of them. From what she remembered, little had changed. The walls were still Government Issue drab gray, the furniture so austere people usually stood. A single-throw rug covered the highly polished yet aged tile floor. It smelled of cleaning solvent, which masked the underlying aroma of Tennessee Sour Mash.

'I don't get paid to spend the peoples' money on myself,' Bridgewater said on numerous occasions.

In her youthful naiveté, Kenna had believed that statement put Malcolm Bridgewater in a political pot by himself, one immune of distrust. Now, she wondered.

"Kenna, I would like for you to meet—"

"Hunter the Terror Treadway," Kenna interrupted, striding forward to shake the general's hand. She detected a whisper of admiration from the military man. "I've read of your exploits."

"And I've heard your name spoken in vain several times around here."

"As you gathered, Kenna, the general also has an uncanny sense of when I am in the office."

"You're always in the office, Malcolm," Kenna said.

"I'm a persistent bastard, senator," the general countered. "I'm not impotent!"

"A hard dick doesn't make a good lover, general. And it could be annoying to the woman not wanting it."

"I think I'll leave now," Dorothy Baldwin said.

The general spun on the ball of his foot, then paused. He turned back, "Chamberlain's successor will back my proposal. With that, I'll get the White House."

"Not in my lifetime." Bridgewater sucked in a cool breath, circled the desk, and shuffled some paperwork.

"Good day, Ms. Hannigan," the general said, marching from the room.

After the outer doors closed, Malcolm Bridgewater lifted his dark-rimmed eyes. Kenna saw the aged man differently than she did the day before. Now, she saw an angry, perhaps beaten man. She wondered if Malcolm Bridgewater had fought the political wars too long.

XV

Kenna's narrow view of Washington politicians and bureaucrats was simple: Of the hundreds of thousands of people who worked for the government in Washington, D.C., it was that too many. Politicians and bureaucrats fed off the toil and sweat of others' hard work. It didn't take a genius to see the absurdity with Lawyers making the laws. Bureaucrats perpetuate their existence by creating unquantifiable value from an indefinable position and by justifying why their job is required, just not by any value-added standard found in the private sector.

In Kenna's mind's eye, Harvey Chamberlain's stone-cold face rolled over to greet her. Tagged and bagged, Chamberlain was now an object, scurried away by bureaucrats eager to conclude an unpleasant interruption in their routine. The papers had labeled Senator Harvey Chamberlain: *'mentally disturbed', 'weak', 'selfish', 'unfit for government service'*. Kenna didn't know Chamberlain well, but knew he was none of those things.

And then there was Charlie.

'Watch his charms, lass,' Wiggy had said earlier that morning. *'Gran Lockwood warned against townies like*

him.'

"Of course," she said, looking at Bridgewater. "You are a creature of habit, Malcolm. I knew you wouldn't be in church, it's—"

"For hypocrites seeking absolution for the week's sins," Bridgewater bawled, annoyed.

Kenna knew it went deeper. For the senator, religion was best practiced during re-election campaigns and Papal visits when there were babies to kiss. Kenna chuckled.

"With your direct pipeline to God, absolution is guaranteed."

Head bandaged, Jimmy McDowell stepped into the room, "You wanted me, senator?"

"Jimmy, I want the car clean as polished boot leather today. There are moneymen in town with time on their hands. I want them contributing to our next campaign."

"Yes, senator," McDowell said. "You'll be able to eat off the floor."

"I don't want to eat with the bastards, Jimmy. Just want their money."

"Of course, senator," McDowell said, turned to Kenna, and shook her hand. "Expected you sooner."

"Stop wasting time, Jimmy!" the old man shouted.

McDowell smiled, "I sometimes wonder why I went to college."

"Four-year party," Kenna said. "A beer later?"

"On me."

"What happened?" Kenna asked, pointing at the gauze patch.

"Obstacle course … wasn't paying attention," McDowell said, going out the door.

Dorothy Baldwin carried a fresh cup of coffee to the senator's desk. "If I'd known you were coming, I'd have gotten you a Diet Dr Pepper, Kenna."

"Won't be here that long, Dorothy, but thanks for remembering."

"You're still just a child, aren't you?" Dorothy smiled as only she could and squeezed Kenna's cheek.

That summed it up: she was still *just a child* to those in the Washington cesspool. As Dorothy grabbed the door, though, Kenna reassessed her dislike of bureaucrats, if only by one.

"I am sorry about Harvey," Kenna said. "I know you were close."

"Dorothy," the old man growled. "Government doesn't stop working because some damn fool put a bullet in his brain."

"Devon Whyte called for the eighth time," she said at the door. It wasn't an exaggeration; it never was. She walked out.

"I should get another secretary," Bridgewater said. "She's known me too long."

"There's a cliché about old dogs and new tricks, Malcolm."

"I view myself more as a leopard," he offered, taking a sip of coffee but never losing eye contact. "Best damn coffee on The Hill."

Kenna inhaled clean air from an open window, "Have you ever thought about leaving Washington, Malcolm?"

"And do what?" The old man stood, cup in hand, and walked over to lean on the wall next to her. Nostalgia overcame him. "I saw her for the first time over thirty years ago. I was standing in the back of an old Ford Fairlane convertible, preaching to a crowd … my children, I called them back then. I saw her in the crowd, and my heart skipped a beat. I should have married her then."

"Why didn't you?"

"Blind ambition, stupidity, call it what you wish. She had no political value. God bless her, though; she has given me more than even my late wife, save our sons. She's been my greatest asset, right out there. What could I have done with her in my bedroom?"

The old man's eyes glimmered as she stared up Pennsylvania Avenue. Kenna didn't respond. Bridgewater glanced at the polished cherry wood clock on his desk. He set the coffee cup on the fireplace mantel and turned to look out the window. A tall portrait of Abraham Lincoln stared down on him.

"More trees and cars now," the senator said. "And our capital smells like a ghetto!"

She had thought the same, "Why have you stayed?"

The senator's brow furrowed, "Until last night, the answer had been to bring someone in to add sensibility to this madness, a strong person able to control this out-of-control machine. That dream died with Chamberlain … too young, I needed more time with him."

"That brings us back to me, Malcolm … and you. What do you want me to do?"

"It's too late. What could you do?"

"Find the truth," she said without emotion.

"Truth? To what end? Add objectivity to misery and insanity?"

The old man eased into his chair with a grunt. As he did, Dorothy entered with a fresh cup of coffee. In her other hand was a cold can of Diet Dr Pepper. She opened it and placed it on a Jack Daniel's coaster on the senator's desk. She didn't offer a glass. She knew Kenna had worked at a bar and never drank from glasses. Both understood their unspoken appreciation.

Kenna furrowed her brow at the senator, "No, to find out what really happened."

"That's up to the U.S. Marshals, now."

"They couldn't find their asses if their mothers slapped 'em on it."

"Just the same, you'd better leave it to them."

"What about yesterday, Malcolm?"

"That was to prevent this, not to come in after the fact and smear a man's name."

"Smear his name?" Kenna snapped but then pulled in the reins of her emotions. "Charlie Sommer thinks he was being blackmailed."

"Probably by him," the old man said, then lifted the cup and blew across the hot liquid. "Besides, if he was, then it's definitely a U.S. Marshals problem. You need to stay out of it."

"What do you know about a man named Bernard Altmann?"

The old man shrugged, "Never heard of him."

A lie, Kenna thought. "Of course, you have. Chamberlain met him at the club. You knew that, and you also knew the Marshals were looking for him."

"So, let them do their job! This isn't your game, Kenna." The senator leaned forward. "Men have killed themselves for less than divorce and blackmail. Sommer must have sensed it. Why else would he ask me specifically about you?"

"What do you mean, *'specifically'*? That's not what he says."

Bridgewater chuckled with a guttural wheeze, "Your father's paranoia is infectious, Kenna. Everything's a plot. Altmann, the German, you say? Did he have a little cropped mustache in the middle of his upper lip?"

"Don't patronize me, Malcolm. A U.S. Senator, supposedly your friend, is dead. You came to me first. Maybe at the same time, Harvey asked Charlie to contact me."

"You put a lot of faith in Sommer, girl. His laundry won't be clean on this. You can be sure of that."

"Are you saying he was involved with Chamberlain?"

"Open your ears. Can't you hear the bedsprings squeaking?"

Kenna bit her tongue, "You've been playing people a long time, Malcolm. Don't play me. I don't give a damn if he's screwing the Pope. Why—"

"The damn fool killed himself!" Bridgewater shouted, slapping an open palm on the desk. "How does one explain that? Is there more we need to know? He's dead!"

Feeling sorry for her father's old friend, Kenna said, "This town has sucked the life from you."

"Chamberlain became weak. The Marshals say he killed himself. That's good enough for me."

"You've contradicted yourself, Malcolm, and misjudged me again." Bridgewater stared across the desk but didn't respond. "You brought Chamberlain into this city. On a white horse, as I recall. You taught him the ropes. He would have confided in you if there was trouble."

The older man's eyes narrowed, "He changed; lost track of what's important in this city ... loyalty to the Party."

Not to the country or the people, Kenna noted. The U.S. Marshals wanted to talk to Chamberlain for two reasons. She was now convinced they were related. Perhaps the squabble between the two agents was a territorial dispute … Or perhaps it went deeper.

"You're reading more into this than there is. The man's dead. Let him rest. You need to go back to Boston."

Kenna recalled the scene, "Harvey Chamberlain didn't kill himself, Malcolm."

The senator stared at Kenna through those aged wise eyes and ran slender fingers over thin white lips. His hands were steady as he glanced at the copy of the Constitution on the wall over his desk. The debate wasn't going as planned.

Kenna leaned forward, "It's a chilling sight, a man on the ground with a bullet in his brain. Have you ever seen that?"

The senator took a sip of coffee and spoke with his lips still on the brim of the cup, "Drink your soda before it gets warm, Kenna. Dorothy will be disappointed."

"You're hiding something, Malcolm. You and Chamberlain were close."

"Believe what you want. Chamberlain never talked to me about blackmail or a German."

"Then, who would he have talked to?"

"Ask Charlie Sommer," he said dismissively.

She was having none of it. "And the U.S. Marshals?"

"This Salvatori fellow isn't in your fantasy world, girl."

"Would a man in Salvatori's position lie and jeopardize his future, his pension? He reports to someone who reports to someone else who reports to the … you follow? He started the investigation, a helicopter lands, a short conversation with a superior, then *let's wrap this thing up, people,'* I believe is what she said."

"Your hatred of politics is affecting your judgment," Bridgewater insisted.

"No, Malcolm, my vision is clear." Kenna walked away and turned at the door. "Unfortunately, what I also see is that special interests and Party interests are more important than truth … and life."

"There's a golf tribute to Harvey this afternoon." It wasn't a request.

"Bring the Marshals' report from last night." Neither was that.

"I can't help you there."

"Yesterday, you were invincible, senator. Today, you are powerless? Get the report!"

XVI

On a hunch, Kenna took the elevator up to Senator Chamberlain's floor. The long, polished halls were quiet, even by Sunday's standards, until she was nearly run over by a young page that slipped on the tile while rushing around the corner towards the stairwell. The girl apologized for nearly laying Kenna out, then hurried off to attend to her senatorial duties.

Kenna paused at the tall, stained wooden door to Harvey Chamberlain's office. She stared at the name, seeing once again the dead man's eyes. She grabbed the polished brass handle and turned it, somewhat surprised it was unlocked.

Inside the dark mahogany-paneled office, she sensed more than felt, something out of place. Was it the silence, the stale cigar smoke, or the slow-spinning brass ceiling fan that flicked shadows across the walls? Her lips drew thin. The gentle whisper of the closing door resembled the hush of the politicians when she aligned her final putt.

Her stomach tightened. Words came to the tip of her tongue when a shadow darted from the adjoining office. The bigger man hit her with a shoulder at a run. Kenna was driven over the top of the receptionist's desk. A computer screen crashed to the floor; Kenna followed it. She landed atop the keyboard on her ribs, knocking air from her lungs. She gasped for breath and tried to stand as the assailant darted out the door. She shook her head to clear her mind.

The vague whisper of a man's voice turned her. A hand against her cheek, she looked up. Charlie Sommer painted a grizzled smile across his face and brushed hair from Kenna's forehead. She didn't move until she had fully gathered her breath. In the light through a window shade, Kenna noticed a red welt creased Charlie's left cheek. Her fingers traced its edge. He winced, touched her hand, and half-smiled. With a painful breath, Kenna sat upright.

"Are you alright?" she asked.

"Nothing a good dose of pride couldn't dispel," he said.

Leaning back against the wall, Charlie ran his fingers through her long hair and flipped it behind an ear. Stretching, she lifted the desk phone from the floor, finding that the cord had been ripped from the wall.

"Did you get that truck's license number?" she asked.

Charlie thought for a moment. "Big man muscular, attacked me from behind when I entered the office. I didn't have a chance."

Few people ever do, Kenna thought, then remembered

the German's grainy photo. "He had building access; there'd be a record."

"That's a lot of people, Kenna. You got in."

"I know Malcolm Bridgewater." She frowned, then pointed across the room to the opposite door. "Avery Gowen?"

"Harvey's counsel."

"Could it have been him?"

"That's two questions, really," he offered. "Could he be involved in Harvey's death? Yes. Could he have done this? Never. If he was running full-stride, that weasel couldn't knock the dust off my clothes with a cross body-block."

He knows football, too. Kenna smiled and helped him up. Charlie straightened his shirt and led Kenna into Chamberlain's private office. One look at the room told Kenna the attacker knew what he wanted. Papers were strewn about, a desk light broken, paintings thrown onto the floor.

Kenna sat in the chair; Charlie's eyes softened as the springs squeaked. She opened the drawers; they were empty.

"The squeaky springs annoyed me at times. Now, I will miss that. Do you think his successor will replace the chair? And me?"

The nostalgia that consumed Charlie passed within a few moments. He was back in-role. Kenna sat on the corner of the desk.

"Who made Chamberlain's meeting with the German, and just who the hell is he?"

"Harvey could have done it himself, or it could have been Avery," he said. "I didn't. What do the Marshals say?"

"They're adamant it's suicide," she said. "Something's convinced them."

"That something could be Malcolm Bridgewater."

Kenna stared into his emerald eyes. "You don't trust him."

"I don't trust anyone in this city."

"Present company excluded, I hope," she said.

"You're not from this city. But I trust Malcolm Bridgewater least of all."

"Why do you say that?"

"He's a lifetime politician and powerful enough to avoid consequences."

Kenna had never thought about her father's lifelong friend like that. It chilled her to do so. She remembered how it had been Malcolm Bridgewater who kept the FBI from arresting her in Chicago, or so Malcolm boasted. But had he?

"Nothing here but junk," Charlie said. "Harvey hasn't been here for a long time. There was at least a month's worth of mail in the in-basket. Everything that was here on Friday is gone. But the truck that hit us didn't take it."

"Who else had access to the office?"

"Harvey's wife and Gowen." Kenna moved so close she sensed the fear that lingered on Charlie's breath. "Watch out for Avery; he's a snake."

"And the wife?"

"A drunk, taking the senator for everything. The divorce came on suddenly."

"Maybe like two months ago?" she asked. Charlie smiled and placed a hand on her shoulder. Her imagination raced. "Is there anything else you need to tell me?"

Charlie Sommer's best game face reappeared. He allowed manicured fingers to straighten his jacket. His foot brushed her calf. Kenna remembered Wiggy's warning with a Cheshire grin; she knew not why.

"We can discuss it over a drink," he said. "I need to get security up here, or they'll think I did this."

Kenna moved her leg and brushed against his well-defined muscles. There was much to enjoy about Charlie Sommer. There was also much to fear.

"Then, tonight at the Clubhouse," she said.

"That would be wonderful."

Her instantaneous daydream said it would be if she allowed it. However, she knew she wouldn't … for many reasons.

XVII

Devon Whyte took a long cab ride to Lincoln Memorial. All the way, the cab driver talked about Senator Chamberlain's suicide. How terrible to leave a wife with a child in college. What a coward, taking the easy way out of his troubles. Why couldn't he stand up like a man and fight? One man's death, his weakness, exemplified the country's leadership ills.

The Party Chairman sat on the steps to the memorial of the greatest president in American history … he preserved the union, freed the slaves … and reflected on his own past. He didn't ask himself what Lincoln would do at that moment. There was no need; Lincoln would never have found himself in this position.

More disturbing, Whyte thought of his youth; they had all been so young. He walked around the memorials for more than an hour before he hailed another cab. On the ride home, the driver's words rang through his ears.

Without speaking to his wife, he limped into his study, trying to ignore the burning leg. Several times, he lifted the phone but always set it back down without punching any numbers. How could he get someone else involved? It had to stop somewhere. He sat in the dim light of his study and ignored his wife's call for breakfast. When she came in to check on him, he slurred that he was okay, which he wasn't, and that he would be out shortly, which he didn't.

For half the morning, the past raged through his brain like a bullet. Eyes affixed on the dormant fireplace, he didn't leave the room. He read the Post articles repeatedly, not believing them, not fully comprehending them. How could Harvey do that? Did he? Each time he read the final line, he realized their past beckoned them. Each time, he felt the German's grip and heard his words. He had prayed he would never hear his name again … Bernard Altmann.

A knock on the door and his wife entered. "Avery Gowen is here, dear."

Whyte met the little man at the front door but didn't allow Gowen inside. Without speaking, Whyte accepted a package. It was heavy, manila envelopes marked with Harvey Chamberlain's name.

"Before things get too crazy," Gowen said. Whyte's mouth firmed as he stared into Gowen's deceitful eyes. "From the senator's past month's correspondence. Thought the Party should go through everything before it's made public."

"Public? Why have you brought this to me?"

"You know why, Devon," Gowen said with devious intent. "Is your leg alright?"

Anger shot between Whyte's temples. "Get out of my sight!"

"I am only a facilitator, Devon. What can I do for you?"

"Die!"

Whyte watched Gowen enter the cab. No sooner had it driven off than a police car stopped in front of the house. Whyte paused as the officer stepped out and walked to the door.

"Mr. Whyte?" the officer asked from the bottom step.

"Yes." Devon moved out to greet him, admission of guilt on the tip of his tongue.

"We got a call this morning, sir … well, it came from the inner city … you know, some kid claiming that you'd been hit by a car." The officer stopped and looked over the chairman's clothes. "And … well … we just thought we should check it out."

"No serious damage, officer," Whyte said and sighed with relief. He patted the young black officer's shoulder. "All my fault. Not watching where I was going. Reactions aren't what they used to be."

"Do you want us to look into the driver?"

"Heavens no. He stopped and made sure I was alright. I didn't think about it, but we need to give that young man a service award or something."

"Will do, sir. Thank you for your time."

Devon Whyte closed the front door and watched as the broad-shouldered officer entered the police car and drove off. Mind in a haze, he walked back to the study, ignoring his wife's questions. For the next hour, he rifled through the documents in the Manila envelopes. For another hour, he stared at the walls, contemplating what had to be done. Exhausted and anxious, he settled back into his leather office chair, lifted the receiver, and punched a number.

"We have to meet, Malcolm. It's about Harvey."

"We don't have time. We're playing golf at two this afternoon."

"I'm not playing golf after this."

"Balderdash! Put your party smile on, Devon. Moneymen are in town."

"Gowen brought me the correspondence from Chamberlain's office for the past month. There's nothing from the German, nothing!"

"Dammit, calm down, Devon! We'll get through this. Be at the golf course. If you're not ... well, God forbid ... you don't have a choice."

"We all have choices, Malcolm."

"Not on this, Devon. Harvey thought he had a choice, and you see where it got him. You come, or I'll have Jimmy drag your sorry ass out there."

Devon Whyte dropped the receiver. He stared at shaking hands, never having seen them do that.

XVIII

The first time Kenna visited Washington, D.C., for an extended period, she was told about an unknown restaurant she fell in love with. Huáng's Thai was a tiny room in Fairfax. To her, it was the best-kept secret in the city, the best Thai restaurant in the world … at least of the ones where she had eaten. How a Thai restaurant ever ended up with a Chinese name was beyond her. She had been surprised to learn it was still in operation.

She and Wiggy sat in the small, three-room building: dining/kitchen, multi-sex bathroom, and a walk-in freezer. It was not quaint. The ambiance consisted of a whitewashed brick façade so close to Highway 50 that, on more than one occasion, cars had ended up in the dining room. With the front door open during rush hour, you were lucky to hear yourself think. But you didn't come here to think; you came here to eat.

Owned and operated by a family of Thai immigrants, the restaurant's food was authentic, so you asked what you were eating only if you truly wanted to know. Here, you ate as well or as meagerly as you wanted. So hot to break a sweat after the first bite, the food could also be toned down by Maxi, the owner, for his 'soft-bellied' American friends.

Regulars asked for Maxi's family dish, a concoction of leftovers, no doubt, thrown together each day and never the same as the day before. Kenna referred to it as food art.

Kenna lowered her nose to the vegetables and hot shrimp … very hot shrimp … over thin rice noodles. The long, slender, dark red peppers in the middle dared her: She indulged, followed by mouthfuls of water.

"Happy to see ya eatin', kid," Wiggy said.

Kenna inhaled several times. "You know food's always down the list for me."

"Thinkin' of Mr. Sommer again, are ya?"

"Well, I am a woman."

"Someday, I'll teach ye how to eat like a townie."

"Drink like a townie, eat like a townie." Kenna pointed to the fork in Wiggy's left hand. "I know; keep your hands away from the intake unit. You Brit descendants are wussies. Real men eat the chilies."

"I'll forgive yer indiscretion this once, kid. Next time, though, might get my Armagh blood boilin'."

"Did yer ancestors wear dresses like the Scots?" Kenna asked, followed by another bite.

Wiggy curled his upper lip. "It made it easier to bear our arses at 'em."

"A pretty site that must've been, given the hygiene of the day," Kenna said in her worst Irish accent; they both chuckled.

Wiggy washed the food down with a gulp of Singha Beer. A toothy grin followed as he swiped at his chin with a red paper napkin. "Ye should finish that, lass."

"I'm just …" Kenna shoved the half-full plate into the center of the table.

"I know, not hungry."

"No, full."

"It happens every time, you know. On one of these cases, yer gonna collapse."

"We don't have to worry about that with you, now, do we?"

"Not on yer life, but ya better be—"

"Stop preaching, Wiggy. Tell me what's in the wind."

Kenna's partner settled the fork and knife on the empty plate and gathered a mouthful of beer. He belched into a napkin, mumbled an apology, and then took another drink. He belched again, the one apology covering all ills for the day.

"Begin with the obvious, the German," Kenna said.

"A blank so far. The name didn't raise any flags with

those I spoke to, but the search just began."

"He's the key and probably our man."

"No doubt. His ties to Afghanistan complicate matters. I'm thinkin' the better way is to go after him through this Gowen, the bloody middleman."

"Agreed," Kenna said.

Wiggy said it from memory: "Cum Laude from George Washington. Law degree from there in one year. Yep, one year, mind ya. Did an internship with Chamberlain while in school and studied abroad for a year in Cambridge."

"That's MI5 breeding ground, isn't it?" Kenna interrupted.

"Don't see a link so far, but he did study foreign politics. He's a slippery character, and it seems a might short on ethics."

"Every politician needs someone to do the dirty work."

"Word is he's more than that and plays the Washington game better than anyone. He has stacks of information on every politician and their family and likes to use it."

"Heinrich Himmler did that to keep an eye on the masses for Hitler." Kenna took a drink of beer. She thought of Bridgewater's comment about Hitler's mustache, then rapidly wiped her upper lip.

Wiggy took another drink. "Anyway, more than a few senators have raised a row with Chamberlain about their phones and computer systems being hacked. They say Gowen lobbied some very large foreign companies and individuals that have, apparently, dumped tidy sums into the Party's political action committees."

"Is that the Marshals line of questioning or the opposition?" Kenna asked.

"The opposition, no doubt. His biggest critics say many of those contributions are illegal, and the companies and people are linked to foreign governments."

"Marshals again?"

"Lotta word salad on Gowen havin' put a little in his own pocket along the way."

"An insurance policy," Kenna said. "Gowen does the dirty work and keeps the others clean. In the meantime, he makes a small fortune for himself and gets government protection. Information like that would be valuable."

"If ye could trace it."

"And if he had?"

"He bein' Chamberlain?" Wiggy asked; Kenna nodded. "It costs a lot to keep someone's mouth shut, kid."

"But none of that tells me why Gowen would kill

Chamberlain," Kenna said, then snapped herself into Gowen's position. "Unless the senator didn't know, uncovered Gowen's game and threatened to expose it."

"Hard to believe Chamberlain didn't know the Party's money trail."

"Not really. My father raised a lot of money for the Party that the hierarchy never knew about, or more importantly, never asked about."

"Dishonestly?"

"Ask my old man," Kenna said, beer at her lips.

"As long as he helps us find Anson Beck, I'll refrain from questions like that."

"So, this is what Bridgewater meant by saying that Chamberlain hadn't been faithful to the Party," Kenna wondered aloud. "Appears to me Chamberlain was going to blow the whistle."

"Would make the list of enemies quite long, my guess."

Kenna hesitated for a few seconds. "An educated one that would require a cover-up."

"More than one person in this city signatory to that theory."

"Agent Edelman?"

"If I read between the lines correctly," Wiggy said. "The

press is beatin' on her like she pulled the trigger."

"Misinformation being force-fed from somewhere."

"Aye," Wiggy said, eyes narrowed. "I'll deal with that when I find out who."

"What else?" Kenna growled.

"I contacted one of the lads at Interpol—"

"Is there anyone in the world you don't know?" Kenna asked.

"Gran Lockwood had many friends, lass." Wiggy raised his glass and took a drink. "It seems there's been some interest in Gowen on their side of the pond since the Taliban fell."

"You mentioned Cambridge; anything connect them?"

"Checkin' that now," Wiggy said stone-faced. "It takes time to develop an international network, but the lad's been active, very active."

"And Chamberlain was blind while this happened under his nose? I don't buy it."

"Could'a been Gowen's charge to keep Chamberlain out of the money loop."

"Until a couple months ago?" Kenna leaned back, contemplating. "Not buying it. Chamberlain and Gowen shared an office. The senator had to be mixed up in it."

"Difficult to get a read on the totality, Fiery. Chamberlain's nose seems clean, at least in the last few months. I think he got in the way."

"That seems awfully simple."

"Maybe he decided they'd gone too far and wanted to clear his conscience."

"What about Altmann, then?" she asked. "A set-up, or here to pedal information to see if Chamberlain would play the game, or keep his mouth shut?"

"Or the hit man," Wiggy's icy words bit into Kenna. "Threatens him with blackmail, arranges for a meet, then kills him: simple and clean."

"Blackmail, murder: Which is it?"

"Unlike murder, lass, blackmail's never simple. But together—"

"We have several angles, Wiggy. The widow, Gowen, and the German."

"Yer forgettin' one."

Kenna leaned on her elbows; "I haven't forgotten. Actually, two: Malcolm and Charlie."

"Me gut says that the lads at Interpol will find a connection between the German and Gowen. Maybe even the bloody German and Chamberlain. One thing's for certain," Wiggy said and continued after a drink, "nobody likes or trusts Gowen."

"I haven't met anyone here I trust either," Kenna said. Maxi's wife, the waitress for the day, overheard Kenna's statement and slapped her on the shoulder. She recanted: "Present company excluded, of course."

It amazed Kenna that Maxi's wife remembered her after all these years. She shot a loud rejoinder at Kenna in Thai, curse words no doubt, as she lifted their plates and walked for the kitchen. The yelling continued in clear view until Maxi slapped a knife on a cutting board. It was the usual banter, a crowd-pleaser, and part of the ambiance, as well.

"Whoever's involved, smells like a rat, kid."

"Is this where I get bombarded with clichés and anecdotes?"

"Ya didn't seem to mind the one about the old hen trying to squeeze out the big egg when all she had ta do was relax." Wiggy brushed his arm over the table. "Would'a helped ya in the windy city."

"No bad memories, Wiggy; let's get back to business."

"Then, let's hear 'bout yer day, kid."

"Met a general trying to take control of the U.S. and the senator who wants us to leave town."

"Still makin' friends and influencin' people. You've always done that well."

"A personal gift from father."

Wiggy said. "The blond-headed lad is a snake charmer, that one."

"No doubt, but the best-lookin' one I've seen in years."

"As was Medusa. Don't be blinded by it."

"Caution noted, again," Kenna agreed. "Did Gowen do anything else?"

"Left a parcel at the Democratic National Chairman's house and saw Bridgewater."

"Did he leave anything with Bridgewater?"

"I don't think he even had time to pay respects. But he spent a few minutes with Devon Whyte before he went about his way."

"Could Whyte be in this thing with the others?"

"Makes fer a nice little band of thieves," Wiggy said. "Whatever it is, Chamberlain stirred the pot. I went into Bridgewater's office after Gowen left. The ole man was yellin' at yer friend from Massachusetts on the phone. Lady Dorothy was kind enough to lie and tell me the good senator was in a meeting. For her to lie, it must be big. I told her you wanted to get together with the senator tomorrow, but she said he was fully booked."

Kenna thought of the U.S. Marshals ripping the evidence from the murder scene and of Salvatori's comments. She had never liked the scent of everyday business in Washington. With every inhale, it now burned her nostrils like an acid nasal spray.

"We can't assume anything, and, as usual, timing's critical," Kenna said.

"Gowen's not concluded his business; he won't be hard to find."

Kenna took a large drink. "Last night, Hobson said he first told Agent Edelman about Chamberlain's body. Yet, she was like a backdrop at the scene."

"Aye. Like her presence was a nuisance to the Italian."

"Go put your Armagh charm to work on her and find out what you can."

"It'll be me pleasure, kid," Wiggy said with a smirk. "You off to the golf course?"

"Yes, a tribute to Chamberlain with Bridgewater."

"I thought that was tomorrow?"

"They moved it. My tee-time is scheduled for 2:00. Call me no later than 2:30. I'm playing with Devon Whyte. Think I'll make a few politicians uneasy, then give the Party leader something to think about it."

XIX

A Mike Savage painting would have shown that they were to be the first foursome of the day, or at least that is how Kenna envisioned it. Their faces would have reflected the confusion that filled Kenna's mind. There would be no cart tracks, no footprints, indeed, no politicians. The late morning rain shower would have streaked the canvas like blood. In the background, people would stare into the distance with black eyes. There would be a dog in the background doing its business on the 18th green.

When Kenna stepped from the Clubhouse into a light mist, the images came back. The light noon rain had driven the fair-weather crowd to shelter. That disappointed her. Apparently, some didn't believe that last respects to Harvey Chamberlain were worth getting wet.

While awaiting her playing partners, Kenna sat on the hillock overlooking the valley below. She inhaled the humidity and absorbed the warm sun as it appeared from behind a cloud. It bounced off the first fairway like a hundred million diamonds spread across a blanket of checkered green velvet. For the moment, the view released the city's stranglehold on her mind.

Carried by a light breeze, the smell of freshly mowed wet grass filled her nostrils. A rainbow stretched across the southern horizon and dropped behind a distant hill. Goosebumps straightened the hairs on her arms. She loved this most of the game, of the places where the game was played. Such venues could, even in the worst of times, offer peace of mind.

Her attention shot away from the game of golf to her other game. Her immediate challenge … Gran's life teaching … was *'to separate the lies from the truth'*. The distinction was nearly impossible to make in this bastion of political subterfuge. Here, it had become normal behavior to lie, to deceive, to lead people into an abyss from which there was no escape. The game, over the decades, Malcolm Bridgewater had mastered.

Kenna had no preconceived notion as to what today would bring. With the rain gone, the crowd trickled out onto the course. Some hearty players had endured the light rain and remained on the course. A foursome putted on the very green where, not much more than 12 hours before, a United States Senator had been killed. She was moved by the lack of sincerity but tried not to show it. There was something wrong, terribly wrong, with all the pomp, with the chest-beating that had initiated the round. It wasn't about reverence to a man, to a fallen comrade, of that she was certain. It was about self-importance, about getting before the cameras. Bridgewater had said it so well … about the church, where God was only worshipped when the kneeling served them.

The initial lunacy of this case went beyond the inept investigating team, beyond the evidence that was literally thrown together and carted off with the same reckless abandon that one would expect when peeling a dead skunk from a remote stretch of highway. Charlie had said it best: A 'vast emotionless void enveloped this city', and everyone in it. She refused to allow it to envelop her, forbid it to become like Chicago.

"Kenna, hop in!" Malcolm Bridgewater yelled.

She turned when the senator stopped the golfcart next to her bag. The old man's expression was not anticipated: the puppy dog eyes of long-lost friends meeting again for the first time in years. It was as if no one had died, as if they had not spoken earlier. It held, though, the wisdom of age and … Hidden deceit.

"I was supposed to partner with Devon Whyte."

"We'll meet him at the tee," Bridgewater said. "I wanted General Treadway to join us, but he's been detained at a meeting … saving the world from Communism or some nonsense."

Bridgewater smiled as he steered towards the 1st tee. She took a sip of water from a plastic bottle, smiled, and waved at the professional women leaving the course.

"What was it the general said about the senator's seat?" Kenna asked. "He seemed to think it could mean a vote in his direction."

"Confidence and speculation aren't the same."

Kind of like your colleague from Massachusetts, Kenna did not say. "Well, I'm sorry the general couldn't make it."

"Even he knows when to declare a truce, girl. As should you."

Threat taken, Malcolm. "It's always troubled me, compromising the truth."

"Come to Washington for a while, girl," Bridgewater said with a straight face. "You will learn many useful things. It could become your greatest ally."

Kenna thought he meant to say 'I' instead of 'It' as they stopped at the first tee. Another cart approached. Kenna stood and took the bottle of water to her bag.

"Do you have that Marshals' report, Malcolm?"

The displeasure registered immediately. "I told you I couldn't get it."

"Then you and I don't have anything to discuss this afternoon."

Kenna moved her bag to the other cart and popped a crick from her neck. Her ribs burned, but it shouldn't bother her game. Introductions were made. Senator Lansford of Missouri joined them, reaching out to shake her hand, followed by Devon Whyte, whose limp did not go unnoticed. The chairman's eyes flicked to Bridgewater. Kenna detected silent, questioning communication.

"Are you alright, Mr. Whyte?" Kenna asked.

"A bump while jogging this morning. The exercise will help work it out." He motioned when she favored her side. "Appears I could ask the same of you."

"Good," Bridgewater said, interrupting the exchange. "Now, let's get to it before they give away our time."

"That'll happen with the cows fly, Malcolm," Lansford said.

"I have admired your writings for many years," Kenna said to Whyte.

"One of the few to have gotten through one." The chairman pulled a white bone pipe from his pants pocket and winced as he tapped it on the heel of his golf shoe. "Do you mind?"

"Not as long as it's a Texas tobacco."

"Since Malcolm's buying a Tennessee blend today."

"Don't give him the option, Kenna," Lansford said. "I've negotiated with him before. Take a hard line."

"Try not to make us look too foolish, Kenna," Bridgewater said over the whine of the golfcart as he accelerated. "This is for fun, not for money."

"Really?" Kenna replied. "I thought it was for Harvey Chamberlain."

At the first tee, the air thickened. By the flip of tees, Devon Whyte was given honors. The big man turned to face Kenna. A bead of sweat appeared on Whyte's brow; he wiped it off with a long, thick, gloved finger. A jerky practice swing preceded an equally jerky hack at the ball. The ball sliced wildly for a line of trees no more than 200 yards out. It slapped against wood and bounded backwards into the thick rough.

"Relax, Devon," Kenna said, teeing the ball on the ladies' tee box. "Like Malcolm said: 'this is for fun'."

Her ball rested within a foot of the miniature statue of the Capitol. With the club lifted over and behind her head, Kenna stretched the previous round from a stiff back, sore ribs, and side. Her neck burned, but she tried to ignore it.

Staring down the 400-yard par 4, she took a practice swing, noting a slight breeze from left to right. Her stance was relaxed and confident. She inhaled the thick, stale air and exhaled slowly just prior to pulling her back swing. 'Keep the mechanics sound', she heard her father preaching, which she did. With a fluid motion, the club-head reached its apex, then gathered speed downward in a precise swing line to make crisp contact with the ball. It skidded along the right side of the fairway, kicking up a rooster tail in the wet grass. It stopped in the rough not far from Devon's ball, exactly where she wanted it. The men didn't notice the pleasure on her face.

"Is this your first time on our course, Ms. Hannigan?" Whyte asked.

"Kenna, please. And no, I played here a few days ago with Malcolm and years ago with the senator and my father."

"That's where I recognize the name, your father, television man in Dallas," the chairman said as he pressed the golfcart into motion, steering the opposite direction of Bridgewater's cart. "Please call me Devon. I'd like to hear your opinion of it."

"If the location of my first shot is indicative of the day, I will like it just fine. Besides, it's all going to change with the planned alterations."

"Yes, I'd forgotten that's why you're here, to report on that and upcoming events."

"The announcement's moved to next weekend," she said. "As for the course, you guys owe the superintendent a raise. He did a great job. It's challenging, somewhat surprising, but playable even for a hacker like me."

They made a swift left turn along the cart path, and then Whyte took a 90-degree turn onto the fairway. He pressed the accelerator again; tires hissed on the moist grass. They stopped 20 yards to the side of Malcolm Bridgewater's ball and remained silent until the senator played his shot. The 3-wood landed 50 yards short of the green in the middle of the fairway.

Whyte raised his voice, "Predictable Malcolm: on the golf course, always in the middle, but never in the Senate."

"It's served me well, Devon, very well."

Lansford lofted a wicked approach toward the green. It bounded over a trap, through some thickets, and disappeared. He took it with reserved anger. Whyte rushed his shot. The clubface met the ball off-center, hooking it wildly. It caught a lucky bounce 70 yards to the left and short of the green, then veered right 90 degrees. It rolled to a rest just outside a sand trap, though buried in thick, rough 10 feet behind the first cut.

"Damn," he shouted.

"My father always said not to allow the game to frustrate me, Devon," Kenna said. "My grandmother always said that patience was the mark of a professional in all things. She also reminded me that Ted Williams only hit four hundred once. That meant he failed six out of ten times."

"Never thought of it like that." Whyte smiled. "That can be said of many things in life."

Kenna played her next shot to the edge of the green. From there, she would have a lengthy chip.

"Shame the announcement was cancelled," Whyte said with a pause. "For the reason it was, that is."

"Yes. Were you close to Harvey?"

Whyte raised an eyebrow, then shifted an uncomfortable stare at Malcolm in the opposite cart. "As close as one can be in this city, yes."

"How did you land in Washington?"

"This is where you come when you can't find a job anywhere else."

"I know better. There are at least twenty Fortune-Fifty companies that could use your talents, but you stay here. Why?"

He puffed on a cold pipe and pushed the cart into motion.

"When I came here, I believed I could make a difference."

"You have."

"Maybe. But the harder I try, the more it feels like a futile gesture of self-indulgence."

"You don't honestly believe that?"

"Ten years ago, I would have given you a definitive no. But today, it may be truer than even I care to believe. Like never before, games are played with peoples' lives. Laws are created that have no cultural or societal benefit. It's all for the sake of improving power bases. Bureaucracy has become so burdensome even the insiders don't know how it works."

"No one can convince me that Malcolm doesn't know how the system works."

"One of a handful of exceptions."

Kenna turned to face Whyte without speaking. She saw another book behind those wise, dark eyes. Who was in it? Just then, she realized that it could be her, as the biggest sucker ever to set foot in Washington: just a snot-nosed kid manipulated by the grand masters.

"Tell me about your relationship with Harvey Chamberlain."

Malcolm Bridgewater played a nice short iron to the center of the green. The chairman glanced at the aged senator; Bridgewater's eyes met Whyte's.

As Whyte stopped the cart at his ball, Kenna stepped out. The ball was buried, and Devon hacked at it. It shot out of the rough, never more than a few inches off the ground, and wound up to the left of the green in the rough again. They drove to the green, getting there long before the other two who were looking for Lansford's ball.

"Harvey and I were friends in college," Whyte said. "We were dependent on each other for more years than I care to think. After college, our careers took similar meteoric paths. It made us closer in a lot of ways." Whyte paused. "Tragedies inside politics come no easier than outside the beltway, Kenna. The loss of a friend is as deeply felt, if not deeper here, where friendships are forged in philosophical belief."

Kenna had stepped into Nathanial Whyte's confessional. Was she suddenly everyone's priest?

"Aren't all friendships?" she stated as much as asked.

"If life were as simple as a conversation, there would be no need for people like you, Kenna."

"No doubt," Kenna retorted.

"If I were to tell you that I no more believed Harvey killed himself than I will hole this next shot, what would you say?" Whyte asked.

Kenna stepped to the edge of the rough. "I'd say, chip out."

Kenna believed that the chairman stared at the impossible task before him, both on the golf course and off. The chairman lifted a sand wedge from the cart and limped close to where Kenna stood. With a deep exhale, he stared down at the shot.

"The saddest thing? Harvey didn't talk to me."

"Troubles with his wife?" There was something Whyte wasn't saying.

"Nothing new. She's a gold digger; he was a manipulator. They accepted their roles, but I suppose the benefits ran out long ago."

"Others have said that."

"What can I do to help? I want to know what happened," Devon said.

"What got Harvey sideways with the Party?" Kenna asked.

"Many things over many years, actually. A changing of the guard, if you will."

"The old moderate establishment isn't liking the swing to a more radical liberal stance?"

"Perhaps," Whyte said. "Harvey and I have been trying for years to bring about change. Now it appears I will fight alone."

A cart whined towards them. Malcolm Bridgewater passed with the wave of a hand. "We're here to play golf, not gossip."

"Why wouldn't Harvey confide in you?" Kenna asked.

"Another time, Kenna. There is more, but I have to know your intentions."

"I'm here to find the facts, Devon."

"A lot of people won't like that if it doesn't suit their purpose."

"I don't give a damn what they like."

"How far are you willing to go?"

Kenna looked askance, noting a determined stare on her playing partner's face. It was a curious question; one she had not considered. But, then again, she never worried about the consequences of her actions.

"Malcolm is the most powerful man in Congress," Whyte continued. "If you discover information that will hurt the Party, he won't take it lightly."

"The truth is hard to repudiate, Devon."

"But often harder to accept, Kenna."

"Harvey may have been involved in some campaign funding improprieties. Know anything about that?"

The chairman did not turn; his shoulders tightened, and he hesitated. "No, why?"

A lie. "Is that what Avery Gowen delivered to you today? Or was it about a German named Altmann?"

"That's absurd," Whyte snapped. "I don't know what you're … any German."

Once again, Kenna knew she had been taken full circle on a conversation. And once again knew the lies and deceit scrambled her brain more than breakfast.

"I believe you're a good man, Devon. Don't prove me wrong."

There was hesitation. "Honestly, I'm not sure I can … now."

Kenna learned a long time ago that the word 'honestly' always preceded a lie. Devon Whyte knew about the German and more than likely knew why the German was blackmailing Chamberlain. The phone in her bag rang; she answered. She listened as Wiggy talked, then disconnected.

"I have to leave," she said, then to Whyte: "You want to help without helping. That's strange, but tells me there's something working on you."

"Where are you off to, girl?" Bridgewater yelled.

"I have work to do, Malcolm." She turned back to Whyte. "Would you see that my clubs are taken back to the Clubhouse?"

The Chairman of the National Democratic Party nodded as Kenna dropped her putter into the bag. Walking away, she felt the stares on her back, like an assassin sighting her through a rifle scope.

XX

The hiss of a golfcart turned her; it slid to a stop. Cheap after-shave gave off a hint of recognition. General Treadway clamped an unlit White Owl between broad yellow teeth. Sweat stains darkened the armpits of his khaki shirt as he leaned thick forearms on the steering wheel.

"We need to talk," the general put it succinctly.

The general's meaning was a double-edged sword, no doubt. Kenna had a feeling she was going to need this military dinosaur. At what price, though?

"I just left my sticks with –"

"Golf can wait."

"I'd be happy to buy you a drink."

"Too early for me," Treadway said.

"Was thinking of something lighter."

"Don't drink the stuff; no alcohol," Treadway added. "Let me show you the ground where men in blue and gray traversed over a century and a half ago."

Without hesitation, Kenna climbed aboard. She liked the military inferences of 'the field' and 'the ground'. These were hallowed places where men spilled blood for what they believed. It was no doubt the true meaning behind

Treadway's words.

At the 1st tee, the starter hailed Senator D'Amato of New York and the Chairman of General Dynamics. The general stopped the cart and jumped out, as would a man 20 years his junior. He leaned into handshakes with the two men. His transformation from military strategist to politician took less time than did his strides to greet them.

Is this whole town like this? Kenna asked herself, knowing the answer.

"The pleasure is mine, general," the businessman said. "I followed you into Baghdad on business in oh-three. I, for one, look forward to you being on the Joint Chiefs."

"Not nearly as much as do I, sir," the general replied.

Kenna was moved by the general's swollen chest. The confidence was not all that far removed from what she had felt going after Anson Beck. Victory at the highest levels could only be achieved by those willing to sacrifice everything for it, be it in journalism, war, or solving murder. Looking at the men together, she wondered about the latter.

"I shoot skeet to relax," Treadway said. "Care to join me some day?"

The men agreed to a time, and Treadway took his seat beside Kenna. The general steered the cart off the manmade paths and through a long line of heavy foliage away from the Clubhouse. The machine growled as it climbed a steep hill that overlooked the Clubhouse 150 feet below. Large houses stood behind them at a distance; several Congressional holes were visible in the valley below. Treadway stood out.

"Beautiful view," Kenna said, joining him. "Never been up here."

"It's good ground."

"Sorry, general, I didn't go to The Academy. I appreciate it for something else."

"McClellan had Lee's Army of Northern Virginia on the run through this valley, but the bastard didn't follow up. It cost the North a quick victory."

"A similar fate to what happened in Afghanistan, I take it," Kenna offered.

Treadway removed the cigar from his mouth, smiled, and turned. "So, you do know history."

"Frustratingly so."

"A lot of politicians think they are better military strategists than professional soldiers. Lincoln had that problem. In a way, though, he was just looking for someone to take the fight to Bobby Lee and not vice versa. It took him three years to find Grant." He chewed the cigar, then lit it.

"More recently, it's a little-known fact that Churchill drove his generals crazy by micromanaging their every move."

"The British didn't seem to come out any less for it."

"It's changed without total war. Politicians stick their noses where they don't belong."

"Civilian oversight is how we prevent dictatorships," Kenna offered.

Treadway's eyes glistened as he stared into the valley. "Were you in the military, young Kenna?"

"No."

Treadway bit down on the cigar and spoke with it clamped between his teeth: "You have a nose for trouble, but do you have the guts to back it up?"

"Looks can be deceiving, general," Kenna said. "Does it bother you that I make decisions without someone else's permission?"

"I do what needs to be done."

"Within the limits of military doctrine."

"Naturally. But a true leader leads."

The general pulled the White Owl from his mouth. He spit, stared at the end, and inhaled. "Philosophy is for pansies in linen suits and silk paisley ties. You don't strike me as the type."

"You don't strike me as a pansy either, general," Kenna said.

"Shame you can't appreciate what's before you like I can," Treadway said, followed by a military grimace. "Chamberlain was weak, had no backbone. He'd still be alive if he had."

Far in the distance, Kenna followed the flight of a ball as it left a player's driver. It disappeared into the trees. *Weekend warriors,* she mused.

"Like I said, a frustrated historian, general. What little I do know, though, helps me know the enemy."

The general gripped the canopy of the cart until his knuckles turned white. "Perhaps I have misread you."

Treadway swept his half-open palm and extended index finger across the expanse before them until it stopped at a gap between the distant hills. He stiffened his finger and stabbed at the air as if tapping a painting. He traced the route of the fairway formed by the natural lay of the land. It was flanked by the high ground to the west and the continuation of the valley to the east. At that moment, Kenna believed General Treadway saw General Stuart forming his cavalry.

"Through there … the gap." Treadway tapped the live painting again. "Stuart had a clear road to Washington until

McClellan cut him off. Yet, McClellan didn't take advantage of his numerical superiority. The question is, why?"

"I've never heard of such an engagement. Did J.E.B. Stuart hold McClellan here long enough to buy Lee time to block the route to Richmond?"

"What could explain McClellan's lack of determination, his failure to take advantage of a superior position and strength?"

"Not all generals are like you … and Grant."

"I have no doubt of that. I admire greatness, Kenna. Stuart was a great leader and a great tactician. McClellan was a great organizer. They both had failures; Stuart's was at Gettysburg, McClellan's perhaps here, in a battle that never took place. But does one mistake supersede a thousand successes?"

"Are you talking about Stuart and McClellan, or you?" Kenna asked. "It's well known you don't back down from a fight, or did you really bring me out here to discuss the Civil War?"

"I've heard that you find things; I think it was," the general said.

"Part of that nose I told you about."

"A word of advice," the general said with a set jaw. He

turned full-face to Kenna and squinted into the sun. "Mrs. Chamberlain is off limits."

"I met Mrs. Chamberlain once, in my teens," Kenna said.

Treadway's protective animal instinct bore into her. She wanted no fight with the general. The truth about Gloria Chamberlain was yet to be known. She hoped the general's convictions were defensible. Treadway followed the government line of the moment: Harvey Chamberlain killed himself … any fool could see it.

"That's what separates me from the fools, general," Kenna said. "If I'm on track, there is one other person who will know I'm right … the killer."

Treadway puffed on the cigar and allowed the smoke to swirl past the top of the cart. He turned back to the valley and inhaled. In Terror Treadway's form, he pressed forward.

"After Baghdad, I was sent to Germany to wipe my ass with my last Purple Heart. Later, I was assigned to military intelligence. My job was basically running black ops into Afghanistan."

"We keep going back many years, general. Is there a reason?" Kenna leaned forward.

"The Washington press set back our intelligence efforts decades in Europe. But, in a strange way, we deserved it.

They proved then that military and intelligence were two words not to be used in the same sentence.”

It was an interesting admission from an intelligence officer. Yet, Treadway believed he had changed that in Europe. Cigar smoke drifted from the general’s mouth as he spoke:

“You’ve been asking about a German named Altmann.”

Kenna’s silent response, *and if I have?*

“I’ll tell you like I’m going to tell the U.S. Marshals. Altmann was a double agent for the Afghani Taliban. We killed him.”

“Is that a collective ‘we’, or you specifically?”

“I organized a rat line with a Berlin church elder, Doctor Christoph Frhein. He recruited people in Afghanistan to work with us inside. We paid them to help Frhein’s people escape. Altmann hunted those who helped as if on a private mission against my team.”

“Altmann’s a German name. Afghani intelligence?” Kenna asked. “Mixed mother and father?”

The general allowed a lazy eye to wander in Kenna’s direction. He tapped the ash from the cigar that fell onto his pant leg. He glared at Kenna as if to say, *‘stop interrupting’.*

“Simply put, I want Altmann if it’s really him,”

Treadway insisted.

"You mean, if you failed to kill him in Europe, you want the first shot at him now."

The steady hand of the warrior raised and pointed to the gap between the two distant ridges. "McClellan's army was ten times the size of J.E.B. Stuart's cavalry force. Had the Army of the Potomac pushed on without hesitation, they could have easily destroyed Stuart's cavalry and carried the field. Instead, the Yankee general was fooled by Stuart's ruse, and the Army of the Potomac came to a grinding halt to await reinforcements and supplies. Stuart then circled completely around McClellan, a feat still studied at the Academy. His cavalry had taken the attention away from Lee and delayed the end of the war at least a year … without firing a shot."

"And this should make amends for leaving Lee blind at Gettysburg?"

Treadway squinted. "You're missing the point."

Kenna stared into the fiery eyes. "No, general, I think not. You aren't talking about Stuart at all. You're talking about yourself, that you won't hesitate like McClellan."

"In Baghdad, I offered a deal to a Republican Guard commander after we destroyed nearly his entire battalion and encircled the balance. When he countered my offer, I finished them off to the man without responding."

"A fair deal, I assume, given he was in no position to bargain."

"That's the deals I cut!" Treadway exhaled out the side of his mouth.

"Is that the deal you cut with the widow?"

The general rested an elbow on the roof of the cart. He took a long drag from the cigar and allowed the smoke to drift from his mouth, not blinking as it drifted into his eyes. He rubbed the edges of his teeth with a thumb; his stare was fixed on *the ground*.

"God, I loved Berlin. Best God-damned beer in the world," he continued without hesitation. "The Methodist clergyman and I got close, very close. He was reluctant, but I convinced him that we should be smuggling information out, not just people. He didn't want to be in the spy business. After a few months, he brought me information about a deep contact in the East. A Kraut that called himself Morningstar."

The general took a deep breath of clean air. A distant celebration at the 17th green did not disturb his concentration. With a middle finger, he brushed another ash from the end of the cigar. A hint of fire dropped and was ground into the dirt by a boot heel.

"Morningstar passed us a lot of good intel, and then one day, he told me he wanted out. He promised a final cache that would be worth his freedom. I was working on bringing him out … hell, I wanted to meet the bastard … when he fell off the face of the earth. I presumed he was dead and discovered later he had been killed by Altmann."

"Altmann killed Morningstar and you killed Altmann. Nice and tidy, end of story."

The general straightened his back. It popped more than once. He pointed the cigar at Kenna. "This is when things start getting nasty. Keep off the German's spoor."

Kenna turned away as her telephone rang. Her facial expression did not change as Wiggy spoke into her ear: "I found our lad's Arlington flat, Fiery. Hurry along."

"I'll grab an Uber. I have a stop to make in Georgetown first. Call me if he goes anywhere. I'll be there within an hour." She turned to the general and hung up. "Are you meeting with Agent Salvatori, general?"

"Yes, at six in his office."

"Mind if I tag along? I'd like to see this."

The general hesitated. He rubbed his chin, inhaled from

the cigar, then spoke as he exhaled. "Hell, a unified front's a sound strategy, young Kenna."

"I'll see you at his office at six. I appreciate what you said about McClellan, general."

The general's expression was blank as he turned his eyes back to J.E.B. Stuart's ground.

XXI

The Uber driver slowed the Toyota Prius in front of the late senator's apartment in Georgetown. Kenna was disappointed; they had arrived too late. As they passed, there were no students idling in the streets, none sitting on the stoop of the two-story flat that Harvey Chamberlain had called home for the last two months of his life.

Yellow 'CRIME SCENE' tape stretched across the front walkway. The street was lined with bland-colored and black-wall-tired government vehicles, the same as she had seen the night before. Armed men and women in cheap suits and Wal*Mart sunglasses ignored the darkness of overcast and stood vigil at the entrance of the fifty-year-old brick structure. They stopped everyone at the tape barrier and sent them away. Pressing against the tape, the paparazzi chattered into microphones, cell phones, and recorders.

No doubt, these meticulous professionals would find Chamberlain's apartment empty. She hunkered down in the rear seat when Salvatori walked from the building. He surveyed the area and lit a cigarette. Kenna believed she could hear the U.S. Marshals' public position: *'There is no investigation'*. Not amused, she wondered, *how long would it take them to raze the entire city block?*

"Want me to stop?" Luis, the middle-aged Latino driver, asked.

"Nah, they're ahead of me, Luis."

"Ma'am?" he asked, confused.

"A long story. I have the second address."

She ignored the question and gave Luis the address that Wiggy had texted. A half-hour later, she met Wiggy on the curb in front of a row house condominium complex in Arlington. The building's façade was a replica of early American style with metal siding and a metal door. It stood as a counterfeit of the architectural flavor of the nation's capital. She knocked; they waited.

With hollow eyes, a thin man of Kenna's height stared out from behind the chained door as if looking through Kenna to the street beyond. Pimpled rosy cheeks held a much too young-looking face in cherubic innocence. Black, stolid eyes told a contradicting story of what was held behind.

The apartment interior was equally phony as the exterior. Beyond the door, Kenna saw a vinyl leather couch. A gas fireplace was centered on a wall of thinly sliced pumice red brick. Plastic silverware was stuck into a half-eaten frozen dinner atop a laminated wood-grained table. Kenna was sure the meal had been microwaved. Gowen balled his stockinged feet atop a Chinese Persian rug. He wiped a bead of sweat off his thin upper lip with a monogrammed handkerchief that had been purchased from a catalog, not a fine men's clothier. His tie was shiny, though not silk, and loosened about his permanent-pressed polyester blend cotton shirt.

"My name is Kenna. I knew Senator Chamberlain."

"I won't hold that against you," Avery Gowen replied. "What do you want?"

"To talk about his death."

"What's there to talk about?" Gowen said matter-of-factly. "He puts a gun to his head, kills himself, and puts me out of work."

"It's never that simple."

"And your muscle-bound friend?" Gowen asked, staring at the entire length of Wiggy's broad frame.

"Is harmless. We travel together."

"Ah, I get it. The journalist who doubles as Dick Tracy or something." His mind whirled. "But you're a woman, does that make you Pussy Tracy?"

"Mr. Gowen, I have a feeling you fit very well into Washington society."

"I try."

Avery Gowen could not pretend beyond the expression on his blemished face. He had stepped beyond that neutral territory coined in World War I as 'no-man's-land'. Kenna wondered, have you gotten into a game you know nothing about? His actions told her Gowen was in fear.

Kenna once again heard Charlie's warning: *'Watch out for Avery; he's a snake'.* "Are you a pretender, Mr. Gowen?"

"That's not a nice way to get invited in, Ms. Tracy," Gowen said. "I was warned you might be coming around, but then I didn't know you were a Private … Pussy until the senator was killed."

"If you are doing that to piss me off, it's succeeding."

"Oh, piss you off, most certainly, Ms. Private Puss." Gowen smiled while lowering the target of his stare.

He masked his fear with sarcasm and confrontation. An interesting game for a man of such small stature. Or …

"Tell me about him," Kenna insisted. "Senator Chamberlain, that is."

"I have nothing to say to you or anyone for that matter."

Wiggy stepped towards the crack in the door but was stopped by Kenna's outstretched arm. At that moment, Wiggy's animalistic instinct to hurt someone permeated his being.

"The Marshals now know what I do. At least they did as of about a few hours ago after Agent Salvatori left." Gowen glanced at the $50 imitation Rolex on the inside of his right wrist. "And they instructed me to remain silent on the matter."

"Does Agent Salvatori know about the business you've done in the East since the collapse of the Taliban?"

"My, that's a long way from home."

"Maybe events that have to do with illegal campaign contributions. Salvatori may find that interesting."

"Funny, he didn't mention that," Gowen said confidently. "Now, if you'll forgive me."

He started to close the door, but Kenna pressed her leg against it. Wiggy's foot provided a second restraint.

"Oh, wonderful. Now, isn't this when you threaten me with one of those Private Dick clichés?" Gowen cooed and chuckled. "Beat me, rape me, make me write hot checks!"

Wiggy's flexed muscles pressed against his understudy's arm. Kenna used the doorframe as leverage to push her partner back. Within moments, Kenna was succumbing to the stronger man's will. She turned; Wiggy backed off.

"I do so enjoy the pain," Gowen challenged Wiggy. "So,

the hard way, please.”

Kenna intervened. “It won’t be so amusing when they learn of the blackmail.”

Gowen backed from the door. Wiggy’s weight snapped it to the end of the security chain, “Agent Salvatori said there wasn’t a case at all.”

“If that were true, why would they ask you to keep quiet?”

“For the widow,” he smiled unconvincingly.

“Or maybe so Salvatori could get the German?” Kenna offered.

Avery Gowen’s eyes softened. He lifted two fingers to his lips, then crossed his arms at his chest. He bit a nail.

Wiggy interrupted: “You’ve done business with the German for a long time now. It’s easily enough proven.”

“Then, there’s nothing to discuss until you have proven it, Lord Armagh.”

“We were hoping to avoid the leg work,” Kenna said.

“And the broken bones,” Wiggy snarled.

“My mother always said that anything worth getting was worth the effort … and the pain,” Gowen said.

“Ya have a mother?” Wiggy barked.

“Are you fucking with me, muscle man, or just trying to

piss me off?" Gowen laughed lightly. "I was instructed to remain silent about the senator's suicide. I'm inclined to oblige."

"Something to ponder in that devious brain of yours," Kenna insisted. "It wasn't suicide; it was murder."

"Murder?" the pretender snapped. "My, you are imaginative. That's not –"

"What certain people want certain others to believe. Salvatori knows better. You and I know better, too."

"This is so confusing: campaign contributions, murder?" An eyelid wiggled. "I think it's time you left."

Gowen took a step towards the door. A bead of sweat appeared on his forehead. He lifted a cell phone from his pants.

"Ya delivered an envelope just like the one on your desk to Devon Whyte," Wiggy said. "What's in it?"

"You're the Private Dicks."

The little man's confidence turned Kenna back to the door, "Your smart-ass routine's a front. Some big prick in prison is gonna love givin' you what you want."

With calm hands, Gowen grabbed a can of Diet Cola. "Politicians that have been here for decades can protect me better than you. This city is made for people like me, Ms.

Puss, not for people like you."

'Where deals are made,' Kenna had heard a thousand times growing up. But blackmail and murder? Confused anger and fear on Gowen's face gave her the answer. No, he's not afraid at all, Kenna thought.

"It's being said on The Hill that you're working for Charlie Sommer. He was fucking the senator, you know." The young man chuckled and flipped his index finger at the door. "Oh, but I see … you've been smitten by Charlie's feline fangs."

"I deal in facts, Gowen, not lip service."

"I like how you said, 'lip service'. But do you Texas girls mean what you say?" he asked with a smile while biting another fingernail. "I take more pleasure from –"

Kenna held back her doubled fist and imagined Gowen's sweaty, skinny body being whipped, his screams of ecstasy echoing through the prison halls. For some unknown reason, Kenna envisioned Gowen's lover in studded leather, high jackboots, and crotchless panties. She shut it off.

"Your game's sick, not cute, and it doesn't work on me."

Gowen frowned. "Then, I suggest you go see Devon Whyte or Malcolm Bridgewater. Your detective thing doesn't allow you to divulge clients, Ms. Pussy. Mine doesn't allow me to kiss and tell."

"We'll see," Kenna said. "And one more thing."

With a single hard impact of her foot, Kenna broke open the door. She took two long strides and stood no more than a few inches from the little man. A well-directed finger was driven into Gowen's bony chest. The little man reeled back but managed to stand firm.

"The next time I see you, chili chest, you better call me by name, or I'll break every bone in your fuckin' body."

As they turned back outside, Wiggy placed a hand firmly on his student's shoulder. "I don't like it when ya take me fun away, kid."

"I didn't think he'd tell us anything," Kenna said. "But he told us plenty."

"Aye, he's up to his nads in this."

"The game's changin', Wiggy. I have an appointment with Treadway and Salvatori. Drop me at U.S. Marshals," Kenna said and flipped a thumb over her shoulder. "I want everything you can dig up on that weasel."

"As good as done, kid," Wiggy slapped her on the shoulder. "Chili chest?"

"All I could come up with at the moment." They laughed.

XXII

Salvatori sat at a government-issue gray metal desk in a six-by-eight glass-enclosed cubicle. The room had one air conditioning vent that provided insufficient airflow. A single overhead light cast little more than a dim shadow over his shoulder. Another desk lamp cast an opposite shadow over his left arm. The agent that escorted Kenna … fresh out of college, she thought … rapped on the window, rattled the door open, and announced her as if Salvatori hadn't expected her. Hands at her sides, Kenna stood motionless and waited for Salvatori to look up. The games.

"What do you want?" the agent asked.

"I was supposed to meet you and General Treadway."

"Just missed him."

Two gift bags, helium balloons, and other assorted items decorated Salvatori's desk. He looked up with droopy eyes and an unshaven face. Sleep had not been his friend the night before. In fact, they looked like the same clothes from the night before.

"These people must like working with you. Fifty, huh?"

Salvatori forced a smile. "The reality sank in too late. I was numb for a while, and then it hit me like a fucking truck:

I'm closer to being a hundred than to being born."

"That's refreshing," Kenna said sarcastically.

She didn't look forward to turning 30 but knew she didn't have a lot to say about it. If the next big birthday came, all the better. If not, well, it wouldn't make a lot of difference.

"I found a good drunk to be the best medicine," he offered. Salvatori was slow to lay a pen atop a mountain of reports. "The general gives his regrets he couldn't stay for *'the fireworks'*."

"When did you get home last night?"

"What the fuck does that have to do with anything?"

"Small talk," Kenna said. "You don't like me much, do you, Agent Salvatori?"

"I don't like your kind, especially."

"What *'kind'* am I?"

"A fancy silver-spoon-fed brat with an Ivy League education trying to tell me how to do my job."

"I never went to a university. After I graduated high school and refused to go to my father's Alma Mater, I went to Boston. There, my grandmother taught me how to be a pest."

"She did a damn good job."

Kenna enjoyed that. "To earn my way, I kept up the estate while learning the art of journalism and my other game."

"Estate? Yes, the reason you're here … your grandmother."

Kenna moved closer to the desk. "Why don't you get to what's really bothering you."

"I have nothing more to tell you than I told the general. Get off this fucking case and let me do my job. I'm gonna get that bastard."

She took a long, hard look at Salvatori. With strong hands, the agent brushed back a full head of straight, dark black hair. The eyes usually said a lot about a man. When Kenna stared into Agent Salvatori's, she saw nothing. His features were harsh, with a five o'clock shadow on a long and slender face. When Salvatori stood to refresh a cup of coffee, he was taller than she remembered. The agent spoke with no noticeable accent, though Kenna detected something deep down, perhaps ancestral.

A quick glance about the room gave her a brief study of Vinny Salvatori, the man. There was a lone photo on his desk: he, his wife, and two children sailing. He was younger, much younger, and she wondered how long ago the photo was taken. A plaque indicated his acceptance into the U.S.

Marshals in 2013. There were no diplomas or certificates.

"Senator Bridgewater says you asked for the Chamberlain file."

"Yes," Kenna responded. "Another set of eyes—"

"The senator doesn't have control over me or my bosses. If I gave you that file, I'd be selling pencils on a street stand. I'm sure you can understand that."

"Not really."

"Don't think I've done my job?" Salvatori rocked back. A dried coffee stain on his shirt convinced Kenna she was right.

"To the contrary, I think we saw the same thing."

"We didn't if you saw a murder."

"Then, why are you so all-fired up after Altmann?"

"Unrelated. I explained that." The agent's eyes drifted to the family photo.

Wiggy had already pulled up Salvatori's record. His education record was sketchy, which wasn't unusual for someone who worked deep cover. At some point after university, Salvatori joined the Army, where he spent nearly two decades in intelligence. He had been a rookie in the Marshals on the stakeout six years before but no rookie to fieldwork.

"Did you know General Treadway in Germany?"

"Never met him until today." Salvatori narrowed a stare, lit a cigarette, and exhaled directly at Kenna. "What does this have to do with the Chamberlain suicide?"

"I was talking about what happened six years ago with Altmann. I assumed the Chamberlain affair was Agent Edelman's problem."

"Not that it's any of your damn business, but I knew of the general. We got directives from his office." Salvatori exhaled and picked a strand of tobacco from his teeth. He flipped a pen in and out like a metronome. "As far as I'm concerned, the Chamberlain issue is dead."

"No pun intended, I assume," Kenna said with controlled rancor. "You showed me Altmann's photo, which I take means you think I can help."

"Why didn't you offer this earlier?"

"I think you know why. Now, things are different."

"That bastard killed two good men."

"Other than the colleague killed on the stakeout with Edelman?"

"Yes, in another life," Salvatori said. "A day doesn't go by that I don't remember that night. I see the faces of their families as they were dragged from their homes. We later found them murdered. Now, all that's left are unidentified plots of ground. I won't rest until I settle this." Sweat beaded on Salvatori's forehead as he leaned forward. "I don't need your help! The exercise at the Clubhouse was for Edelman."

"Looking at the bags under your eyes, Agent Salvatori, I'd say you need all the help you can get. Personal vendettas cloud judgment. Don't let it get you killed."

"I have no intention of allowing that to happen."

Kenna didn't move. "Why would a wanted foreigner risk traveling into this country to sell some antique documents?"

"The oldest game in the book, bribery."

"And all these years, I've been told that was prostitution." Kenna turned to the door. As she grabbed the handle, she looked over her shoulder. "Does Agent Edelman believe Senator Chamberlain killed himself?"

"It doesn't matter what Edelman believes. Get the fuck out of my office!"

"I'm like a cow, Agent Salvatori. Push me one way; I tend to go the other."

"Right into the slaughterhouse." Salvatori lifted his face. His left eye twitched a few moments.

Kenna stared into eyes she had seen before, in photos taken by her grandmother, and of victims and criminals she had seen this close. It reminded her of what she saw in the mirror every morning during a tough case … such as this one. She didn't like this man much and knew a bureaucrat out of control had the potential to be her worst enemy.

Kenna walked from the room as several of Salvatori's fellow workers gathered outside his office. At the elevator, Kenna turned when a group of piercing, out-of-key voices erupted in a special rendition to the tune of *'Happy Birthday'*.

"You're as old as a shoe … like leather all blue," the chorus began. "It's too bad you can't move … now that you're an old fart, too."

'Closer to being a hundred than to being born,' Kenna thought and caught a disconcerting glance from Agent Miriam Edelman.

XXIII

'You better change your ways, daughter, or one of these days, someone's gonna knock that arrogant chip off your shoulder.' Kenna had heard from her father more than once.

'Don't confuse arrogance with confidence, father. I'm the byproduct of a proud, cocky Texan.'

'You're the Irish offspring of your mother's mother,' father had said of Kenna's venture into what he called *'the surreal endeavor of crime detection'*, and on rare occasions, *'you're totally opposite'*.

'Because most people think she was perfect, or because you despised her?'

'I despise what she is turning you into,' he had said in finality.

As the sun settled and Kenna walked from the U.S. Marshals building, she couldn't help but think what had brought her to this place, this day. Gran was kind, easygoing, and pristine, but she had a dark side Kenna had only seen the once … Anson Beck.

Criminals never forget it, usually from behind bars. Hers was the personality Kenna acquired. Combined with father's, it led to an oft-volatile mixture. At a young age, though, she learned to control her inner conflict. Looking up to Salvatori's office window, she wondered how much longer she could maintain the discipline.

'She wanted you to be more Irish than American,' father had said. *'I wanted you to be a Texan.'*

'Then, you both succeeded.'

But her father had not seen it that way. As a youth, she spent many summers in Boston. Gran lived in the 19th century stone manor house that overlooked a great valley. There, Gran had taught her the art of *finding things*. Exploits chronicled in her leather-bound books gave her an astute and deep insight into the criminal mind. Kenna often thought of how easy it would have been to be on the other side of the law. No doubt, she would have been very successful.

But she had gone Gran Lockwood's way. Even so, she had not chosen Gran's expertise, art, antiquities, and jewels. Canvas and paint, chiseled metal and stone, pearl and diamond necklaces were a creation of man. Human death was more like a black hole, a void, and murder, the destruction of the Creator's perfection. Art was a known; it remained after theft. Death was not; it was absolute. So, she chose human flesh and bone and the idiosyncrasies of the human mind. At Gran's funeral, she promised that someday she would delve into her leather-bound books and try to solve the cases Gran had not … after finding Anson Beck.

Kenna kicked a rock, sending it down the asphalt. It rattled into a storm drain grate. She only wished this case was that simple, but nothing was the truth, nothing real. Everywhere she turned, those who swore friendship and honesty were lying.

"If you can't trust 'em, they're not friends," she mumbled, thinking of Gran Lockwood.

She stared at her scarred knuckles and winced at the bruises. How many years had she taken off her life? Would she ever do as she promised Gran; would she finish her work?

'Ye have to live as much for Gran Lockwood's game as for reporting, kid,' Wiggy had said more than once. *'She's right, ya know. Hers is the greatest game of all.'*

The evening sun cast shadows across the street. She leaned against a streetlight to hail a cab. The game, this game, was running circles around her like Chicago. A car stopped; she didn't turn until the top electronically rolled back.

"I'll buy that drink if you tell me what's on your mind."

Charlie Sommer, the perfect male specimen, wore freshly pressed casual clothes. He fit well behind the wheel of the bright red SL320 Mercedes and knew it. Puckered lips said *'take me'* without moving. Revealing a fluff of chest hair, his Polo parted as he leaned over to open the passenger door. For an instant, Kenna's eyes flashed electricity as she slid into the passenger side.

"If you've seen the traffic in Hong Kong, you know what's in my head," she said.

His hand enveloped hers. "I can help. Let me in there."

"Ha," she chuckled and forced a smile. "Philosophizing. I think General Treadway said it was for pansies."

"You're no pansy. Besides, I want to know how you think."

Of course, he did. They all did. To clear her mind from his looks, she explained her philosophy on the basic nature of a case. Actually, it was Gran Lockwood's. *'A criminal is a criminal simply because that is what he is. It's not because of some profound societal influence, and certainly not because his mother spanked him as a child.'*

"You must have a great view on world peace," he chuckled.

"Yeah, it can't happen. Thucydides' comparisons of man and war in the book *The Peloponnesian War*, applied to our modern world, put it like this: Two people have two differences of opinion; Two differences of opinion create arguments; Arguments start fights; Fights lead to battles, and battles to war!"

He laughed at the simplicity of it until she convinced him that such simplicity was exactly what they were dealing with. It didn't mean that the case was simple, only that the basis of the crime was simple.

'Find the basis, Kenna, and you will find the truth,' was another of Gran's axioms.

Gran's wisdom steered Kenna's mind through the whirlwind of confusion that ran amuck in this cesspool, the U.S. Capital. Confusion was the criminal's greatest weapon; he knew where he had been and where he was going. She knew only where he had been.

"I'd love to hear what you think of our judicial system."

She was saved when her cell phone buzzed. *Or was it that she was thrown back into the cesspool?* she wondered.

Wiggy had watched the dead senator's remains taken out of the morgue; no autopsy had been performed. They refused to answer any questions about the suicide and said the widow would explain everything at a press conference. When asked if he could look at the physical evidence, Wiggy was told there was none.

"I said, what do you mean, *was none*'? Truckloads of it were hauled away from the golf course," Wiggy said over the cell phone.

Kenna was numb, her mind off the specimen behind the wheel. She had become an ice cube that would not thaw. Charlie's words passed through her brain without processing. That was until he mentioned Agent Salvatori.

Charlie had been more than intimidated by Salvatori; bullied was a better word. The agent had come to the office when Charlie was boxing belongings and shoved a photo in his face. When he turned away, Salvatori pushed him against a wall and demanded answers. Bad turned to worse when Bridgewater joined them. The two cornered Charlie and demanded answers to questions of which he had no knowledge. It was then he refused to talk, regardless of how physical they got.

Kenna's mind flashed to an image of Salvatori strapping Charlie to a chair and beating him with a nightstick, though she knew it hadn't happened. Charlie's dislike of Salvatori increased his blood pressure; there would come a day.

"Just left him stuffing his face with icing and white cake while Harvey Chamberlain's remains were burned to ash," Kenna said.

"Salvatori's motivation is personal and beyond reason,"

Charlie agreed. "Soon, Harvey will be bottled for display on Gloria's mantel and toasted by a whiskey-soaked mind."

A chill awakened Kenna's dormant hormones as Charlie grabbed her arm. She fought against it, uncomfortable. Though she admired his maneuvering, she fought off the attraction. *One day, there will be time and opportunity to mutually take advantage of that*, she hoped.

"Take me to the Clubhouse," she said and changed the subject. "How did you find me?"

"Pretty in a tomboyish way, intriguing, somewhat stand-offish."

"That's not what I meant."

Without responding, Charlie leaned across the console, pulled her face to his, and pressed his pouting lips against hers. He was warm, moist, everything she envisioned. Her body responded, but she forced herself away. *No, not now!*

"I want your help," he exhaled.

"Everyone does, with conditions."

"I have none."

She licked the kiss from her lips. "You just gave me one."

"That's a benefit, not a condition."

"Trust is dangerous, often deadly," Kenna warned.

"So, it's happened. Avery Gowen and Gloria Chamberlain got to you."

"No, it's just caution." Kenna hesitated. "It's too convenient, too quick."

"That a man and woman should be attracted to each other?" he asked. "You've been hanging around Avery Gowen too much."

His words were followed with a smile she enjoyed. The knot in her stomach loosened. There was something extremely right about this man, or she was extremely blind. In Washington, D.C., either was possible. Wiggy's caution boomed in her ears.

"I also have a way of getting things, Kenna. Especially things I want."

I bet you do, she thought. Their stares locked. "Look, Charlie—"

"When I was a child, I got very sick. For over a year, I was bed-ridden. Others fed me and cleaned me. I swore if I survived that as an adult, no one would ever have to take care of me." He leaned closer. "Check it out. See if I'm lying."

"I had everything given to me."

"No, you didn't."

"Oh?"

"You didn't have your father's love," he said; she turned away. "I'm sorry."

"Don't be."

The only way she would have had that love would have been to attend Rice University and journalism school. Then, back to Dallas to become one of the automatons of the great Texan's television conglomerate, tearing down the walls of legality for a pot of gold.

"It's just … that." He lowered his stare. "I am attracted to you. I had no way of knowing when Senator Bridgewater gave me your name …"

Charlie's emerald eyes fixed on her as if lasers. He weakened. He had gone to Avery Gowen's apartment to confront him. When she and Wiggy arrived, he changed his mind and followed her.

"I'm glad you did," she offered. "But leave Gowen to Wiggy."

"He doesn't frighten me."

"My grandmother always told me that *starving animals eat their own*."

He folded his lips into a perfect pout and moved with the agility of a cat across the center console again, pulling her face close. He brushed an arm against a firm breast, a hot breath across her neck. He pulled her face against his own, their lips pulsating, their tongues lashing like the rigging of a sailing ship in a stormy sea. Her hand fell on his chest, fingers probing, exploring.

With a racing heart and great effort, she pushed away. The longing in his eyes said their desires were mutual. Ignoring the need for oxygen, their lips locked again. Her eyes opened, as did his, and each stared into the depths of their respective souls.

She forced a separation. He reached for her face; she resisted. *Fool,* she thought.

"What's the matter?"

"Later," she exhaled. "There will be another day."

Deep from within, her passion beckoned, yet she again resisted. Her swelling breasts strained against the blouse. She leaned back against the seat, panting, placing her delicate tongue against the heart of her upper lip. A few moments later, she breathed more easily, then slowly.

"Grandmother was on a case in Hong Kong and became involved with an MI6 agent. She was nearly killed because of it. I swore that would never happen to me. I went against that credo once, and it almost got me killed. It did the man I could have loved."

Charlie placed a hand against her cheek, inhaled once hard, and then brushed her long hair behind an ear. She took his hand and kissed it.

"I'm sorry," she said.

"No need to be. Perhaps a taste of things to come."

With a lengthy sigh, Charlie straightened his back. He placed the car into drive and pulled away from the curb. While watching the street …

"The dragon lady will have his seat, you know."

"Yes, I believe she will," Kenna agreed.

'Absurdity will become reality,' Gran Lockwood said. It now engulfed Kenna.

If the Party wanted a special project in one of their leading senator's constituencies … cut a deal. If the military wanted a new weapon system … cut a deal. That wasn't the Founding Fathers' vision but had become 20th century Washington politics. Favors begot favors. It was the power and the failure of the two-Party system. The Founding Fathers assured checks and balances on the branches of government. But many years ago, the Washington elite discovered a way to circumvent the proletariat and Founding Fathers: There were no checks or balances on the two Parties! Kenna focused …

Sunday traffic was light. Even so, Charlie attacked it aggressively. Unlike Wiggy, his moves were smooth and precise. He swept across lanes fluidly; didn't cut across. The Mercedes ate up the miles like Kenna had never experienced in traffic around the nation's capital.

"All without a public vote," Charlie said as he steered around a series of delivery trucks.

For a fleeting moment, Charlie sounded a lot like Gran Lockwood. Kenna looked at him differently now, though cautiously. He drove into the country club and parked near the main entrance of the Clubhouse.

"Gowen took a package to Devon Whyte this morning. Any idea what it might have been?" she asked.

"Probably what we and the intruder didn't find in the office. He's working all angles to get a higher position in the Party," he said and hesitated, "and will do anything to get it."

Kenna was certain Charlie was wrong. Gowen was in it to line his own pockets. There was no doubt he had initiated contact with the German, the perfect dealmaker, devious and unscrupulous. It was the main reason the Party put him in Chamberlain's office. What Gowen didn't realize was that he was also the perfect fall guy, which was the second. It was going to crash down on him very hard when it came.

"The intruder didn't get what he came for," Charlie said out of nowhere. "I have an idea what the guy wanted."

She stiffened with a silent, *What?*

"Harvey didn't trust Avery and kept everything from Gloria. A couple months ago, he told me if things got strange, he would find a way to get a message to me."

"And?"

"After Salvatori and Bridgewater confronted me, I went home and checked my recorder. Harvey left me a message."

Kenna checked the timeline in her head. "That's impossible."

"I didn't check it after I saw you at the Club last night and didn't this morning before I went into the office. He left it about an hour before he was killed last night." He looked down and inhaled. "He knew it was going to happen."

"Why didn't you call me?"

"I couldn't. When I heard his voice, I froze. I couldn't do anything." He shook uncontrollably.

"What was the message?"

"Chamberlain bugged Avery's phones at home, the office, and his cell. He left me a recording at a local mailbox facility."

"How did Altmann know it existed?" she questioned. *And came after it in the office,* she wondered.

"Avery must have known," he said. "I was frightened. I thought we could go together."

Kenna's mobile phone beeped. At times, she hated the inconveniences of modern society and answered to find Wiggy on the other end. Her face tightened.

She disconnected and brushed the back of her hand across Charlie's cheek. "Go get the recording. Just make sure you aren't followed."

He grabbed her arm. "I'd feel better if you came along."

The weaker side of Charlie Sommer was less radiant than the strong. It seemed out of place. "The way you drive, you don't need me. Just make sure you aren't followed."

"I can't get to the box until tomorrow morning, and I don't feel comfortable going home." An instant later, he stiffened. "I don't want to fail. I owe Harvey too much."

"You won't fail," she said and stood from the car.

It was then she knew Malcolm Bridgewater and Avery Gowen were wrong about Charlie Sommer. Kenna's insides crashed together like too much Mexican food and Tequila. Hand on the car, she gathered her breath before she leaned into the window.

"You said Bridgewater questioned you in the office after I left. What did he want?"

"For me to convince you to drop this case."

XXIV

Kenna walked along the shaded cart path toward the superintendent's shed. She found Roots Hobson leaning on a golfcart, animated and boisterous, barking instructions to a group of groundskeepers. When Hobson finished 5 minutes later, the groundskeepers sped away in their carts. Kenna joined him.

"I understand you make your last rounds about this time. Mind if I tag along?"

"Aye, I'll show ye how I found the senator."

"I just want to see how you work," she lied. "I'll buy the beer afterward."

"Just don'a bother me while I'm thinkin'. And I expect ye to buy the whiskey."

The cart sped into motion. Kenna carried on with small talk about his youth in Scotland. She had watched Hobson putt prior to the interview with the professionals and was surprised how his crippled hands manipulated the club with the fluid elegance of a master. The expertise came from knowing that the short game was the most important in the sport.

"So, Roots, the nickname ... from your work?"

"Ney, when I was a wee lad."

A cool, humid breeze ruffled the trees and brushed Hobson's longish gray hair. Silhouetted by the sun, the Clubhouse darkened on the horizon. The sun lingered into the deep shadows of dusk as they headed to the first tee.

'Contrary to classic illogic,' Gran Lockwood had told her, *'the truth of a crime is often not found at the scene.'* The criminal makeup, what Kenna called the *good looks* of the crime, were often found in the peripheral elements unrelated to the actual scene. These involved the personality of the criminal and the mistakes the killer made while believing in his own invincibility. It was all part of building the crime pyramid. Gran Lockwood had taught her that, as it related to art. Remarkably, the same principles applied to murder.

"Ye ever 'ear of Bill Marriott?"

"As in hotels?"

"The one," Roots said with a sparkle in his eyes.

Most people did not know that the Marriott Empire started in D.C., with A&W Root Beer stands. According to Hobson, he was employee number three, behind Bill and his wife. He acquired the nickname from his friends who came into the shop and ordered *'Rooties'* from the *'Rootie Man'*, which was later shortened to *'Roots'*.

"One helluva bloke."

"So I've read," Kenna said.

One more lie: She had read about the life of J. Willard Marriott, the founder of the hotel chain. He opened his first A&W Root Beer stand in 1927 in D.C. Bill Marriott, his eldest son, was yet to be born.

"He helped me get this job, he and the good senator."

"Chamberlain?"

"No, lass, from Massachusetts." Hobson held up his hands. "That's how I got these, workin' for his family."

Kenna turned back to the course as Hobson stopped at the first green and marked it for pin placement the next day. The old man walked the circumference of the green, checked the bunkers, and returned to the cart. As he pushed it into motion, he scribbled on a chart.

"Funny how things that happen in our youth stick with us," Hobson said. Kenna crumpled a brow. "That when you decided to become a copper?"

"Nah. I was the one everyone turned to for help." The events in her early 20s contradicted that statement. But that time was locked away, never to be known by Roots Hobson or any other suspect. It was between her, Wiggy, and Anson Beck.

Hobson turned a glare for an instant. He stopped the cart at the 4th hole and stepped out. "Are you as good a copper as you are on television, reporting on sports?"

"Better, I believe."

Hobson was delving into her past as much as she was his. There wasn't really a reason to keep up the dialogue; nothing the old man said would be of value unless he made a mistake. Hobson's lies were a rambling of witticisms, beginning with being born in the U.S. Kenna lost interest; Hobson got the message.

Hobson turned to the 4th green and located the hole placement. He did not seem as meticulous on this hole as he had on the previous three. He stepped into the cart and pressed it into motion before he sat. Kenna wanted answers.

"So, do you believe the senator was murdered?" she asked.

"Na for me to say," Hobson said matter-of-factly. "The pushy Italian seemed to think so in a way. Gave me his card."

More mixed signals, but from whom: Hobson or Salvatori? Kenna ignored the old man's thoughts and interrupted before he could continue:

"One thing is curious; tell me again how you found the body."

"Just as he was before they took him away."

"That's not really what I meant."

"Wait'll we get there, lass and I'll point it out to ye," Hobson insisted. "Right now, I got me work to do."

Kenna admired the detail with which Hobson approached his profession. Perhaps this work ethic had come from the time working for the senator if she was to believe the story. Kenna was certain of one thing: the superintendent had not been in the United States since childhood.

As the evening inspection carried on, Kenna saw that Hobson expected no less than perfection from his ground crew. The superintendent was a professional as much, and most likely more, than was she. Where Hobson was totally committed to his job, being a television reporter was more of a dedicated hobby to her. She admired the old man for that.

With a daily log in one hand and a 50-foot tape measure in the other, Hobson stopped at every green and, refusing help, measured the new hole placements for the following day. He marked them with a small orange flag on a metal rod stuck in the green. Occasionally, a smirk creased the red cheeks when, staring back at the fairway, a particularly difficult pin placement pleased him. He walked the circumference of each sand trap, applying the finishing touches to several with an under-the-breath curse at incompetence. Several times, he adjusted sprinkler heads for precise coverage. He walked back to the cart only when satisfied.

The sun had fallen behind the Clubhouse as they drove around the sand traps at the 17th green. The aged hand placed a red mark on the miniature map of the course. Simultaneously, he stopped and stared along the edge of the sand traps. He cursed.

"The bloody mowing team's passed through here like a hurricane. The 1st cut of fairway rough along the entire course is in horrible shape. I dragged the blokes out last night to fix their shoddy work, and, by God, I'll do it again!"

"I hadn't noticed."

"You bloody well don't get paid to notice!" The old man slammed his open palm on the scorecard plate at the center of the steering wheel. "By damned, I'll fire every last one 'em."

"Wouldn't it be better to tell them what you want?"

"I don't get paid to talk, missy. I get paid to keep these grounds. And keep these bloody grounds I will, and it will be my bloody way."

"Why don't you gather them all together and—"

"I'll throw one of the dossers off a bridge; that'll get their attention." Hobson grimaced. "Brilliant idea, Kenna."

"Your Scottish is rearing its ugly head, Roots."

The old man was not amused. He wiped his brow with a wet golf towel; his face relaxed. Kenna pointed to the surgically scarred hands.

"Is that what kept you off the Tour?"

"A meat grinder when I was helping with a party for the senator's family." Hobson stared at front and back of both. "Just started to learn the game, too. Can't swing a long stick now with any authority."

"That when you took up this work?"

Hobson turned. "Ye ask a lotta questions, Lassie."

"It's a character flaw."

"I would guess it goes with the profession. Even so, these ..." he lifted his hands, "aren't me favorite topic of conversation."

"Don't discount your accomplishments out here, Roots," Kenna said, waving at the grounds. "This course is as good as any I've ever played."

Hobson turned the conversation around to be about the failure of the PGA to give him full recognition. Yes, the evidence was here, but just like Capitol Hill, the PGA was a massive bureaucracy. Kenna shook her head: *There was that word again, bureaucracy.*

"I see where you're goin', and I don't like it, Lassie."

"Just making a statement."

"Ye know it was the late senator's influence that kept me from gettin' the recognition."

Wiggy had found that tidbit of history. It seemed Chamberlain and the Tour president were college roommates at Northwestern. Kenna silently sat as Hobson stopped the cart at the 18th tee. Her numbing stare was attached to Hobson's hands as they wrung the steering column. In them, she saw both power and grace. Beyond that, she saw …

"That must have angered you a great deal."

"Never liked the man. He wielded power like a sickle, cutting the legs off we insignificants along the way. Like the bloody British."

Kenna paused again. "Doesn't seem like the Chamberlain I knew."

"I see it in yer eyes." He paused at length, staring at his hands. "I could'a killed him with me hands had I wanted. But I didn'a. He wasn'a worth the effort."

"A lot of people been telling me that lately."

Hobson pushed the cart into motion towards the 18th green. Kenna pointed to the right: "Pull up over there, will you?"

"So, ye didn'a offer to buy me a whiskey for me looks."

The Scottish brogue came and went. Kenna couldn't help but wonder why. Something rumbled at the pit of her stomach. The cart slid to an abrupt stop at the edge of the trees a hundred feet from where Senator Harvey Chamberlain fell. The evidence of death was gone. Now, a circle of white groundskeeper's tape designated ground under repair.

An ominous orange tint streaked the horizon as the sun settled. It set ablaze a long, thin line of high cirrus clouds that hung over the top of the Clubhouse.

"I want to continue this, but know you have to fire all your help."

"Aye, I like yer way of thinkin'."

Kenna pointed at the trap. "The timing's wrong."

"Timing?"

"You found the body, went and called, turned off the sprinkler system, then brought the Marshals out here, right?"

"What ye gettin' at, Lassie?"

"You had to go back out with your crew to fix something.

What was it?"

"Lotta things, Lassie."

"At the 18th?"

"Aye."

"Who went with you?"

"Some of the lads went to the tee box. They did their work but saw nothin'. "

"But you went to the green, why?"

With a crooked eye, Hobson released the brake. "I'll be back in a few minutes."

"Don't bother. I'll meet you in the bar. By the way, I have an open book if you need help mowing tomorrow." Hobson did not laugh.

The old man steered around the green at full speed. The cart tires spun on the wet grass. Within a few moments, the cart was gone, as were its sounds. The sprinkler system clicked on with a staccato rattle. It startled Kenna, the noise louder in the shadows than she thought it would be. She moved away from the spray.

She knelt at the edge of the trap, ignoring the spray of cold water as it tapped on the ground nearby. She ran her fingers through the fluffy white sand, then the thick new sod at her feet. The stream of water passed; she folded it into her fist to wash away the sand. Kenna's eyes lifted to the trees, a good hundred feet away, and the darkness within.

Evidence of the crime was long gone, filed in some government warehouse where it was now boxed for eternity or already destroyed. She wanted a feeling. What Harvey Chamberlain felt … she turned to the trees as the sprinklers rattled leaves … when the bullet … wind whipped through her hair, chilling her … entered his brain.

Kenna stood where she believed Harvey Chamberlain had stood … alone. No, with the killer. Across the lake, Clubhouse lights came on. Why would Harvey meet someone here, possibly someone from the club? She tried to recall the faces that night; there were so many.

Sprinkler noise would hide an approach. She turned back to the rustle in the trees and heard the U.S. Marshal yell again: *'Footprints in the trees.'*

Why hadn't Salvatori reached the same conclusion as her? Yet, he hadn't said that … the helicopter … he had been ordered. Could the political establishment order an agent, as well as every politician and newspaper, to see what the hierarchy wanted? The history of the Washington Post said that was impossible, but it was a new day, a new administration, and definitely a new game.

The city was no longer a game, she corrected herself. *It was a madhouse.*

She walked to the edge of the trees, turning as the main fairway sprinklers burped, then howled to life. From where she stood, the major orifices propelled steady streams of water 30 yards. She clapped, then clapped again, surprised that the gushing water and trees muted the sound. She couldn't see the veranda where she and Wiggy had stood that night with so many others. The dying sun fell behind the top of the trees.

Was there significance in the timing of Chamberlain's death: the night before the announcements? An important vote of the Country Club hierarchy? She shivered.

Kenna snapped a leaf from a low limb and walked into the trees. She guardedly stepped through the muddy newly planted sod that, before the senator's death, had been thick with firm, mature grass. She grabbed a tree, then kept going until 20 feet into the trees and away from the thick fairway rough. She spun towards the green as the shadow of darkness cast a blanket over Harvey Chamberlain's resting place. She closed her eyes to see the scene …

Footprints on the green, two sets: one coming, one going. They had been different, but how? The Senator's body position, the gun, and the blood in the sand all screamed at her.

In her imagination, she snapped back to the night before, two men arguing. She strained to see where she had been standing and wondered if she had seen the killer. Did Chamberlain have another later meeting with the German here? And why? Why?

She sensed more than saw the movement to her left, deep in the trees. She jumped the opposite direction and slipped on the newly placed sod. The brief flash of light preceded by an instant the indistinguishable thud of the bullet smashing into the tree at her right and the muffled pop of a silenced gun. The sting of torn flesh on her forehead brought her hand up.

Throwing herself away from a second flash and into the darkness, she raised her arms to break the impact as she fell. She slammed against the exposed root of a tree; air shot from her lungs. Frozen by pain, she tried to jump up. The assailant beat limbs from his path towards her. Another flash, contact with something solid, and the whine of a disfigured bullet tumbling out of control into the trees. A stream of light searched the darkness. She forced herself up ... *move, quickly!*

Controlling a scream, Kenna ran to the left and kept low, dodging the light thrown outward from the attacker. It was opposite her now. She reached for her pistol, cursing when she did not have it. She paralleled the attacker's heavy footsteps in the underbrush. Breathing echoed in her ears: her own. A pulsating locomotive filled the trees: her heartbeat.

Suddenly, the shadow darted headlong into the black, away from her; she followed. She spoke no words. The attacker stopped and turned; the pistol was leveled. The brilliant flash, a miss, and the singing bullet again. Kenna bounded into the man with a flying block; the gun fired again. With a crack, she slammed the attacker into a nearby tree. A shriek pierced the silence as a tree branch snapped from impact.

Stunned, Kenna rolled to the side, gasping for breath, positive something had been broken. For the moment, she was unable to move. She coughed, flinging tree limbs from her face, kicking at the underbrush. She fought for breath, tasting blood. Mud blurred her vision. She wiped it away and lifted to a crouching position to stare at the killer's eyes behind a black mask. Before she could, a golf shoe slammed into her chest. She fell but rolled away. At the same instant, they spotted the pistol between them.

Kenna dove first, falling an inch short, fingers grappling, pawing for that extra reach. She lifted the gun and raised to the prone position to fire. She blinked hard as the sprinklers died in the fairway, and the man's running footsteps fell

distantly silent in the night shadows.

229

XXV

Kenna stumbled into the superintendent's building. She didn't know why she walked this far; her mind spun. Hobson was the only one to know she was at the 18th. Was it him in the trees? The employee locker room was dark and empty. She leaned against the doorjamb to catch her breath. Her pectoral muscles throbbed like she'd been shot with rock salt on her father's Texas hunting ranch. Warmth covered the left side of her face. She wiped at it and drew back a bloody, muddy hand. She lumbered to a bench between the lockers and collapsed.

For what seemed an eternity, she fought off impending unconsciousness. With short, choppy breaths and an occasional splash of water on her face from a nearby sink, she fought it off. Briefly, fear of death chilled her. Elbows on knees, face in hands, she eased away the Adrenaline rush that pumped her chest like a steam engine.

Instantaneous reactions had saved her life. She leaned back against the lockers, trying to suck in a deep breath, but pain made her settle for quick spurts. No, sound judgment had saved her life. She lifted a shaking hand, wondering once again what she was doing in this city. She was supposed to be looking for Anson Beck and covering the announcements!

Fear saved your fucking life! she screamed inside.

It was then she noticed the gun was still in her hand. She pressed a cheek against the cool, light gray tiled wall. Once again, the dark, hollow eyes of her adversary appeared. She cursed, not having seen them completely. A big man, strong and thick ... *the same as in Chamberlain's office?* she asked herself.

Not since staring down the barrel of Anson Beck's Uzi had she come so close to death. She tried to discount it with a chuckle, knowing it wouldn't work.

The smell of sweaty feet and anti-bacterial cleaning agents filled her nostrils. She cringed and lifted her left arm to take off her shirt. Her ankle burned as she untied a shoe. Undressed, she stepped into the nearby shower and turned the water on hot, very hot. Head directly under the spray, she allowed it to blast away the mud and run down her back. She ignored the pain in her scalp and forehead. With each brush of soap across her breasts, she winced. She looked down; a group of small puncture-wounds in her breasts seeped blood. A jagged object from her face brought up her hand. She brushed over it lightly; blood covered her fingers.

It's not radicals anymore, and it's not Chicago, she thought. The fact that Chicago turned to murder didn't matter at that moment. No one had taken a shot at her then. It had been knife play, equally deadly, but at least hand-to-hand. She had learned the latter from Wiggy during their summers at Gran Lockwood's. That training undoubtedly helped her in the trees.

Once again, this game had changed in shape, color, and intensity. Her mind whirled in constant circles, trying to focus on the facts, concentrating on Gran Lockwood's peripherals. The gun remained with her, though she was nearly certain her assailant was gone for the night. It was supposed to have been a quick shoot and scoot; her fighting had spoiled the party.

As soon as those thoughts left her brain, gunshots echoed again; she spun into the darkness and flinched. Grabbing her side and the wet gun, she cursed as Roots Hobson banged an interior door closed. He strolled towards his office but paused before entering. He rifled the sheets of paper on his inspection clipboard and paused at one in particular. Just then, he looked up, noticing the running shower.

"You blokes need to be about your way," he yelled and then froze.

Kenna stepped from the shower, grabbed a towel, and patted the chest wounds. It left patterned red bloodstains on the white towel. She eased taut muscles from one position to the next, pleased that nothing seemed seriously injured or broken. It had felt different in the trees. Her heartbeat eased; her anger did not. As she stepped out from behind the lockers, Hobson entered his office and hung the clipboard on a nail. He turned to finally see her.

"What the bloody hell happened to ya?"

"Unexpected visitor in the trees."

Wrapped with the towel, Kenna stepped to a sink and mirror. A deep two-inch long gash ended no more than an inch from the corner of her left eye. The jagged end of a half-inch-long wooden splinter protruded from her face. As she eased it out, blood spurted across her fingers and cheek. She dabbed the cut with the towel. Hobson lifted the first aid kit from the wall. He allowed a quick glance to his lit office, which was neat and tidy.

Kenna accepted a bottle of peroxide and allowed it to hiss and boil as it cleaned the long cut. Unlike advertised, it burned. A healthy glob of Neosporin was squeezed into the wound, and then Kenna forced the wound together with her index finger and thumb. With shaking hands that calmed, the old man applied clear wound closure strips. Kenna barely felt the touch. A large wound bandage covered it completely.

"Ye better have a clinic look at that, Lassie," Hobson said. "Or they'll start callin' ye *Scarface* on the tele."

"Not funny."

"What happened there?" the old man asked, pointing at Kenna's chest.

Kenna dabbed the chest wounds with peroxide. "Happened too fast, but I'd say a size ten."

The old man dropped to a nearby bench, took off a shoe, and lifted the sole to the mirror. "Not bloody like these. Would'a been old metal spikes. Don't use 'em anymore."

Kenna held the spikes up alongside her wound. The pattern was similar, a near-perfect match, but too small. Roots provided her a clean set of groundskeeper's overalls. She gathered the rest of her clothes in a plastic trash bag and followed Hobson outside.

On the cart, she turned a blank stare to the old man. There were a thousand questions on the tip of her tongue and a thousand more rattling around her brain. Eventually, she would work through them all. The last would be answered when this madness was over when they reached the top of Gran's pyramid.

Hobson steered the cart along the path that followed the 1st fairway and a stand of trees. The electric engine whined as they passed the tennis courts and turned towards the Clubhouse. Kenna was quiet; much of what Hobson said fell on inattentive ears.

When the old man went out and checked the course before he found Chamberlain, it was past 10:00. Wiggy verified that Chamberlain had been on the veranda until well past dark. The senator's signature on the bill for his drinks verified the time as 10:20 pm. He had consumed eight double Jack Daniels and water since about 8:00 pm, not too long after Kenna and Wiggy had gone to their rooms.

"As I drove to the first tee, I saw the senator stumble from the Clubhouse," Hobson said.

Kenna's eyes turned lazily. *Another lie?* "And in all our conversations, you didn't think that was relevant?"

"I had work to do, Lassie. I've seen the senator in that state before."

"I'm talking about after his death, not before!" Kenna insisted.

"I didn'a see where he went."

Anger boiled within Kenna with such intensity that she fingered the pistol in the pocket. *If I started killing all the liars, eventually the entire city would be gone,* she thought but brushed it away as quickly. It was like herding cats, getting anyone to tell the truth in this place.

The old man's astute eyes flipped to the side. He steered

the cart onto the concrete apron outside the entrance to the Clubhouse and stopped. Kenna grabbed her side from the sudden jolt and eased out.

"Please continue," she requested.

"I was running late with me rounds, takin' extra care to make sure the bloody course was perfect for the lassies. When I came to the 18th, I saw a big man, like the senator. When he saw me, he walked into the trees."

"Did you talk to him?"

"Nay. He was drunk; the sprinklers started. I saw no need to interrupt him. I minds me own business. Ye learn that in this bloody city and at this bloody golf club."

That contradicted everything: both men were drunk? The only thing it could possibly explain was the time discrepancy she believed existed.

"That meant the senator was in the trees through the entire cycle of the sprinklers. How long would that be?"

Without expression, Hobson ran weathered fingers across the short stubble of that morning's shave. "I had 'em set at eighteen-minutes, if I recall."

Plenty of time to start and end an argument, Kenna thought. *But that's too long unless someone else entered the picture.*

The possibilities were endless. Because of his superior's infinite stupidity, Salvatori had destroyed any physical means of finding the truth. That missing block of time banged against the inside of Kenna's head. It had been too long from the time that Roots Hobson first saw the senator, his death, and when he led Salvatori to the body. Kenna stared into the past, seeing the senator's body the instant before the coroner zipped him into the body bag. The eyes … no, his position … there was something.

It hit her like a truck. The sand! Rake marks surrounded the body, not like the ground crew had done it. It had been done after Chamberlain was face down after he was dead. Whoever was there with Harvey Chamberlain moved him. The killer was looking for something.

XXVI

The phone call came a little after seven. Kenna answered though she didn't want to. She listened for a few moments and then forced herself from the bed. She went to the bathroom, relieved herself, brushed her teeth, and dressed in a workout suit. She paid little attention to the mirror. As she walked out into the main room, Wiggy met her.

"Who was that, kid?"

"Reporters' meeting; I'll be right back."

Two hours later, Kenna returned to the room. Over that time, she had answered more questions about her condition than what the meeting was about. Wiggy was working on his computer when Kenna stepped back into the room. It was the first good look he had of her that morning.

"So, that's why ye were in bed so late," Wiggy said and stood. "Let's take a look."

"Don't bother, Wiggy," Kenna said and held up a hand. "I have a feeling we've just begun to make friends."

"Do ye need a doctor, kid?"

"No," Kenna said with a wrinkled smile. "He'd just want to stick a needle in me."

"The meeting?"

Kenna threw an envelope on the table. "The announcement's been postponed for two weeks."

"What 'bout the suite?" Wiggy asked.

"We're staying until we figure this out."

Kenna left the room without speaking. Pain punctuated every movement. A long shower helped, but Advil would do the trick. Standing with a towel around her, applying new wound strips to her head, she looked in the mirror, not pleased. For a long moment, she thought about her lifelong dream, wondering if it was ever to be.

"Quit whining," she said to her reflection. "You have work to do."

Kenna entered the main room casually dressed for the day. Wiggy sat behind the computer. From that point, his eyes never left the screen. Kenna took an orange juice and a banana from the bar and walked to the veranda. She slid open the door, not surprised by the activity on the club grounds and amenities.

"You have to be one-of-a-kind, Wiggy," she said without turning. "An aged guru with that thing, compared to your counterparts. I envy you."

"You're the one-of-a-kind kid. Young and no interest in

it, not even a tablet.”

Kenna frowned and smiled. “It’s called computer illiteracy.”

“Truth is often ruthless.” Wiggy took a swallow of coffee.

Kenna tried to grasp the intricacies of the computer, but the logic … as the computer geeks called it … escaped her. Everything seemed to be a contradiction. Years ago, her frustration mounted until Gran Lockwood pulled her aside and jammed a long, slender finger against Kenna’s temple: *‘This is yer computer, Kenna. More is stored in here than can ever be put in a machine.’* From that day, she left the *machine* work to Wiggy.

“You’re the anomaly at hacker conventions, or whatever it is you computer pirates call ‘em when you get together.”

“Like whiskey, lass, we improve with age.” Wiggy’s thick fingers danced across the laptop keys as he spoke.

“That’s good because you weren’t any good at crime.”

“Oh, but if I was so inclined now, I could hack us to riches in a week.”

“You could make more money telling companies how to beat guys like you.”

“I don’t do it for the money, lass. I do it for the Grand

Ole Dame."

Kenna's stare remained on the golf course. The trees were still. Players and golf carts moved across the grounds. Sprinklers were dead. She grimaced and leaned on the balustrade. Once again, she was reminded that Gran was right: *Wiggy's a good man.*

In her mind's eye, she saw the nation's monuments to its Founding Fathers and war heroes: Washington, Lincoln, Jefferson, Vietnam, and finally, World War II. They were testaments to great men and women of vision, comrades in arms, willing to fight against all odds for what was right, to make the ultimate sacrifice. Today, though, the monuments were the antithesis of what the nation's capital had become and just how far her country had fallen.

She thought of the general. "How long's it been since you could walk around this city at night without being mugged or robbed?"

"Before the bloody politicians occupied it," Wiggy said. "Mind you, it's no different anywhere else in the world."

"You know, you could be right."

"I am bloody right."

"What's up with Agent Edelman?" Kenna asked.

"A very unhappy lass," Wiggy responded.

"Could tell that Saturday night at the 18th." Kenna bit off some of the banana and finished the orange juice. "She might be feeling like I do about now: We might have been able to help Chamberlain before he ended up face down in the sand."

"He had many opportunities to get help before we got here, kid."

"Yeah, but that doesn't make it any easier to accept."

Wiggy walked across the room, took a water bottle from the refrigerator, and tossed it to his student. "Drink this; you've been in the bloody sun too long."

"I'm not in the mood."

"And I'm not in the mood for this rubbish. None of us could'a stopped what happened to the senator. Don't let it bring ya down like Chicago."

After Gran's death and Chicago, she walked away from everything: this work and reporting. The incidents became her personality, her life. Hell, she had become it. This one was grabbing her gut the same way. She took a big drink, breathed, and then lifted it again.

"I hear you," Kenna said. "I have to get out of here, so keep it short."

Wiggy walked back to his seat. "I've nearly completed

the background checks.”

“Tell me something about this damned German.”

“Nothin’ to tell yet. The name’s undoubtedly an alias. It’s as if he never existed.”

“That’s the way spies operate.” Kenna rubbed her chin. “Anything worth telling?”

“One I never would have imagined.” Wiggy lifted an eyebrow at the computer screen. “But first … seems ya were right about Gowen. Chamberlain suspected him of something, maybe someone using his homosexuality against him.”

“That’s a throw-back to the Hoover years; it’s too archaic. You saw his expression at the apartment. It’s something else.”

“Aye, for starters, Chamberlain contacted the U.S. Marshals.”

“The reason for Agent Edelman’s interest, perhaps,” Kenna said. “So, information was passed to her, and she acted on it.”

“I’m having lunch with her today; I’ll find out more,” Wiggy said.

“Pinch her hard about this campaign funding, Wiggy.” Kenna ignored the pain that had yet to subside. “And find out what she and Hobson talked about before Salvatori got to the 18th. Hobson's full of hot air and thinks he's avoiding us by expelling it."

"I have me way, Fiery," Wiggy said. "The lass first, she needs someone to talk to."

"That golden tongue is what I'm counting on." Kenna chuckled, but it swiftly soured. "If Chamberlain contacted the Marshals, Charlie Sommer had to have known."

"She gave me some dates from the senator's computer. I tried to break into the Marshals' system to see what I could get. No luck yet, but give me time. I'm hoping Edelman will help."

"Too many unanswered questions, Wiggy."

"Fight the paranoia, lass. Not everyone's a criminal," Wiggy said.

"Couldn't prove it by me. Did you check her out?"

"Aye. Nothin', lass. As for the sickness as a wee lass, she had rheumatic fever. Her parents discovered it too late, and it nearly killed her. She was in hospital for most of a year. Records indicate she weighed fifty-five pounds at age twelve. I'd say she's made up for that handsomely."

Kenna exhaled. "Anything else?"

"Nothing funny where Charlie's Mercedes is concerned.

Chamberlain checked." Wiggy leaned back. "He clerked weekends and at night to pay for it."

Kenna relaxed inside a little. She *was* like Gran. "Back to Gowen. What then, after the Marshals and Edelman got involved?"

"A black hole."

"If Chamberlain suspected him of something illegal, why would he keep the little twirp in his office?"

"Could'a been working with the federal lads. You know, keep yer friends close, yer enemies closer."

"Would make sense if Charlie said they had responded." Kenna stared at the golf course without seeing anything. "So, Chamberlain has a change of heart a couple months ago and asks the U.S. Marshals to investigate Gowen. The program is handed over to Edelman, who involved Chamberlain more deeply than he probably wanted? Wow!"

"Chamberlain might have demanded anonymity," Wiggy said.

"That Edelman couldn't guarantee," Kenna responded. "How about total confusion? Or she was also involved from the beginning and was looking for a way out? Not necessarily to save her career, but to do what was right?"

"That's what the blond-headed lad said. Edelman could

be protecting him."

"Either gives Gowen a reason to protect himself … you know, hungry animal. What did they suspect him of doing?"

Wiggy flipped a few keys, and the screen jumped wildly. It flashed up a format that showed everyone involved in the case. He pointed to the middle of the screen as if Kenna could see it from across the room. He double-clicked on Gowen's name to open another screen.

"He called Europe a great deal. Those calls coincide with a lot of cash flowing into the Party from offshore. And Gowen's name or a PAC he manages show up as the major contributors on most of 'em."

"The PAC money could be key. We know they were building a war chest, no doubt in the millions. If Chamberlain wanted out, the PAC money in his name would go with him."

Wiggy looked up, dumbfounded. "What you sayin', kid?"

"The money he didn't spend on campaigning would go with him when he left office."

"Bloody hell, I didn't know that," Wiggy barked. "That's a helluva motive if someone wanted that money to stay with the Party."

"Just like Charlie said, Gowen does good for the Party and is shoved up the bureaucratic ladder."

"He doesn't seem the type."

"Hell, the entire Party hierarchy could be involved," came Kenna's response without really thinking about it. "They could buy an election with the money, so what's the difference? And if illegal?"

"Legal or not, the majority of the public doesn't know about keepin' the PAC money."

Kenna drank from the water bottle, thinking out loud, "What if Chamberlain wanted to change the law and make it that the money had to be returned or remain with the Party?"

"You just expanded our list of suspects, kid."

"Yes." *Is that why Devon Whyte went silent on the golf course?* Kenna wondered. "If Gowen facilitated the deals, he must've raked in handsome middleman's fees."

"Not here in the States, at least not that I can find."

"If the money's coming from abroad, a smart man keeps it off-shore."

"And he's not daft," Wiggy agreed. "I've made contact with friends at Interpol—"

"You mean drinking buddies," Kenna interrupted.

"Pubs are used for more than simply drinkin', kid. It's a

sociable event by which we discuss matters, be they important or trivial."

"And when it's over, you roll home in the streets."

"It often takes a bloody long time to reach agreement," Wiggy said with a smile.

Kenna turned away from the course. "The more we do this, the more we learn just how great Gran was at it."

"People from Africa to Hong Kong owed her favors, as do the lads at Interpol. She pulled their tails out of the sow's slop more than once. I put a rush on 'em; they're good for it. Afterall, the favors are now owed to you."

Kenna remembered the foot slamming into her chest, wanting back that moment in time, knowing it was never to be. She wanted to smash the attacker's skull with the butt of the pistol, or to break a tree limb over his back, to hear bone shatter at impact. Now, as much for her as for Harvey Chamberlain.

"Ole Hobson intrigues me a great deal," Wiggy offered.

Kenna raised an eyebrow. "How so?"

"He bloody-well fooled me. From the ole country, he says, Scotland. Actually, he's from Ireland, son of an Irish Catholic in Belfast. It's his mum who's Scottish: a liberal sympathetic to the plight of the Irish Catholics and all the downtrodden masses, as the rhetoric goes. She converted and married Hobson's father a few weeks before the boy was born.

"Seems the father had links with the IRA," Wiggy continued. "In a skirmish with the British Army, he became a statistic at the receiving end of a British bullet. She took the lad, then in his teens, and went into hiding in England, where they lived until 1990. I can't find how, but that's when she died, and he came to the States."

"In '90? Are you positive?"

"That's what the Interpol lads say," Wiggy said, "with some help."

Kenna's ears pricked. The convoluted became stuck in a quagmire, and it made it much clearer why nothing ever got done in Washington. This was how deals were struck in this city. Plots and subplots to every tiny bit of legislation made sure that nothing was ever accomplished. After all, it was better to do nothing than to make a mistake.

Her stomach curdled; was this case as impossible? Suicide was the simplest for Chamberlain and everyone else. Murder required obstacles to be overcome. It was easier not to buck the system but to flow with it. For Salvatori, it was easier to obey orders, ignore the evidence, and go with what the hierarchy dictated as *the facts*. He had a pension and a family. Don't defy the powerful politicians and the press. Chamberlain's death was suicide, plain and simple.

Kenna wondered if Salvatori was the smartest of all and she the biggest fool.

When the agent confronted Hobson, there were no kind words by either. One believed he was doing his job; the other believed that his job was being destroyed. Neither wanted to give an inch; in the end, the United States Government won the day.

"Before he came to the U.S., he was a groundskeeper at Cambridge." A pause. "You heard me right, kid. The lads in London said he was at Cambridge in the late eighties."

"So, how did he end up here?" Kenna asked.

"The superintendent's sponsor was the good senator from Massachusetts," Wiggy said. "But yer blond lad says it was Chamberlain helped Hobson get this job."

Kenna's face furrowed. Within a few seconds, it was afire, heart pounding as if she had run a mile or been hit by a Taser. *Why would Hobson lie about that?* Especially since he said that Chamberlain kept him from getting Tour recognition. Nothing added up.

"Perhaps it's a good time to see the senator from Massachusetts … and ask him," Wiggy said.

"I agree."

"Do you want it to be by appointment?" Wiggy asked, knowing the answer.

"Hell no, I like surprises."

XXVII

Wiggy parked the rental car in the lot outside Carl's Crab Shack on the Virginia side of the Potomac River. A sign over the door read: 'Get the Crabs at Carl's'. It was in the flight path of National Airport, but by the afternoon crowd, it was obvious the noise was no distraction. In a way, it added to the ambiance. A plane roared overhead as Wiggy entered the restaurant. Walking through, he saw the jet descend over the river towards the runway.

At the Clubhouse, Kenna gave him some ribbing about clean, pressed clothes and combed hair. Their exchange had been good comic relief. And then Kenna gave him the pistol.

'See if Agent Edelman will run it; we might get lucky.'

Carl's was a colorful place of Art Deco design and lighting. For a moment, he thought he had stepped into a bar in Miami. *Wishful thinking,* he thought. A moment later, he saw Agent Edelman on the outside patio.

She was well made up this day, with her hair down. A sleek cotton dress fell over her shoulders, revealing a cleavage Wiggy had either not seen or been too blind to notice. He wondered where she hid the SIG-Sauer. He paused in the shadows for a few moments and watched her movements. Calm and collected, she sipped a beer and looked up as the next jet flew overhead.

While she was distracted, Wiggy approached the table. "Dressed like that, lassie, ye need a new line of work."

She started to stand but didn't when Wiggy took her hand gently and pressed a kiss against it. A waiter joined them but paused. He waited until Wiggy sat before he placed a drink menu on the table. Wiggy simply pointed at Miriam Edelman's beer and placed the linen napkin on his lap. They sized each other up silently until Wiggy's beer was brought.

"You clean up nicely, Mr. Heffernan."

"Oh, this ole thing," he said, pulling out the shirt. "Had this for … must be since me school days."

"Thank you for coming," she said.

"I recall that I asked you."

"May we say it was a mutual invitation, then?"

She smiled, as did he, and they toasted. Their conversations at the Clubhouse had been all business and curt. They both saw the same thing that evening, and that was murder. Wiggy was hesitant to broach the subject; she was hesitant to discuss her frustrations. Requesting the day off, she needed to think about the past and how it related to her future.

"I'm starvin'," he said to break an uneasy silence. "And it is a crab shack."

"One of my secret getaways," she said, sat upright, and lifted her glass. "May I order, then?"

Within fifteen minutes, a bucket of spicy steamed crabs was thrown on their newspaper-covered table. Bibs were tied around their necks. The waiter instructed Wiggy in the art of stripping a crab, which began by beating it with a mallet as if the Boston native was a novice at eating. For another half hour, they ate and drank their fill. Wiggy made a joke about what Kenna called *the intake unit*, which brought a smile to Edelman's face. As the debris was cleared away, the waiter provided them with bowls of lemon water and clean napkins. More beers were delivered.

"Saturday night convinced me to evaluate my career," she opened up, not really knowing why.

"How so?"

To Wiggy's surprise, Miriam Edelman started from the beginning. She grew up idolizing her father. He and his father before him had both served on the Baltimore police force. There weren't many Jewish officers on the force, but her father encountered little racial prejudice because of his professional attention to duty. He instilled that quality in his only child. They both wept hard when her mother died from an extended fight with cancer, but he loved her even more for the strength and emotional support she provided in her youth.

Abraham Edelman, though, could not fight off the loneliness that engulfed him when Miriam went to the University of Maryland. Even before graduating from high school, she knew her path would be Criminal Justice. She accomplished that and attended Maryland on full scholarship. Her dedication in the classroom equaled her father's on the streets. The nights were lonely for both; her father's health deteriorated at an alarming rate. After being sworn into the U.S. Marshals, her first field assignment took her to Portland. Five years later, one of the last events of her father's life was when his daughter moved back into their old home in Baltimore. She still lived there.

"When I saw Senator Chamberlain lying motionless in the sand, it made me think of everything my father taught me."

"Aye, duty and honor above all else," Wiggy said, taking her hand. His soft touch surprised her.

She smiled. "When I saw Kenna in Salvatori's office, I wanted to talk to her about our conversation."

"At the room Saturday afternoon."

“Yes, and so much more,” she said. “I paused my story … it happened about the time I returned to Baltimore.”

“Perhaps six or seven years ago,” Wiggy stated more than asked.

“You are a terribly attractive and insightful man, Wiggy,” she said, squeezing his hand. “Yes. What I want to show you is where I believe all of this began.”

XXVIII

Tightening the thumb screws on Roots Hobson again had to wait. Wiggy had dug deeper into the superintendent's background but had more to do, specifically about his mother and father and immigration into the U.S. Like the Chamberlain murder, segments of time were missing from Hobson's life. No cute anecdotes or lies about Bill Marriott could explain these now, and Hobson knew it. Like everyone else in this madhouse, he was buying time, but for what?

Perhaps Kenna's greatest question was of Avery Gowen's time at Cambridge, which was where Chamberlain spent a year in the late 80s. Prior to Gowen's attendance, Chamberlain gave a personal reference on Gowen's behalf. Lighting the fire of her curiosity was Interpol's interest in the pretender. Everything about Gowen piled into an all-around gut-wrench that suggested he was involved so deep there was no way to extricate himself. If Gowen was, indeed, running scared, he just might be vulnerable enough to talk. To accomplish that, Kenna knew she had to break down Gowen's veneer of hard-ass that he laid on thick as peanut butter.

'Get enough dirt on them; they'll eventually want a bath,' Gran had said.

The struggle in the trees changed her entire attitude about this case, as well as her approach to it. More importantly, it had changed her. She wouldn't forget the pain in the ribs, the soon-to-be scar on her face, the large lump forming on the back of her skull, or the cleat-wounds in her breasts. The gunshots that nearly killed her still rang in her ears.

Even so, today was a new beginning. Over the last 30 hours or so, she had taken a lot of things at face value when she shouldn't have. *Ignorance is a sore that can't be healed,* Kenna thought. She had fallen and gotten back up again but knew she was allowed that a finite number of times. In Washington, D.C., she believed that was only once.

She moved to the room bar and picked up the Washington Post, again staring at the lead story:

Unconfirmed investigations are underway into the late Saturday night shooting death of Illinois Senator Harvey Chamberlain. The U.S. Marshals issued a formal statement ruling out foul play, confirming the senator's death was suicide. No suicide note has been found in the senator's Arlington home, at his office, or at the scene. The senator's wife has been unavailable for comment. Sources at the scene

...

Why did the American press play word games with everything? *'Unconfirmed'* really meant no one knew anything. *'Foul play'* was murder. Why don't the *'formal statements'* and the press just say that?

A light tap on the door; her eyes lifted. She opened it to the faint whiff of clean skin and smiled before she saw him. With a blank expression, Charlie Sommer entered.

"You owe me a drink, but since it's early, I'll settle for coffee."

How did he know I was in this room? She wondered.

His masculine steps clicked on the stone foyer, then hissed across the carpet. He wore Bond's suit and tie again. His developing shiner and the bruise on his cheekbone puffed his chiseled face. In those imperfections, though, he maintained strength. In a macabre way, it became him. However, his manner said that he wanted someone to pay for those beauty marks.

Kenna spun and walked away from the door; her ribs shrieked; her heart pounded. Shocked when he saw her injuries, he lightly took her shoulders.

"Are you alright?"

"Nothing a few months convalescence and whiskey won't cure," she answered.

"If you need a nurse, let me know."

His smile was as warm as his touch. She envisioned kissing him hard, but decorum forbade it. The pounding in her head the pain in her side and ribs, agreed with the decorum. Charlie traced fingers around the bandages on her forehead. They were frozen, as if in time, without moving before she backed away; he understood.

"Did Altmann do this?"

"Didn't get this truck's registration, either."

Charlie's eyes narrowed; emotion welled at the corners. He wiped it away with a thumb. Kenna hesitated, surprised by the weakness, sensing that Charlie hated displays of emotion.

You are a complex man, Charlie Sommer, or a master gamesman. Which, I wonder? Kenna thought. *Or is it both?*

"Hazards of the duty, Charlie. Nothing serious."

"At least now we know we were right," he said.

"They're starting to feel the pinch. Now's when it gets dicey."

"If we are to follow the U.S. Marshals' lead that it was suicide, then why would the attackers still come after you?"

"You've answered your question with one," she countered. "A lot of people want what Altmann's peddling, and they're willing to do whatever it takes to get it before we do."

"The value of life seems to have lessened in the last few days," he said.

Or increased, she didn't say. "Normal, logical humans only kill others for self-preservation. But we're dealing with a criminal's mind here that will kill for a buck. Only, now he's desperate."

"After what I've seen, I'm beginning to believe your philosophy."

"If we live through this, you'll be a full subscriber."

Charlie's expression asked, *if we live through this?* Kenna moved around the bar, put coffee in the coffee maker, added water, and flipped it on. Charlie leaned on the bar across from her.

"Senator Bridgewater called about an hour ago. He doesn't give up; told me to forget this *'incident'*, he called it. And demanded I talk some sense into you."

Burning acid rekindled the fire in Kenna's gut. "What else did he say?"

In his best bravado, "That *'Chamberlain killed himself, and that's that. You're meddling in something that will only get you hurt.'*"

"Bridgewater said that?" she asked, thinking. "That's the second time someone's threatened us under the guise of offering advice."

She rubbed sweating hands together and stared into his eyes. She saw fear, which was surprising until she remembered the attack in Chamberlain's office. If she hadn't interrupted, Charlie Sommer may have also *committed suicide*.

"I didn't know what to say," he said. "He's involved, isn't he?"

She poured two cups full. "Cream or sugar?"

"Neither, but I will take a computer."

Kenna turned with the two cups. Charlie held a memory chip. "From the postal box."

"Have you listened to it?"

"Waiting to do it with you," he said.

She set her laptop on the bar and inserted the memory chip. The hiss of a blank recording hummed from the speakers; she raised the volume. A mechanical voice broke the silence:

'14:07, June 21, 2019.'

She looked at Charlie. "The Friday before Chamberlain was killed." *When I saw the argument,* she thought.

'Avery Gowen,' the firm voice answered the phone. In the background, reggae music played.

'When was the last time you were in Germany?'

"Has to be Altmann," Kenna said.

Gowen: *'Where are you?'*

'Dulles.'

'You could be identified,' Gowen insisted; the music died.

A flight arrival announcement over a loudspeaker in the background, then: *'Not likely, Avery. That was many years ago. I don't have much time.'*

'We agreed I would coordinate everything and make the exchange,' Gowen bawled.

'This is too valuable. Have you made the arrangements?'

Kenna paused the recording. "Okay, Gowen's in this with Altmann, but he's very anxious."

"The little bastard," Charlie hissed.

"They played you like everyone else, Charlie. They were betting you wouldn't interfere."

The recording, Gowen again: *'I'll arrange the meeting ... when?'*

'The senator likes golf, as I recall. Set it for the veranda

bar at Congressional tomorrow. There will be a nice crowd there, lots of faces.'

'You need an invitation.'

'We've known each other a long time, Avery.'

'Risky, don't you think?' Gowen warned. *'And unnecessary?'*

'Make the arrangements.'

"Now we know who set it up," Charlie said.

Kenna pushed pause. "Did Gowen tell anyone else about the meeting?"

"If I didn't know about it, I doubt anyone else did."

"Not Bridgewater, not Dorothy Baldwin?" she asked. He shook his head. "Then, after Gowen arranged it, Chamberlain called Bridgewater to discuss it."

Kenna pushed play. There was a crackling pause; then the recording continued with the mechanical voice: *'15:09, June 22, 2019.'*

"The evening after Chamberlain met Altmann," Kenna said.

A pause of five seconds before Gowen: *'He can't raise the money.'*

'Help him, Avery,' the German demanded. *'We are meeting again.'*

'I have enough on my plate.'

'Find a way before our meeting. Tell him to go to the Party.'

'I've tried; he won't.'

'Remind him of the PAC funds and convince him it's the only way!'

'And if I can't?'

'Don't let me down. I've come a long way to finalize this deal, and I don't mean just the miles.'

Gowen: *'The U.S. Marshals have been asking about the agent's death six years ago.'*

'It was only a matter of time.'

'And your conversation with Chamberlain. They know you're here!'

'How do they know I talked to Chamberlain? Only you and I knew about that?' The German chuckled, one Kenna would long remember. *'You disappoint me, Avery. I thought you were smarter than that.'*

Gowen: *'But I didn't—'*

Altmann interrupted: *'It's of no consequence, I assure you. I will conclude my business quickly and be gone by the time they sift through the rubble. Unless you do as I say, you will be found in that rubble.'*

The recording finished. Kenna ejected it and set the chip on the bar. Charlie's hand fell on hers; she pulled away. There was something wrong; she couldn't pinpoint it but felt it.

Charlie pressed that strong body against her and pulled her face close. The aroma of coffee on his breath was warm and sweet against her skin. They both trembled. He kissed her cheek. She wanted him as much as she believed he wanted her. The rush of womanhood nearly exploded inside her … *control* … she pushed away to arm's length and stared into his eyes.

Charlie's phone beeped. Hesitantly, he looked at it. "That's the mailbox drop. Another package was just delivered."

"How can that be?"

"Somebody's obviously delivering them," he said. "There was no postage on this one."

Kenna thought for a moment before a name came to mind. "Get it and play both for Wiggy when he returns."

"What about you?"

"I have other things to do," she said.

"You always have something else to do."

She lowered a stare at him, not liking that comment.

"Don't get needy, Charlie. Nothing comes before finding out who killed Harvey Chamberlain. First off, I'm going to pay my respects to the widow."

"That will be a treat," he said sarcastically.

"Later, Devon Whyte is having an impromptu gathering at his house in honor of Senator Chamberlain," she said and raised a hand before he could say anything. "I'm going to meet Bridgewater, Whyte, and the senator from Massachusetts. The three of them with you would be like pitching gasoline on a fire. I want answers."

"You won't get them, with or without me."

She knew that. *I just want to see who squirms first ... and the most.*

XXIX

An hour later, Luis, the Uber driver, stopped in front of the early American home where Harvey Chamberlain and his wife had lived prior to their separation. Nestled among tall Virginia Pines on a hilltop of Langley Forest, the home was easily ten times the value as when the senator bought it after his second term. Chirping birds and wind brushed through the foliage in a peaceful hush, the antithesis of Harvey Chamberlain's life and, certainly, his death.

Luis leaned over the front seat, "I'll wait out here."

"Thanks, Luis. Doubt I'll be very long."

Kenna stood from the car and stretched soreness from her ribs. She inhaled sweet air, unlike the cesspool of the city just a few miles away. As she exhaled, though, she sensed that the pleasantries were about to end. Her finger touched the doorbell; a minute later, the large double door opened. She half-expected a servant.

"Ms. Hannigan, I assume," Gloria Chamberlain said from inside.

"You were expecting me?"

"At some point," she said and surprisingly waved her inside.

Taking a step past her, Kenna's nostrils flared from the heavy whiff of whiskey. The room was unmistakably Harvey Chamberlain … or had been. Evidence of this had already been stacked in boxes around the room. Congressional photos, humanitarian awards, and diplomas were spread everywhere.

"Most people would allow a widow time to mourn," Gloria continued with a waved hand, without question intoxicated. "But I guess people like you don't know courtesy."

People like me? "If you would like me to come back another time—"

"The great Harvey William Chamberlain planted the political kiss of death on my lips, Ms. Hannigan, sealing my fate in 1995. He brought me to this God-forsaken hellhole where I have since been controlled by his destiny. That has now changed. I am forty-six, young enough and attractive enough to do what I want."

To get what I want, Kenna thought she meant to say. Gloria's point-blank candor left little doubt there was no love lost by the senator's death.

Gloria Chamberlain's boasting was not without merit. She was attractive at 46, though an innate fear of growing old was her weakness, a tragedy in and of itself. Tall, she carried a well-proportioned feminine frame. Short, business-cropped brunette hair held a touch of gray at the cusp of her ears. Noticeable traces of youthful beauty defied the bags under her dark brown eyes. Some of that youthful vigor had been resurrected by a plastic surgeon's scalpel. It had worked, leaving a more seductive stare. *Or was it evil?* Similar procedures had lifted sagging cheeks and chin; other hidden parts of her anatomy were upright and firm.

Confident arrogance left no doubt that Gloria believed she could manipulate her way into any bedroom she desired. It seemed to be this city's trademark. Charlie Sommer flashed through Kenna's mind.

The morning Post had yet to be opened; the headline about the senator was facedown. At a little past two in the afternoon, it was not difficult to pinpoint Gloria's greatest weakness. Whiskey and water sat on the table. Ice in the glass said it was not left over from the night before. Initially, Kenna believed the alcohol dependence was fueled by grief. Gloria's stinging initial diatribe changed that thought; Charlie Sommer's analysis of her might have been on the mark.

A chrome-framed black and white photo of the late senator and a military man remained on lone display on the fireplace mantel. They were both young, so very young.

Other men and mountainous desertscape filled the backdrop of this intriguing flash of the past.

"I didn't realize your husband and General Treadway were friends."

Gloria lifted an eyebrow and broke into reserved laughter. "Then you don't know the general very well, and you damn sure didn't know the senator.

"If ever oil and water, it was those two," she continued, laughed, and took a large drink. She shook a finger at the picture. "They knew each other in a paradoxical way. I suppose it could have been hatred. Someone once said a man should keep his enemies closer than his friends."

"My father," was all Kenna could say.

"The senator kept that picture to remind himself how much he hated the general, I think. The ravings of a madman have no logic."

"You believe your husband was mentally disturbed?"

Gloria chortled into the drink. "Or, he was gay. God knows he didn't touch me. But as you can see, most of what the senator left behind is being shoveled into the bad memory files."

Her blunt demeanor took Kenna aback. To Gloria, both men worked only for political profit, never for meaningless personal or emotional reasons, such as love. Or was Gloria reflecting on herself? According to the philosophy garnered at the bottom of a glass of Jack Daniels, that was why political marriages were hollow, without meaning, without fulfillment.

Gloria allowed a guarded smile. "The senator's weakness was his inability to use his power for personal benefit. Benevolently misguided, he believed he was elected to perform some intrinsic good for mankind."

"I notice you haven't said my husband or even spoken his name. Is there a reason?"

"I am coping, Ms. Hannigan."

How long would it take her to eliminate the past, to blot out her husband forever? Icy hatred shot as much from Gloria's eyes as from her mouth. Within a few days, the late senator would be nothing more than an ink stain on marriage and death certificates.

It was unhealthy to judge people for what or who they were or even wanted to be. Distractions were simple; discovery was not. As much as Kenna suddenly disliked this irreverent, lifeless piece of scalpel-molded flesh, she pressed on.

"I'm sorry," Kenna digressed, incapable of stopping

herself. "But wasn't Harvey doing good for society?"

She took a drink without answering. "The late senator and I haven't loved each other for a long time. Our relationship was one of mutual benefit. He had what he wanted …" She waved a hand across her body. "And I had what I wanted, his power and this city at my feet."

"From *'God-forsaken hellhole'* to the *'city at my feet'*? That's quite a transition."

"Washington is a contradiction, Ms. Hannigan. You will discover that over time."

I believe I already have. "It sounds like you will miss it."

A drink, a blink, and the flutter of dull eyes: "Who said I'm leaving?"

Kenna walked to the mantel and lifted the photo. "So, you don't hate Washington?"

"Everyone has a love-hate relationship with this city. I adapted, as I did with him. I lived my life making the most of an unfortunate situation."

As you will this one. "Are you happy he's dead?"

"An inappropriate choice of words. You can surely do better."

What Kenna heard was different. To Gloria, Harvey Chamberlain no longer existed beyond drunken rhetoric. Her words were those of confusion in a mind floating in booze. For Gloria Chamberlain, it was paramount to finding Ponce de León's Fountain of Youth. She had so much to live for but was flushing it all down the toilet as processed whiskey.

"Frankly, your candor is troubling, Mrs. Chamberlain."

Only then did Gloria Chamberlain realize she was still wearing a nightgown. She reached out to touch Kenna's hand and laughed. Her touch was cold; Kenna withdrew.

"Please excuse my obvious bad taste, Ms. Hannigan. I was boxing up the late senator's belongings."

"I understand, and again, I apologize for coming by at this time."

"I am willing to help."

The grieving widow she had yet to see, or just a Washington game? "You already have."

"I've always spoken my mind. Besides, I would do anything for Malcolm."

Malcolm had called Gloria before the late senator was killed. Presumptuous, but also Malcolm's style. Did anyone say no to the great Senator Bridgewater? Kenna leaned against a chair. She hated being played, which intensified the deeper she sank into this Washington game.

"Anything, Mrs. Chamberlain?"

"Gloria, please. Malcolm said you were, and I use his words, *'looking into the senator'.*"

"You mean your husband."

There was a moment of silence before Gloria snapped her head up and jeered: "Yes, good old Harvey. Out to change the world, Harvey. When, in fact, it changed him. What do you intend to investigate, Ms. Hannigan? Good old Harvey puts a gun against his good old head and deposits a bullet into his good old brain. Good old Harvey, the loving husband and father, leaves a widow with a daughter in private college. Always thinking of others, the good old bastard."

She took a large swallow of whiskey and, with a quick glance over her shoulder, stumbled to the sideboard for another. Sun struck the widow's cheekbones. The youthful beauty Kenna saw in the shadows was now crumpled and wrinkled by alcoholic reality.

"How about you?"

"A little early for me," Kenna said.

"You sound like the senator. Are you judging me, Ms. Hannigan?"

"No, I just don't drink this early."

"I love drinking in the afternoons, mornings too. It's the

only way I can cope with the rest of the day." She laughed and moved to her left; the wall helped with balance.

"Some people don't think your husband killed himself."

"Fools. I certainly hope you aren't one of them."

"I'm paranoid, so I must be a fool, Mrs. Chamberlain."

"Paranoia and naiveté are often confused, Ms. Hannigan. The senator killed both when he killed himself."

"That's pretty deep for me," she said. "Did he do it because you were leaving him?"

"Over me? God, that's funny," Gloria said with a short-lived chuckle.

"Men have done stranger things over women, and for lesser reasons."

"If that was meant as a compliment, go to hell," Gloria snapped. "The senator killed himself over his own miserable failures."

"You're avoiding my question, Mrs. Chamberlain."

"Harvey never thought of anyone but Harvey. Even in death, he has forgotten about me and his daughter."

"Hatred is a strange way to mourn the dead."

"I mourn the living, Ms. Hannigan. The dead are gone, free of the Harvey Chamberlain's of the world."

"I heard the pending divorce was rather heated."

Gloria inhaled, swelling her surgically youthful chest, and slapped her glass on the fireplace mantel. Half the drink spilled. She made no effort to clean it.

"A personal matter overplayed by a press hungry for headlines. So, tell me how a reporter becomes a private investigator."

"I don't think of myself in that way, Mrs. Chamberlain. I liken it more to a proprietor of a lost and found department." *Or at least that's what Gran always said,* she thought.

"Dealing in human lives?"

"No, in the dead."

There was a long silence as Gloria Chamberlain took another drink and dabbed at her eyes with a handkerchief. A portion of the sentiment seemed genuine. The alcoholic rhetoric rambled on:

"Though the senator and I were not in love, we didn't hate each other. People have interpreted his actions as trouble at home. Nothing could have been farther from the truth."

"You weren't living together," Kenna said, confused.

"He wanted to work through his problems on The Hill, somewhere other than here. I accommodated him."

"Is that typical around D.C.? To live apart, I mean?"

"One of this city's many political diseases. His career supplanted his private life and certainly our marriage. I was better being the wife of a U.S. Senator than anything else. I accepted that because I knew and loved his work."

Kenna shook the confusion from her ears. It had, indeed, been a love-hate relationship, and she had experienced it all in a few intoxicating minutes. Any truly grieving woman would have thrown her out of the house after her first question. Gloria relished brandishing every gruesome detail of their sorted life.

"Seems like a lousy reason to be miserable," Kenna said.

"Before I met the senator, I was nothing and had nothing," Gloria said, ignoring her. "He changed that. Now, I am an educated woman, as knowledgeable about Washington as anyone they could bring in to replace him."

A shock wave rifled through Kenna's body. She saw the photo and placed her left hand on the arm of the sofa. The general's words and confidence in Malcolm Bridgewater's office echoed in her ears once again.

"I don't mean anything disrespectful, but it's logical," Gloria said. "Washington doesn't stop moving because of one man's death, Ms. Hannigan."

"So, I've heard."

"Are you here to see if I killed my husband?"

"Did you?"

Gloria chuckled again. "I like honesty in a woman."

Living in Washington must have made Gloria Chamberlain a very lonely person. To her, the men and women in Washington were not dishonest; they were driven. Kenna held up a weathered hand. Numb, she took several steps towards the door; Gloria moved in front of her.

"Oh, and you were doing so well, Ms. Hannigan."

The game infected the entire city, not just Malcolm Bridgewater. Gloria was lifeless, soaked in booze, trying to maintain some semblance of youth. It was sad, extremely sad.

"The senator killed himself. Why do you insist otherwise?"

"I don't believe I've said anything to the contrary, Mrs. Chamberlain. I deal in facts, and the only fact right now is that your husband is dead."

Regardless of how Kenna antagonized Gloria, she allowed it to roll off her back. Was it because of the booze or that she was totally insensitive about her husband's death?

"Shot by the hand of a fool … his own." Gloria finished

the glass of whiskey with one gulp and then glanced out the window as a drab brown government-issue Cadillac stopped in the circle drive. "Now, if you don't mind."

Kenna caught Gloria's quick glance in the mirror over the mantel as she escorted her to the door. The doorbell rang. Gloria pushed up her breasts and opened the door with a large smile.

"Good afternoon, Mrs. Chamberlain. I tried calling, but your line appears to be off the hook, or so the Telephone Company said. If later would be more convenient."

"Not at all, general, come in."

It was then Kenna noticed Gloria Chamberlain wasn't wearing undergarments. It also struck her as odd that there was no one else in the house, especially the daughter. This coincidental meeting shed some light on her statements and actions. It said a lot about the photo on the mantel. She intentionally stared at it when Treadway entered. The smell of animal attraction overpowered the whiskey-laden air. The handshake between the general and Gloria lingered with constant eye contact. Kenna awaited a kiss that did not come.

"General Treadway, an honor again, sir," Kenna said, extending her hand.

"That it is, young Hannigan." The general glanced at his

host before looking at Kenna. He grasped Kenna's hand with usual military bravado, then turned to the widow. "I wasn't aware you knew the most famous woman in Washington this weekend, Gloria."

"Famous? Because she's a reporter?"

"No, she's here to solve the crime of the century." The general smiled and stopped short. He showed no outward sign of why and turned back to Kenna. "I could use a lesson or two in facing the camera, young Hannigan. Never good at playing the press game. How about it?"

"Something tells me you play every game well, general," Kenna said with her best double entendre and turned for the door.

XXX

Miriam Edelman parked the Ford Explorer on the empty street in front of an abandoned brick warehouse. The rundown neighborhood was as empty as the street, lined by vacant tenements and small warehouses. She and Wiggy stood out. A brilliant sun boiled them in the high humidity. Thick, tall shrubs whipped about like swirling waves in a heavy breeze.

Edelman's eyes were heavy as she took in the area. Save the missing buildings, the scene had not changed much. The entire area was overgrown, with weeds surrounding the warehouse. Perhaps fittingly, a stand of cardinal flower grew near the front door. She remembered the young agent who died that night with a heavy heart.

"So, this is where it started?" Wiggy asked.

"If you mean by Altmann, yes," she said. "At least, for me."

"We didn't know Altmann was an ex-German agent with Afghani ties until Salvatori joined us. Here, we learned that Altmann obviously had friends."

"Just as you described," Wiggy said, waving his hand toward the building. "I can see that night, lass."

She stepped to the aged building and slid open a rusty bolt on the tall dual swinging doors. It snapped open; she swung the doors out. Wiggy accompanied her into the darkness. Trash fluttered past in the breeze; they paused. Cardboard enclosures stood along the center aisle, ragged blankets and clothing inside them. The building had become home to squatters, the homeless, and drug addicts. Now, they were alone.

"Six years ago, it was Salvatori's first assignment with me since joining the service," she said. "He and Craig, the rookie, were to wait inside. I was outside."

"Only three people for a known terrorist?" Wiggy said, recalling a similar night with Kenna when they had gone after Anson Beck, just the two of them.

"I objected, but it was Salvatori's call. He convinced the section chief—"

"Brock Anderson," Wiggy interrupted.

"Yes. Only Salvatori had seen Altmann, who believed he was going to meet someone who could connect him with Senator Chamberlain."

"But not for blackmail back then," Wiggy said. "To kill him for the betrayal in Afghanistan."

"That's what Salvatori believed." Edelman paused,

looking up the street, re-enacting the events as they happened. "It was dark, no streetlights, there were no cars. Salvatori and Craig entered to take their positions for the ambush. Just as I took my position in the rear, all hell broke loose inside.

"I rushed for the door," she continued, "but Altmann broke out the side, firing inside. Wearing a hoodie, Altmann spun on me and fired, knocking me to the ground."

"Good thing ye wore the vest, lass."

Bleeding, Craig ran out first, followed by Salvatori, also wounded. Edelman fired, hitting Altmann in the arm. He screamed, fired behind, and spun towards the rail tracks. Craig went down, dead. Salvatori collapsed. Edelman gave chase down the embankment, over fences, and onto the rail yard.

Concealed behind a train car, Altmann fired. The bullet hit Edelman in the shoulder, just above the vest. A second hit her in the thigh; she collapsed to the tracks. As Edelman lifted her gun to return fire, Altmann ran behind the train cars into the night.

"Lying on the tracks, bleeding, watching Altmann run away, I remember thinking he didn't look nearly as imposing as I imagined he would," Edelman said.

"This all sounds very familiar, lass."

"How so?"

Wiggy stood with Edelman at the fence overlooking the rail yard. A train passed slowly. Their first attempt to capture Anson Beck had ended in a similar fashion, with him being the one to collect the bullet in the chest. He had no vest. If not for Kenna, he would have bled out.

"The contact Salvatori expected never arrived," Wiggy said. "Or that was the contact, and it was Altmann that never showed."

"Whoever, I hit him. His failure here could be why he's waited until now to return," Edelman offered.

"He went back to the drawing board. He learned from his mistakes and has now refined his approach." Wiggy surveyed the rail yard. "He'll make other mistakes, though. Count on it."

"Thank you for today. Revisiting this was what my sanity needed."

They turned for the Explorer. "Ya mean you've not been here since?"

"No. While I recovered, Brock Anderson took over the case."

"Aye, I know all about it," Wiggy said.

She took his arm as they walked to the Explorer. "And how is it you know so much, Mr. Heffernan?"

"I have my ways, lass," he said with a smile.

"I have no doubt," she said and returned a smile.

Senior Agent Brock Anderson was promoted to deputy director after Agent Calvin Craig was memorialized. Anderson took over Edelman's case like a man on fire. He was in front of the cameras daily, but every question was answered that the *'investigation is underway'* and there *'is no comment at this time'*. After several months and then a year, the case lost its luster and fell into the cold.

"Aye, but the day is young, lass," Wiggy said and kissed her cheek lightly with a smile. "I like it that ya don't mask your scent with a perfume."

She straightened, surprised. "Always preferred au naturale."

As much as Wiggy wanted to forget this city and go to Boston with Kenna to be with the memory of Gran Lockwood, he could never abandon what they had begun. The grand ole Dame would never forgive him.

"Did they ever find the weapon that killed the agent?"

"I don't know," she said. "I was taken completely out of the loop."

"Reprimanded, you mean to say," Wiggy said without malice.

She appreciated his honesty. "It took me a long time to get back into the field."

"Aye," he said and handed her a flower. "And they've thrown ye right into a cauldron of boiling shite."

She forced a chuckle. "You have a wonderful way with words."

"Why did Altmann pick here to meet?" he asked, taking in the entire area.

"I always believed someone scouted it for him," she said. "Deputy Director Anderson might have the answer to that."

Anderson would be unavailable, of that Wiggy was certain. He also knew his work was cut out for him. There had to be a trail of ownership on this land, and now there was another person of interest to investigate.

"We are dealing with masters of deception, lass," he continued. "Masters, indeed!"

"One of my men died in that fight, and I didn't back him up. In a way, Salvatori has blamed me for that."

"There's no *in a way* to it."

What Wiggy saw in Salvatori at the 18th green was hatred toward Edelman, pure and simple. He understood her actions and frustration. No, it wasn't her fault, but there was no way to convince Edelman until he and Kenna proved it.

"Before the ambush, Salvatori told me that Altmann killed his family in Germany," Edelman said.

Yes, the fuel behind the obsession, with Gowen the common denominator. "Did the senator call you about his meeting with the German?" Wiggy asked.

She shook her head and looked up. "That's what I don't understand. Two weeks ago, he was on the phone to me daily, and then he fell off the map."

"With no explanation," Wiggy said and did not ask. "Which in itself explains a lot."

She smiled. "That it does."

"So, ya aren't just a pretty face?" He placed a hand on her cheek. "On Saturday night, everything changed."

She ignored the compliment with a frown. "Everything fell into the cauldron."

Wiggy countered, "You are too professional not to inform a superior about the senator's calls and eventual silence."

"Which is when Salvatori came into my office and said we had an appointment at the Clubhouse."

"To meet Kenna, no doubt." She agreed. "And Gowen

… why haven't ya clapped him in irons?"

"Ask those of authority," she offered. "They say they will get him when this is all over."

"That's not what he thinks," Wiggy said. "So, why would Altmann kill Chamberlain when he was trying to blackmail him? Dead men don't pay."

"There's only one explanation."

"Aye," Wiggy agreed. "If the good senator didn't pay, someone else would."

She turned away. "I could have prevented all of this."

"It was organized long before ya got involved, Miriam." He looked back to the warehouse and put an arm around her. "But if ye have some time this afternoon, perhaps we could think this thing through."

"I was thinking the same," she said. "I have some Irish stout at my place."

Wiggy lifted out a plastic bag with the pistol. "You should check this against the past."

"Where'd you get this?" Edelman asked, taking the bag.

"Kenna has a way of bringin' out the best in lads."

XXXI

Senator Chamberlain's office door handle turned. Charlie Sommer's attention turned away from packing personal items into a box. He tensed when the door opened. Adrenaline flooded through him as a strand of yellow light dissected the room's grayness, and a man stepped forward. Relaxing, Charlie dropped a stack of files into the box.

"I feel your beady eyes locked on the side of my head, senator," he said.

Hands on his hips, Bridgewater's eyes rummaged through the shambles of the office. His glare eased past Charlie into Chamberlain's private office. Little had changed from his last visit, though it appeared much of what had been thrown around was now stacked neatly on the dead senator's desk. *You are good for something, Charles*, he thought.

"What have you done here?" Bridgewater demanded.

"What do you want?" Charlie insisted.

"I wanted to talk to you about Harvey, but right now, I'm concerned with what I see."

"Collecting the last of my belongings," he said.

"Looks like you've been rummaging through Harvey's private documents."

He had expected this from Gowen but not Bridgewater. The elder statesman had not been in Chamberlain's office in several years. Those who had business with the omnipotent Malcolm Bridgewater went to him.

"What someone else did on Sunday," Charlie snapped.

His eyes went to Gowen's door, the thought of the package delivered to Devon Whyte. His mind flashed to what he had seen before Harvey's death and what he had seen the day after. It all ran together in a blur. He was certain of one thing: after Harvey Chamberlain's death, the hint of cheap aftershave told him that Avery Gowen had been here before him.

"Say what you want, my boy," Bridgewater insisted. "Only two people with the most to gain from Harvey's death. His wife to get rid of him and you to cover up your past."

Jimmy McDowell came through the door just as Charlie lunged forward. The agent stuck out a hand and grabbed Charlie's arm, which stopped his fist a few inches from the senator's face. Bridgewater did not flinch.

"Unlike you, there's nothing to hide in my past," Charlie snapped, instantly calm.

"We'll see what the Marshals have to say about it all."

"He's standing right beside you." Charlie snapped his

arm away as Bridgewater walked to the door. "You worked with Harvey; you knew!"

For months, Charlie had felt the contradictions and gamesmanship on both sides of the aisle. The past few months had deepened the fissure between the Parties. There was no truth in Washington, D.C. It was as if he were outside gravity's effect, unable to control simple body motions everyone took for granted.

The old man turned back into the room. "But I didn't kill him. He took care of that himself."

Charlie took an immediate step forward and directed a perfectly placed backhand across the cheek of the most powerful man in Congress. McDowell froze momentarily, then jerked Charlie aside in a standing arm bar.

"Calm down, Mr. Sommer," Jimmy insisted. "This isn't doing any good."

Charlie looked up into the bigger man's eyes and saw something he never had … understanding. His anger subsided when McDowell loosened his grip, turned away, and grabbed the door handle. Charlie straightened Bond's suit, then spoke to Bridgewater:

"We should be burying you, not Harvey."

"Your wish will come all too soon," the aged senator

said.

Charlie stomped back to his desk and sat heavily. Without hesitation and without looking up as the door closed, he continued to box his belongings. His heavy eyes circled the office. Activity in the hall filled his ears. It was as if he could hear Senator Chamberlain barking on the phone, as he so often did. He threw the last of his personal belongings into the box, flipped off the desk lamp, and stood.

In the hall, Bridgewater paused for a long moment. He placed a hand on McDowell's chest. "Go in there and give him some friendly advice, Jimmy."

Before lifting the box, Charlie looked back into the senator's private office. He would miss him; hell, the country would miss him. His eyes shot to the door and then back into Chamberlain's private office. Bridgewater hadn't come to talk to him at all. He had come to go through what remained of Chamberlain's things. Had he missed something? Charlie startled when the door opened, and McDowell stepped inside … the recordings!

"I need a word," McDowell said.

Charlie walked back to his desk when the big man approached. As he did, the office door opened again. The retiring female senior Democratic senator from Kansas entered. She walked straight to Charlie and gave him a hug.

"I heard you were in the building, Charles," the senator said. "I wanted to come by and tell you how sorry I am."

"Thank you," Charlie said with great emotion. "I was just leaving with my personal belongings. Mr. McDowell offered to carry them to the car for me."

"That's nice of you, James. Mind if I walk along?" the senator asked. "You know, Charles, if I wasn't retiring, you wouldn't have to leave. If you ever need anything, call me."

"Thank you, senator. You don't know how much I appreciate that."

As the three walked out the door, McDowell glared at Charlie, but his expression was impossible to read.

XXXII

Kenna knew from experience that politicians didn't like having their private gatherings crashed. She was seldom welcome when her father's political friends were in town; however, there was one marked exception. When wives were present, she was paraded around like a prize calf at the State Fair to prove how cute a young daughter the great Texas television magnate had produced. With growth came inconvenience. Once she reached puberty and cute was replaced by teenage awkwardness, she was confined to her room or shuffled off to a movie. After driving age, she was sent out with the great man's blessings and $20 in her pocket. She had a feeling she was about to find out just how inconvenient she was now.

The contemptuous glares of more than one hypocritical snob greeted her when she entered the private caucus of the Democratic Party elite. Had looks been guns, she would never have made it out of the foyer of Devon Whyte's Victorian home. Without passing Malcolm Bridgewater's name, she probably wouldn't have gotten past the gang of U.S. Marshals at the front wrought iron gate. She was surprised Jimmy McDowell wasn't one of those on guard.

It was not a black-tie affair, but tailored suits and ties

were mandatory. As the self-important noticed her presence, conversations became hand-covered whispers, undoubtedly about how Kenna did not fit and was certainly not welcome. She stepped forward; they backed away as if she were a contagion. She neither smiled nor frowned. *No fear.* Gran Lockwood had taught her that, too.

Devon Whyte met her at the edge of the foyer. "This is a private affair, Ms. Hannigan."

"You look smashing in battle dress, Devon," Kenna said of the black jacket and red bow tie. "We were interrupted on the golf course."

Whyte escorted Kenna to his private study. The door closed to darkness before he flipped on a single, green-shaded light in the corner. When asked if the discussion could wait for another day, Kenna offered to talk to Malcolm alone.

Kenna inhaled alcohol and stale pipe smoke. Her eyes stung, but when she took a good look around the room, she saw the real side of Devon Whyte. A copy of the Declaration of Independence was above the mantel. His historical taste was displayed from artwork to reading material, classical to modern. He was diverse, with one exception.

"Nothing from Africa," she said as much as asked.

"I am not one to be in vogue, Kenna. I am an American; that is my heritage." Whyte leaned on the desk. Diamond cufflinks glistened in the light.

"Those look expensive."

Whyte tugged down his jacket to hide them. "Are we here to discuss my clothes, jewelry, and collections, or something else?"

Whyte stared at the dormant black fireplace centered in the stone wall next to his desk. He lifted an Ivory pipe from an Abalone shell atop his desk and stuck it between his lips. Full cheeks were sucked into his face as he inhaled. Darting eyes circled the room but never landed on Kenna until he shoved a lighter into the bowl and drew the flame into the tobacco.

"A fire takes the chill out of the air. One would be most appropriate today," Whyte said.

"Nixon used to take the chill out of the air year-round."

"Nixon may have been a pompous ass about most things, but he taught our Party a few things. It's unfortunate some of us weren't paying attention."

"Whatever that means."

"You know, he and Jack Kennedy were friends before they became rivals for the White House."

"They had a mutual enemy, communism."

"A lot like us. I didn't like what you said at the golf course, Kenna." Whyte lifted a decanter on the sideboard and poured two fingers of Scotch whiskey into a square glass. Kenna lifted a hand to decline. "But I suppose I had it coming. I want to help."

"Make sure that's really want to want before offering, Devon."

He exhaled. "My mind was made up two holes after you left. I grew weary of the cross-examination."

"Yesterday, I asked you what Avery Gowen brought to your house. What was it?"

"If I told you that you were right, would that be enough?"

"I'd like to see the information."

"I was going to bring it to you, but this—" he swallowed the whiskey.

Before Whyte could continue, the door opened. Red eyes glared across the lip of a glass as, unannounced, Bridgewater barged into the study. A bodyguard shut the door with authority, but not before staring at Kenna. She was unmoved; *it was time for the fish to squirm.*

"You have some gall, dropping in uninvited," Bridgewater said as if it were his house.

"There are things missing from the Chamberlain puzzle," Kenna started. "You met with him Saturday. Was that before or after you talked to me?"

Bridgewater hesitated. "Neither. I didn't meet with him."

The lies continue. "That's not what Avery Gowen says."

"If you believe him over me, you need your head examined," Malcolm said and cleared his throat. "I came to see you. After that, I had dinner, then went home. Ask Jimmy."

"I will. So, you didn't speak to Chamberlain on Saturday?"

Bridgewater glanced at Whyte, "Am I stuttering?"

"Chamberlain was at the Clubhouse for an extended time before he was killed. That's been confirmed by a waiter."

The old man crinkled his face and rested a hand on the back of a chair. "I'm not sure what you're fishing for, girl, but you're in the wrong pond. Nobody here had anything to do with Chamberlain's death. He killed himself."

"Because he was being blackmailed?"

"Perhaps," the elder statesman offered. "Maybe he was tired of fighting Gloria."

The story going around was that Harvey Chamberlain was a quitter, though he was always considered one of the strongest senators on The Hill. In speeches and writings, Bridgewater and Whyte had boasted of Chamberlain's fortitude, as had senators on the opposite side of the aisle.

"Harvey Chamberlain took the easy way out and put a bullet in his brain. Accept it."

"Is that what Gloria Chamberlain said he would do?"

Bridgewater frowned and cleared his throat. "What do you mean?"

"She talked to you before Harvey put that *'bullet in his brain'*. But yesterday, you told me you hadn't talked to her. Why did you lie to me, Malcolm?" The fissure of deceit deepened.

"What she and I discussed has no bearing on Harvey's suicide."

"You expect me to believe that now?"

"I think you're frustrated that the announcement was called off. You're dreaming this up as you go along."

"Reality, no dream!"

"You're way off the mark, Kenna. Chamberlain dug his own grave. I won't help you drag a respected man's name through the mud. He's done enough damage by himself."

Kenna shook away the contradiction, "Whose name, yours or his?"

"We need to get back to our guests," Bridgewater said to Whyte and turned.

"Not yet. Actually, I came here to talk to the Massachusetts senator."

Anger and reluctance swelled Bridgewater's face. He set his drink on a sideboard. Abraham Lincoln stared down at him from the far wall between two velvet-curtained windows.

"That isn't going to happen," Malcolm insisted.

Kenna grimaced and glanced across to Whyte. Meek and hesitant, the chairman rolled the whiskey glass in his large palms.

"I'd think the U.S. Senate would have an interest in the truth."

"Oh, but we do, my girl," Malcolm replied, then sipped his whiskey. "That's why we have the U.S. Marshals."

"You're trying to turn a tragedy into a scandal. It's real!"

"You're rambling, Kenna. Perhaps you should go back to Boston before you're consumed in your own imaginary black hole. Chicago comes to mind." The old man swallowed his drink hard, but his eyes remained fixed on Kenna. "I'm a veteran of the political wars, my girl. You know you can't run roughshod over me."

"And you know how far I'll go to get the facts, Malcolm. I'll get my answers, with or without the Massachusetts senator's help."

"Perhaps there is another time, another place better suited for this conversation," Whyte suggested in compromise.

Kenna slowly turned to the chairman. "Your reluctance to help says a lot, Devon. You talk of self-empowerment to your people when you, yourself, can't crawl out from under the thumb of your Party's power brokers. Why don't you write a book about that?"

Whyte lowered his chin and stared at Kenna through those cavernous eyes. His wide nostrils flared, and a large hand balled into a fist. A chill of anticipation crawled up Kenna's spine. At that instant, she wondered how far Devon Whyte would go.

"As a child and then a young adult, I grew up having faith that our country was in good hands with you two." Kenna stared at both men. "Now, I see that my confidence and beliefs were youthful idealism based on ignorance."

Bridgewater chuckled and pushed out his whiskey glass. "We're all grown up now, little girl. Act like it!"

Malcolm had a history of crucifying those who fought

against him. Kenna's own father had said as much. She knew then that she was going to discover firsthand if that assessment was true.

The Washington games are played year-round, she thought. Fronted by the *best* this Party had to offer, it was frightening in a way. She was not frightened of them; she was frightened by the knowledge that this was the political *best.*

"I want to ask the Mass senator about someone who says it may not have been suicide."

"What are you saying?" Whyte asked with furrowed brow.

"The U.S. Marshals were looking for Chamberlain before he was found dead. They questioned me about a German that Chamberlain was seen with earlier in the day and about you, Malcolm."

"That's old news! Get to the point!" the senator snarled.

Kenna smirked. "The reason for or result of their conversation may have been a reason to commit murder. My source says the U.S. Marshals found clues but have since destroyed them."

"Balderdash! And who is this witness?"

And now the hammer. "The Mass senator helped him into

the United States back in 1990. The son of an IRA terrorist killed in Belfast."

The chairman's blank face turned slowly to Malcolm. A siren passed in the distance outside. The green tint of the single-shaded lamp in the far corner strained against the deepening shadows of emotion.

"This fucking inquisition is over!" Malcolm Bridgewater stomped from the room.

XXXIII

Kenna walked into the Clubhouse bar. Appropriate given her mood, it was dimly lit along with the veranda. She sat at the bar and ordered a beer; her phone buzzed. She stared at the text message: *'wl b L8'*. She stared at it for a long time until the bartender set the beer in front of her.

Kenna looked at the message, shaking her head. "Why the hell didn't he just call?"

The bartender chuckled. "It's a new age, Ms. Hannigan."

"Where people don't talk, just punch numbers and letters into a phone."

Kenna flipped her phone to silent; she wanted to think without interruption. In a way, she was relieved that the internal struggle between duty and beauty was momentarily avoided. She couldn't allow her attraction to Charlie to hamper her objectivity. As she took a drink, the words from Devon Whyte's house rolled like thunder through her brain.

She toasted the photos of previous tournament champions that aligned the bar inside a glass display case. *Oh, to have a life of only one career?* she thought. *And to be a champion at something!* She envied them … somewhat. And wondered if they did her. She chuckled … *no one is that foolish.*

"Mind if I join you?" came a familiar voice over her shoulder.

In the mirror stood the reflection of a confused, angry man. Kenna asked herself if she was the one confused, and was the look on her visitor more of determination? Her own reflection was the sorrier of the two: cuts and bruises. The mirror provided a particularly interesting view of Agent Salvatori. The difference between these looks and those at his birthday party was obvious … exhaustion. A shower had helped her, but Salvatori smelled like he'd lost the soap bar.

"I'm in no mood for a grilling, but I've heard it said that it's a free country." *Until the politicians have their way.*

"Somebody must not'a liked the way you comb your hair," the agent pointed at the cut above Kenna's eye.

Salvatori leaned forward to order an ale. She forced an unconvincing smile. The thick head of Salvatori's drink flowed over the lip of the mug and formed a ring on the mahogany bar. Salvatori took a drink, wiped the tan foam from his lip with the back of his hand, and set the mug down in the same ring. The bartender wiped down the bar and placed the mug onto a stone coaster that bore the Country Club's insignia.

"Lager woman myself. Never got used to the heavy stuff. Too much like having a steak with my steak," Kenna said. "So, which category do you fall into, Agent Salvatori?"

"Me? I've always enjoyed the heavy stuff."

"Not what I meant." *Enough of this bullshit.* "I understand you get your rocks off pushing people around."

The agent turned an eye. "So, Sommer came crying to you. I had questions; he had answers and didn't want to share them."

Kenna detested men who believed their physical power gave them Carte Blanche to use it at will. She rested her drink on the bar. With doubled fists, she turned but had second thoughts. Gran Lockwood would have told her to *'pocket the attitude'*. Salvatori raised a hand, nodding more to himself than to her.

"Hey, I got a little out of line, but I didn't hit him. He knows something about this case but isn't talking. And he's probably keeping it from you, too."

"What case?"

"Altmann. It's the only case."

Contradictions flew from ear to ear, as did the wind in the trees, but Salvatori remained consistent. There were so many players telling so many lies she needed Wiggy's computer to track them.

"Why are you here?" Kenna asked.

"Seems the director was into his fifth martini at the party with Senator Bridgewater when you paid a visit. He calls my boss; my boss calls me; he suggests I talk some sense into you."

"An unfortunate waste of your time."

Salvatori's hand fell on Kenna's arm. Their eyes met. "They run this city. Fuck, they run the country! They make and break people like us every day!"

"Parasites!" Kenna said without emotion. "A society governed by the lawless who make the laws?" A chuckle. "Am I insane, or on the wrong side?"

"The Romans practiced it over a thousand years."

Kenna's eyes narrowed as she took a drink. "That's it! I figured out what's eating at you. I follow leads wherever they take me. You don't like that because you've been ordered to ignore the obvious."

"Your simplicity is refreshing, if foolish," Salvatori countered. "I'm but a pawn in a political world. I do what I'm told."

"Following the lemmings over the cliff—"

"Dragging you with me, screaming and kicking if I have

to," he interrupted.

"Is that a threat?" Kenna asked, immediately realizing it wasn't the right thing to say.

"Threat?" Salvatori said with a grin against his ale. "This case aside, if you go after one of the suits at the party today, they will destroy you."

The voices had been mumbled, distant, when Whyte ushered her to the door. Eyes followed her as if she were the corpse on a gurney being wheeled from a crime scene. Outside, the internal chill of a hot June breeze stung her like a morgue.

"Stupidity knows no fear," Kenna said. "Chamberlain—"

"Is dead! A suicide! From that political position, I will never waiver."

Salvatori had basically said the same in his office, except for the word *political*, his canned speech. She needed a drink with Wiggy but turned to Salvatori's rumpled expression.

"Then, why isn't your partner convinced?" she asked.

"Edelman's not my partner."

Salvatori took a large drink and turned the trunk of his body perpendicular to the bar. His thick hand remained wrapped around the mug. A finger of his free hand spun around the top; he licked the foam from it. The heavy hairs on the back of his hand masked thick blood vessels.

"She talks too much and obviously doesn't give a shit about her pension."

Wiggy's conversations with Edelman portrayed the opposite, something deeper, dedication. Edelman felt the bureaucrats crushing her from all sides, just as they did.

Salvatori's confrontation meant he had become not just the hierarchy's errand boy but also their mouthpiece. The *Romans* at the party had been afraid to confront her, so they sent their *Centurion*, Salvatori. For some reason, she felt a slight bit of sympathy for him. Succinctly, no professional should be cast into the role of bootlicker.

Logic dictated the widow would benefit from Chamberlain's death. And if *logic* dictated truth … Gloria Chamberlain did it or hired it done. That simple: case over, solved, lock her up, everyone can go home. It was as if no one in this city cared; and Salvatori was chasing a ghost from his past. Wiggy confirmed what Gloria had told her earlier while drunk: she and her husband's problems began long ago. There was no evidence of things turning violent, but since when had evidence mattered in this city?

Salvatori exhaled sharply. "You made Chamberlain's suicide larger than it ever should have become, Ms.

Hannigan.”

“Quoted from the Party Caesars, no doubt.”

“I’m hunting Bernard Altmann, which makes our objectives different,” Salvatori countered.

“Unless Altmann killed the senator, you are correct.”

“You’ve been reading too many detective novels. The bad guy was dead on the ground in front of you, not running away in the trees.”

That statement hit Kenna like a brick. Chamberlain was soon to be labeled the *‘bad guy’* in the press. Every speech made by the Caesars would now put personal blame on him. The new label would become what Malcolm said: *‘the fool that killed himself’*.

“The obvious isn’t always the truth, Kenna,” Salvatori said, interrupting her thought.

“You’re burning up what few brain cells I have left, Salvatori.”

“Not the first time in this town someone’s been misled.”

You mean like tonight, Kenna did not say. Somehow, she chuckled at the absurdity of it all. If she listened to the Party Caesars and Salvatori, Charlie Sommer’s perfect body had done a number on her, and this was Charlie’s way of getting back at Chamberlain, a lover who scorned him. Gloria, the despondent widow, was telling the truth. In the end, Gowen would be the good guy, and Malcolm would be crowned president.

She flushed those thoughts out of her head and downed half a beer in one gulp. *Get me out of here!* She screamed inside.

There was something Salvatori didn't want asked. The same held true with Hobson. The call about the senator's body went to the local police, not the U.S. Marshals. Wiggy said the dispatcher confirmed that Hobson made the call. The question begged why, but it was better asked of the old superintendent.

"When you physically got to the body, the sprinklers were off and had been for some time. Blood was still pooled in the sand. I questioned Hobson about that, and he said he turned them off when he discovered Chamberlain."

"That was smart," Salvatori said and exhaled hard. "Look, we've been over this, and I'm in no mood to rehash it. I came to tell you to stop crashing parties."

Salvatori's eyes flicked to the windows that overlooked the 18th green. Kenna gathered her new lager and allowed the cool mug to soothe sore hands. She wanted to swim in it.

"When I arrived, there were two sets of footprints across

the green, and only two: One led to the body, one led away."

Salvatori finished his drink. "So?"

"Nobody has ever said that the senator's body—"

Agent Salvatori's cell phone rang to interrupt. Kenna straightened from the bar when Wiggy appeared in the mirror and hurried her direction with urgency.

"Fiery, something's come up."

Kenna ignored the strong hand around her arm as Wiggy pulled her away from the bar. Her attention was on Salvatori. The agent hooked his cell phone to his belt. His face firmed with determination, eyes directly on Kenna.

"Interesting you visited Devon Whyte's residence today, Ms. Hannigan."

"Why?"

"Agent Edelman just called, kid," Wiggy said. "Whyte apparently left the house shortly after you did. They just found him under the bridge across the spillway by the 6th green."

XXXIV

The same army of governmental ants … some mistook them for *'investigators'* and *'evidence specialists'* … arrived with the same vengeance as they had with Senator Chamberlain's death. Once again, they were directed by Agent Salvatori; however, this time on a golfcart. Sirens blared, and lights flashed like the Las Vegas Strip. Engines raced, and tires spun across Roots Hobson's horticultural masterpiece, tearing the finely pruned grass off the manicured fairways. They smashed sprinkler heads and crushed bushes. Flowers exploded like grenades. Only one man cared; no doubt, Roots Hobson watched the destruction from some venue, cursing as only a pretend Scotsman could.

Another cliché came to Kenna's mind: *The dead tell no lies.*

Back on the veranda, Kenna toasted black America's true warrior in this madhouse of political iniquity. Though she wished Whyte well in the great beyond, what would the chairman say now? As a man of humble roots, Devon Whyte would have wanted nothing more; he would have said his job was incomplete. But Kenna knew her first impulse was wrong upon meeting Whyte: the chairman was anything but a simple man.

The killer had made a mistake. He had panicked and taken a second victim. Now, there was no suicide to confuse the obvious. Now, there was only murder; *at least to me,* she corrected herself.

She made an excuse not to accompany Salvatori to the death scene. She didn't believe in *I told you so's.* Wiggy accompanied Salvatori out. Kenna envisioned Devon Whyte bound by the hands and feet, face down in the creek, and Salvatori talking about suicide, with the Caesars standing alongside, questioning why Devon Whyte would kill himself like that.

Kenna believed she could see the Washington Post headlines: *Democratic Leader Drowns Self in Two-Inch Deep Spillway. They shouldn't have made the spillway so deep*; she heard the city of liars screaming, blaming Congressional Country Club for the death. *Tear it down, tear it down,* would be the battle cry throughout the city. Where would it end?

"By building Gran's pyramid," she mumbled to herself.

'This fucking inquisition is over,' she kept hearing Malcolm Bridgewater say. Now, that meant more than just the finality of a meeting. It had meant the end of a good man's life.

The bar cleared with remarkable speed as the ambulance

chasers rallied on the veranda, fascinated by the array of flashing lights. Drinks were pointed. Excited voices proclaimed what had happened, how it had happened, and why, though none could see anything and knew less. Kenna was saddened by the display of absurdity. It reminded her of the movie *Rollerball* and the cheers from the crowd each time the steel-sphere-wielding Jonathan crushed a man's skull.

A rush of cool air spilled across her. It was sweet to the senses. She swallowed the last of her beer and went down the stairwell. Once outside, the night embraced her. Her mind rushed back to Malcolm Bridgewater's words. She stepped beyond the Clubhouse into the night, noticing the light was out above the exit door.

A trail of taillights streamed across the grounds from the Clubhouse in the direction of the 6th. *Perhaps a picture of those taillights, frozen, taken with an open aperture from the roof of Congressional, was the true reflection of society,* she thought. *Or had Rollerball become reality?*

She was tired of this city; Washington was draining her of energy, of will. But now there were two dead. One had been the original target; the other, a man who perhaps knew too much. She couldn't help but think of Cambridge at that moment and questioned how it all tied together or if

Cambridge was this case's, MacGuffin. Too many lies, not enough facts.

In the mind of one, though, there was total logic to the murders. And eventually, it would all make macabre sense, even to her.

'To catch one, become one,' Gran Lockwood ordered from the grave.

Her words were prophetic. They didn't mean to become a killer; they meant become one with the killer's thought process. Panic had set in, threatening to close off the killer's passageway to freedom. When paranoia overtook the thought process, desperation bred mistakes. This was the criminal's mind at work. Devon Whyte's death proved it.

She stopped at a tree and leaned on the trunk, head back against the rough bark. Gran had put it best:

'Humanity has two pure states: the instant before birth, the same before death. The former is nothing short of a miracle, the latter a culmination of life's experiences, be they kind or cruel, short or long. Unlike birth, death is not a site to behold or to celebrate. It is the essence of man itself: hollow, void of emotion, silent, and cold.'

Irony and absurdity defined the deaths of Chamberlain and Whyte. In a way, she supposed that made her absurd for being obsessed with finding its truths. Not a pleasant revelation but a reasonable one, if not real.

Darkness engulfed her like a large hand as she turned down the 1st fairway towards the superintendent's shed. It was time for Hobson to come clean about Cambridge, his entry into this country, and the Mass senator. She wanted the truth, knowing she might never get it. She followed a series of stone steps, followed by the noise of the crowd on the veranda. As the sounds died out along the cart path, she noticed the small building was black, empty for the night. She grabbed the door, surprised it was unlocked. Clubhouse lighting trickled through the trees. Even from across the front nine, flashing lights of the emergency vehicles pierced the darkness from the 6th green and spillway.

Night took on gray, unrecognizable shapes when she entered. Black blotches melted into the shadowy forms of lockers; chrome handles took on a rustic haze against the whole of night's abyss. Stacked on a bench against the far wall, white towels were illuminated in an outside light from the mirror where she had examined her wounds.

"Roots?" she asked into the night.

She hadn't expected a reply and received none. She sat at the end of the lockers and wiped sweat from her face with a towel. Devon Whyte had known something about Harvey

Chamberlain's death. Perhaps that was what the chairman was coming to tell her. Or was there another reason he was now face down in the spillway?

Kenna had to forget Chicago, as Wiggy had said. Forget politics. And even for the time, forget Anson Beck. Those past events had tainted her vision, clouded her judgment, and weakened her resolve. Her family's friendship with Bridgewater had charged an instinctive fear from childhood. No more!

She stood and walked past the lockers to Hobson's office door. Gran taught her years ago how to pick a passageway lock. The principle remained remarkably unchanged, and within a few seconds, she was inside. Open mini blinds allowed a single yard light to streak the room. She looked outside. Nothing moved.

Had the same person who attacked her also left Devon Whyte face down in the spillway by the 6th green? And what about Chamberlain?

She turned to the room, to the signs of a struggle … no, a fight … to the death. Blood of dragging fingers streaked the surface of the desk and paperwork. Walls and desk articles were splattered and streaked. Glass was broken. It was only then the putrefied smell reached her nose. Her eyes flashed through the grayness of the rapidly enclosing room.

File cabinets had been opened, blood on the handles, and the files rifled and strewn across the floor. Desk drawers had been emptied, the drawers themselves thrown into a corner. She circled the desk, avoiding the high-backed wooden rocker, pausing when light from outside brushed across her eyes. It was not all that dissimilar from the way the light had struck her face when she stood at the sand trap looking at Harvey Chamberlain's lifeless remains … and his eyes. A single siren turned her attention but a moment.

Whyte *'left the house shortly after you did'*, Wiggy had said. The words registered like a thunderbolt. The chairman had left the party before it ended. And who *found him*? Forensics could match the blood, but before that happened, she was positive the office would be wiped clean. Kenna pondered the thought of Hobson actually firing an employee and that employee pitching Whyte into the water.

The ramblings of a lunatic mind, she thought. *'Become one!'*

She reached for sore ribs, remembering the impact on the computer and then against the tree. She felt once again the impact of the golf shoe on her chest. She winced at the silenced gunshot reverberating through her ears. The gun: why hadn't the assailant fought for the gun?

Despite what Salvatori said, they *had* seen the same

thing. Salvatori was doing what he was ordered to do. If there was a head to roll, Kenna had a feeling that shit ran downhill right into Salvatori's office. And no doubt, heads would roll by the time she was done.

She flinched as the air conditioner kicked on. She straightened and took a deep breath. Had Hobson gone out again to meet someone? Or had the killer caught him with Whyte and followed him here after killing the chairman? Or had the Marshals not yet located the superintendent? Her heart pounded, remembering Hobson's words at the 18th green:

'I'll throw one of the dossers off a bridge; that'll get their attention.'

The drone of chirping insects beat in her ears like spears, slapping the shields of a thousand Zulu warriors. Her mouth dried; her tongue thickened as she tried to swallow. The killer had been in the trees all along. Kenna and Hobson had been easy targets had he wanted to kill them. Looking at the blood, she thought of her own: what if the attack and the shots fired in the trees had been only a warning? Kenna remembered Bridgewater's verbal warning to Charlie.

The attacker hadn't wanted to kill her at the 18th … he wanted Hobson. They had surprised each other. A killer with intent would have stood his ground and blown her brains out.

This one had not. *Why?*

She walked into the employees' locker room to retrace her steps from earlier. She moved to the bench in the shower area and sat. Distant voices outside surprised her; she had not heard them before. From the bench, she walked to the shower and awaited Hobson's arrival, just as she had before. She turned on the shower and allowed the steam to rise. In her mind, the voice shouted as she toweled off, then looked up as … she saw it!

Kenna hurried to the office and lifted the clipboard from the wall. In the light of the window, she rifled the sheets. About the tenth sheet down, she paused. It was not a record of cup placements, sprinkler schedules, or ground repair requirements. The paper had creases where it had been folded. She hesitated but a moment before removing it. Her heart raced. Hobson's life and perhaps death were in her hands.

The blood that surrounded her: a long interrogation process. Someone had not talked. The killer had not gotten what he wanted … perhaps this sheet. Hobson's body was out there somewhere, as well.

Kenna shivered and made her way to the door. Stepping into the outside light, she didn't do so without first looking into the darkness. At a quick trot, she took the footpath towards the Clubhouse. Her running steps ground on the stone pathway and pounded into her ears like the rock drum solo from *Inagodadavita* by Iron Butterfly.

Why were they finding these things and the Marshals weren't? Even considering their previous actions, she had been blinded by the preconceived notion that they were out to find the truth. Blood … whose? Once again, she thought of basic forensic testing. Would it ever happen, even after she told Salvatori what she found, or would it be blocked by the powers-that-be? *Become one!*

The trees were silent; the wind fell away. A lone cricket chirped like the irritating beep of a recorded phone call. Tonight, she took it as nature's warning signal.

XXXV

The media frenzy was in full swing when Kenna made her way back to the Clubhouse. Regardless of the measures taken by the U.S. Marshals, the local police, the FBI, and any other group with official or unofficial jurisdiction, the media always found a way to infiltrate a scene.

Without being there, she could hear the blitz of questions: *'Is there a connection between the chairman's death and the senator's?' 'Was it a similar weapon to the one that killed the senator?' 'Was the body found by the same person that found the senator?' 'Were there any witnesses?'*

She wanted to feel sorry for Salvatori, but it came with the territory, as it did to everyone who wore a badge. That was the beauty of what she did. She faced the paparazzi only when she thought it would help. There had been no instance to date where she felt their *'help'* was warranted. To the contrary, she preferred to avoid them, even though most of them considered her a colleague.

She entered the suite to find Wiggy staring at the computer screen, fingers nimbly flying across the keyboard. A half-full pint of ale rested on a coaster next to him. Since returning from the scene of Whyte's death, he had been on the phone and on the computer, searching for any relevant background information on the players of this drama. He yawned.

"Oxygen to the brain, kid."

"For me, it's lack of sleep," Kenna countered.

Kenna passed him with a lager and went to the window to look out over the golf course. Flashing lights in the distance were like giant fireflies darting across the general's *good ground* and reflected from the lake between the 6th and the Clubhouse.

"If Hobson wasn't mad about the grounds before, he's gonna be now," Wiggy said without looking up.

"If he's alive," Kenna said and took a drink. "Superintendent's shed is a forensic paradise."

"Ya tell Salvatori?"

"Wasn't in the mood for hearing how Hobson was into some satanic cult. Sent him a text."

Wiggy raised an eye and stopped typing. A broad smile crossed his face. "Well, the lass has finally joined the Twenty-First Century."

"Don't know if it came out legible or if he even got it."

"If not, you'll have time later."

Kenna lifted the clipboard document from a pocket. Something said it was significant, what Gran Lockwood would call *'the heartbeat'* of a crime. Red, yellow, and white lights backlit the paper like a disco ball as she lifted it to arm's length. She folded it along the same lines as the original folds and shoved it back into her pocket.

Wiggy filled his glass with ale and joined her at the window. "I'll make a proper Eastie drinker of ya yet, kid, and get ya ta drink from a glass."

"Never happen, you know I worked in a pub in Chicago."

Though Wiggy was curious about the paper in Kenna's pocket, he knew not to pry. Once she had digested it, she would share it. Besides, Wiggy knew he had enough on his plate and didn't want to get distracted by other issues. He went back to the computer and rubbed the stubble of his wide chin.

"Who have we heard the truth from, Fiery?"

"Maybe half-truths from Charlie and Edelman," she said. "Not sure about Salvatori beyond suicide."

Wiggy told her of the afternoon with Agent Edelman and his feelings at the scene of the stakeout six years before. He knew something was wrong with it all but couldn't put a finger on it. She had told him as much as she legally could, he felt, but there were holes that needed filling. When he left her house, she gave him a taste: Jimmy McDowell.

Interpol had found no hard leads on foreign bank holdings for Avery Gowen. Wiggy assured Kenna that the Interpol lads had ways around numbered accounts. They had, however, found a frequent communication stream from the U.S. to a recipient in the East. The recipient changed addresses often, or it was multiple recipients. They both believed the former.

There had to be a link, an *'umbilical'* that tied campaign contributions together with the senator and chairman. The obvious was the political Party, but how would Hobson be connected to the Party elite? The Mass senator? Given the disparity of class, it seemed unlikely. It had to go deeper than that.

"Lads from MI5 rang today," Wiggy said. "Hobson never worked at Cambridge, never existed at Cambridge. His papers were falsified entering the States."

Kenna lowered her beer. "In this convoluted cesspool of liars, that surprises … who? Obviously why Malcolm didn't want me discussing the subject with the Mass senator."

"Goes beyond that," Wiggy continued. "They say Hobson was followin' in his dear departed dad's footsteps."

"IRA?"

"Seems they haven't built the walls high enough around Derry to keep 'em all in."

"Immigration couldn't have known that when he entered the States."

"Na, but I'd bet a year's salary the Mass senator bloody well did."

"You don't make a salary."

Wiggy hoped to have confirming information by morning. So, along with everything else, Hobson was directly linked to the IRA. The bizarre was rapidly becoming Gran's *absurd*.

"Have you heard from Agent Edelman?" Kenna asked, staring at the carnival being played out in the night. "I mean, since your extended lunch."

"It'll be tomorrow, kid," Wiggy said. "She's good to her word."

Was anyone in this city good to *their word?* She stared out at the darkness, thinking of General Treadway. For an instant, she saw the encamped Civil War Armies ready to do battle come the sultry morning. A shroud of mist lay heavy nigh the ground, fuel oil lamps and ground fires providing an ominous pulsating glow in the trees. She smelled the smoke of burning wood and spent black powder. A banjo and mouth harp rang in her ears from the enemy encampments. Horses neighed, anxious for the morrow's charge. Screams of the wounded filled the air, as did the intermittent hush of death. The latter echoed loudest.

She didn't like bartering for the truth. Would working in this damned city taint her forever? Or was she the dinosaur?

The room phone rang. Wiggy answered, placed his hand over the receiver, and whispered: "He beat ya to the punch."

Kenna forced the receiver against an ear and spoke firmly into the mouthpiece: "I'm surprised it took the esteemed senator so long to call you."

"Even Malcolm Bridgewater has a limited number of favors to burn."

Kenna could see her father, Cuban cigar clamped between gold-capped teeth, resting back in his favorite handmade chair that overlooked his sprawling estate just outside downtown Dallas. Caesar in all his opulence. *He was leaning forward now to get serious, perhaps dipping his feet into a pot of gold he had swindled out of clients earlier in the day.*

"Or was it your friend from Massachusetts?" Kenna asked.

"Let's get to the point, girl." Derick Hannigan cleared his throat; *he was serious now.* "He tells me you're out to destroy the good name of the Party."

"There's an oxymoron if ever I heard one. Malcolm's been breathing the air out here too long, father. He's lost."

"I've known Malcolm Bridgewater longer than you've been alive. He's never lost." Cleared throat again, *ready for attack.* "Why are you looking into the Party?"

"Malcolm has confused my search for finding out why Harvey Chamberlain was killed with trying to give his … correction … your blessed Party a black eye. He should be helping me find the truth."

Derick Hannigan hesitated. *Some gold must have fallen on the floor out of reach.* Kenna heard the shift of her father's large muscular frame. She saw the old man's face redden, though thirteen hundred miles away.

"Yeah," Kenna continued, "that word got Malcolm, too."

Their discussions and arguments could go on endlessly until one of them called it quits or her mother broke in to play referee. Today, Kenna was in no mood to cry *'uncle'*. Her father would be the consoling businessman at first, wanting what was right for his client … that being the Party … while wanting what was good for him … more of that gold soaking his feet. Then would come the fatherly advice about talking some sense into her.

"Harvey Chamberlain's death was no accident, and damn sure no suicide," Kenna insisted.

"You appear to be alone in that assessment."

"Too much says otherwise, especially now."

"Now?" her father asked, circling around as would any true warrior of the boardroom.

"When did you last speak to Malcolm?"

"A couple hours ago. I had a late-night dinner meeting."

"Then, you haven't listened to the news?"

Derick hesitated. "No, why?"

"Because Devon Whyte was found dead this evening."

There was a long pause. An exhale filled the phone, and the cigar dropped into an ashtray. *Her father stood, looking out over his domain.* The television clicked on in the background. *Does Caesar see Rome burning?*

"My, God," her father whispered, trying to listen to the news and his daughter simultaneously. "What do you know about this?"

"I think Devon was killed for the same thing Harvey was … possibly illegal campaign contributions."

"What … what illegal contributions?"

"My initial information says the money came from abroad, brought into the country by a Party confidante." She swallowed. "What do you know about this, father?"

"Not a damn thing, but I intend to find out."

Usually, when her father said that, he meant it. Perhaps for the first time in his life, Derick Hannigan was going to help his daughter. *We'll see,* Kenna thought.

"I follow my gut, father. That's one thing you taught me."

"I find it hard to believe Bridgewater would keep this from me."

"He might, if he's involved."

"And if he isn't?" countered the best television executive in Texas.

There was another long pause: An internal battle in her father's brain between Party and family, which Party had always won before. Kenna suspected it would win again.

"I want to know about the funding," Kenna insisted. "And I'll get the proof on the murders, whether Malcolm was involved or not."

"Malcolm says you're beyond reason."

"Murder's an unreasonable business, father!"

"You won't find the guilty in Malcolm Bridgewater's

office."

How could a man whose life was dedicated to the gathering of information be so blind? Or was that what the statue of Lady Justice really stood for, turning a blind eye to the truth? The man who investigated murderers and twisted the Constitution for his benefit hesitated. And, so, they entered the last act of their typical conversation.

"For Christ's sake, listen to yourself!" she insisted. "Murders mean nothing to you?"

"Great men in great societies make great sacrifices, Kenna."

"You've lost your mind. Hell, the world's lost its mind. Ted Bundy's victims' families will sleep better tonight knowing they made a *great sacrifice*'! "

"Don't be absurd," her father insisted.

Kenna slammed the receiver onto its cradle and lifted a cold beer from the refrigerator. She drank half of it before she breathed. She looked at the clock and rubbed red eyes, hoping she could sleep. A deep exhale followed; she knew the answer.

"I take it he wasn't in a cooperative mood."

"When is he ever … and Malcolm?"

Kenna's phone buzzed with a text. "Appears Charlie's

coming with a surprise."

"Nothing surprising in this bleedin' city, kid."

Almost as soon as Wiggy said it, there was a knock at the door. Instead of opening to the handsome face of Charlie Sommer, she was greeted by the sleepless glare of Agent Salvatori.

"You got my text, I take it?" Kenna asked.

"I hate that shit."

"Is there anything you don't hate?"

"Italian women with big boobs."

Kenna smiled. "Can't help you with that, I'm afraid. You need to smile more."

"I'll do that while we ride to the superintendent's shed."

"How did I know you were going to ruin my night!"

XXXVI

At 11 pm, Kenna sat in a wet swimsuit at the table alongside the pool. Other guests swam calmly; she watched without paying attention. Bloodshot eyes confirmed she hadn't slept. It was not an unusual occurrence; one she handled by any numerous means. After arguing with her father as a child, she'd split wood for the fireplace until Mother came out and shuffled her to bed. *Thank you, Father,* she thought.

Like a boxer beating a heavy bag, she liked any activity that helped clear her mind. Tonight, she needed it more than usual, but pain prevented it. It was the only time she forgot about everything. It was mental therapy for their other game, paramount to staying alive. Gran Lockwood called it the *'alternate energy source'*.

"Thought I would find ya out here," Wiggy said, eyes equally bloodshot.

Flipflops with puppy dog ears propelled him across the patio and into the light. The orange and yellow horizontally striped robe made him look broader than actual.

Kenna leaned back in the chair and cursed. Wiggy pulled off the robe to reveal matching swim trunks. He jumped into the pool and, at the edge, turned to Kenna.

"Jump in Fiery, work off some of that aggression."

"It's right here," she said, tapping a finger against the side of her head.

"Get in here," he insisted. "We'll work it out together, always do."

Kenna jumped into the pool beside him. She stretched through the pain into the Australian crawl for a lap. With Wiggy pushing from beside her, she changed to backstroke for a lap.

"Push it!" Wiggy insisted.

With a grunt of pain, Kenna powered into a lap of breaststroke then changed for a last leg of butterfly. They met at the edge of the pool. A waitress brought bottles of water.

Wiggy swallowed a mouthful. "Damn, thought that was beer! Ya Father will never change, kid."

Charlie Sommer had been right. Kenna had never had her father's love, and she doubted if Mother had either. Had she always been second to the Party, as well? A marriage of convenience, as everyone in this city had tagged Gloria and Harvey Chamberlain's marriage?

"It's a good thing father only has one kid, or I'd

recommend we kill the other one."

"Some blokes would recommend we do that to the one he has."

"Yeah, but they're in prison, so what do they know?" Kenna turned.

"All but one," Wiggy said. "But his time is comin'."

The lines of sleepless nights streaked their faces. "How many years have we taken off our lives, Wiggy?"

"It doesn't matter, Fiery."

"Guess not. Never wanted to die in a comfortable bed, anyway."

"Aye. We'll go out like the Grand Ole Dame. God grant her eternal peace."

"So, she can be bored for eternity?" Kenna said. "Nah, she's here with us."

Wiggy took another drink of water. "So, as the grand ole dame preached, time to *'peel the grape'.*"

"Will this be the one, Wiggy?" Kenna asked, ignoring his gran-ism. She floated on her back, thinking.

"Gran Lockwood wouldn't like hearin' ya talk like that, kid."

"I'm not sure I like hearing it either, but this damn city—"

"Aye, take Washington off my travel maps."

Kenna turned as her mentor pulled himself from the water, then helped Kenna out. They sat at the table; the waitress brought beers. Wiggy took a big drink with an "Ah."

"Remind me to vote against all incumbents next time," she growled.

"Yer brain's workin' overtime, Fiery. No other reason you'd be out here at the witching hour."

Kenna fought the pain and straightened. From inside her robe, she lifted the paper taken from Hobson's clipboard, unfolded it, and handed it to Wiggy.

"From Hobson's office," she said. Wiggy's eyes danced across the page:

THE CHESS CLUB

The King -

The Queen -

The Rook -

The Knight -

The Bishop -

The Pawn -

"Beaten you a few times at the game, as I recall," Wiggy said and took a drink. "But I don't know many who beat the Grand Ole Dame."

"Have you thought of what she'd do now?"

"Not worry about what others would do and do what's right for you." He looked up. "Regardless of what yer bloody father says."

"And if he's right?"

"He isn't. If ruinin' the Party needs to happen, then it needs to happen. They aren't above the law simply because they're bleedin' politicians. If they've made a bed with the devil, they have to sleep with him."

"And that's what Gran Lockwood would say?"

Wiggy leaned back. "Aye, after knockin' ya alongside the head."

Kenna grimaced. "I've never been this … Bridgewater … I just can't believe it."

"It isn't anger yer feelin'. It's that analytical mind fightin' itself to put this mess into proper order. Relax, it'll come."

Kenna took a drink. Wiggy moved the paper over the imitation candle in the center of the table. Kenna tapped the paper.

"Something about Hobson," she said.

"Aye. That bloody terrorist isn't missing; he's hiding." Wiggy turned back to the list. "The Chess Club … pieces of the game. Means nothin' … but somethin' …"

"The paper's not old, just a bad copy."

"Nay, that it exists today suggests it's a copy of somethin' old, Fiery. Otherwise, it'd be in a bloody computer."

"But what? The pattern how all the pieces are aligned on the left. There's a hyphen after each, then nothing."

"Could be anythin'. Bad formatting by someone with a typewriter. That dates it, lass." Wiggy lifted the paper against the light and traced down the page with his index finger. "This straight-line shadow here says they tabbed past the line."

"The line? Where someone laid a piece of paper when it was copied?"

"Aye. Hiding something." Wiggy rubbed his unshaven jaw, sandpaper against wood.

Kenna took another drink. "People's names to coincide with the Pieces. Altmann's selling their lives, but there's something else."

Wiggy did not interrupt through a long, silent spell.

"He's selling information that each one of them wants," Kenna added.

"Or his silence," Wiggy added.

Kenna leaned on her elbows. "Murder to get this from the senator and Whyte."

"Yer right, lass," Wiggy agreed. "Hobson?"

Kenna tapped the page again. "Unless he's dead, too."

For the first time, Salvatori had admitted that a murder had been committed and that it had been Devon Whyte. As forensic experts combed Roots Hobson's office, Kenna had been silent. Within a half hour, they found one of Devon Whyte's cufflinks covered in blood. The agent lifted it with gloved hands and placed it into a plastic bag. Whyte had not been killed at the creek; he was tortured in the superintendent's office and taken to the small bridge at the 6th green in a golfcart. The killer abandoned it on the other end of the course.

"Which tells me the killer didn't get what he wanted." Kenna stared into the dark night beyond the yardlight.

"Ya said Devon Whyte offered ta help."

"Our brief conversation in his home led me to believe he was coming to give me something, perhaps the information Gowen took from Chamberlain's office."

"Then, why Hobson's office?"

Kenna paused. "To confront Hobson first? He could have wanted me to meet them there after they talked."

"If it was Hobson, why wouldn't he have taken this?" Wiggy flapped the paper.

"Too many questions, Wiggy. Simply, I don't know," she said. "Unless … he intended to come back, clean the office, and retrieve it then."

"Or he was interrupted … and ran."

"We need to know what was blanked out, Wiggy. Chamberlain knew, Hobson knew, and Altmann knew." Again, Kenna paused. "You're right: Altmann was selling his silence."

"And when Chamberlain didn't buy, he moved on to the next buyer, Devon Whyte."

"A logical progression if we're right. Look at the pieces." She traced the shadow with a finger. "Was Altmann working down the list?"

"He wanted a lot of money. It had to be very powerful people. He would start at the top: The King?"

"The bloke who runs the group; maybe put this Chess Club together."

"Okay, but what's the significance of The Chess Club?"

Wiggy yawned. "If ole Hobson's alive, he's holdin' the key. Looks to me like this has somethin' to do with Hobson's background."

"I wouldn't kill two men because one of them didn't mow the greens properly. You said it earlier: his father's footsteps."

"So, you think Hobson, Whyte, and the good senator were all tied to the IRA somehow? And it started with this bloody Chess Club?"

"I don't know what to think. Does this damn Chess Club even have anything to do with it, or is it another ruse?" Kenna grabbed the beer, took a drink, then stared up at the black sky. "Malcolm was angry, then went silent when I confronted him about the IRA."

"But how did Whyte figure in?"

It clicked in Kenna's brain. "The one thing they all have in common … Cambridge."

Wiggy mumbled. "Exactly."

Kenna lifted her glass to his. "The Massachusetts senator has ties there. Chamberlain attended, as did Whyte. Roots said he worked there in 1989 and '90, wasn't it? But we know he didn't. Is the key why he lied about it?"

"No sleep for me tonight. I have to find him." Wiggy

turned and raised the paper. "What about this, kid?"

"You keep it; it's better in your hands," Kenna said. "Thanks."

"For what?"

Kenna pointed to the flipflops. "Nice try."

"One of these days, I'll get ya a pair. They have remarkable powers." They laughed together, though hesitantly, and then Wiggy turned away. "Hurry along, lass. The blond-headed lad is waitin' fer ya in the room."

Wiggy disappeared into the darkness. Kenna finished the beer and walked for the Clubhouse. The conversation with her father was still afire in her brain. She prayed for her mother's sake that the old man wasn't involved.

The marble foyer of the Country Club was silent as she made her way to the room. Her side felt better when she stepped through the door then turned to close it. Cool air fell against the back of her neck. She was tired and needed sleep if only a couple hours. She detected something; it was sensory, a smell. She inhaled, smiling; *nothing cheap about this cologne*. He was illuminated in the light leading to the bedroom.

"I owe you two apologies," Charlie said. "The first for standing you up tonight; the second for being needy. Neither will happen again."

The terrycloth robe draped over her like a cirrus cloud. "Accepted."

"Besides, I have something for you."

I was hoping you would say that, she thought. His eyes danced over her long, slender body, her glistening flesh. She argued with herself over the merits of his next move, but female desires fought against logic. *Gran Lockwood, rescue me!* she screamed inside. She took the initiative and stepped to within a few inches. His warmth. He smelled like a man; she flinched.

"What's next?" Lips brushed his chin.

She turned without talking. His full red mouth beckoned hers, yet she struggled with her conscience, with her professionalism. His lips fell against hers slowly; she lightly caressed his bottom lip with her teeth. She moaned and pulled back.

"I promised to nurse you back to health."

"That could take a while."

His embrace was hot and strong. She disregarded the pressure of his arms squeezing her ribs. Pain could never overcome this pleasure.

"I'm up to the challenge," he cooed.

She slowly pushed away. *You're insane,* she screamed to herself. He stared at her, understanding. "No, it's not right … when …"

He kissed her hand. "Then, we'll have to talk about Avery Gowen."

XXXVII

TUESDAY—DAY 4

When Kenna awoke with the sun, she stayed under the sheet and tried to doze. As was typical, it didn't happen. Getting out of bed and into the shower took a while, but she managed. Standing under the running water, previous nights came to mind like happening now. Her wounds had all bruised. She ignored the jagged cut on her forehead; if she took off the strips, it would only bleed. *The Chess Club* flashed before her like her reflection; *find the significance.*

"You should put a new dressing on that cut," Charlie's voice cooed from the bedroom.

She stuck her head out the door to see him, fully clothed, standing at the door. Morning light through the windows lit his face in a brilliant aura. He was more handsome now than before. *How is that possible?* she wondered. She always looked like a truck ran over her in the morning, even when one hadn't.

"I promised to nurse you," he continued.

She gathered all her willpower and retreated into the closet to dress. "All I have is cereal and a couple bananas."

"No coffee?" he asked, feigning great disappointment.

"Come on, I'll buy the breakfast."

Within a half-hour, Kenna and Charlie strolled into the restaurant arm-in-arm. She was greeted warmly by the maître d' and several waiters. Nose buried in his computer, Wiggy sat at a large round table in the sun near a window. A waiter swept empty plates from around him as they walked up. He glanced up, annoyed, as Charlie pulled out Kenna's chair.

"Aye, and don't ya two look grand today," he chuckled, "all multi-colored and bandaged."

"Not funny," Kenna said.

The intake unit had made short work of Wiggy's morning ritual of three eggs up, as many bangers, tomatoes, and a pile of beans with toast and lots of butter. He grunted and patted his stomach.

"The vein-cleaning experts are going to love you someday, Wiggy," Kenna said with a smile.

The waiter placed a Diet Dr. Pepper in front of Kenna. Raising the eyebrows of both men, Kenna asked for a Spanish omelette and Tabasco. A joke was made; she patted her stomach and said that she was a growing girl.

"Just a coffee and bagel for me," Charlie said.

"Agent Edelman phoned," Wiggy said and handed

Kenna a piece of paper with an address on it. "She'll meet you at the coroner's office to look at Senator Chamberlain's personals. Also said she had something else for ya."

"So, how was your date?" Charlie asked, followed by a sip of coffee. "Oooh, heaven."

Wiggy didn't like the question or the situation between Kenna and Charlie. She felt his discomfort and waved it off, *talk later*.

Why Agent Edelman opened up with Wiggy was complicated. Perhaps she saw the failure of six years before as hers to bear. On the other hand, Salvatori's anger and doggedness were single-focused … revenge. According to Edelman, Salvatori was on a short leash with the director, which was why he flew out to Congressional.

"Working with Salvatori again can't be comfortable for her," Kenna said.

"She's convinced he isn't just out to avenge the death of his partner six years ago," Wiggy said. "She thinks it's more of a personal vendetta that Altmann killed his family."

"I hadn't heard that," Charlie said.

The office photo, Kenna thought. "If that's the case, his obsession has reason."

"Aye, Fiery—"

"Fiery?" Charlie interrupted with the bagel at his mouth.

"Nickname, lad," Wiggy said, annoyed. *Stop interrupting.*

"Personal vendetta, messy stuff," Charlie added. Wiggy's glare made him wish he hadn't.

"Speaking of guns?" Kenna asked.

"She's tryin' ta keep it quiet."

"It won't be for long," Kenna said.

Wiggy recapped his discomfort at the site of the ambush six years before, but there was work to be done. Edelman was checking on land ownership while Wiggy looked into Deputy Director Anderson's history.

"Anderson? There's a piece of work," Charlie interrupted. "You think Gowen is greasy, well, Anderson's the definition."

"How so?" Kenna asked.

"Always working the senators, a quintessential bureaucrat."

Salvatori's single focus kept him from seeing the complexity. It wasn't just about Altmann, though he might be the central most important element. Everything in the Chamberlain case began with the Party hierarchy and a golf course superintendent. And now Devon Whyte's murder was thrown in the middle of the mix. These things were the foundation of Gran Lockwood's pyramid.

Motionless for what seemed an eternity, she stared at her reflection in the window. An ulcer the size of a watermelon formed at the pit of her stomach.

"Anderson's who she and Salvatori argued about on how to approach the case six years ago," Wiggy said. "According to Edelman, Anderson doesn't like the direction Salvatori's gone with the Chamberlain case."

"Salvatori's a loose cannon, Wiggy. We have to watch him."

Kenna stared across the table. Bond finished his bagel and coffee. It kept her stare on him now. But the physical alone was not what made him an attractive man. True beauty was inside, like Bond, and that confused her. Like Gran would have said, Charlie was already up to his eyeballs in this. That led to an uncomfortable situation, making it difficult for her and Wiggy to do their thing. She had to move him on.

There had been a lot right about the night before. She resisted what female hormones demanded. There had been passion, but it was now greater as a result of self-respect, of knowing what they had done … no, hadn't done … was right.

That said something for them both, good or bad, she believed. Or did it say more about the case? Desperate people take desperate measures to reach a natural human comfort level, which in most cases is contentment. Or was it like her father said: *'Great men in great societies make great sacrifices.'* *'Pansy shit'*, the general would say.

She and Charlie had, indeed, discussed Avery Gowen. Charlie had gone to the drop box and retrieved the new recording. Not only had Gowen contacted Altmann, but he had been contacted by Hobson. After he moved Chamberlain and took the Chess Club, he raked around the body. Document in-hand, Hobson joined the extortion game if he hadn't been in it from the beginning. Wiggy now had another assignment: find out who delivered the tapes to the drop box.

"Your eyes say you haven't slept," Kenna said to her mentor.

"Don't get paid to sleep," Wiggy said, pleased by Kenna's empty plate.

Kenna shoved the empty plate forward. "Speaking of Hobson—"

"He's a slippery one. He'll be mine before the day's out, or he'll be out of the city."

"Not likely if he wants a retirement."

"We have two disappearing angels," Charlie interjected.

"Yes, Gowen," Kenna agreed. "We have a whole new barrage of questions for him."

Wiggy didn't waste time and begged off. Once fed food as well as assignment, he was nothing short of Gran Lockwood's *tenacious bulldog*. Kenna was once again reminded why Gran thought so much of him. *I would like to have seen him in his youth*, she thought.

"What do you want me to do?" Charlie asked.

"Study the recordings with Wiggy," she said. "Then, stay out of the way."

"I didn't realize I was."

She allowed a hand to fall on his cheek. "Two dead, and you were the closest to Chamberlain. They have to believe you know what he knew."

"Why don't I go with you?"

"Three's a crowd with the people I'm going to see. Besides, I plan to bring this to a head, hopefully today. It could get messy."

"It's already messy."

"Yes, but we have unfinished business." Kenna squinted into the rising sun that framed two recent arrivals.

XXXVIII

An enduring waft of whiskey told Kenna who it was. She tapped the face of her watch as if to check that it was still running. She turned into the inebriated eyes of Gloria Chamberlain, drink in-hand.

"I've been waiting for you to finish your breakfast, Ms. Hannigan," Gloria said. "I didn't want to upset you on an empty stomach."

"I operate well on an empty stomach, Mrs. Chamberlain." She pushed her chair back to stand but hesitated when Gloria's hand fell on her shoulder.

Unsteady, her slender body waved like a flag. "Please don't bother. This won't take long."

"That's hard to believe," Charlie snarled.

The widow ignored her enemy. "Ms. Hannigan, the late Senator, was from small-town America. Rather cliché, isn't it? Senator grows up an all-American boy. Right, Mr. Sommer?"

"Not when you think about it, no," Charlie said. Innocence died; fangs were exposed. "I know your husband's background better than you, Mrs. Chamberlain."

"Yes, no doubt." The widow took a drink and chortled with most of it still in her mouth. A well-placed index finger against her cheek, she spoke to Kenna:

"You see, Charlie's always been good at uncovering men's weaknesses. Oops! I guess I could have left off the last word, couldn't I have?"

Unamused, Kenna thought of two children bantering back and forth in a dispute of *takes one to know one*. She grabbed Charlie's arm, only to have it jerked away. Kenna saw the unspoken words *you killed him* at the tip of Charlie's tongue. Kenna's *it's not worth it* glare forced him back into the wicker chair, arms folded over his stomach.

"Relax," Kenna said softly.

The man behind Gloria … Kenna knew the type … remained silent. The weight of a briefcase leaned the thin man to the right. The morning sun brought a bead of sweat across a five o'clock shadow that would have made Nixon's look like a baby's butt. He lifted the briefcase to the adjacent table. Brushing long, greasy, thick black hair from his forehead, he opened the case to pull out a red folder.

"Red folders are always a bad sign," Kenna said to Charlie with a smile.

"This is Kenneth Walford, my attorney."

"The greasy hair and open palm gave him away," Kenna said evenly, neither looking at nor particularly acknowledging the attorney's presence.

Gloria lit a cigarette and exhaled at Charlie without apologizing. A patron at a nearby table reminded Gloria that this was a non-smoking restaurant. The advice received a contemptuous glare.

"Perhaps you should leave, Charlie," Kenna said. "I believe Mrs. Chamberlain has come to see me."

"Nonsense," the widow snapped. "I think the little whore should hear this."

The widow's retort drew the attention of more than one couple having breakfast; several stood to leave. Words were had with management, fingers pointed, and apologies made.

Kenna interrupted: "State your business, Mrs. Chamberlain. You're running off the clientele."

"If I may," Walford interrupted. "This is getting us nowhere, Mrs. Chamberlain."

Gloria flattened a palm against her hip and turned an angry stare at the man in the plain black suit and brown knit tie. She wiped whiskey from her hand onto her dress and leaned on a chair for stability. Her hand slipped, and she almost fell. Kenna's eyes never left her; pity became embarrassment.

"As you wish, Kenny. I'll … shut up, then."

She jabbed her glass against the young man's black suit. Whiskey slopped onto his starched white shirt. Eyes on the damage, the attorney withheld the retribution undoubtedly filling his mind. He was, after all, paid for doing so.

Kenna withheld comment. There was a great deal to learn from this moment. The exchange turned cold; she silently thanked Gloria for that.

"Very well," Walford said. He pulled a thin-bound set of documents from the red folder and slid them across the table. "I have secured a Restraining Order on behalf of Mrs. Chamberlain—"

"Way too early for any judge to be awake, and in Montgomery County, no less. Your connections and favors owed do run deep, Mrs. Chamberlain."

"This Order prohibits you, Ms. Hannigan, from prying into the personal life of Mrs. Chamberlain, the late senator, or the senator's suicide. You are restricted to talking to Mrs. Chamberlain only before counsel and only if arranged by counsel," the attorney said, lifting a stray eye. "And that would be me."

"There's a problem, counselor," Kenna interrupted. "I'm

not looking into the senator's suicide."

Walford looked askance to Gloria, then back to Kenna. "How do you mean?"

"I am looking into Senator Chamberlain's murder."

"Everyone but you says my husband killed himself," Gloria said in anger. "Yet, you alone persist with this ridiculous fairytale. Why?"

"I don't believe in fairytales," Kenna said and drank the last of her Diet Dr. Pepper.

"Then, you will end up in jail!" Gloria slurred with bravado.

"The solitude will give me time to think," she said, a slight pause, "without these annoying interruptions."

After Gran Lockwood's murder, Kenna's first investigative trip became a nightmare. She had gained the radical group's trust in a manner she never imagined possible. But she lost it because she slept with a woman she trusted when she was blinded by something close to her emotionally. It would not happen here.

"I have one question, Mrs. Chamberlain since your counsel is present, and I wish to abide by this Order for the moment."

Gloria's alcoholic gaze was distant; she hadn't heard

anything the attorney said. On the verge of unconsciousness, she rolled her bloodshot eyes to Kenna. "Y … es?"

"Did you and the general make a deal?"

"That's none of your business."

"It's possible motive which makes it my business."

"Do I have to respond to that?" Her head floated along behind the question.

"You don't have to respond to anything, Mrs. Chamberlain," the stained black suit responded.

"She's afraid to," Charlie said, sitting upright.

"Look all you want, Ms. Hannigan," Gloria growled, leaning on the table. "You won't uncover any fucking skeletons in my closet."

"Interesting choice of words," Kenna said. "You were leaving your husband because he wanted to change the Party, didn't he?"

Gloria brushed the drink from her chin with the back of a hand that was wrinkled, blotched with liver spots, and lined with thick blood vessels. Kenna hadn't noticed that before. Gloria pointed the glass at Kenna like a pistol.

"Everything was fine until this last election. He argued with Malcolm and disagreed with the Party's platform."

"He knew about the campaign contributions, didn't he?"

Kenna insisted. "I want the truth!"

"Dammit, Gloria, don't answer!" Walford snapped, grabbing her arm.

"The truth in this city? You're the only fool who doesn't see it," Gloria snapped, throwing off her attorney's hand.

She jabbed a finger against Kenna's chest, and a long, painted nail punctured one of the holes put there by the attacker's golf cleat. She refused to acknowledge the sharp pain.

"Tell your client to get her hand off my chest, counselor."

"Gloria, please," the little man pleaded, pulling her arm back, only to have his hand slapped away. He spun to his briefcase. "Enough!"

Gloria's action turned the manager and waiter; both approached the table with intent. Walford took her by the arm. Kenna held her hand out to the manager, who was within 10 feet, and stopped.

"If you expect me to follow your Court Order, Mr. Walford, you better have an army of police following me."

"So, you intend to disobey the judge's Order?"

"It is my intention to find the truth. And if the good widow is a key suspect, I will do what I must, whether it violates this Order or not."

"That is unfortunate, Ms. Hannigan."

"And that's too damned bad," Kenna advised.

"This is not your typical case. Certain provisions of the law protect the widows of our public officials. Her privacy may take precedence over some of your rights." Walford glanced down at the Restraining Order. For Kenna, the sucking sound of the leach continued: "Or at least one judge believes. And that's all I need. You are a dangerous woman, Ms. Hannigan."

"You're right about that, counselor. Especially to those who fear the truth."

Gloria was unstable. Kenna stood, pushed the attorney away, and forced Gloria upright until the dilated pupils lifted. She tried to leave; Kenna didn't allow it.

Her head rolled back. "I'm doing this at the advice of a very good friend."

"Treadway?"

Gloria laughed and then wiped drool from her chin. "Malcolm, you fool."

Kenna shook her. "Don't you want to know what happened?"

"I already do."

XXXIX

Kenna felt the same hatred she had felt at 21 in Chicago. She was in the rear of Uber driver Luis's Toyota Prius. As much as she tried, he would not speed through the dark, rainy street. She wanted, needed excitement at that moment. He told her to relax, to watch the intermittent wipers. Street filth spread across the windshield and reminded her how much she hated this city. Though day, headlights occasionally flashed across her face in Luis's mirror; once again, she didn't like what she saw. She leaned back, taking Luis's advice, and corrected herself: *It was a stronger hatred than she had felt in Chicago.*

In the Windy City, it was a group of malcontents whose single weapon against what they feared was hatred. Now, it was the country's political elite, the educated and wealthy, who made decisions that affected every American's daily life.

She bit her lower lip, nearly drawing blood, cursing. They wanted her anger to take away her control. She hit her leg so hard it sent a shock wave of pain through her right arm. *Solve the murders! Forget these bastards!*

'What murders?' she heard everyone but Charlie and

Wiggy screaming. And the question posed itself again: *was everyone else was right?* A nice, neat suicide packaged for everyone? Hardly! There were too many loose ends, too much peripheral garbage. It was murder, and one person alive knew the facts of what happened. If nothing else, she owed the truth to Harvey and Devon.

Christ, why do I owe them? Why must there always be some higher good to accomplish? She screamed inside. But Gran Lockwood would not stop preaching, even from the grave. Kenna wanted her to shut up just this once, knowing she wouldn't.

'Most men are judged by what they do for themselves, Kenna,' Gran had said. *'How much money they earn, their worldly accomplishments. Like your father. You must strive to be judged by what you do for others. That is the better final analysis of a woman.'*

So, it was Chamberlain and Whyte that also had a hold on her from the grave, and there was no letting go. She wanted her actions to be for them but knew it had to be for her, just like when she defied her father and refused to attend university. That's when Gran's *'rippling tide of emotion'* pulled her to do what was right if only in her mind, to do what was best for her.

She forced herself to feel it today. Just like then, she

knew that ignorance was not confined to those of lesser means or education level. Hatred was also preached at handmade cherry dining tables in elite multi-million-dollar mansions. At the highest self-proclaimed class-levels of society, the *truth* was thrown around like the gospel in a prayer meeting.

Kenna entered his life like a firestorm and tried to convert him to the right way, not sexual orientation, but of legal vs. illegal. Kenna had fallen for him, just as she was now falling for Charlie. A first love's deceit teaches a harsh reality: *Don't rely on anyone else. Always be prepared to stand alone.*

The parallel of then and now was deceit. There was a pinprick of doubt today. Had she thoroughly analyzed the events, the potential danger, and the consequences? Gloria Chamberlain and Kenneth Walford had suggested not without saying so. Charlie said there was no need. Kenna's previous work left wounds with friends and family that took years to mend and remained an unhealed scar with her father. They were both such stubborn, cynical bastards. Deep inside, Kenna knew she still had not forgiven him, as much as he had not forgiven her.

Devon Whyte had been right in one of his writings: '*Equality is the offspring of civility*'. It was not a product of nature, as Hitler professed; or cultural influence, as some university professors preached to the mindless minions in their classrooms.

She had taken things too lightly; had believed in a misguided way she was dealing with honorable people. There was no civility, no honor surrounding Harvey Chamberlain's or Devon Whyte's murders. Even though she wanted nothing more than to have the peripheral disappear to leave the dead men in the center, it would not happen. It could not.

Information whirled through her brain like a tornado, filling Gran's pyramid. They were all-encompassing. None would go away until she identified the killer … or killers. Even if that meant pointing to the ashes of Harvey William Chamberlain and saying that Malcolm Bridgewater was right; the murderer was dead in front of her. But what then of Devon Whyte? It was the latter that wrenched at her gut, and her gut had yet to be wrong. Whyte face-down under the bridge proved beyond doubt there was a murderer at Congressional Country Club.

Gran's *'higher good'* pushed her into the unknown, toward the wholeness that would come only after success or after death. She shelved that for another gloomy day.

Luis parked across from a block-long, bland stone-faced

government building. She inhaled, hoping that Miriam Edelman was not another of this city's deceivers. Meeting Wiggy and taking him to the site of events six years before had said she was a woman of her word.

"No need to wait, Luis. I'm meeting someone that will give me a ride back."

With deep apprehension, Kenna stepped from the car and hesitated. Luis waved and drove away; she walked to the building. This repository of hidden secrets was an enigma. Rumor had it that classified evidence on John Wilkes Booth was held inside: Evidence that proved some of his convicted co-conspirators were innocent. What would she give for a glance at that, knowing that the evidence concerning the death of Harvey Chamberlain could soon be buried as deep or deeper?

She entered a steel-barred foyer and pushed a buzzer at a black plate glass window on the left. Surveillance cameras twisted back and forth at the corners. A woman's tin voice demanded:

"Name!"

"Kenna Hannigan."

"Purpose for your visit?"

"I have an appointment with Agent Miriam Edelman of

the Marshals Service."

"One moment," cackled the box.

She spun when a car turned onto the street and accelerated out of sight. She hadn't seen a garage door or a parking lot and questioned where it had originated. The heavy, humid air brought a bead of perspiration to her upper lip. She loosened the top button of her sports shirt.

"We have no record of you being contacted by Agent Edelman."

"I was supposed to meet her and review the articles found on Senator Chamberlain. She was also to have arranged for me to speak to the coroner."

"One moment."

She didn't like it when plans took a detour. After several minutes, the door buzzed, a lock clicked, and the heavy steel opening swung out. She stepped into a long, narrow, barren foyer. With hesitance, she walked to the glass booth at the far end. A stunning black woman spoiled her striking features with a perpetual frown. Her expression displayed the contempt Kenna believed most government workers held for their jobs. The target of that contempt was usually aimed at the taxpayers responsible for their salaries.

"You should be in New York selling your face to a

fashion magazine," she said to break the ice. It didn't. The woman's response was a deep glare.

Kenna presented her driver's license and signed in. She turned when the heavy door behind closed. Another door opened to her right without so much as a whisper. An instant before, it had been a wall. A rush of cool air whisked hair from her forehead.

A small, round man, whom Kenna recognized from the night at the murder scene, marched into the foyer. Medium-length graying hair was bowl cut around his head. He wore large round spectacles and a white medical smock. He extended a puffy hand.

"My name is Peebles."

"Kenna." The grip was clammy.

"Yes, Agent Edelman asked me to see you."

"Thank you for your time."

The words did not extract an emotional response as Peebles led her through a metal detector into another room. Kenna blinked hard. The bright white tiled floor matched the white walls … *Clorox,* she thought. She struggled to see the white leather couch and chairs that faced each other across the white coffee table. Nausea settled in as they sat in the overstuffed chairs. A five-bladed white ceiling fan pushed air across her face. For a long second, she concentrated on the brass plate at the heart of the fan.

"Feel like I should ask for a White Russian," Kenna said sarcastically.

Peebles' expression did not change. He leaned on the arm of the chair and crossed his legs at the ankle. His hands were folded together over his ample belly.

"What can I do for you, Ms. Hannigan? I understand you're looking into the senator's death."

"And Devon Whyte."

"Yes, equally tragic."

"That's what I understand. I didn't see his remains. How was he killed?"

"Who?"

"I'm sorry, Devon Whyte. The cause of Senator Chamberlain's death was obvious."

"There will be a press conference this afternoon on Chairman Whyte, as I understand."

"But you were there. And I'm here."

"It's unfortunate, though, the rules we must follow."

"Can you tell me what was found on Senator Chamberlain?"

"Not from memory. Everything was gathered by the

Marshals."

"Isn't that who you work for?"

"Yes, but we analyze the dead, Ms. Hannigan, not evidence," Peebles offered. "All I saw was a wallet, keys, money clip, and cell phone, you know, the usual stuff."

More lies. "Did you help them with the remains at all? I mean, beyond the obvious when you bagged him and put him into the wagon?"

"No. I arrived, they cleared away his body, and we left."

"You didn't check to see if it was anything other than suicide?"

Peebles smiled. "That's their call, not mine."

"So, what was the cause of death, if you could tell that?"

"A single bullet to the temple usually does the job."

"How about trajectory?" Kenna asked.

"No exit wound, so I would say it's pretty messy in there and would be hard to determine, anyway."

"Care to venture a guess?"

"Guessing isn't part of my business, Ms. Hannigan. I'll leave that to you guys."

You of lesser intellect, Kenna thought he meant to say. "Is it odd that you weren't asked to perform an autopsy?"

Pebbles straightened his back and leaned forward with a snicker. "It's the position of this office, Ms. Hannigan, that Senator Chamberlain killed himself."

"That wasn't said with much conviction, doctor."

"Nonetheless, it is our position."

"As directed by whom?"

With great hesitation, Peebles lifted his eyes over Kenna's shoulder.

"By me, Ms. Hannigan!"

A tall man in a dark blue pinstriped suit entered. He held himself too sure to be a government librarian. His clothes were too finely tailored to be a storage keeper. A full, neatly trimmed beard presented him as a contradiction to the stereotypical government employee.

"At Congressional, the helicopter," Kenna said.

"Brock Anderson, deputy director." He did not offer a hand.

The greasy one, she thought. "I was expecting Agent Edelman."

"Agent Edelman has been reassigned," the deputy director said straight-faced. "She was working outside the parameters of her assignment and attempting to process a weapon that wasn't involved in any investigation."

Another alarm went off in Kenna's head. Was that what happened six years ago? How could it possibly be determined the weapon *'was not involved'* … if they didn't process it? *'The parameters of her assignment'*: What the hell did that mean? Kenna's gut feeling once again became the ulcer.

"Nice work." Kenna turned for the door just as Peebles stepped out. "You guys are good at appearing and disappearing."

Anderson's blank expression was like a still-painting. "Your amateurish implications are disturbing, Ms. Hannigan. What I know is that Agent Salvatori says you've been intruding into an ongoing investigation."

"I'm curious as to why looking for the truth is *'intruding'?*"

"I'll rephrase: We cannot allow you to continue in that direction."

"The only way you can stop me is to arrest me, Deputy Director Anderson."

A larger, younger agent without expression on a square face joined Anderson. His short-cropped brown hair matched the tailored suit that covered an inverted pyramid stature. His education appeared to be mastery in the art of dismemberment.

"Have it your way," the deputy director said. "But coming along without a struggle would be better."

Eyes on the younger man, Kenna said, "No doubt."

"Then," Anderson said, pointing through another door opened by the young agent.

"Why is it that everyone around here is afraid of the truth?" Kenna asked and followed Anderson out the door.

The deputy director of the U.S. Marshals did not respond. Just outside the door, the agent pushed Kenna into the back seat of a black Chevrolet Suburban with blackened windows. It was surreal as a garage door fashioned to look like the exterior skin of the building opened. The armed chauffeur drove out into a sudden rain. *Fitting,* Kenna thought.

"The truth is what we seek," Deputy Director Anderson said. He adjusted the visor from the passenger side of the front seat to see Kenna pinned between two agents.

"Then, you should be working with me, not against me."

"Different styles, I'm afraid, vinegar and molasses. You seem to torture people for your truth. We tend to find evidence."

Kenna leaned forward, feeling the pressure of the young

strongmen's forearms easing her back against the seat. The Washington bureaucratic smirk remained affixed to Anderson's cheeks.

"It'll never work," Kenna said.

"What won't?" asked Anderson.

"You won't be able to frame me for Devon Whyte's murder."

The smile. "We have no desire to *'frame'* you. We want to find the truth."

"Vlad the Impaler eventually got to the truth he wanted, deputy director. But by the time he did, the entire enemy city had been slaughtered, and the skulls of the victims were stacked as high as the walls."

Elbow on the seat back, the deputy director turned. "But he accomplished his task, didn't he?"

XL

The interrogation room was the antithesis of the Clorox room. Kenna pushed the uncomfortable wooden chair back with a squawk on hard tiled floor. The sound bounced around the barren, high-ceilinged, concrete block room. She stood and squinted into the bright lights that blinded her like a World War II Gestapo interrogation.

"We don't want to create a national incident here, Ms. Hannigan, but—"

"You're working on one, Deputy Director Anderson," Kenna retorted, her face stretched thin with anger. "And a nice lawsuit."

"You aren't under arrest."

"Then, I'll leave."

"When you have answered a few more questions," Anderson replied.

"You don't understand what you've done, do you?"

"Excuse me?"

"As much as I wanted to walk away from this, I can't now," Kenna lied. "I owe it to Harvey Chamberlain and Devon Whyte—"

"We'll see if we can't change your mind," Anderson interrupted.

"To discover who's been running this cover-up from the beginning."

"There is no cover-up, Ms. Hannigan." The deputy director cocked his head again with a bureaucrat's smile. "Indeed, there is no case."

The company line. "To someone with eyes closed, I agree."

"Then, enlighten me."

"That would be like trying to explain colors to a person who has never seen. Get my drift?" He didn't. "You tell me I'm interfering with an investigation, and then in the next breath, you tell me there is no case. Which is it?"

"Perhaps we are talking about two separate issues."

"I've been here four hours and answered every question you've asked without due process or even a glass of water!"

"I am aware of your legal rights, Ms. Hannigan. But the death of a United States Senator may have national security implications. That allows me certain privileges."

Kenna chuckled, having heard that before. "That's an overused threat. One minute, you want questions answered about Chamberlain, the next about Whyte, the next about

Hobson. Then you say there is no case at all … again, a big circle jerk."

"Oh, there's a case, just not what you think."

Make up your mind. "Not now. Your people destroyed the evidence when Chamberlain was killed."

"Killed himself," the deputy director corrected.

"Right. Tell me: Did Devon Whyte kill himself, too?"

"That has yet to be determined."

"Yeah, I forgot. You guys destroy the evidence first when looking for the truth."

Anderson wiped a finger across the bottom of his mustache. He sat on the corner of the small wooden table and rested his hands on a knee.

"The obvious reason for our misunderstanding is you are the one who needs convincing. We are dealing in facts. The latter has proven invaluable in the resolution of the Chamberlain matter."

"This is ridiculous."

"Our position is supported by fact," Anderson said. "Moving on: You were the last person known to have been with Devon Whyte and the superintendent named Hobson. Were you also the last with Senator Chamberlain?"

"You said Chamberlain killed himself. You guys can't

even get your story straight. If you can't do that, deputy director, how the hell do you expect to convince me or anyone else on the outside?"

Anderson ignored her. "Do you see a connection where Hobson and Whyte are concerned?"

"A correction, perhaps. I didn't see Chamberlain until he was face down in the sand," Kenna snapped. "There were several of us in the room when I was with Chairman Whyte. When I left his house, he was still with Senator Bridgewater and the others."

"That's not what we think happened."

"You guys are thinking?" Gran Lockwood was screaming at her now, '*Pocket the attitude!*' "Pretty obvious why you don't know what's going on."

"Your belligerence isn't helping your cause any, Ms. Hannigan."

"My cause?" Kenna smirked. "What the hell is that?"

"In the meeting with Whyte, witnesses say you threatened not only him but Senator Bridgewater and the senator from Massachusetts. Indeed, that Chairman Whyte had you removed."

"That's a lie. I never threatened anyone. I promised them, like you, that I will find the truth."

"As for Hobson, you were seen with him a few hours before we found his office bathed in blood."

"Forensics has verified that the blood was his?" She and Salvatori already verified that Devon Whyte had been killed there and taken to the spillway.

"In process, Ms. Hannigan. But I believe the finding will be just that. When that happens, it will make you a prime suspect."

"That's some brilliant investigative work, Deputy Anderson. Hobson dropped me off at the front door of the Clubhouse. That's the last time I saw him."

"You look like you've been in a struggle, Ms. Hannigan. Who was it with?"

"I see it coming. I struggled with Hobson, killed him, and left him where no one could find him. Right?"

"Is that a confession?" Anderson asked.

"Hardly," Kenna snapped, biting her tongue on a string of curse words. "You won't ever be able to frame me."

"You have to admit it looks bad. We found blood on several towels in the locker room, as well. The lab is testing those. What if it comes up yours? Would you call that circumstantial or real evidence?"

"I'd say clueless."

"You seem to be the only one with marks and knowledge of Hobson's death."

"Dead? I never said he was dead. Have you found him?"

"Looking," Anderson said.

"Let me see if I understand this," Kenna said with a half chuckle that belied her sudden nervousness. "You haven't identified the blood as his, haven't even verified he's hurt, and yet you're saying I killed him?"

"If not, we certainly want to prevent this from happening."

"God, you live in a bad video game," Kenna said, recalling similar words from Malcolm.

"We have witnesses, Ms. Hannigan."

"So do I!"

"A convicted art thief?"

Kenna stiffened on the comment about Wiggy. "A better man than you will ever be."

"These things add up," Anderson continued, ignoring her. "In your world, would those facts, as you say, draw you to a conclusion? Or are you in the video game?"

Kenna didn't say what she really thought. There was more at work here than she ever could have imagined. Washington's tentacles tightened about her throat.

"There is another issue," Anderson slithered. "As we see it, you have violated the Restraining Order placed on you by the unfortunate widow."

"So, you guys are also street cops? You've either never met the *'unfortunate widow,'* or this goes beyond the Restraining Order. You can't push me out of the way like your subordinates, Deputy Anderson."

"I'm thinking of your future. Not only in what you investigate but in journalism."

"You and Malcolm Bridgewater need to get new lines, deputy director. I didn't listen to him, either." Kenna turned a glistening stare to the mirrored wall at her right and squinted. "You have put yourself and your position here in jeopardy."

"It is you who are in jeopardy, Ms. Hannigan. I am simply doing my job."

"So were the SS camp guards in Auschwitz, Deputy Anderson."

A curled-up eyebrow was the bureaucrat's response. The deputy director leaned forward onto the back of a chair and licked his thin lips. That smile returned; Kenna wanted to bust it open with a bat.

"You are interfering with an on-going investigation, Ms.

Hannigan. That is the issue, nothing else."

"Is that of Senator Chamberlain's death, or is there something else?"

"Something else, as you know," Agent Salvatori said from the open door. "I warned you to stay out of my way on this. Sorry I'm late, Director Anderson."

"Nice work with Edelman," Kenna said evenly to Salvatori.

Anderson responded, "Leave Agent Edelman out of this. I will deal with her."

So, I misjudged her, Kenna thought. It wasn't Edelman that set her up. And perhaps she had misjudged Salvatori. Another blue-ribbon day in the U.S. Marshals' growing list of failures.

Anderson leaned onto the table. "We take orders, too, Ms. Hannigan."

Kenna turned to Salvatori. "Ever heard that?"

Kenna stared back into the mirrored wall not more than six feet away. A main nerve had been hit, and perhaps she had drawn blood, their blood. And Deputy Director Anderson had just played into her suspicion; *we are all being manipulated.*

"Aren't your orders to find the truth, deputy director? I

think that's what you said."

Anderson turned to leave but stopped at the door. "Our job, Ms. Hannigan, is to stop people like you from disrupting an investigation that has national security implications. We deal in issues of more importance to this country than a suicide."

"That includes cutting deals with people who break the law?"

"We don't cut deals, Ms. Hannigan," Anderson insisted.

Kenna shuttered with a chill that shot up her spine to bury itself at the base of her brain. General Treadway said nearly the same. As the door closed behind Anderson, she turned to Salvatori. The agent pulled out a Camel no filter and lit it.

"Isn't this a smoke-free building?" Kenna asked. "Do you agree with Anderson?"

"I warned you."

"That's not what I asked."

"Unless you haven't noticed," Salvatori said, pointing the cigarette around the room. "This is our forum to ask the questions, not yours."

"I've answered enough questions."

"I'll have Altmann soon," Salvatori said and exhaled into

the return air ventilation duct. "And I can hold you long enough to make that happen."

Kenna knew the truth these men and other Washington insiders didn't want told. She wanted Altmann as much as anyone. They said they weren't afraid of her reviewing the evidence from Chamberlain's death but kept it from her. She was told she could talk to the coroner, only to have Peebles ushered from the room. Her one ally inside the ivory tower, Agent Edelman, had been conveniently *'reassigned'*. And then there was the deal cut with Avery Gowen, which none of them would acknowledge.

It was then Salvatori finally said something new: "What you can't get through your thick skull, Ms. Hannigan, is that you aren't meant to know."

Those words rattled between her ears like the bullet that scrambled Harvey Chamberlain's brain. Beyond those words, perhaps there was no *why*. Perhaps it simply *was*.

Wiggy opened the door and smiled when he pushed aside a U.S. Marshal escort and walked into the room. Kenna stood from the chair. Reviewing documents, Deputy Director Anderson entered on Wiggy's heels.

"Ya have a bad knack of findin' a skunk in the flower garden, kid," Wiggy said.

"To the contrary, Wiggy, the skunks seem to have a knack of finding me."

"Ms. Hannigan is free to go," Deputy Director Anderson forced from his mouth.

Kenna turned to an enraged Salvatori and said, "You should have listened to me. Now, you've pissed me off."

"I'll tell you a final time," Salvatori hissed. "Stay out of my way."

Kenna knocked Salvatori's cigarette from his hand and ground it out with a heel. "I hate fuckers that blow smoke in my face."

"Ya need new friends, kid," Wiggy said as they walked from the room.

"I need a few months in Belize." *With Charlie,* she didn't say. "How did you manage that?"

"I made a call."

"Malcolm?"

"No. This is a city of deals, lass. I had to make one … with yer father."

Kenna froze. "Father? And he agreed?"

"Aye. He made a few calls last night and found out you weren't blowin' smoke up his arse. Agent Edelman called to tell him you were here."

"We owe her big."

"A single malt, perhaps," he said with a smile.

"Maybe more than one. I'll let you buy, depending on what the deal with father costs?"

"You won't like it. He said she wants you out of D.C."

Kenna swallowed hard. Everything was being sucked into Bridgewater's black hole of Washington politics. She could not allow that to happen, regardless of what she owed anybody.

"It won't be the first time I've defied him."

"He knows that, kid."

Salvatori watched them leave. As Kenna and Wiggy walked outside, Kenna smiled and blinked against the sun. She looked back at the building. In Salvatori's office, what she saw hadn't really registered until just then. She now knew it was what she hadn't seen that mattered. The one glaring piece missing from that night six years ago: The Chess Club.

XLI

Kenna followed Wiggy to the rental car and nearly tripped over a man who walked in front of her. With quick reflexes, she grabbed the man's hand that was buried in his jacket pocket.

"What's the matter with you?" the man insisted, pulling out his cell phone.

"Nothing," Kenna apologized.

The case, this city, was getting to her: no, had gotten to her. Before, she never would have reacted like that. Wiggy swiped a parking ticket off the windshield, walked away, and slid it under the wiper of a government-issue sedan. With a chuckle, he returned to the rental car and slid in behind the wheel.

"What the bloody hell did they want?" Wiggy asked thumb over his shoulder.

"To make sure I include them on my Christmas list."

"Letter bombs aren't my specialty, Fiery," Wiggy said and steered into traffic.

"Might want to re-think that after this case."

"We'd die old before we had the time to make as many

as we'd need."

Kenna turned to see Wiggy's eyes in the rearview mirror. They flashed back and forth, ahead and behind. In the side mirror, a standard-issue government sedan pulled onto the street behind them.

"You have definitely made friends, kid."

"What else do they have to do?"

"Blow up a religious sect in Montana or something!"

"Don't get me started," Kenna said.

In keeping with the insanity, Gowen had disappeared. If the guys in the building behind had anything to do with it, she knew who'd be blamed. Even her father wouldn't be able to help her if that were the case.

"I have a lead on the old terrorist," Wiggy said. "Didn't realize it until this afternoon."

"I'm confused, Wiggy."

A quick *'no shit!'* glance said a lot as Wiggy steered through traffic, then watched their tail. "I thought you'd have it all pieced together by now, kid. I was thinkin' of takin' the afternoon off."

"Close … real close." Kenna grabbed the door as Wiggy's movements in traffic were erratic, a warning of what was to come.

Footprints across the green … one set coming, one going … kept running through her mind. Everyone saw them, even the U.S. Marshals. Hobson made them; she was positive. But if the killer wanted something off Chamberlain … the Chess Club list … why hadn't he found it? Because Hobson already had it? No, because the killer wasn't looking for it. The German had said on the tape that he had it to sell; that was why he met Chamberlain on the veranda Saturday. It said that the German was selling something else … campaign contributions? Or, as Wiggy suggested, his silence about both.

Something once again told her that her attacker in the trees had wanted Hobson, not her. Otherwise, she would have joined Chamberlain and Whyte in the great beyond. Chamberlain's death had been clean if there was such a thing about murder. But Devon Whyte had put up a fight or had been beaten viciously before he had a chance to fight. Two different murderers? Or two different reasons?

"Chamberlain was no hero," Kenna said, thinking aloud.

Wiggy knew to let her mind buzz. He had something else … and worked the traffic as well as one could in Washington. It was always slow at best, a parking lot most of the time.

From Charlie's latest recordings of Gowen

conversations, they knew what Kenna suspected was, indeed, fact. Hobson was now in the market to sell the information. He had become the second in line of that game. Or were they working together?

"I know I've gone back and forth, Wiggy, but we have to find Gowen. He knows about the recordings."

"He's on his own, or he did it."

"There's another option," Kenna said.

"Aye. We could find him with a bullet in his brain."

"He won't do us any good like that."

"Chili chest's not the type to stay on the run for long. He feeds off this plastic society and has friends."

They passed a VW minibus full of young skinheads. Kenna remembered photos of when such vehicles were reserved for the longhaired generation, covered with peace signs, and left a trail of odd-smelling smoke. How things had changed.

"The blokes in the U.K. followed-up about Hobson's background. There's something very interesting," Wiggy said. "But right now …"

Kenna turned. Wiggy's eyes flashed to the rearview mirror. A red light loomed ahead. Kenna inhaled sharply for what she knew could be the last time. She was about to object when Wiggy snapped the wheel to the right, throwing the car between two trucks in the right lane. Kenna grabbed her shoulder belt and slammed her other elbow against the armrest. Multiplied by the g-forces of the turn, her stomach muscles screamed when her body smashed against the door.

A truck horn blasted a few feet from Kenna's right ear when Wiggy snapped the wheel to the right again, darting into the far-right lane. Kenna's stomach and the heavy automobile lunged into a left-hand power slide past a turn-island. As Wiggy recovered from that move, he stomped the accelerator and then braked hard to steer left in front of a line of stopped traffic. More blasting horns greeted Kenna's pending death as the crazy Eastie accelerated hard to the next street. He caught a green light and filed into the heavy noontime Washington traffic that snaked onto an overpass. Once on the other side, he spun the car up an on-ramp and folded into traffic going the opposite direction than they had two streets over.

Wiggy glanced into his mirror and smiled: "Bloody amateurs never made the first turn."

"My stomach didn't either," Kenna said. "Let's go back and get it."

Wiggy laughed. "You're an ole maid sometimes."

"I wish you'd tell me before you do that."

"Impulse, Fiery. What Gran Lockwood loved about me. Besides, it'd take all me fun away." Wiggy checked the mirror once again, then, with similar flash, turned into a parking lot marked by Golden Arches. "I'm starved; how about lunch?"

"Cotton candy after that rollercoaster ride."

Wiggy jerked around a car pulling from a parking spot. Kenna gripped the door handle so hard the tendons in her hand burned. The trunk of the approaching car dropped as it screeched to a stop. The driver yelled something.

"Ya want anything?" Wiggy asked, ignoring the other driver. "Didn't think so."

With a moment of indecision, he ordered, paid at the first window, and collected his food at the second. He handed Kenna a Diet Dr. Pepper and didn't notice the hand gesture delivered out the window of the car they nearly hit.

"Good thing we're not in L.A.," Kenna said. "They shoot drivers like you out there."

Leaving the lot, Wiggy turned into traffic, then up an on-ramp to I-395, which was jammed with traffic. He piloted the car steadily into the far-left lane and accelerated to 40, braked to zero, then accelerated again in keeping with the flow. He steered around a slower car to cut off a string of traffic. Blasting horns.

"Didn't see Charlie Sommer at the club."

"He's not on a leash."

"Maybe not, but he oug't ta be," Wiggy said with a mouthful of Big Mac.

Wiggy was meticulous about his work, often to the point of repetition. It made for fewer mistakes and, on more than one occasion, accounted for new details. While eating and driving, he went through Hobson's background again. With fluid accuracy, Wiggy detailed the connection between the superintendent and the Massachusetts senator. Chamberlain helped influence the governing board of the Country Club to hire him, though Hobson's background was not verifiable. It was also Chamberlain who arranged false records from Cambridge.

"But we didn't know it all. Let me back up." Kenna knew that was her cue to shut up. "We know the Massachusetts senator's father was related to one Paddy O'Leary in Belfast. Had I known that, I would have made the connection a lot earlier. Paddy O'Leary was a lieutenant in the IRA, mind you, and was killed during the Belfast ambush of the British in '75. The good Catholic lad had a wife of Scottish descent and a son who survived. They left Ireland and went to England, where she and the boy took her maiden name—"

"Hobson," Kenna interrupted.

"Aye," Wiggy said. The intake unit consumed the second half of the Big Mac. Before it was all chewed, he continued. "Seems they got some help for many years from their long-lost relatives in the States. The story is that, when the boy matured in England, the senator from Mass got the lad a job at the University where the family provided a large endowment."

"Cambridge!" Kenna said. "So, we've come full circle. Why isn't there a record of him?"

"In due time, lass." Wiggy took a drink of coffee. "Bloody awful stuff. Seems the lad never put in a day's work at the campus, as Hobson, that is."

"Explains why MI5 couldn't find record of it."

"Seems so. No pay records on a Mathew Hobson. They did say that he got the nickname *'Roots'* at Cambridge, though. Logic would say, because he was good at keeping grounds."

"That's not why you're talking."

"Gran Lockwood came short on teaching you patience, didn't she, kid," Wiggy said. "So, ya want somethin' new, without all the foreplay. Ya must disappoint the lassies and lads.

"So be it," Wiggy continued. "Hobson was on the watch list through MI5 in the late 80s and early 90s. The nickname *'Roots'* came about because he used to root the sewers and plant explosives, or so they believe. They say that's how he mangled his hands when a blasting cap discharged early. They never proved any of it, though.

"Years before," he continued, "his father had befriended a young fellow Irishman and good Catholic named Father Jonathan Michael Bergen. MI5 connected the lad and his mother to the good Father in England."

"I've heard that name before."

"You should've. He's the bloke who bombed Harrods in the name of God and Irish independence."

"Yes. That's when Gran was called in to help assess the damage and find what was stolen during the looting. You're holding something back. You're right, no foreplay, out with it!"

"It's confirmed that Father Bergen used Cambridge as a base of operations while in the U.K. Socialism, cloaked in liberal democratic dogma, all that rubbish. He operated via a code name within terrorist circles.

"Are you ready for this, lass?" he continued. "He was known as the Bishop."

The Chess Club list flashed before Kenna's eyes. A terrorist's name linked not only to Roots Hobson but Chamberlain's death. And what about Devon Whyte, the Black Knight? She checked her excitement momentarily.

"You said *'was'*?"

"Died in prison about six years ago."

Kenna nodded apprehensively … *six years*. "The timing ties with Altmann's terrorist plot. How long was the Bishop in prison?"

"Not long. And you'll love this one: he committed suicide in his cell."

"'God *loves a good mystery,*' Gran Lockwood always said. Cambridge and suicide."

French fries flew across the mentor's lap when the car hit a bump. "There's something else about the Bishop, though. While in prison, he had only two visitors. One being our recently departed senator from Illinois. The second, a German."

"Altmann?"

"They didn't know at the time. If Altmann he used an alias. They didn't think about it because he visited the Bishop not long after the senator did."

"But that doesn't—"

"They ran a background check later and found that the man fit the description of a suspected German agent working in Afghanistan, but that was all they found. No surveillance photos or identification."

"Like this case," Kenna said. "Where we going, anyway?"

"The Pentagon. I took it that you would want to know more about Father Bergen."

"And?" Kenna pried, finally taking a drink of Diet Dr. Pepper.

"Ingenious footwork is taking you to a general in the Pentagon who was instrumental in bringing the Bishop down." Kenna almost threw up the drink and turned. "One in the same, Fiery, one in the same."

XLII

Wiggy turned into the Pentagon, the monstrous office complex that fed America's military-industrial complex. Thousands of cars were crammed bumper-to-bumper in the endless parking lots. People in uniform and civvies shuffled in and out of the structure with intent.

Wiggy dropped Kenna at the guard gate and drove off. Light rail whizzed past on the tracks across the highway; car traffic filled Kenna's head. All the activity made her dizzy. She looked up at the building, having been here once before during a high school senior class trip.

Kenna entered to the buzz of bodies, men and women on a mission, knifing through the stark halls. Endless pedestrian highways of polished stone and painted walls reached as far as the eye could see. Those human highways were crammed with uniformed men and women escorting business-suited men and women into the void. It left little doubt that this was, as proclaimed, the largest office complex in the world. To Kenna, that meant the biggest seat of bureaucratic stagnation, and therefore waste, in the world. She stood before a young Hispanic corporal at the front desk, rigid at perpetual attention.

"According to the general's aide, an urgent meeting came up, ma'am," the corporal said. "He asked the purpose of this meeting and if it can be delayed."

Kenna was not to be denied. "Please tell the general the Bishop isn't dead."

Never took his eyes off Kenna as if examining the enemy, the corporal turned back to the phone and spoke in a muffled whisper. He disconnected the call and shoved a register out the security booth window.

Inside the security entrance, Kenna was photographed, fingerprints scanned, and she was led through metal detectors where a Visitor's badge was hung over her neck. She had an older one in a scrapbook somewhere … from the time before metal detectors. A young, armed Filipino Marine private appeared from nowhere. Escort duty was his; Kenna followed.

They rode two elevators, walked forever, it seemed, and made their way through a maze-like path that she could never duplicate or backtrack. With a heavy breath of anticipation, she was ushered through the glass door of a plain office and directed to a leather armchair. She did not sit; the private remained at attention at the door.

A smartly pressed lieutenant stepped from a heavy wooden door on her left. The young officer's name, W.

Shipp, was printed in white block letters on a black nameplate pinned just above his uniform pocket. He walked forward stiffly and stopped, heels together. They exchanged greetings without shaking. W. Shipp dismissed the private, who snapped to attention and spun out without speaking.

"The general asked me to see if there is anything I can do to help you, Ms. Hannigan. He is extremely busy today, and such an impromptu appointment—"

"I must have piqued his interest, lieutenant, or I wouldn't have gotten this far," Kenna interrupted. "Why don't we cut to the chase, as the general would say, and tell him to see me … it's about the Bishop."

"I don't tell the general to do anything, ma'am," Shipp corrected with a raised eyebrow.

"Of course. My apologies," she said.

Shipp backed away and walked stiff-bodied through the heavy wood-glass door. Within a minute, he returned and motioned Kenna inside.

Greatness permeated the large, manly room. It was that of a powerful human being, a man in charge of every aspect of his life and the lives of those who reported to him. Certificates of Commendation decorated the walls, as did memorabilia from heads of state around the world. Letters from Presidents Bush, Clinton, Bush the junior, Obama, and Trump were in plaques atop a cherry credenza, positioned around a small American flag on a glass tube *pole*.

"Have you come to arrange that lesson you promised?" the general asked, standing to shake Kenna's hand.

"You know why I'm here … the Bishop."

Treadway hesitated. "I like a woman that cuts to the chase, but I'll hold you to that lesson on camera face time."

"Everything in this city revolves around a deal; yours is cheap." Kenna's eyes took in the presidential commendation letters. "I'm impressed, general. But you seem to be missing one." When no response came, "Is that an indication of what the past administration thought of you?"

"Politicians come and go, Ms. Hannigan," the general offered. "Military men are accepted or shunned based on whether they kowtow to their master's whims."

"That's off the record, I take it," Kenna said, not waiting for a response. "You were all but placed in the *'necessary evil'* classification, I suppose."

The general allowed a rare crack in his otherwise chiseled stone features. "Now, what's this about the Bishop?"

"I understand you were instrumental in bringing him

down."

"My unit was, yes."

"From accounts I've read, you're being modest," Kenna said, never having read anything about it.

"Good military men are not *'modest,'* young Hannigan. We do our duty. I commanded the intelligence unit that discovered the Bishop's terrorist ties to the Taliban and their connection to some in German intelligence. That was Morningstar's biggest coup."

"Tell me about him."

The general looked at his watch. "I'm meeting with the Chief of Staff in a few minutes and don't have time for a history lesson."

"Then, why did you agree to see me?"

"You are a necessary evil," Treadway said, another crack in the stone. "You said the Bishop was alive; that's not true."

Kenna frowned. "What did the Bishop have to do with the Chess Club?"

Treadway narrowed reddening eyes, followed by a rapid series of breaths. His lips tightened to a thin line. "Nothing."

"I don't accept that, general," Kenna countered. "There's more you're keeping from me."

Treadway hesitated and chewed his unlit cigar. "It took

us several years to run the Bishop's group down. I don't recall any mention of a *'Chess Club'* other than rumors."

"Enlighten a dumb Texas girl in the big city and all."

"You're slicker than cow pies, young Hannigan. So, you can cut that good ole girl crap with me." The general snickered and shoved two red folders into a briefcase. Neither's eyes waivered. He continued:

"The rumor was that the Chess Club was a small group of students who studied weekly with the Bishop at Cambridge. They discussed the philosophical aspects of terrorism, communism, governmental overthrow, and other radical bull shit."

"The Cambridge Five back in the fifties and sixties, as a model?" Kenna said. Treadway was silently impressed by her historical knowledge. "Did the Bishop confirm or deny that?"

"Never got the opportunity to ask him," Treadway said.

"You never met him or saw him, even though your group brought him down?"

"That's right. Morningstar led him directly into British hands. It's how we wanted it. At that time, the British needed a victory over the Taliban."

"Unfortunate for you, in a way."

"Not really." Treadway leaned on his knuckles, allowing his beribboned chest to puff out if just a little. "It never went beyond that while I was in Europe. An order from on-high."

"So, no one … meaning you … even knows the identity of the students involved with him?"

"Affirmative … to my knowledge."

"You've been in Washington too long, general."

"Meaning?"

"Meaning that ten years ago, you would have said *'hell yes'* or *'hell no.'*"

Treadway smiled with a lengthy pause. "In Baghdad, I'd have just kicked your ass until you understood."

"Why do you think it took so long for this to surface?"

"Don't have the slightest idea. My operation ended with the Bishop imprisoned."

"You mean when he died in prison?"

Lieutenant Shipp opened the door. "General, your meeting with the Joint Chiefs is in ten minutes. And you are set for an interview with Ms. Hannigan at noon tomorrow."

"Right," the general said. The lieutenant circled Treadway's desk to collect the stack of folders and the general's briefcase.

"Ah, the quid pro quo, general," Kenna said. "I warn you

that I don't pull any punches in an interview."

"As I don't in my answers." Treadway walked around the desk.

Kenna waited for Shipp to walk out. "How was it you came across the Bishop?"

"How could that have anything to do with the Chamberlain affair?"

"That's what I want to know."

"You've asked about two parts of my past in Germany that I can't answer. Twenty years …" Treadway paused for a long moment and pulled a strand of tobacco from his teeth. He stared out the window at the ground. "I'm still pissed with a system that went wrong. And you, young Hannigan, are leading me into a trap you can't shut."

"And the Bishop?"

"Is dead."

Kenna followed the consummate soldier away from the desk. How many people knew, really knew, what clicked inside that military brain? One. What did this man have in mind for the streets of their cities that gave Bridgewater so much concern? Order? Or was it more?

Treadway raised an eyebrow. "You have a propensity for sticking your nose where it doesn't belong. You should stop questioning everyone about a murder that never occurred."

"I said before, you've been here too long."

"Your intelligence is based on supposition. Refine it to convince others."

"War *is* supposition, isn't it, general?"

Treadway scowled but appreciated her foresight. "In a way."

"They say Gloria Chamberlain is interested in her husband's seat. A man like you could help her get it."

"If she's qualified, they may give it to her. That's politics; I'm a military man."

Kenna allowed a long, lingering smile. "If that wasn't politicking in Bridgewater's office, I don't know what is, general."

"I have one question," Treadway said. "Just what the hell are you doing playing detective when the best minds in that field are already on top of the Chamberlain death?"

"A hobby of mine."

"Well, don't let that hobby get you killed." Cigar clamped between yellow teeth, the general smiled. "I like you."

XLIII

Kenna walked across the Pentagon parking lot to the guard booth and asked about where her Uber ride would be. The guard made her sign the mandatory forms in triplicate and showed her on a small map where her ride waited … across the parking lot. She worked up a sweat walking there.

She walked toward Luis's Toyota Prius, appreciative but also wanting to take the wheel herself. She enjoyed the fact that Wiggy didn't know her real side behind the wheel. Someday, she would show him the Lewis Hamilton inside her. She hesitated, staring at the Pentagon, wondering if the general's last words had been a threat. Or, like Avery Gowen, was Treadway just in too deep? She doubted the latter.

Never had she questioned herself as much as she had in this city. Weary from lack of sleep and continuous mind games, she felt the end was close but accepted the fact that she didn't know where the end was. *'Sleep when ye've won,'* Gran Lockwood would have said.

Luis handed her a bottle of water; she leaned against the car to take in the sun, not recalling Washington ever being this hot. A bank of clouds formed to the east; it smelled of rain. Humidity slapped her across the face as she grabbed the door handle. A car stopped behind.

"Do you believe Lee Harvey Oswald killed Kennedy?" The accent was German.

"Ma'am?" Luis asked, easing open his door.

Kenna motioned Luis to stay in the Prius. She swallowed hard, just then realizing she was without a weapon. She turned to see the German for the first time. The bold features held the German's face like stone. He stared through Aryan eyes that penetrated her inner soul as if some supernatural power. Images of Nazi World War II concentration camps burned into her mind.

"That's what the Warren Report said," she forced out.

"Things seen are often wrong."

"I suppose there's some kind of deep meaning to that," Kenna offered.

"I came to pay my respects to the general, only to find that he was occupied … apparently with you." Altmann watched all angles of the parking lot without moving his head. "Elaborate ruses are often the most difficult to detect."

The game being played by Bernard Altmann was convoluted, at least to everyone looking at it. But this meeting was not random. It was part of an organized plan.

Heart racing, Kenna took a step towards the vehicle. A trace of Aramis aftershave drifted into her nose.

"You are becoming troublesome, Ms. Hannigan," the German said, eyes electrified, encompassing his surroundings. "Had you not gotten involved, I would already be gone."

"A role I play well, Herr Altmann, or so we've been quasi-introduced," Kenna replied. "The other times we collided, there was no time to talk."

"Please allow me to conclude my business, Ms. Hannigan. Had my desire been to end your life, rest assured you never would have known it."

Kenna believed him; the prior incident had already convinced her. The shots in the trees had been a warning. That they had fought had not been part of his plan. Charlie Sommer's office had been a different matter altogether.

"It is sometimes an unfortunate necessity in our business to act swiftly."

The words *our business* hit Kenna full-face. The German's chilling blue eyes brought back memories of all the evil that Kenna had seen in her early 20s. Hatred remained in its purest state for some; yet she didn't believe that was the case for Bernard Altmann.

"I must be going. It appears they discovered that I borrowed someone's automobile." The German's eyes flashed toward the mirror. He flinched and turned, his hand on the steering wheel, then pointed at the security cameras. "They have seen enough of us. Good luck."

Kenna was about to question the closing statement when a car lunged at them from the front and screeched to an abrupt halt. Kenna jumped back as Altmann's car catapulted forward, ramming into a government-issue Chevrolet. A uniformed man leaning out the driver's door was thrown to the pavement 20 feet away as the car spun around her. He struggled to stand but fell. Kenna's head slammed against the Prius. Luis jumped out, yelling for her.

Altmann's car careened around the wreckage, then spun 90 degrees through the parking lot, bounded over a curb, and slid on the green grass of the parkway. It flew into the traffic of the south Rotary Road and rammed into a convertible. Both cars spun; traffic shrieked to a stop. With a puff of smoke, Altmann accelerated along the shoulder. Government cars raced out of the parking lot, red lights flashing, sirens blaring over roaring engines, and reached the off-ramp.

Men brandished weapons, aiming them at Kenna and Luis. She raised both hands and was pulled to her feet. Luis was thrown against the Prius and cuffed.

Blood filled Kenna's mouth; she cursed. On the street, nothing moved but the *borrowed* car that sped along South Washington Boulevard. Pursuit ended before it even began. Through clouded eyes, Kenna had no doubt Bernard Altmann planned that exit.

A gun was placed against the back of Kenna's skull. Handcuffs were snapped on her wrists. Curses filled her ears; she turned as the German's *borrowed* car disappeared into the distance.

XLIV

Avery Gowen brushed an unkempt strand of hair into place with the delicate sweep of his right palm. His clothes were rumpled and dirty, the air tainted with his unwashed body. He wore black tennis shoes caked with mud that had left a trail into Bridgewater's office. He shifted uncomfortably in the hard chair.

"How is it you managed to survive this long?" Malcolm Bridgewater insisted.

"I did what I promised, senator," Gowen insisted. "Now, it's your turn. Kenna Hannigan is involved because of you, not me."

"The way you've messed up this entire thing, you should be joining Harvey."

"My secrets won't travel with me to the grave, Malcolm," Gowen guaranteed.

The old man leaned forward onto aged white knuckles. Bridgewater was no longer in control, and he knew it. Eyes that drooped into blue-black bags still showed no fear and stared down on Gowen like they would a servant or a field hand. His hands shook; his skin was pale. Yet, he missed nothing, attentive to Gowen's every move, his every word.

"You threaten me, and that's exactly where you'll be going," the senator from Tennessee promised.

"You've known from the beginning what I wanted, senator."

Bridgewater furrowed his brow. "And I get?"

"What I told you over the phone. This, and I believe you have something for me."

Avery Gowen lifted a manila envelope from his shirt and placed it on the desk. He did not release it. The senator lifted his cell phone, dialed a number, and spoke into it. In the time it took Gowen to drink a glass of water, his phone beeped. He pulled up the message.

"Transaction confirmed," Gowen said with a smile.

"I should have had Jimmy deal with you when you involved the German."

"Jimmy's on a wild goose chase, Malcolm," Gowen sneered. "I made sure of that prior to coming. Besides, how was I to know the German knew Chamberlain?"

"With the amount of money I just transferred, you should have known."

"I seem to have gotten what I wanted, anyway," Gowen grimaced. "There's one more thing."

Gowen pulled his manila envelope back a few inches

before Bridgewater lifted an envelope from his jacket pocket. The senator hesitated a few moments, staring at the official seal on the outside, and then threw it across the desk.

"Don't be such a pompous ass, senator. We're born of the same hypocrisy."

"Balderdash!"

"The difference is I will stick my balls out to play the game."

"Get out of here. If I see you again or find out that there is mysteriously another copy of this somewhere, I'll have Jimmy dump you in an acid vat."

With a grin, Avery Gowen stood. He opened the second envelope, pulled out the letter, and read it. "Thank you, senator. It's been nice doing business with you."

Bridgewater grabbed the manila envelope and pushed himself up from the chair. He walked to the corner of his office, where he opened a closet, removed each document from inside the envelope, read them, and fed them into a shredder. When the shredding was complete, he carried the trashcan full of paper strips to the fireplace. There, he fed them into the flame until heat radiated against his face. Within a few minutes, the fire had died to a few flickers fighting for air; all the paper was consumed. He stirred it with a fireplace poker until every ember died.

At his desk, the senator from Tennessee sat in silence. Dorothy brought cups of coffee and poured Tennessee Sour Mash into them. They toasted and drank with confidence … like they always did.

XLV

With hand-written orders from the general, Lieutenant W. Shipp had rescued Kenna and Luis from Pentagon security. Favoring her burning side, Kenna leaned out of the military Chevrolet into a light rain and closed the door. Without hesitation, Shipp drove the car away. She rubbed her wrists that burned from the handcuffs. Atop the hill off Schley Drive in Arlington Cemetery, Kenna watched through the rain as a brown Cadillac turned off Memorial Avenue. It pulled to a stop not far from her at the edge of the grass.

Without an umbrella or slicker, the general stepped into the rain. The stone-faced military man marched across the manicured grass between the perfectly aligned cross headstones. He stopped at the headstone bearing his father's name and looked up, savoring the weather.

A lump appeared in Kenna's throat when she walked across the sacred soil to America's fallen heroes. Weather was as unpredictable as this case. The skies opened with great intent; buzzing rain filled her ears. She joined the general at the cross, noticing the name.

"These simple markers are more a tribute than any fancy

mausoleum," Treadway said, staring at his father's name. "Their exactness in form and function speaks of the ultimate sacrifice made by each person buried here. Officer or enlisted, man or woman of every race, each paid the same price for freedom and for this country."

Rain folded off the brim of the general's cover, as would tears from saddened eyes. The general turned into the rain to face Kenna. He was expressionless; generals do not cry.

"My mother said he was a great man," Treadway continued.

"Would she have said the same of you?"

The Potomac River was but a thin black line through a gray fogbank of battle smoke into which the rows of white crosses disappeared. Swallowed by the heavy air and storm, the sounds of traffic were like a distant army converging on their position. Hidden by the low clouds, planes passed overhead to National Airport as if on strafing missions. This, Kenna believed, was what General Treadway saw and heard at that moment.

The general's pressed uniform of a few hours before was now soaked and crumpled. He was unmoved. Glossy eyes embraced the permanent encampment of dead. Kenna saw the military man looking back on Afghanistan, perhaps even more on Germany.

"There are few men alive who could clean the latrine of these heroes," Treadway said.

"Even you?"

"Especially me. But I think I've done something right today."

"What?"

"You're here, aren't you? And not in one of the U.S. Marshals' interrogation cells."

"Doing what's right is sometimes the most difficult," Kenna said.

"There comes a time when honor and duty override personal interests, young Hannigan. Something the politicians in this city will never understand. And something bull-headed bastards like me sometimes forget."

"Why did you bring me here?"

"I owed you something."

"Something he would have wanted you to say," Kenna said, nodding at the grave.

"I'm not a romantic. But in essence, you might be right." Treadway clasped his hands together at his waist. "My wife and I were married for thirty years before she died. The only time we weren't together on Sunday was when I was on duty. It was the thought of her that drove me to what I saw as excellence. I wanted her to be proud of me.

"In Iraq, the thought of her kept me going," he continued. "When together, we never missed church. After services, she always made roast beef, onions, potatoes, carrots, green bean casserole, and rolls. It wasn't her favorite meal, but it's been mine ever since mother made it. And by God, I can still taste it."

"But it's been a while, hasn't it, general?"

"When I lost her, my life became hollow. Both female inspirations in my life were gone. There was no one for me to make proud, I suppose."

Pansy shit, Kenna thought: *A chink in the armor.* "Was Gloria a substitute?"

"It didn't start that way. We became friends when the senator *'got weird'*, in her words. Then, yes, I believe it became mutual. She was a field of flowers in this mud hole until the bottle got in the way."

"So, you confided in her your deepest secrets."

"Initially, yes."

"But when Chamberlain was killed, you knew you had made a mistake."

"I knew that long before Chamberlain's death." A thumb wiped rain from his watch.

"She saw you as her means to stay in Washington, to get her husband's seat. She threatened to tell the Joint Chiefs your deepest secrets if you didn't help her."

"She didn't have to. I would have given her that in exchange for her vote. The bill is too important. But that's not the way it was."

"No? You convince the President not to close the bases in Illinois. That means no layoffs, keeping her husband's initiatives in place, and you get her vote on the bill."

Treadway leveled a stare. "It's that simple to you, isn't it?"

"The simplest is usually the most logical, but sometimes the hardest to realize."

The general's eyes narrowed. "Like Afghanistan."

Kenna thought once again about Treadway's plan in Afghanistan. The general would owe her that one-day.

"Gloria hated him, you know, but she didn't kill him," Treadway said.

Treadway turned away, staring at a car that drove slowly past. A young boy in the backseat waved. Terror Treadway saluted; he was a mere mortal, after all.

"When I met Bridgewater the other day, I put on a mask and played politician. God, I hate that part of this job."

"You were better in the field."

"You know the enemy in the field; kill the enemy, no questions, good versus evil, no wrong, only right."

"But you fucked up!"

Treadway leveled a Machiavellian stare. "A minor lack of proper information that should have quickly been remedied."

"But it wasn't. For the general's star, you reported both Morningstar and Altmann were dead. But they weren't. So, you had to cover it up."

"It wasn't for my star! The politicians wouldn't let Morningstar go, said he knew too much, was a liability. So, after I heard Altmann was killed, we made a deal and arranged for Morningstar's disappearance."

Kenna faced him. "Was the man in the car Morningstar?"

The general stared without responding. Perhaps it was denial, perhaps an admittance of truth. She didn't breathe for the longest time. Treadway pulled off his cover and allowed the rain to dampen his short hair. A brief sense of appreciation creased his face.

"You're a good intelligence man; wish I'd had you in Germany."

"Your chair on the Joint Chiefs is being pulled out from

under you, general." Kenna hesitated, then insisted, "Morningstar!"

The general looked at his father's marker and swallowed hard. "Morningstar gave us more information than anyone before or after. If this fella you met said he's Morningstar, he's lying. Morningstar wouldn't come out in the open, not to you."

Kenna saw the tactical genius at work. The general was undoubtedly working a dozen contingency plans for every conceivable attack. But was the thought of his old workhorse, Morningstar, coming back to the barn one of those possibilities?

"Why not?"

The general's face crumpled. He wiped rain from his eyes with a forefinger. "Things were different during the war against terrorism, especially in Afghanistan. There was a lot of shit being scattered in the wind."

Kenna looked at the grave again, then at the general. No such man could stand on the soil of a fallen hero … father or not … and lie.

"You're forgetting something," she said. "You took a risk for Morningstar."

"Doctor Frhein put it in place. Morningstar wanted

protection."

"Earlier, you said *'we'* made a deal with Morningstar. What did you mean?"

The general froze. "I'll tell you when you're wrong."

The fiery eyes leveled on Kenna, though not as strong as before. "You were getting resistance from your detractors here in Washington for letting Morningstar run free after all those years working for us. He knew our most intricate intelligence details, didn't he?"

"Perhaps better than anyone in the East."

"But the detractors, the senator from Massachusetts, Harvey Chamberlain, and Malcolm Bridgewater, demanded we not let him go. They wanted him exposed with all the others. What they didn't know, though, was that you were about to bring down the Bishop."

Treadway raised only his eyes into the rain without blinking. In battle, a lot can happen in the time a man blinks. Fear was born in the unknown, that instant a man's eyes closed when a bullet traveled through space and drove into his brain.

"So, you cut them a deal," Kenna continued. "Morningstar goes free in exchange for the Bishop."

"There is—"

"Morningstar was cut loose, his identity lost forever. But before the British could be convinced to release the Bishop, he conveniently killed himself." For the first time, General Treadway was speechless. "Who confronted me at the Pentagon, then?"

"Altmann."

"How can that be? You said that your men verified Altmann was dead. So did Salvatori."

"Dammit, I know what I said!" The general stiffened, then flexed his fingers and calmed. "Twenty years ago, I would have stuck a pistol in your mouth, blown your fucking brains out, and thrown your carcass in the river. All this would have ended with that."

"Twenty years ago, you might have won that fight, general."

"Don't think I still can't, young Hannigan."

Kenna had no intention of finding out. She had forgotten about the pain that racked her body. Now, it was replaced by a chilling numbness throughout her entire being. Was this her body warning of pending death?

"I only want the truth about Senator Chamberlain and Devon Whyte. You can take Altmann, or whatever his code name is this week, out in the trees, rip his head off, and shit in his neck for all I care."

"If I find the bastard, that's exactly what I'll do."

There was a lengthy pause. Treadway's hand was atop the cross that bore his father's name. *"Taps"* played in his mind. The entire Army of the Potomac converged on the positions held by J.E.B. Stuart. The general looked up with red eyes and hesitated but an instant.

"I was up for promotion from Europe to the Pentagon, what I had worked for my entire career. I couldn't afford a blemish on my record. But I was being flanked, both by Morningstar and our own government."

"So, personal pride won out over duty."

"Hell, our own press betrayed our agents in Europe, and no one here did a damn thing about it. At one point, all our agents were going to mutiny if we didn't protect them. That would have been disastrous."

"But the Joint Chiefs wouldn't have seen it that way."

"Bull shit! I did what was right. If they want me, they can come get me. Proof is hard to come by in the covert world, and that's the way we operated. The way it will remain … on a need-to-know basis."

"And *'into the valley of death rode the six-hundred'*—"

"General George Marshall said: *'I can't expect loyalty*

from the Army if I do not give it'," Treadway snapped.

Kenna moved in for the kill. "Chamberlain knew Morningstar was alive because of the swap with the Bishop. He thought Altmann was dead because you had it verified, right?"

"Yes," the general said.

"But now, we discover that Altmann may be alive."

"And looking to deal with you, it appears."

"He could easily have killed me in the parking lot. Why didn't he?"

"He wants you to keep the Marshals out of it, or at least wants them more concerned with you than him, until he finishes why he's here."

"And why would that be, general?"

Kenna felt J.E.B. Stuart challenging the left. Treadway pulled out a cigar. Staring up into the rain, he allowed it to wet his face. He bit off the end of the tobacco, spit it into his palm, and pocketed the waste.

"Everyone in this city has something in their past to hide, young Hannigan," Treadway said. "Suffice it to say that Morningstar put us ten years ahead of the Taliban, maybe more. He got people and information out we never could have. I didn't betray that loyalty to anyone; I damn sure won't now."

"Not even for the murder of a U.S. Senator?"

"Not even the president's!"

"I've come too far, general. I'm the one being flanked."

"Then, live with the consequences."

"The last time, it was *'die with them'*."

"As you see fit," Treadway said, turning to the brown Cadillac.

Kenna watched the aging warrior enter his chariot and drive off. The general's car turned off Schley Drive. Caesar stared back at her from the driver's window. Kenna imagined the general looking back at Afghanistan that way when he shipped out.

She lifted her face to the rain as a touch of blue eased through the gray line. Like a child, she allowed the rain to fall onto her tongue. Once again, it tasted like dead fish. She wanted to spit but couldn't on such hallowed ground. With disgust, she swallowed.

Treadway had divulged the monumental mistake he made in Europe that could never be made right. Someone else had to do it for him. Kenna knew that the general had intentionally spoken around the issue to allow her to draw the correct conclusion. They had gone full circle on

Morningstar, only to eventually get to the one man who had the biggest reason to kill Harvey Chamberlain … Bernard Altmann.

By meeting, Kenna believed that Terror Treadway was giving her permission to go after Altmann. The general had done so without saying it, without admitting the German was alive, without saying that he had failed in his duty. What the general wanted more than anything was to protect his career and Morningstar's identity. Perhaps, in a strange way, Treadway was trying to regain his father's respect; even say he was sorry. She believed the general had done just that.

My God, it was that simple, Gran, Kenna thought. The man who killed Chamberlain was Bernard Altmann, and all the peripheral was a smoke screen created by everyone else with something to hide.

"I hate this fucking city!" she screamed to the thousands of dead who could not hear.

XLVI

In a conference hall of the Clubhouse, Kenna sat through Gloria Chamberlain's press conference. Tear-soaked eyes caked with make-up hid her intoxication … and not her grief … as she spoke of the late senator's greatness. She did so without ever mentioning his name or calling him *'my husband'*. He was referred to as *'the senator'* or *'such a great man'*.

Red, white, and blue ribbons were draped from ceiling to floor. At the back of the podium stood U.S. and Illinois flags at half-mast. She wore a black tight-fitting dress … too short for mourning … that displayed her well-sculpted figure from top to bottom. The black cap was in bad taste; it was similar to what Jackie wore when she buried Jack.

"Why are men of such great vision always the ones to die early, swept from their mission on earth into the great beyond?" Gloria bellowed. "Why do programs for the poor, for the working, for the enlisted grades of the military have to suffer in an economic system created for the wealthy elite? Better yet, why can't these programs not just continue but flourish?"

And who better to do so? Kenna thought with contempt.

Gloria had been right in a politically hypocritical sense: she didn't believe a word she spoke, with one marked exception. Someone should carry on Chamberlain's work. Someone should keep the torch of eternal hope alive for those who sought deliverance from the slums and to the Promised Land of Devon Whyte's America. But the late senator and chairman's voices said it so much better and without insincere drunken conviction.

The crowd was riveted as if listening to the reincarnate of the senator himself … obviously the same speechwriter. At her side, colleagues from the Party smiled and pumped their heads up and down like bobble head dolls at a ballgame. Bridgewater was first to applaud when she finished, fueling a standing ovation. There were no questions asked by the press … adlibbing, not her forte … for she was too grief-stricken. At the end, though, there was time and enough self-control for lots of smiling, palm pressing, and cheek kissing.

Confident from the acceptance, Gloria strode to the back of the Clubhouse conference hall and stood at the exit. New believers wished her well as they passed, offering never-to-be-accepted assistance in her time of grief. As these men and women left the building, their heads bobbed up and down, and their fingers snapped into the air. They were convinced Gloria Chamberlain was her late husband's replacement.

Kenna watched her movements, amused at their absurdity, although completely understanding. The kiss placed on her cheek from none other than Malcolm Bridgewater confirmed the afternoon as the greatest display of human hypocrisy and calamity Kenna had ever witnessed. The Tennessee *'Mouth of the South'* stared her down when she walked out.

The thought of confronting the self-appointed Senator of Illinois unsettled her stomach. When Kenna left the room, she believed she could have walked straight to Gloria's journey's end and ordered the drink for her. Doing so did not appeal to Kenna at the moment.

Gloria knew her husband was being blackmailed and went to the one man with whom she had always confided: Malcolm Bridgewater. According to Kenna's father, that had begun when Gloria was but a teen as a page. She and Bridgewater had a sordid, hot affair that drove the senator's wife back to Tennessee, from which she would never return. She would die there a few years later. It was the senator who introduced the young beauty to an up-and-coming Senator from Illinois. For the guarantee of a good life, Gloria agreed to supply Bridgewater with information on her husband if he ever strayed too far from the Party line.

When Harvey wanted to expose the illegal campaign

contributions, she defied him. She betrayed the only man who ever loved her, thereby remaining an inconsequential fish in the cesspool of the nation's capital. In the end, her betrayal indirectly cost the senator his life.

She was a waste of good air, Gloria Chamberlain. For, in the end, she believed her husband had a choice. *'Until the instant that bullet entered his brain, Ms. Hannigan.'*

Kenna hurried outside and caught Bridgewater politicking with a group of *moneymen*. They made unfriendly eye contact, but Kenna was undeterred. Jimmy McDowell was nowhere to be seen, and Kenna believed she knew why. When the meeting broke up and Malcolm turned to walk away, Kenna cut him off.

In her mind, Kenna saw the lights flooding the golf course, the government issue vehicles destroying all in their wake. She felt deep sorrow for Harvey Chamberlain.

A naïve young man had not known what awaited him on The Hill when he won the seat back in 1997. Proudly, it had been a Democratic hold that election. Chamberlain was a Democrat cast in the mold of Devon Whyte's American dream. He believed in the righteousness of America, of its people, and the responsibility of government to all the people. As a young senator, Harvey Chamberlain had no way of knowing that twenty some years later, he would be set up for the biggest fall of his life: his own death.

Blackmail had turned to murder as a means to political end. It corrupted the nation's halls of government from bottom to top. Kenna had no desire to fight the battle to right the wrongs within the political system or those involved. They could clean their own latrines.

There was, however, one exception.

"Life's fragile, Malcolm. I see it in your eyes. Can you feel it? What little is left of your conscience is fighting you."

The politician had broken a three-decade-old family trust with lies and deceit. Bridgewater's stare was like two silent daggers. A single hot, broken breath. The senator looked beyond Kenna toward the swimming pools and the 11th tee box.

"Two murders, not one, and now maybe a third, all over illegal campaign funding. Chamberlain was buying Altmann's silence with the Party's approval. You thought involving me would help with the cover-up. Then, too late, you realized that Altmann wasn't in the mood to negotiate, and I wasn't playing along either. That's when you changed."

"Balderdash! You don't know what you're preaching."

"Gowen funneled the money into the Party for this last

election, possibly the one before," Kenna said, and knew it went way beyond that. "When Gowen informed Altmann, things got messy. Money became the issue more than life. No, Party became the issue. Why did you betray Harvey Chamberlain?"

"Harvey Chamberlain … betrayed his country."

"There's a difference between betraying your Party and your country, Malcolm. He wanted to expose Gowen's work."

"It was Harvey's idea!"

The old man leaned forward, his lips thin, his eyes narrow. Age spots were pronounced against ghostly white skin.

"You might as well have pulled the trigger, Malcolm."

"I didn't force him to …" The old man raised a shaking finger to Kenna's face. "This is over! Do you hear me? Over!"

"How can it be over, Malcolm? There's still a murderer out there."

"Dammit, don't be such a blind fool!"

"Fool?" Kenna said calmly, though wanting to scream it. "What's more important than the truth?"

"We are not in the business … of telling the truth! We

are in the business … of running this … God damned government!"

Kenna's greatest fear had become reality. There were no honest men in Washington. Her old family friend wanted her to back away from multiple murders. Malcolm Bridgewater had become a cold, ruthless Caesar in a city where the death of a few people was akin to taking a piss in the gutter.

Here, Kenna knew she was considered nothing more than a sentimental fool. Gran Lockwood was once again right: *They lead themselves into the moors to be eaten by the wolves.'*

Kenna pulled a memory stick from her pocket and twirled it between fingers. "This is what you want, right Malcolm? The Avery Gowen recording about the contributions. And you thought you got it all when you bought the paper."

"It cost us a fortune."

"Not nearly enough," Kenna said. "He mentions your name. I think I'll see what honesty is worth."

"Honesty is for life … outside the beltway, girl."

Kenna stiffened and shook her head. "My God, I think you mean that."

"It's reality, not fiction," Bridgewater said, suddenly

weak, sitting on a nearby bench.

"Wiggy discovered how Gowen collected the illegal foreign campaign contributions, how he made all of the transfers," Kenna said, leaning on a chair. "We know how Gowen was paid and when. More importantly, we know where and by whom."

"How can—"

Kenna interrupted: "Did you know that your messenger boy pilfered a few million off the top while the money was on its way here?"

The old man's eyes narrowed; he lifted a frail finger. The once imposing political giant nearly collapsed. "You—"

"Interpol is helping until we sort through this mess. Gowen will never see a penny of that money."

"But you—"

"I haven't stuttered, Malcolm. Gowen set up the meetings, not only between Chamberlain and the German but also with Devon Whyte."

"What … does that have to … do with … me?"

Senator Malcolm Bridgewater allowed his hands to fall slowly to the arms of the bench. Mortality was pronounced across his body, as Kenna had seen at no other time. The old man gathered the strength to look up and coughed. He covered his mouth and sucked in a breath. Another deep throaty cough followed; he expectorated over his hand. Shaking, he wiped it clean with an expensive monogrammed handkerchief. It seemed fitting. Hollow, tired eyes lifted.

"I … cannot allow you to make this … public. It will ruin … too many people." The old warrior extended a wrinkled hand. "Besides, he … is long gone. You've … won."

"I said all along, Malcolm, all I wanted was the murderer." The old man looked blankly at her. "You should have listened."

Wide-eyed, Malcolm Bridgewater's stare was confused. He was alone. The old man's eyes narrowed as Kenna stepped forward. A hand trembled outward and grabbed the memory stick. Kenna did not let go. Bridgewater grabbed Kenna's arm hard. Kenna released her old family friend's hand. The youthful vigor evaporated, and Bridgewater turned ashen, leaning back, breathing irregular. His chest pounded, his hands and lips white and trembling. Kenna placed the back of her hand on Malcolm Bridgewater's forehead. It was cold clammy. The senator shoved it away and forced himself upright.

"Don't stop her … from getting … the seat. Don't … stop it. She must … have … his seat," the old man insisted, followed by a few quick, shallow breaths. "Dorothy—"

"She isn't here."

"Please tell me … you won't … stop it," Bridgewater whispered, balled Kenna's shirt in a fist, and pulled her close. "Don't let them … make it public!"

For a moment, Kenna imagined covering Bridgewater's nose and mouth until he stopped breathing. She flicked thin hair off the old man's forehead.

"This fucking city's a sickness, Malcolm, you miserable son-of-a-bitch. What have you done?" Bridgewater's pulse was racing, erratic. "You never deserved the White House.

"You told me that in this city, you don't make friends, you make deals," Kenna continued. "Since I no longer consider you a friend, I'll make you a deal."

A strained glare asked the unspoken question.

"You and I both know what's on this stick isn't the half of it. My condition is this: Everyone involved must resign their position or retire within four months. If all of you don't, I'll take it public, and I'll get every one of you impeached … beginning with you."

XLVII

Kenna stood behind the corner brick pilaster of a south Baltimore row house. Roots Hobson plodded down the middle of the block and passed a family Ice Cream shop that advertised *'Shaved Ice'*. Hobson yelled something into the door, raised his thumb, and laughed. He smiled at a young red-haired mother pushing an infant in a stroller.

Hobson crossed the street and walked to a red brick building that leaned ever so slightly toward the alley. Age cracks zigzagged up the front wall, and tar streaked the side where it was stained by years of water runoff. Tall window trims were faded, weathered, and chipped. Windows of the top two floors had long ago been boarded.

Kenna wanted to believe many things about Hobson but knew Gran Lockwood's analogy applied: *'A criminal is a criminal simply because that is what he is.'*

Wiggy was angered that he hadn't seen his mistake about Hobson. On the Clubhouse veranda, the superintendent had lit his pipe with a stick match from the pub he now entered. The old man visited the Senator from Massachusetts several hours ago. Was Roots Hobson's day of reckoning upon him, or had he been guaranteed protection that no one could undo?

A Guinness sign above the pub's door was held by a single bolt; painted letters below it read: *'O'Leary's - All Irish Since 1990'*. Removing her sunglasses as she entered, Kenna paused to allow her eyes to adjust to the darkness. Heavy air struck her, thick with smoke and the 30-year-old stale aroma of spirits. The room was long and narrow, with wood floors and cracked plaster walls. A leaning bar with foot rail stood before a single row of five tables on the left. Two single-bulb lights dangled from the 14-foot-high ceiling, providing a yellowish glow that never reached the floor. Dull but natural light filtered through an aged, unwashed curtain.

Curious stares filled Kenna with a rush of unfamiliarity. Old and young alike, they were men who hadn't touched razors in a week and whose Guinness was in their hands before breakfast. Hobson blended well, though totally contrary to his position at the Country Club.

Kenna made her way to the bar and ordered a lager. She got a frown in return, and a stout slid before her. Roots Hobson tossed a coin on the bar. Glass raised; Kenna did not turn when an elbow touched her.

"Call yer lap dog. I've had better men than Heffernan after me. And none of 'em got close."

"Yet, here I stand."

Hobson leaned against the bar. "Ye should be askin' if what yer riskin' is worth it."

"And what am I risking?"

Hobson shrugged and responded softly, "Everythin'."

"You're a long way from Ireland, Roots."

"Look around, cailín … not as far as ye might think."

Kenna wanted to ask about Hobson's mother but saw no need. She knew what she wanted. His mother had taken him away from the street thugs of Derry, away from the IRA. They had made a new home in England, where, as MI5 reported, she apparently died. At that point, young Hobson fell off the map.

Or, that was the story, what everyone was supposed to believe, perhaps the Mass senator most of all: *'A criminal is a criminal …'* Wiggy uncovered more.

When Hobson's mother moved her son to England, it was not to be away from the Derry thugs. Soon after her husband's death, Roots' mother fell in love with Father Bergen, whose IRA philosophies and activities were legendary. A man of many cloths, Bergen was far removed from the priesthood but had the credentials to mask his true intentions. Together, they took the young lad to England to be Father Bergen's instrument of will. Roots' mother did not die; she and Bergen disappeared into the Eastern Bloc after her son was put in place at Cambridge. After that, contact came through Bergen's biggest financial supporter in Germany: Bernard Altmann.

"Your problems began in England, right?" Kenna asked.

The terrorist turned aged eyes, hand firm around his whiskey. "They're not problems, lass, when they're solutions."

Idealism is the birthplace of terror. Kenna believed someone once wrote. Conversely, though, *birth itself was often the foundation of terror and tyranny.*

Hobson narrowed those aged eyes. "If ye've never fought for freedom, lass, don't criticize the means or the methods."

"Your mother buried one of her men in the fight for freedom. She didn't want to bury another."

"*'Peace through political process'*, she preached, God bless her misguided soul."

"Have you ever asked yourself if she was right?"

Hobson slapped his glass on the bar. "Ye can't negotiate with the fuckin' British!"

"Here, here," every man in the pub bellowed, followed

by the clank of mug against mug, the thud of hands against wood.

"So, she contacted your cousin," Kenna said. Hobson winced. "An influential American political family that pulled some strings to get you work at Cambridge. But you never worked there; never gave up the cause."

"Couldn'a give it up, ye mean, lass. How's a man give up the fight for what he believes?" Hobson bit his lower lip and stretched his hands as if to hide the scars.

"It's a bad memory," Kenna said and pointed at Hobson's hands. "It crippled you."

"Ye've stuck yer nose in the way of the butcher's axe, lass."

"Harrods or Deal Barracks?" Kenna asked.

"Aye, another British lie." Hobson took a drink. "And what do ye know about the bloody fuckin' British other than the bloody fuckin' Queen?"

The balance of Hobson's tirade fell into Kenna's subconscious as that word rumbled through her mind like a freight train. The *'Queen'*! The *'bloody fuckin' Queen'*! She sucked in a mouthful of air, followed by a jolt of stout … Harrods … Deal Barracks … the Queen!

Hobson paused and took a drink. "Yer diggin' yer own

grave."

"It all makes sense now. I didn't know until a few hours ago that you had been in contact with Chamberlain over the last month."

Hobson snickered. "Yer dreamin', lass."

"You knew Chamberlain was going to be at the 18th on Saturday night. You went to discuss a particular problem he was having with a German. He wanted to talk to you because you had known each other a very long time ago, and he thought you would help him deal with it."

"I think that's about enough, lass."

"But when you crossed the green, you found him dead. You took the list from his pocket, crossed the green again, then went and called the police. I didn't remember it until later that the footprints going away from the senator left traces of sand. So, you see, there really isn't any lost time. You had to rake the trap after you moved him and before you left."

Hobson's strong grip fell on Kenna's wrist. The smell of Hobson's fury filled her nostrils. It was a combination of fear, of hatred, and of revenge. A thick gray eyebrow lifted a glassy glare. Hobson stuck a callused finger into his fresh drink, stirred twice, and then licked it. When he didn't answer, Kenna pointed to the old man's hands and continued:

"You started this work when you came over from England. But you had no credentials, so they were created for you. Rich, influential people have the power to do that."

"Ye don'a really want to open the coffin, lass! Ye just might fit inside."

"You had plenty of reasons to silence Chamberlain and Whyte. Especially if they were threatening your U.S. safe-haven."

"There's no threat."

"Not now," Kenna agreed. "Not unless I tell the press about the deal that brought you here."

Silence followed. The front window brightened from the evening sun. It was humid and hot. Sweat moistened Kenna's underarms and the pit of her back. Blade hitting metal, a small fan behind the bar squealed. A young couple strolled hand-in-hand to a small fountain at the building across the street. They hugged and kissed.

Hobson's hollow black eyes stared beyond Kenna for an instant and through the tall glass entrance door, perhaps to a place and a time far away. What was it Hobson saw: failure? Failure to kill a Queen he and his *freedom* fighters despised more than everything and wanted to kill at the risk of being killed themselves?

"That was a fuckin' British lie, lass!" Hobson digressed and twisted his hands in the light. "This happened because I couldn'a do Harrods, not because I did!"

"Then, you were there?"

"Nay. I didn'a have it in me blood. But the bleedin' British blamed me. That's how I got these."

"So, the British tortured you?" Kenna knew Roots Hobson had been perfecting this story for many years.

Hobson sipped his whiskey. "Much like ye, young lass, they wanted information. They didn'a get it either."

"So, you puff out your chest, bragging that the British destroyed your life without anything to show for it? I don't buy it."

"It's ye who says I have nothin' ta show for it."

The terrorist's credo set Kenna's soul afire. Terror was an instrument of good. Hatred for good, hatred justified the cause and the means. Kenna looked at Hobson's hands once again: a bomb-maker's hands. The Queen … what could have been with her scattered in a thousand bloody pieces on the street in front of Buckingham Palace? Had they ever thought of who the targets would be if all their enemies were exterminated?

"The Chess Club!" Kenna insisted.

"It's a long time ago, lass. They aren't important," Hobson lied.

"The blackmailer thought so. You must have thought so, too. You tried to sell it to the Party through Avery Gowen."

Hobson inhaled his whiskey and laughed. "Correction, lass: I didn'a need ta sell it. They bought me silence long ago."

"And Gowen?"

"Let's say I was asked to work with the lad," Hobson said.

"They bought Harvey Chamberlain's silence, as well."

"Aye. But as ye said, ye see who's standin' here."

"Let me take a stab at it, then. The King, Bernard Altmann, German agent, planned it." Hobson did not bite. "Father Bergen organized a private study group, and the Bishop put it together. Chamberlain was the Rook, working to become a member of the American Ivory Tower crowd. Whyte was the Black Knight, a youth brought up in an era of racial hatred, but he didn't believe in violence.

"For several months, they debated theories of Social Equality and injustice," Kenna continued. "They talked about passive protest, of Gandhi, and of Martin Luther King; as well as armed insurrection: Lenin, Che Guevara, Mao, and Ho Chi Minh. They theorized on how to transform the West into the Utopian ideal."

"You all but said Father Bergen was a terrorist. Why would he work with allies of the fuckin' British?" Roots Hobson stopped with a glimmer.

"What easier way to get to the Queen?" Kenna looked into the mirror. "I can see it as plain as you in the glass."

"And what be the end of this fairytale?"

"I just want the King, the German. And I want you to help me get him."

Hobson narrowed those ancient eyes. They were wrinkled and worn from years of sun and perhaps even the detail with which he had previously worked. Another drink followed, and the brush of a long strand of hair behind an ear.

"So, ye think it was the King, lassie? Well, that's nigh on impossible. The King was killed years ago by U.S. agents in Europe."

"That's what you all believed, and that's why two of you are dead," Kenna said. "The King's come for paybacks for being betrayed."

Hobson's laugh was half-naked. "I will tell ye, lass …
only because I like ye … that the business with Chamberlain
and Whyte has nothin' to do with the Chess Club. And
nothin' to do with the King. Leave it at that."

"Your eyes say otherwise. Everything says otherwise."

The campaign funding issue crept into Kenna's mind's
eye. Was there more? Did the *serpent's will* slither deeper
than even she and Wiggy believed possible?

Hobson pulled the glass to his lips and swallowed the
drink. He shoved it towards the young bartender, who
undoubtedly doubled as a bouncer. When the glass was
returned full, the young man didn't move away; he leaned
on the bar in front of Kenna.

"And now, I'll be drinkin' alone, lassie. One way or
ta'other."

Kenna turned but paused as outside air filled her nostrils.
Once again, the smell of dead fish filled her. She dropped
money on the bar and pointed at Hobson's glass.

"You said it was impossible that the German's returned.
I don't agree. I think he wants to find who betrayed him a
couple decades ago. Maybe he would also like to know who
betrayed him six years ago.

"So, you see, you were the benefactor. In a way, all of

you were," Kenna continued. "Your cousin cut a deal that brought you here and kept you from rotting away in Hull Prison."

The old superintendent was silent, not liking the direction she was going. He rolled the glass and took a sip. A quick glance to the bartender, then to his other friends.

"To get you out, your cousin had to give up the King and many others from the fight in Derry. You're the only one who walked away free."

A rumble of low voices filled the room. Hobson's reaction was one of calm, but fear filled his eyes. "That's a bloody fuckin' British lie."

"We'll find out soon enough. Because he's coming for the rest of you unless I get him first." Kenna finished her stout and slapped the mug on the bar. "Even though you can't help me, it's ironic that it'll be a dainty lass such as me that saves your miserable life."

"I can take care of meself, lassie."

"Not this time, me boyo," Kenna chortled. "You may be farther from Ireland than you think, after all. Altmann's alive and coming after you," Kenna said. "With that, Bishop, I'll leave you to your drinks … and prayers."

XLVIII

Kenna walked along the narrow path through the dark trees, two bottles of beer in-hand. Jimmy McDowell sat alone on a bench thinking, an elbow on a knee, hand pressed against his cheek. It was hot, muggy. Sweat glistened on the outside of the brown glass as she handed it to him.

"Mind if I interrupt?"

"A beautiful woman bringing beer is no interruption," McDowell said, looking up. "But I said I'd buy."

Kenna moved into the shade of a tall White Oak. She stared at an array of Black-Eyed Susan in a nearby planter and pointed at McDowell's shoes.

"I didn't know you were a golfer, Jimmy."

"How I relax."

"Relaxing … a lifetime ago," Kenna said, took a sip, and savored the ice-cold American brew. Her eyes did not leave the agent.

She had lost track of the body parts that ached. Thinking of each new pain made previous ones reappear. She rolled the bottle on her forehead and on the back of her hands to soothe away a foul mood. Clouds formed overhead; they smelled of rain … no, the damn dead fish.

"I should have stuck to journalism."

"You don't believe that," McDowell said.

"You're right. I should have taken my inheritance and gone to the Bahamas to live on the beach."

McDowell stared through the trees and chuckled, more of frustration than humor. "What I would have done."

"If not for the higher duty, eh, Jimmy?" Kenna said. McDowell snickered. "You've been AWOL … and missed Gloria Chamberlain's press conference."

"No stomach for it … too much to sort out."

"Like, why you didn't stop Chamberlain that night."

McDowell looked up through swollen red eyes. "I tried."

"And now you think, not hard enough."

"I don't know what to think," McDowell said.

"Chamberlain actually came to you first, didn't he?" she asked. The agent hesitated and took a drink to mask it. "You two had become close over the years, perhaps even closer than your relationship with Malcolm."

"It was different."

"Yeah, he had something you wanted," Kenna said.

"He promised me the truth about what happened to my

father if I helped expose the campaign contributions." McDowell took a drink.

"But there was this intense loyalty inside fighting against you, wasn't there?"

"Malcolm's always been good to me—"

"Until Harvey told you about the campaign contributions. Then, you realized that maybe you had been used like everyone else."

"Things are never what they seem, Kenna."

"Like in Chamberlain's office with Charlie Sommer when I interrupted," Kenna said to McDowell's surprise. "I owe you for the bruised ribs."

"I didn't mean to hurt you; just didn't want to be caught."

"A couple bumps, nothing major," Kenna said. "You were looking for the report Chamberlain promised you."

"Yes, but it wasn't there. Now, I guess I'll never know." McDowell turned.

"I hate to say it, Jimmy, but you're probably right." Kenna took another drink and pointed the bottle. "And that's why you agreed to deliver the recordings to Chamberlain's drop box."

"Agent Edelman set up the wiretaps and got me the recordings," McDowell said. "We kept it hush-hush; the way

Harvey wanted it."

Kenna now realized what Deputy Director Anderson meant by Agent Edelman *working outside the parameters of her assignment'*. No doubt, Miriam Edelman would become another victim of this Washington game. Hopefully, she had a bargaining chip up her sleeve. If not, she was positive Wiggy could help find one.

"Well, you made the call, Jimmy."

"I was thinking about my wife and son." McDowell took a drink. "It was easier when I was single. I was stupid then."

"No," Kenna corrected. "You were young. It's always easy to overlook the obvious when you're young … or just blind. Avoiding the reality of what we don't like comes with the territory."

McDowell shook his head. "I worked hard to be the best. I owed Malcolm that in return for how he helped me."

"At one time, Malcolm Bridgewater was a great man." Kenna hated using the past tense.

"Still is," McDowell insisted. "His priorities have changed."

"Sorry, Jimmy, but you're wrong. And I think you know it. His priorities have remained the same, as have his methods. It's the world around him that's changed. Malcolm refused to make the transition or was incapable of making it.”

“It’s no different for any of us, I suppose.”

“To change.” Kenna raised the bottle, and they toasted. “Only time will tell if this makes you a better or a bitter man.”

“So, what happens now, Kenna?”

“That depends on you, Jimmy. You have something I want.”

“Yeah, I know, could cost me my career.”

“Probably will. But you’re here, which indicates you’ve weighed that option.”

McDowell turned a sharp stare. “Guess so.”

“I know Malcolm’s been like a father to you. He’s been like an uncle to me. Betraying him is like betraying your country. But—”

“He reacts to things now without thinking of the true consequences. He wouldn’t have done that twenty years ago.” McDowell flipped his arm across the back of the bench. “He got sucked into this game without realizing there wasn’t a way out.”

“Don’t let the lost old man façade fool you, Jimmy. Malcolm knew exactly what he was getting into.”

"When I say he didn't know, I mean it. Chamberlain came up with the plan years ago, but he never implemented it. Someone, an outsider, brought Gowen in to do that. Financial need outweighed good conscience."

'An outsider' resounded through Kenna's mind. "It outweighed legality, Jimmy."

McDowell hesitated, knowing Kenna was right. "Chamberlain wanted the Party to maintain control of the White House so badly he bet everything on it. He wanted a Party dynasty."

"He wanted to be the next president, Jimmy. And Malcolm agreed."

"Exactly. The Party was willing to do anything to make that happen. Gowen acted on his own and got the money they needed to win. Nobody questioned it then. Hell, I didn't either until a couple days ago."

"What happened?"

"Chamberlain came to Malcolm and said he was being blackmailed by the German." He paused, reflecting, swallowing more beer. "I was there. Malcolm was furious."

"You would be, too, if you saw your life's work going up in smoke."

"He made everyone leave. He and Chamberlain were

alone for a long time. I've never heard the old man yell like that. It lasted over an hour before they were joined by the Massachusetts senator and Devon Whyte."

"After Malcolm came to see me?"

"No, before. They were in there most of the morning, and when they came out, Malcolm was a changed man." McDowell leaned forward to plant his elbows on his knees. "That's the first time I heard Altmann's name. I was told to get the Marshals involved, quietly, discretely, but quickly."

"But Chamberlain wanted to pay him to get rid of him."

"Right. He changed course and wanted me to help him cover-up the campaign contribution issue. But what could I do? The damage had already been done."

"So, you did what Malcolm wanted and contacted Miriam Edelman?"

"No, Vinny Salvatori. Miriam had already stuck her neck out enough," McDowell said. "I had known Salvatori since he entered the service and felt I could trust him to be my eyes and ears on the inside."

"What happened next?"

"That's when Malcolm took charge."

"Of the cover-up," Kenna said and did not ask.

McDowell hung his head. "Yeah. A day he regrets now,

I think. But he was just trying to save the Party."

"No, to buy the presidency." Kenna paused when a golfcart sped past.

"Politicians in the past have taken unnecessary actions to preserve their power base. This is no different," McDowell said, very close to pleading.

"That doesn't make it right, Jimmy. Why did Malcolm drag me into this and then abandon me?"

"When Charlie Sommer came to Malcolm asking questions about Chamberlain, Malcolm passed your name. We thought you could help defuse all of this. That was before Chamberlain was killed. His death changed everything."

"This is all old news, Jimmy, and not what I'm looking for."

"They believed they could control it up front. It was Malcolm's plan to buy enough time to get everything they needed."

"For what?"

"To make it all disappear."

"What do you mean, *all*?"

"When the game changed, that's when Malcolm started using you. They learned that Altmann wasn't here simply to collect for helping on the campaign funding. He wanted more."

"What?"

"That's when Malcolm took me out of the loop," McDowell said. "When the operation went black, I knew everything had gone wrong. It became his own private war."

"With others, the body count," Kenna said. "Who can tell me what Altmann's after, Jimmy? Malcolm won't."

"There's only one guy."

"You mean, besides the killer," Kenna corrected.

"Right," McDowell said, swallowing the last of his beer. "Avery Gowen was the middleman for everything. He was in constant contact with the outsider and went to Germany, funneled the donations, even sought out the Asian investors."

Kenna didn't like the way McDowell used the word *'investors'*. But if what he was saying was true, then they were investing. And if it were true, foreign governments, manipulating the U.S. political system, were buying influence with the U.S. Government. People got executed for that during wars, hot or cold.

"You keep saying *'outsider'*, who do you mean?"

"He was Gowen's private contact. None of us ever knew

him or what he did."

"How do you know this about Gowen?"

"Miriam Edelman: We've been friends a long time." McDowell paused. Jimmy's eyes said that he and Agent Edelman had been more than friends at one time. "She was onto him before being reassigned."

"Tell her thanks. She's helped more than once."

"I hate to say it, but everything points to Malcolm."

"It does, at that. I was with him after the press conference. And when I left, I got the distinct impression he had put on a show just to get rid me."

"I'd help, but—"

Kenna held up a hand. "You need to do some personal damage control, Jimmy."

"No, I need to help you end this."

"Not if I fail."

"Gowen won't talk unless you persuade him."

"I agree, but he's gone underground … deep. If Wiggy can't find him, he's buried."

"That's why I'm here," McDowell said, standing and holding out a piece of paper. "I can't do much, but I can give him to you."

XLIX

Avery Gowen stepped from the shadows of the dimly lit bar, stopped to look both ways down the street, then dropped down the single step to the brick sidewalk. He leaned into the light, misty rain that flicked past the streetlight like fireflies on a kamikaze mission directly at him.

Kenna flinched to move forward, then paused alongside the old stone building, cursing. Gowen was not alone. The late senator's co-conspirator looked different, stronger than Kenna remembered. The facial features were chiseled, the stride that of confidence. It was in stark contrast to the arrogant, misguided little man who stood before them at the apartment. The pretender was apparently a master at changing outward appearances like TV channels, allowing an opposite double to surface at will.

Just like the argument on the 18th green, she thought. Kenna stepped through the shadows on the opposite side of the street, concentrating on Gowen's every move. A would-be lover was jerked into his grasp but a half step behind. Kenna was not surprised when Gowen threw the smaller man against a tan stone building, pinning him there with a hand locked on his throat. Gowen said something Kenna could not hear, then kissed the young man hard on the lips. It was anything but passionate. An umbrella concealed their embrace for a lengthy moment. Kenna anticipated a lifeless form slumping to the pavement next to Gowen, another victim of Washington's vicious games.

Kenna again recalled the meeting at Gowen's Arlington flat. The great pretender, Gowen, had fooled her, Wiggy, and most of Washington's self-proclaimed aristocracy. Gowen's game was not weak; it was manipulation, power, and control.

The smaller man rejected Gowen's forceful advance, pleading momentarily. Gowen struck his face open-handed. The younger man's eyes bulged; parted lips were poised to protest as the pretender struck again. Cowering, the partner wept, lifted a hand to the side of his face but did not move away. Gowen raised a backhand to strike again, then paused and lowered his partner's hand to kiss it. The chameleon held the shaking hand against a cheek for a long moment, saying something again, then looked up and gently rubbed the point of impact on his would-be lover's skin.

Gowen laughed, whipping the rain from the younger man's hair and forehead. He patted the companion on the cheek as he would a dog, then kissed his snout. There was laughter from the pretender, hesitantly from his would-be victim.

Kenna had seen actions like this before and found herself void of emotion. Realizing she had put her ultra-conservative Texas upbringing behind her, she knew that Avery Gowen was nothing more than another suspect, another potential witness, another source of information: a very important one, at that.

Gowen's slick words and soft eyes may have deceived a would-be lover this evening, as they had Kenna and Wiggy, but no more. Kenna was wiser to the city's ways than that night standing next to Harvey Chamberlain's lifeless body. Smarter than when she had walked into Avery Gowen's ingenious plastic world. Mostly, she had learned the games and their harsh realities.

Yes, it was the games that fueled this cesspool of hypocrisy that ran the country. Kenna found herself being more frightened about the bleak prospects of her nation's future than she was of failing to solve Harvey Chamberlain's murder. She was certain the latter was but a hair's breadth away. She would fail only if she joined Chamberlain in what Rod Serling called the *'totally unconscious void'*.

She was so close she could smell it, and the killer knew it. They all knew it, every politician, every pretender, and yes, even her father. Fear penetrated their once impenetrable domain. She was about to tear down the imaginary walls that separated the political aristocracy from the ordinary man and expose the hypocrisy that American politicians deemed as their inalienable right.

Kenna was not afraid of the unknown or of death. *'It is the only constant of life,'* Gran Lockwood had often said. Forget taxes, don't pay them if you don't want too. You just must be willing to go to jail … *'But there is no avoiding the Grim Reaper.'*

The ulcer announced she was in for the fight of her life in the next few minutes. Why had she come alone? She should have known better and brought Wiggy. But she had accepted Gowen's vulnerability; they both had. Now, there was no turning back.

Kenna stepped from the shadows and dropped off the curb. Gowen's partner locked onto her. Gowen reacted to his lover's protective posturing; his stare spun. His make-up was rain-streaked; Gowen's face a caricature of Alice Cooper. She stiffened with doubled fists.

"Pussy fuckin' Tracy!" the pretender shouted.

Gowen's voice was no longer meager, no longer pleading. Kenna lifted her hands from her pockets as the two *lovers* walked back towards the bar. She angled across the street and lengthened her stride to cut them off. They did not run. Kenna reached the alleyway at the corner of the building, three steps before them. She stopped and held out a hand.

"We have to talk."

"You have a short memory," Gowen said, sidestepping behind his partner.

"You were involved in the blackmail, maybe even the killing of Chamberlain and Whyte."

Gowen remained behind his partner. A shield. "There's nothing you can do about it!"

"Put you in jail for a very long time."

Gowen laughed, deep and throaty, followed hesitantly by his partner. "My insurance policy from the big man says not."

"Altmann may have something else to say about that."

"Everyone's paid. It's over."

"Maybe not. You're a loose end. A piece of business, I think he said. Do you honestly believe he'll wait to find out if you betrayed him?"

"But I … oh, Puss, you wouldn't," Gowen said, wagged a finger in the air, and licked his lips.

Kenna took a step forward. In life's defining moments, Gran had told her many times, *'Always be prepared for the moment.'*

"I forgot to ask: have you checked your foreign accounts this evening?" Kenna smiled inside. "I think you will find them frozen."

Gowen pushed his partner forward and followed with a guttural yell. Kenna grabbed the lover's jacket, amazed at the thin man's strength, as she tried to throw him aside. The lover's hand went for Kenna's throat, but Kenna grabbed the arm and spun the lover around and into Gowen. At impact, the pretender grabbed Kenna's shirt. They death-danced in circles.

A folded umbrella slammed against Kenna's wrist at the same time her left leg was kicked. A sharp pain rifled through her thigh. If not for her grip on Gowen, she would have gone down. The lover jumped onto her back as Gowen turned. It was then she saw the rage in Gowen's eyes.

'The Israelis call it Krav Maga, Fiery. You may need it someday,' Wiggy had said.

Gowen swung, but Kenna caught it with a forearm and delivered an elbow to the small man's chin. Gowen stumbled back but lunged forward again. Kenna corralled him in an arm bar and forced them all into the shadows of the alley. The lover drove a fist against the back of Kenna's head until Kenna scurried backwards, slamming the lover against a wall. The leach's grip failed; he peeled off and slumped to the pavement.

Driving her shoulder into Gowen's solar plexus like a heavy bag, Kenna slammed the pretender against a dumpster; it jolted back a full foot. Gowen shrieked as air shot from his lungs; he crumpled to a knee. Kenna turned to the lover on her left as a fist caught her full across the mouth. Her lips numbed; she tasted blood. The lover swung again, wild.

Discipline. Kenna ducked, taking a glancing blow off a shoulder. She avoided a knee snapped at her groin and kicked the inside of the lover's planted leg. The blow landed square on the inside of the little man's knee. A snap echoed off the brick alley walls as the lover screamed and went down in a pool of stagnant water.

"You bitch! You fucking bitch!" the lover yelled. "You broke my leg!"

Kenna turned back too slow as Gowen lunged. Gowen's forehead caught Kenna in the numbers. The force drove them over Gowen's partner. They fell. Kenna's head slammed against the pavement; Gowen jumped atop her.

The dull impact of fists sent white flashes across Kenna's vision. Her right hand brushed something hard. She gripped it and rammed it into Gowen's exposed ribcage. The little man reeled back but turned a wild fist that cracked against

Kenna's jaw. Again, Kenna slammed the stubby metal pipe into Gowen's ribs. Gowen fell to the side, gasping for air. Kenna rolled to a knee, but Gowen ripped her shirt and scratched at her eyes.

Kenna swung the pipe with all her remaining strength, slamming it into the pretender's ribcage. The impact drove Gowen facedown onto the pavement like a dead bird. He wheezed for breath; his eyes lifted, still conscious. He reached for blood that poured from a broken nose. Kenna thought she detected a macabre smile on the pretender. With the pipe in her right hand, she gathered Gowen's lapel in a fist.

"We can do this all-fucking night if you want. Or you can tell me how to contact the German."

Gowen wiped blood from his face with the back of a hand. His eyes faded in and out, but the smile remained. "Fuck … you."

Kenna pulled him closer and raised the pipe again. Gowen flinched; the smile disappeared. "How do I find him?"

"You're the Puss!" Gowen snapped, then paused to stare at his would-be lover still reeling in the water. His eyes softened, a long pause. "He'll be at the Watergate tomorrow afternoon. He has unfinished business."

"What business?"

"Find out yourself, Puss."

Gowen pushed away but was unable to get free. Kenna dropped him and, with a foot, pushed him over backwards. The pretender's head smacked against the brick wall, but he lifted defiant eyes. There was no pain now, only pleasure.

"You need help, Avery?" a deep voice came from the end of the alley.

Kenna turned to see a mountain of a man blocking the only way from this trap. She raised the pipe. "This isn't your affair."

"It's my bar. That makes it my affair," the man said, then turned to Gowen's would-be lover.

"If you want to be in business tomorrow, drag that piece of shit out of here. Gowen and I have more to discuss."

Gowen motioned the big man away. The screaming lover was lifted from the pavement and taken around the corner. Kenna turned back to Washington's best pretender as the sounds softened to rain tapping the pavement about them.

"It was his idea years ago," Gowen offered, blood flowing from his nose and mouth. "He sent me to Cambridge. I saw an opportunity. Everyone was panicked; they needed money. So, I made it happen. And then the stupid bastard got religion or something.”

“You’re wrong, Avery. But you didn’t listen. What changed was when you involved Altmann.”

“That’s who he wanted me to contact!”

Everything spun in circles so much even the key players couldn’t keep track of it. Gowen had been fed to the wolves at Cambridge but had willingly joined a conspiracy from which he planned to prosper. Lying in an alley with a broken nose and ribs undoubtedly painted a different picture than Avery Gowen had in mind.

“Six years ago,” he continued. “Altmann failed to blackmail Chamberlain.”

Kenna lifted Gowen’s ripped shirt to reveal gunshot wounds in his upper chest. “That’s where you got these. You were the middleman, wounded by Edelman. That failure opened the door for him to return and do it again. Only this time, it led to murder.”

“I had no part in that!”

“Then, why all the charades? Why not come clean?” Kenna insisted.

Gowen’s stare narrowed. He leaned forward. With the pipe, Kenna pushed him back against the wall. A steady stream of water from a leaky gutter high overhead splattered against his shoulder. Gowen ignored it and the pipe, his stare on Kenna.

"What does the German have to do with the murder?"

"Ask him, not me."

Gowen spit blood. The pretender's breathing was broken; he lifted a hand to push the pipe away. Kenna allowed it.

"You don't get it," Gowen insisted. "Not like you said. God dammit, it's about—"

A dull thud into Gowen's chest stopped him at mid-sentence. The report of a pistol exploded in Kenna's ears as Gowen's mouth froze open, his eyes widened, and a hand lifted to his chest. His eyes lowered to blood that flowed through his fingers. His mouth moved without speaking; blood spewed from his mouth. Gowen slumped to the side with a whimper.

The back door of the bar opened, casting light into the alley. Kenna spun to the silhouette of a hooded man at the entrance of the alley an instant before the next shot. The bullet whined from stone wall to stone wall, disappearing into the distance. She threw herself behind the dumpster as another shot rang in her ears, followed by two more. The bar owner dropped with a thud down the two steps beside her.

Kenna lifted the big man's gun to fire, but when she looked up, the hooded killer was gone.

Kenna crawled to Avery Gowen, who grabbed her wrist with a bloody hand.

"Cam … bridge," was his last word.

L

For several hours during the night, Kenna answered police questions at the scene. For once, no U.S. Marshals arrived, though she had no doubt they would soon enough. Had they, the ulcer said she would never have seen daylight again.

The owner had been wounded, though not badly. Kenna turned over the man's gun to the authorities. They acknowledged the weapon was a different caliber than killed Avery Gowen. Just past midnight, she was allowed to go, with instructions not to leave the city, as if she had anywhere else to go. She cursed when she stepped into Charlie's Mercedes.

"Looks like I need to brush up on those nursing skills," Charlie said.

"Can the humor."

Charlie understood the signal for, *I need silence* and drove. Kenna pointed when they rounded a corner in front of a building with a neon sign that read, *'ALL-NIGHT DINER'*.

"First one we've seen open," Kenna said. "I need to think."

"And I need coffee," Charlie agreed.

They walked inside with the late-night crowd and took a booth. Though they tried to mask it, their presence was peculiar. A woman named 'Wanda' came up with a pot of coffee. Everyone in the place watched her and them. Almost pleadingly, Charlie reached out the porcelain cup with both hands.

"You alright, honey?" Wanda asked, eying Kenna, then Charlie.

"This is my cousin," Charlie said. "She was in a car wreck this evening."

Wanda grinned and turned away. "See a lotta car wrecks in this joint."

"Cousin?" Kenna asked.

"She never would have believed lover," Charlie said after a sip of acidic coffee. "Kidnapper, perhaps, but never lover."

She still felt his earlier kiss on her puffy face. She watched him, hoping she wasn't falling in love with him. *Your lifestyle is not conducive to permanence*, she reminded herself.

"When Altmann attacked you the other evening, what happened … exactly?" Kenna asked, though knowing it had been Jimmy McDowell.

"You keep saying, *'Altmann'*. How do you know it was him?"

"I don't, but we have to sort through it," Kenna said, knowing otherwise. "We've been through this, but what was he after?"

"Harvey's records."

"Records of what?" *Was he going to tell her the truth?* she asked herself silently.

Charlie's eyes rolled up. He leaned on a window but forced himself to remember. Letters were scattered across the sofa cushions. The rest of the room, though, had basically been cleaned of all things belonging to the late senator. Desk drawers were empty, as was the safe.

"I didn't go back until we were attacked," he said, hanging his head. And then he looked up. "The list Hobson had?"

Kenna shook her head, reviewing the Chess Club in her mind. Was it the *'who'* or the *'what'*?

"He didn't need that. It was either the bait or the distraction."

"Bait … distraction?" Charlie asked, confused.

'Organized mass confusion,' Gran Lockwood called it!

"There is something of greater importance."

Kenna fell silent, remembering that first night on the veranda when Charlie walked from the shadows. Instances and people were filling Gran's pyramid: suicide … murder; evidence … none required; Chamberlain … Altmann; Whyte … the green and bridge; Hobson and Gowen … the pretenders.

"I don't understand," Charlie said.

"Drink more coffee; it'll come to you," she said. "Altmann was blackmailing Chamberlain, but the senator was trying to work himself out of it. That first afternoon, when Chamberlain met Altmann at the Clubhouse—"

"Harvey called the office right after that," he said, lifting his face.

"Remember it," she demanded. "What did he say, exactly?"

Charlie's voice was light. "I could tell he was upset. He was distant, rambling, and said he was going to make a trade with the German. It was as if in passing; then, he hung up."

"A trade … of what?" she asked.

"Whatever, it was worth five million dollars to Altmann … and worth killing."

Charlie lifted a blank expression. Kenna tried to ignore

Charlie's features but couldn't. She paused, shaken, his attraction taking her breath as it had the first night. She cursed herself for being so distracted. *Think!*

Chamberlain wanted a trade; Kenna slapped her forehead with a palm. Altmann: The one who betrayed him in Germany! She remembered the conversations with Bridgewater, Salvatori, Altmann, and the general. She had been blind! It had been right in front of her all along! They had all told her, but she hadn't listened. She grabbed Charlie's arm, pulling him from the booth.

"It's at his house!" Hurrying for the exit, she lifted her phone. "Wiggy ..."

LI

"Slow down!" Charlie screamed over the roar of the Mercedes' engine.

Tires bawled as Kenna slid around the corner. The Chamberlain home loomed ominous in the darkness. She shut off the headlights and coasted to a stop along the street a hundred feet shy of the circular driveway. The closest neighbor was another two hundred feet further down the street.

Wind whistled through the trees when she stepped out and tossed Charlie the keys. A heavy mist stuck to her face and was low to the lantern-style streetlamps at the distant corners. From where she stood at the center of the block, they offered no illumination.

"Stay out here," she said, disliking the scowl she received in return. "Anything crazy happens; call the police first, Wiggy second."

"Why isn't he here now?"

"He's looking for Dorothy Baldwin. No one can find her."

"Oh, my God," Charlie said, hand on Kenna's arm. "She has to be okay."

Kenna turned to the dark home where once had resided one of the most powerful men in the land. It seemed fitting that no lights were on, that only the wind spoke through the trees. She felt naked without a weapon, going into a home where another murder may have already taken place. She had never carried a gun but swore from this day forward she would.

Her hand inadvertently fell to the wrought-iron fence; it was cool and wet. She listened to the blackness again, only to hear the rain in the leaves, like that of a distant troop of cavalry. Her footsteps softened as she hopped the three-foot-tall fence and landed on the moist grass. Ignoring the pain, she walked around a stand of hedge.

Kenna expected activity in the house of a fallen senator the night before his arranged interment, but there was none. She avoided the front door and moved to the back of the house. Two cars sat in the driveway: a Lincoln driven by Gloria Chamberlain and a drab-colored Chevrolet Lumina. Perhaps the daughter had decided it was time to help her mother. Her hand on the hood of the latter said it hadn't been there long. She walked to the front door. It stood partially open; the frame splintered. An instant later, grunts of pain and shattered glass broke the silence.

She stiffened and pushed the door open just as a hooded

shadow darted across the front room. She cursed her stupidity, then leaped forward to intercept it. The shadow spun her direction but slipped on a throw rug. The assailant's gun fired into the ceiling.

Kenna hit him in the shoulder as the big man landed facedown hard. The pistol reported no more than a few inches from Kenna's ear. Ringing exploded into her ears as she grabbed the assailant's arm and slammed it against the fireplace hearth. The gun fired again, shattering a front window. The weapon flew across the floor.

The attacker pulled Kenna over and slammed an elbow against her chest. Air exploded from her lungs. The attacker grabbed a fireplace poker from a stand and wheeled about. Kenna turned as a brass object flashed down at her. She raised an arm to block the impact. The loud crack of broken bone deafened her an instant before pain erupted throughout her system. The assailant swung down again. She rolled to the side; it slammed into the floor.

Kenna kicked the man's legs out from under him, driving him to the floor. She kicked again, the groin; he buckled and groaned, looking for his pistol. The assailant kicked Kenna's face. She jerked the gold Lion Head ball marker from her pocket and slashed his face; he screamed.

The ceiling light flashed on; the room spun. Through

fuzziness, Kenna saw the hooded attacker whirl about. Charlie stepped through the front door and into the foyer. He shouted, then yelled, as he was smashed against the wall with an impact that folded him to the floor. Blood appeared at the corner of his mouth; he reached for his head.

Through dimming vision, Kenna watched the assailant turn back and lift the gun. A pistol fired from an adjacent room. A window shattered. The assailant turned. Gloria Chamberlain entered the room, stumbled against a wall, and fired again. The bullet ripped through the man's arm, splattering the wall with blood. Thrown sideways from impact, he dropped his pistol. He slapped his hand over the wound and then dodged when Gloria fired again.

He snatched up photographs and a packet of papers from a nearby box and darted towards the back door. Gloria spun to fire again. The bullet struck the dinette hutch, shattering it, spraying the room with glass. She stumbled forward and fired again. Her knees buckled; she collapsed against the wall, her face slapping the floor hard.

Kenna focused on the door; the intruder was gone. Again, she cursed.

Charlie wheezed. Kenna forced back the pain in her fractured arm and stood. The Chevrolet's engine raced. Its bumper showered the pavement with sparks as it bounced over the curb. Kenna tried to focus on the tag, unable to as the car sped into the night.

Charlie rolled to the side, then reached up for his bleeding mouth. Kenna picked up the assailant's gun and shoved it into her pocket. She placed a hand against Charlie's cheek. He jolted to a protective posture, then hesitated, recognizing her.

"I need your help with Gloria," she said.

Kenna leaned against a wall for a few breaths before making her way to Gloria. Kenna lifted the gun from Gloria's hand and set it aside. Gloria twitched once. Unconscious, her face was bloodied, her eyes nearly swollen shut. The savage cuts and bruises of a pistol-whipping streaked and darkened her forehead and cheeks. Her hands and wrists were bloodied as if raised during the struggle to protect herself. She was breathing, and for that, Kenna was relieved. Slowly leaning against the wall at her side and cradling her arm, she lifted the cell phone and called 911. Her eyes closed; she jumped as Charlie's hand brushed her cheek.

"Can you take care of her?" she asked between gritted teeth and slumped to the floor. "I need a nap."

There was but a brief hesitation before Gloria's mortal enemy, Charlie Sommer, walked away. He returned from the kitchen with cool, wet washcloths that he placed on Gloria's and Kenna's foreheads. He wiped away some of the blood on Gloria's face and pressed the cloth against the deepest of cuts. A blanket was placed over her.

"I should let the bitch bleed to death," Charlie mumbled. "She started all of this."

Kenna didn't tell Charlie that he was wrong, that the general was wrong, that everyone was wrong. She hadn't the energy. A few moments passed before the late senator's wife opened her eyes. She strained to lift her head and stared through one glazed eye.

"He … was not … worth … saving," Gloria mumbled.

Kenna disliked this woman, even in her pathetic, beaten form. "You're wrong. Every life is worth saving." *Even yours,* she did not say.

"Who was it, Mrs. Chamberlain?" Charlie took the words from Kenna's mouth.

Gloria grimaced through the blood and coughed. Her chest heaved. "I thought … he was … dead."

"Who?" Kenna asked, leaning back to ease the throbbing that now reached her head. It didn't work. Distant sirens spelled relief, but that did little to comfort them now.

"So long … ago." Gloria forced one eye open; the other

did not react. "He must … have … killed Harvey."

Kenna moved closer, consuming a large inhale with even the slightest movement of her broken arm. She settled it onto her legs, then placed a comforting hand on Gloria's forehead.

"Was it Altmann?" she asked.

She opened an eye briefly and smiled once. "So … you … know."

"What did he want?"

Gloria's eyes bolted open briefly. She screamed, then cried. "Silence … he wanted … silence!"

Charlie dabbed the stricken woman's forehead, then looked up at Kenna. "Silence?"

Gloria Chamberlain pointed to the empty, broken picture frame on the mantel and the boxes of pictures scattered about the room. Her head slumped to the side, unconscious.

LII

Charlie Sommer allowed a pained smile as he brushed the sweat from Kenna's forehead. His face was painted in the colors of a fight. Kenna didn't like it or the swollen bottom lip. She touched the flaw, recalling how earlier she had enjoyed a slight imperfection. This was not slight.

Charlie flinched but tried to hide the pain. "Is this really how you live?"

Drugs numbed her, and she hated it. Arm in a blue fiberglass cast, she reached for the water jug on the nightstand.

"How long?" she mumbled.

Charlie raised a glass and straw to her lips. "Four hours since we arrived. You woke up once before. Don't you remember?"

"Nope."

"Too bad. We had great sex, and you made all kinds of promises." Kenna forced a smile. "Wiggy's on the way. He didn't say if he found Dorothy Baldwin."

She stared out the window, surprised the sun was up. Rain was apropos. Sheets of water flowed across the glass like rivers of silver. Lightning flashed. Enhanced by the contrasting pristine white of the hospital, grayness held the room.

"*Twilight Zone*," she mumbled.

Charlie found no humor. "At least in the end, the absurd would be absolute."

"How's Gloria?"

"They don't know yet."

Charlie didn't look up when the door opened, casting a long light across the bed. A nurse checked the chart, Kenna's pulse, and smiled. The latter was a gesture seldom practiced in the bring 'em in, get 'em out mentality of the American medical profession.

"That arm's going to start hurting in a few hours," the nurse offered.

Kenna nodded. "Something to look forward to."

"The doctor says you should stay tonight, but your choice. You're the one that's been yelling about leaving since you got here; just let me know."

"I'm letting you know," Kenna insisted.

The young woman turned to Charlie. "From the looks of you two and the other woman, you need new friends."

"Obviously, we don't have any friends," Charlie

responded.

The nurse shrugged and walked out. Kenna's mind whirled, recalling the attacker. There was something different. Her gut said that several people knew more than they had ever let on, Malcolm Bridgewater most of all.

She didn't realize she'd fallen back asleep but awoke to Charlie's hand around her good arm. She rose to an elbow, cringing in pain. Charlie propped her up on the edge of the bed, though she was leaning on a pillow. She was mentally uncomfortable; a piece was still missing. A drink of water and her eyes brightened.

"The photo was gone," she mumbled.

"What photo?" Charlie asked.

"Chamberlain and Treadway in Afghanistan … on her mantel." She strained to remember it: two enemies locked forever in a camera's frame.

"She loved them both," Charlie offered.

"No, there was something in the photo that only she, Treadway, and the killer understood," she countered.

"Another we'll never know here in *The Twilight Zone*?"

"Will she live?" the yell from the hallway demanded, marked in its brevity by the crunching sound of an intake unit.

Charlie's protective glare caught Kenna by surprise. "She's not dead yet!"

"I'm alive," Kenna said and raised to the edge of the bed. "The Krav Maga helped."

"Aye, knew it would eventually." Wiggy pushed open the door and met Charlie's glare. Appreciative, he smiled and nodded. "While you've been lyin' on yer backside, I've done yer dirty work so we can get the bloody hell out of this fuckin' city."

"We aren't going anywhere," Kenna snapped, rolling to get out of the bed.

"Just like the Grand Ole Dame, leavin' before the doctors clear you."

"Then, it's nothing new. I'm gonna finish what we started," Kenna said with a harsh cough.

"You aren't gonna do it on yer arse. Like the Grand Ole Dame said, Fiery, *there be more important things than playin' with cameras'.*"

Wiggy winked. Kenna propped herself upright with her good hand and pulled her broken arm over her lap. A bolt of pain shot from her shoulder to her skull. She hesitated … *overcome it, overcome it* … and then motioned to the closet.

"You can start by getting my clothes," she insisted

"Aye, kid," Wiggy nodded with a grimace that turned to a broad smile. He dropped a bag on the bed. "Brought you clean things from the Clubhouse."

It came to Kenna at that instant. The plan was brilliant. The assassin didn't have to kill Chamberlain to get what he wanted, but he had. Gran Lockwood's, *'Truth loves a patient woman,'* rang through her ears. Had Kenna not heard her from across the great beyond, she never would have seen it, and the murderer might have gone free. The door opened slowly as Kenna stood from the bed and pulled off her hospital gown. Standing there in only her bra and panties, she blushed.

"For God's sake, Kenna, I feel like I changed your diapers," Dorothy Baldwin said. "May I come in?"

"You already are," Kenna said, flinching when Wiggy pulled up her pants.

"Could we talk alone?" she asked.

As the door closed, Dorothy Baldwin's perfectly powdered and polished face was marred by the opposite. Lines of age wrinkled the mask of white. Streaks of black mascara crossed her cheeks like road maps. A patchy camouflage job had taken place moments before she entered.

She had always been devoted, but now she had been

betrayed by the man to whom she had dedicated her entire adult life. Anger settled at the pit of Kenna's being. Or was it that damned ulcer? Malcolm Bridgewater would pay for this moment; one that Kenna feared would someday awaken her in a cold sweat.

Politicians never learned. Their vanity disregarded mistakes made by past generations as those of lesser men. Devon Whyte was partially right: the Party had not learned at all.

"I'm sorry about that," Dorothy said, pointing at her arm.

"A few months rehab." Kenna cringed while Dorothy helped pull a shirt over the cast.

"Is … it over?" Dorothy asked.

Kenna closely examined the frail, devoted public servant. It had been so much easier when Dorothy first came to Washington. Malcolm was young, determined, and brash. But most of all, his energies were channeled in the right direction. Kenna felt sorry for Dorothy most of all.

She sat on the bed, imagining she was at the glassed table on the Clubhouse veranda, listening to a doomed man plead for what now appeared to be his life. She thought she could hear Harvey Chamberlain and Bernard Altmann. Would Chamberlain be alive today if Altmann had agreed to the trade? What if Charlie had asked for help long ago? What if Gloria had loved her husband more than the bottle and what his power offered? She washed away the thoughts; especially her final one of Dorothy Baldwin pulling the trigger to kill Harvey Chamberlain.

The present demanded facts. And the facts were that Chamberlain was dead; so were Devon Whyte and Avery Gowen.

"Could I have some water, please?" Dorothy asked.

Kenna handed her a glass. Dorothy took a sip and set it on the rolling side table. She forced a smile, which Kenna found uncomfortable.

"Better if it was a Jack Daniel's," Kenna said.

"Malcolm's favorite."

"I'm sorry to say it, Dorothy, but I've heard it all."

"When you called and said you were coming to Congressional, he was preparing for a special event."

He got one, Kenna did not say and sensed that on the tip of Dorothy's tongue was the pending betrayal of her champion. It was equivalent to Nancy betraying Ron, or better yet, JFK betraying Jackie. As Dorothy spoke, the words filtered through Kenna's mind like so many others she had heard over the past few days. Dorothy's tears and deep inhales brought Kenna's emotions to bear, but hers were different. Pity became anger.

Dorothy had told Malcolm to come forward and to stay away from Gowen. Chamberlain was afraid of something when he went to Malcolm, but no one knew what … only Gowen. They were both dead. It had been a closed-door meeting with Devon Whyte. There had been shouting, calls made, and Chamberlain had stormed out. But all three were dead.

"Then," Dorothy continued. "Malcolm asked Harvey if, and I quote, *'are you going?'* Harvey said, and I'll never forget it: *'What the fuck else can I do?'*"

Kenna heard the first curse word Dorothy had ever said, but it fell hollow on her mind. None of what she said mattered. It was a last futile effort to save, not admonish, her champion.

This sordid episode of murder really began when Harvey Chamberlain met Bernard Altmann on the veranda of Congressional Country Club, not twenty years ago, or six years ago, and certainly not months ago. That was when Bernard Altmann knew he had to kill Harvey Chamberlain, and Kenna was sucked into the cesspool of Washington, D.C.

Dorothy Baldwin hesitated for a long time and took a sip

of water. Kenna read her hesitancy as a battle between loyalty and truth. Or was it? Deceit and lies ran deeper than she ever imagined. Dorothy was frightened for Malcolm, of that Kenna was positive, but she was also frightened of Avery Gowen and what no one else had known.

Kenna moved aside her internal feelings and took a good look at Dorothy, taken aback. It was like Dorothy's words were a recording, one with excessive background noise. Her eyes drifted to another time, a more valued past. She cried subtle tears Kenna had never seen this strong woman shed. She handed Dorothy Baldwin a Kleenex box. Kenna felt none of her sorrow. All of this was leading to something she already knew. Dorothy was pleading for Kenna's compassion while knowing she offered none.

"He was determined to save the Party, even at his own expense," Dorothy offered.

Her eyes focused on Kenna briefly. The tears fell again, followed by another sip of water. Kenna shifted the cast to a more comfortable position. Her first hunch had been right. Malcolm had fed her to the wolves: *'Hook, line and sinker,'* Bridgewater would say in his good ole boy vernacular. Yet, there was no good ole boy left in Malcolm Bridgewater. It was also what Dorothy Baldwin had discovered at the cost of her undying loyalty, her belief in the man, and in the system.

"All I care about is finding who killed Harvey, Devon, and Gowen. How everything else shakes out is not my concern."

Dorothy squeezed her hand. Those motherly eyes settled on hers. The tears were gone. "Thank you."

What Kenna heard was hollow; it saddened her. "Do you think Malcolm knew something that could have kept Harvey and Devon alive?"

Dorothy hesitated. For the moment, Kenna wanted to believe that she was reliving her youth with America's most powerful politician. "Yes."

"Then, why didn't he do something about it?"

"He thought he had," Dorothy said. Kenna froze, anticipating her response. "He got you involved."

LIII

There was no reason to rush to the Watergate Hotel. Altmann would wait for her now. After all, Kenna was his last obstacle. She stared through the glass enclosure of the ICU. There was the peripheral to deal with. As Gran Lockwood knew, it now controlled *the serpent's will.* Gowen had said it: *'Everyone had been paid.'*

The shuffle of feet on tile was but a hush. Earlier, Wiggy had escorted Dorothy to Malcolm's office; then, he was taking Charlie to the Clubhouse. Kenna told only Wiggy where she was going and that he was to meet her at the Watergate once she verified the German was there.

She wanted a shower, and smelled of the alley, even Avery Gowen's blood. She ran fingers through matted hair, a thumb over the top of her lip. The drugs that numbed the pain were wearing off; she ignored it as best she could. There was no time to wallow in self-pity.

For a lengthy time, Kenna stared through the glass at the motionless Gloria Chamberlain. Plastic tubes from an I.V. and respirator ran from a drip into her arm, oxygen into her nose. A blood pressure cuff was wrapped around her opposite arm, and a small lighted clamp was affixed to an index finger. Both fed her vital signs into a machine of gauges, lights, and paper read-out that told of her stability or lack thereof. Fresh bandages wrapped her head to where Kenna only saw one eye and her lips. Gloria's left leg was in a cast and elevated by a cable lift.

"Looks like our teaching date is off," Treadway said and joined her.

Kenna's no-comment glare spoke enough.

With sad eyes, he looked into the room. "The doctor says she'll live. There'll be challenges, but she'll live."

Kenna allowed silence to linger for a moment. "I want a favor."

"Lost my taste for favors these past few days."

"It's not a request," Kenna demanded.

"Which makes it a demand," he said. "I'm listening."

"Gloria knew about the illegal campaign funding and saw how it was tearing the senator apart. She went to Bridgewater, who tried to silence her. Then, she tried another angle, and that was you.

"Your facial expression at Arlington said I'd breached the wall of lies," Kenna continued. "You will have to deal with what your father would think on your own."

The general was spellbound and mumbled when Kenna

tapped him lightly on the chest.

"She saw Harvey falling apart, torn between duty to the Party and the law. She begged him not to buck the Party, to keep the contribution scheme quiet. After all, it had been his idea at Cambridge. When he refused, their publicized separation started. But little did they know that Avery Gowen already had the game in full swing.

"At the same time," she continued, "an unrelated event tore at Chamberlain's insides: the reappearance of Bernard Altmann, the King of the Chess Club. The senator fell deeper into depression as he struggled with how to manage the new threat. Gloria knew her time in Washington was about to end. She confided in you again to help with Altmann."

"There was little choice," he said with mixed emotions.

"When blackmail became reality, your next step was to contact Morningstar. You had to warn him that Altmann was alive. The next thing, Chamberlain's dead, an apparent suicide, or so everyone was supposed to believe. I became the fly in the ointment."

"Are you insinuating I had something to do with Chamberlain's death?"

"No!"

"The demand?" Treadway insisted.

"The Bishop didn't die in prison. The Massachusetts senator brought him out when you brought out Morningstar. Both got new identities, new lives."

"That's preposterous."

"Afraid not, general," she said. "Think about it. That was about the time the Taliban fell, total confusion in Afghanistan. Precisely when you gave Morningstar the all clear. The same time, Altmann formulated his plan. That's when you all thought Altmann had come back to blackmail Chamberlain and, later, that he had finally been killed in Europe."

"What are you getting at?"

"I'll give you the proof you want," Kenna said. "Call Morningstar. Tell him I want to meet him in three hours."

"Where?"

"He'll know."

"And if he refuses?"

"Tell him I know Altmann's identity."

"If you know that— "

"Just do it, general."

Hesitantly, the general punched the numbers. He had a brief mumbled conversation, then hung up.

"What made you so sure I could contact him?"

"In Europe, you let Morningstar go, even though your political detractors forbid it. You sent him into hiding and didn't keep track of him."

"I couldn't. It was the deal with Doctor Frhein."

"So, six years ago," Kenna continued, "you had no way of knowing that Morningstar had been driven underground in Germany by Altmann before you had a chance to get him out. Indeed, Altmann thought he had killed Morningstar. You also had no way of knowing that Altmann posed as Morningstar when you thought you brought Morningstar out."

"Whaaaat?" came the confused response. "How the fuck—"

"So, you didn't know you brought out the wrong man. The guy that met Chamberlain at the Clubhouse that morning was not Altmann but the real Morningstar."

"I don't—"

"He thinks you, Chamberlain, and everyone else betrayed him. He came for revenge." Kenna paused as the gruff features of the iron man wilted. "He started with the campaign contributions, but what he really wanted to bring out was the Chess Club and their dirty little conspiratorial game, wasn't it, general?"

Another silence. "Good, God. He's not Morningstar!"

"Wasn't it, general?" The general's silent, dejected, *yes.* "And now, he's going to exact his revenge by exposing the campaign contribution plan dreamed up by the Chess Club. Even if your appropriations bill passes, how will it look to the Joint Chiefs that you were totally in the dark on the Morningstar … Altmann swap?"

"You … have … no proof."

"I don't need any," Kenna said. "You didn't know it, but the first time you called Morningstar to warn him that Altmann was alive and coming to the States to blackmail Chamberlain, you were actually passing the information to the one man who had a reason to kill Harvey Chamberlain."

"I didn't …" Treadway weakened.

"You told Altmann. With Morningstar alive, Altmann had no choice but to kill Chamberlain to erase the past. It was that or be exposed. He had to keep killing the Chess Club until he eventually got to Morningstar."

Treadway leaned against the ICU glass. "What do you want me to do?"

"You already did!"

LIV

Rain darkened the Washington afternoon as Kenna walked into the black edifice of the Watergate Hotel. *A fitting location,* she thought. She passed the garden restaurant, amused in a strange way that the German had stayed here. She stepped from the elevator and looked both ways down the hall. Her tongue was thick as she knocked on the German's door; not surprised it was propped open by the safety latch inside.

Bernard Altmann straightened from packing a bag. "I've been expecting you, Ms. Hannigan."

"Herr Altmann," Kenna said sarcastically. "Or so we were incorrectly introduced."

The German placed a pair of pressed trousers into the suitcase, followed by his toiletry bag, and closed it. He smiled, took a seat in a red parlor chair, and crossed his legs.

"Should I refer to you as Morningstar ... or perhaps Erhard Forst?

"Bravo, Ms. Hannigan. As you wish," Morningstar said, impressed. "As you Americans say, this has apparently been a perfect game."

"The Party got what it deserved. Actually, they paid

twice for your bit of history," Kenna said.

"Twice?"

"Yes." She thought of Avery Gowen. "You weren't the only one to get what you came for."

"No romanticism, though. You know, suitcases full of hundred-dollar bills, running from the hounds, guns firing, avoiding the searchlights, ducking through the barbwire, high-speed car chases." The German chuckled. "Simply a boring wire transfer to a foreign account."

"We may have both been born a half-century too late."

The German laughed. "It was, however, worthwhile watching the senators from Massachusetts and Tennessee writhe as the exchange was made."

"After all these years, it must have been quite satisfying. It's too bad Avery Gowen became expendable?"

The German furrowed his brow. "Expendable?"

"Killed last night while telling me how to contact you."

"Unfortunate," the German said, unmoved. "Contrary to his lifestyle, Avery was a man of fortitude, much like you, Ms. Hannigan. Beginning six years ago, he carried out my plan to the letter."

"The perfect chameleon," Kenna agreed. "It took balls to pose as the target in a U.S. Marshals setup, not knowing if he would come out alive."

"Yes, it was the only means to convince everyone that Bernard Altmann was, indeed, alive," the German said. "I admired Avery for that, which is why I allowed him to *earn* a great deal of money while he administered the campaign contributions portion of the plan."

"I understand your motive," Kenna said honestly. "It's unfortunate it turned to multiple murders."

"Unforeseen circumstances in an imperfect world, Ms. Hannigan," Morningstar said matter-of-factly. "But you: I would like to have met you under different circumstances. Alas, my time here is finished."

"What makes you think I will allow you to leave? You just blackmailed some very influential people."

"I believe it is called quid pro quo ... the trees at the country club."

"And if it had been Hobson, not me?"

"The outcome, at least for him, may have been entirely different," Morningstar said. "I had no business with you."

"A warning," Kenna said. "But you are an important piece to this murder case."

"Not your style, I think you would say. And since you are here without police or even your compatriot, you must have solved your case without any further need of me." Morningstar's eyes softened. "It doesn't bring back my family but provides a measure of satisfaction to have ruined the men responsible."

"In a bizarre, if even hypocritical way, I suppose I should thank you," she offered.

"Or I you for allowing me to complete my mission."

"That was for my benefit as much as yours," Kenna said. "I have known for some time that you weren't Bernard Altmann."

"Even before we met at the Pentagon?"

"That sealed it. Altmann would never have taken the time to talk."

"Yes, I suppose not." Morningstar smiled, then continued in a voice laced with heavy German. "The use of his name, though, was to my advantage. My objective was strictly financial."

Kenna smiled. "With a little revenge thrown in for measure."

"Of course," Morningstar said and mirrored Kenna's smile. "What good is life without adventure? When the Senator from Illinois and their little club leaked information to the Taliban that got my family killed, I decided to ruin him and his Party. I wanted him to look over his shoulder his entire life in fear of when I would pull the trigger to end his miserable existence.”

“But you had no intentions of ever killing Harvey Chamberlain.”

“It is far better to torture someone with fear, Ms. Hannigan. He thought he had ended it years ago, but I brought the fear back.”

“You’ll be disappointed to learn that Harvey Chamberlain didn’t betray you in Afghanistan, or six years ago, and certainly not this week.”

The German’s expression stiffened. “Please, elaborate.”

“He couldn’t. There were other powers at work. Your two-fold mission complicated things.”

The German leaned forward. “I think I understand.”

“Chamberlain offered you an exchange—”

“How did you know that?”

“A little birdie told me,” Kenna said.

“What about it?” The German swallowed hard, then stood. He walked to a sideboard and poured a glass of schnapps. He inhaled the bouquet, took a sip, and leveled his stare. “So, you know that I sold more than my silence over illegal campaign contributions.”

"You wanted to expose the Chess Club's other plan, as well as the players."

"Oh, Ms. Hannigan, I sorely underestimated you," Morningstar said. "But I didn't come here to relive history; I came to this country to *sell* it. I have accomplished that."

"There was no plot to kill Chamberlain six years ago, or any other senator."

"To what end? The Taliban had long before crumbled. A bit of subterfuge in order to initiate my overall plan to avenge the deaths of my family."

"Reverting to blackmail."

"Business, Ms. Hannigan, business." Morningstar moved to his right, eyes shifting. He took another drink.

"Gowen played the Marshals as well as the senators," Kenna said. "The intent was to make them believe that Altmann was alive and the one they should fear."

"He pulled it off perfectly," the German said.

"He had them running in circles by the time you implemented the first Chess Club plan."

"Yes, campaign contributions."

"With one exception."

"Oh?"

"He played both sides."

"Unfortunate," Morningstar said without remorse. "Had he stuck with the original plan, he would have been a very rich man, not a dead one."

"Time will tell, but I have my doubts if your work will destroy the Party."

"The weakness of the American system is the weakness of the people in power."

Some think it's the people who vote them into power. "It's our way, Morningstar. The Malcolm Bridgewater's permeate Washington. Though you played them like a master, the Party will do what it must to facilitate damage control."

"I see," Morningstar said, reflecting. "Yes, Americans are a strange species."

"The night Chamberlain was killed; you were to meet him at the sand trap?"

"There were two who met Senator Chamberlain that evening, but I was not one," Morningstar said. "When I arrived to conclude our business arrangement, the senator was dead. The U.S. Marshals were there, so I left with all haste."

"You didn't see the parallel?"

Morningstar squinted, then refilled his glass. "Parallel?

Elaborate."

"The betrayal."

The German set the glass on the sideboard without speaking. He turned his back to Kenna as hatred boiled within.

"Gowen arranged for the meeting with Chamberlain."

"As said, Gowen was invaluable to my mission," the German replied. "I required guarantees that Chamberlain would involve the Party hierarchy."

"But not until he absolutely had to."

"The only guarantee of success was to expose everything."

"But there was one thing you didn't anticipate." Kenna cleared her throat, moved alongside the German, and stared out the window. "After you came forward two months ago, perhaps they manipulated you, not the other way around."

The German's eyes narrowed to where his eyebrows joined together at the bridge of his nose. "Continue."

"You were to take the fall for Chamberlain's murder, then die yourself."

"I killed no one."

"In the words of a good American prosecutor, *'convince the jury'*. You had the motive: Chamberlain double-crossed you in the past. You had the drive: blackmail. And dead, you'd never convince anyone of your innocence."

"They would never have heard the story," Morningstar whispered and nodded. "Gowen's other side."

"Dead men tell no lies," Kenna said. "Bernard Altmann, arisen from the grave, would really be dead this time. Or so it was planned. The living would benefit from that."

"The senator's killer," Morningstar said.

"That's why Chamberlain was killed. It was the only way to force you to stay until they tracked you down," Kenna said. "After your meeting with Chamberlain, the killer knew you were alive. It would have all ended that evening with you dead beside Chamberlain, but Roots Hobson discovered the body before you arrived."

"Yes ..." the German hissed. "Who?"

"The King of the Chess Club, the man who actually betrayed you in Europe."

A grimace creased the chiseled Teutonic features: "That ... that's impossible."

"Not impossible, Morningstar. He is alive."

"So, the leader of their little Cambridge clique lives!" His past flashed before him with a shiver.

"What was the Chess Club's other plan?" Kenna asked.

"Perhaps another time," the German said with a shrug. The former double agent smiled and turned. "The king's new identity, please."

"I think we should allow that honor to fall to General Treadway." Kenna needed a little time.

"And if he refuses?"

"He won't. Altmann betrayed him, too, remember." *But I will get to Altmann first.*

"The King ..." Morningstar's eyes brightened, "... escaped." He crumpled his brow and gritted his teeth. "And now, I have the general to find. You see how cheaply they got off, Ms. Hannigan."

Kenna could not comment as Morningstar lifted his suitcase and walked to the door. She turned for a moment but did not speak and lifted a hand in a goodbye salute. The German disappeared into the hall. It had been the perfect plan ... almost.

"He's gone to find Treadway, Wiggy. That gives us time," Kenna said into her cell. "Get to the Clubhouse and make sure Charlie's okay. You know where I'll be."

LV

In the darkness of night, Kenna leaned on the very tree where the bullet had ricocheted into the distance and sent the sliver of wood into her face. She peeled away a piece of loose bark, wondering if the tree would be scarred for life, as would she. Constant rain fell from dark, low-hanging clouds, resounding through the trees like a swarm of locusts. Water seeped into the top of her cast, but she ignored it.

The Clubhouse was an apparition through the gray haze of the storm; she longed for its roof and warmth. A beer sounded good about now; no, a hundred beers sounded good about now. And a jet to take her to a beach with Charlie Sommer. Anything to get away from this case.

She was driven, as always, to finish what she started. It was an affliction bestowed upon her by Gran and, to a degree, her father. When others told her to let go, she held on for dear life. When they told her to go away, as had Malcolm Bridgewater, she became the immovable object. Right now, though, something inside said she should have taken Jimmy McDowell's advice and gone to the islands.

Kenna inhaled heavily. It was time. She opened her phone. "What's the story, Wiggy?"

"He blind-sided me when I walked into the room," Wiggy said, groggy. "Charlie was gone when I woke up. I'll be down shortly."

A bolt of lightning rocketed across J.E.B. Stuart's *ground*, another shortly after near the 18th green. They illuminated the trees, brightening the shadows. Electricity lifted her wet hair and tingled her flesh. The crack of thunder physically moved her; ears rang for a moment before clearing.

"It's dangerous to be on a golf course during a thunderstorm," a man yelled from beyond the trees.

Kenna didn't flinch and yelled back, "For those who fear death."

While hidden in the trees, she turned to see Charlie, rain-soaked and bloody, no more than 20 feet from her, with Agent Salvatori's bandaged arm wrapped tightly around his neck. Charlie struggled until Salvatori jabbed a non-standard issue pistol against his neck.

"So, that's why we never heard about the forensics on that pistol!" Kenna yelled. "When Edelman turned it in, you took it from evidence."

"I should have killed you when I had the chance, Hannigan," Salvatori said. "As for Sommer, he was careless but predictable. A simple phone call, and … well … I profited from his stupidity."

"Kill this bastard, Kenna!" Charlie screamed.

Kenna now recognized the physical features that had bothered her so much about Salvatori. He wasn't Aryan like Morningstar but was more Afghani, clearly not Italian. The thick black beard and hair were natural, but the stubby nose had been altered by surgery as much as had Gloria Chamberlain's body. The clincher had been discovered by Wiggy: Agent Vinny Salvatori never had a family.

Another lighting strike and the long roll of thunder. Kenna flinched, then straightened to allow water to run across her face. The cast weighed her side like lead, but she ignored it. She jumped when a hand fell on her shoulder. General Treadway placed a finger over her mouth, tapped his own chest, and motioned to the left in a circular motion. He then tapped Kenna on the chest and motioned to the right. With his other hand, he put it against his lips and then flapped his thumb and fingers together, *Keep talking*. Kenna acknowledged.

"Maybe, but your luck has run out. My notes tell it all, and Wiggy never gives up."

"Your associate is indisposed at the moment."

Kenna remained against the tree and watched the general run to the left. His steps were hidden by the rain and Kenna's words. With the general out of sight, Kenna moved to the right.

"You missed Morningstar when you killed Chamberlain," she yelled. "He's still out there, alive, and knows you are, too. You'll never be able to rest."

Salvatori/Altmann fired into the trees at Kenna's voice. "The killer of a U.S. Senator, political Party head, and murderer of a U.S. Marshals' agent against the entire U.S. Government? I don't give him much of a chance."

Salvatori/Altmann was trying to maneuver around the mess he created. He wanted to change his position on Chamberlain's death from suicide to murder and wanted everyone to buy into it with the flip of a hand. *In this city, it could happen.* The first siren bit into the night. *Dorothy,* Kenna thought.

"And then, there's the Bishop."

"Come on out, Kenna. Mr. Sommer grows anxious," Salvatori/Altmann said and fired into the trees once again. "The Bishop slipped on a bar of soap in prison."

"No, still an air-breather," Kenna said. "At least, his replacement is. Unfortunate, you didn't meet him before he came to the States."

With a large breath, Kenna stepped from the tree line. Rain sprayed her face. Her eyes bore into the German/Afghani's.

"He's alive. You betrayed him in Afghanistan and Germany to have Treadway get you out. He nearly died for something you masterminded. At the time, the general didn't know there was a connection between you and the Bishop. The Irishman also knows you're alive."

Altmann/Salvatori tightened his grip on the pistol and Charlie's neck. "You're lying!"

"None of this started until Agent Edelman reported to her superior that a German named Altmann was running an illegal campaign contribution network into the U.S. You recognized the plan. You knew Morningstar had survived, just like six years ago, and you had to bring him out into the open to kill him.

"In short," Kenna continued. "Your charade as Morningstar and as Vinny Salvatori is over. You're about to hang for the murders of Senator Harvey Chamberlain, Devon Whyte, and Avery Gowen. We'll clean up the rest, like your partner six years ago, later."

"You've forgotten something," Altmann/Salvatori said,

lifting the gun against Charlie's temple.

"Fiery!" Wiggy yelled from the cart path in the distance.

It took away Altmann/Salvatori's concentration. She and Charlie made eye contact. Fear bulged his eyes, his breathing choppy. Their eye contact was knowing. She forced a grimace and nodded quickly.

"How's the wounded arm, Altmann?" Kenna asked. "I didn't think Gloria could hit you either."

"You two are the only loose ends."

She heard the rustle of underbrush through the rain. Kenna moved only her eyes as Terror Treadway burst from the trees. Charlie went totally limp and slipped out of Altmann/Salvatori's wounded arm to the ground. An instant later, the gun fired, missing his head by a millimeter. Kenna was on the move.

Altmann/Salvatori spun and fired at the general; the bullet tore through Treadway's arm as he landed atop the double agent, throwing both men into a tree. Mud and water sprayed the area as they hit the ground. Charlie scampered towards Kenna.

"You betrayed me, you bastard!" the general screamed.

They rolled, loose sod sticking to them as if glue. With his wounded arm, the general pulled the killer to the side. He slammed a fist against Altmann/Salvatori's face, then threw him headlong into a tree. Altmann/Salvatori screamed from the impact on his wounded arm; the gun erupted.

Kenna felt heat in her shoulder; she was thrown back and fell. Her head came to rest in a pool of water. Charlie went to her, but she pushed him away. She blinked hard. *Am I dead?* She turned over as the general slammed a fist against the agent's ribcage.

Altmann/Salvatori shouted as air exploded from his lungs, but he spun the weapon and fired. A bullet shattered the general's tibia. Treadway fell but dragged Altmann/Salvatori down to the ground by the throat. The double agent lifted the mud-caked gun to fire, but when he pulled the trigger, the barrel exploded in his hand, showering both men with shards of hot steel. He screamed and lost hold of the general.

Treadway spun; his hesitation was momentary. He lunged forward, once again gripping Altmann/Salvatori's throat; he squealed for air, throat popping. Altmann/Salvatori snapped the butt of the gun against Treadway's temple. The general faltered and was driven into the mud by another blow.

Kenna forced herself up and lunged at Altmann/Salvatori's arm as he raised the damaged gun again. Kenna slammed her cast against it in mid-swing; the butt of the weapon slammed into a nearby tree. Altmann/Salvatori knocked Kenna to her knees with a stiff backhanded fist. Rain drenched Altmann/Salvatori's mud-streaked face as he knocked the general facedown into the mud, then turned on Kenna again. Altmann/Salvatori stretched his neck, fighting for air. With a bloodied hand, he pulled another pistol from his back belt. He kicked the unconscious Treadway away and lifted the weapon.

"You're done, Hannigan," Altmann/Salvatori said.

"Correction," Kenna said.

Kenna raised a pistol from her waistband, aimed, and pulled the trigger. The bullet hit Altmann/Salvatori dead center in the sternum, a second in the stomach. Altmann/Salvatori stumbled to the side, grabbed a tree for stability, and spun from the underbrush. He turned and fired wildly, but the bullets streaked into the trees and rain. Altmann/Salvatori's pistol dropped to the side; he didn't fire again; he couldn't.

The ex-Taliban agent stumbled over a fold in the land. He reached out to break his fall too late. A look of startled confusion filled his eyes, much as the senator's must-have Saturday night. Bernard Altmann, the King of the Chess Club, staggered from the brush and landed face down in the very sand trap where he had murdered U.S. Senator Harvey Chamberlain, the Rook.

Favoring pain in his chest, Wiggy staggered from the trees; blood rain-streaked on his face. His shirt was ripped open, revealing a Kevlar vest. Charlie crawled to the general, whose breathing was labored. He lifted Treadway's head onto his lap. There was a grimace of satisfaction on the military man's face when he opened his eyes.

"Got that … bastard … finally."

"I was counting on one of you showing up," Kenna said to the general and Wiggy.

"Only way I could … keep Morningstar's … identity secret," Treadway said.

"The Joint Chiefs won't like that much."

"Fuck 'em." The general grimaced, then gripped Charlie's hand in a manly handshake. "Thanks."

"When ya get well, Fiery, I'm gonna break yer neck for takin' this chance." Wiggy knelt beside Kenna and examined her wound. "Now, can we get the bloody hell outta this fuckin' city?"

Kenna leaned against a tree and stared up into the rain. As she wiped her eyes clean, the final breath left the King's chest. Ironically but fittingly, the sprinklers clicked to life on the 18th green of Congressional Country Club.

EPILOGUE

Kenna stepped from the cab at the entrance of the Watergate Hotel. Inhaling Washington's rancid air brought back memories she cared not to relive. She had spent her recovery in the cool air and sanity of Boston. Her favorite bartender at her favorite corner pub made the time more comfortable. He turned out to be an excellent typist who made chronicling the case much easier than it would have been with her broken arm, gunshot wound, and mangled fingers. Kenna stretched her arm, now free of the cast. The bullet had passed through her shoulder but broke bones on the way. She was healed, save the nasty scars that would remind her of this event for the rest of her life.

Wiggy would be happy to know that her father picked up the story. He rapidly buried it in the archives, which she totally anticipated him doing. That wouldn't make Wiggy happy … perhaps one thing she would keep from him for the time being.

Kenna smiled, pleased Wiggy had been preoccupied. Miriam Edelman had secured a position with the Israeli Defense Force, and Wiggy was helping her with the transition. After all, Wiggy had friends everywhere. The general provided a professional recommendation from his new posting at NSA.

Kenna's parents visited during recuperation. She and her father had several good days. To both, that meant they spoke without arguing. It was the first time in years they had achieved that, and they agreed to continue their efforts toward mending their relationship. Her mother had cried when they kissed goodbye at the airport.

The next day, Kenna paid a visit to the family plot and had a very long, private vigil with Gran Lockwood. Without her past guidance, there was no doubt she would have traveled back to Boston in a box to join Gran in the afterlife, be it Rod Serling's or some other version. It was at the grave she received an email from Wiggy:

Have a lead on Anson Beck through Mossad. He's hiding in one of our old stomping grounds. Worked on our cover with your father ... will put everything into motion. So you know, Beck was at Cambridge the same time as Avery Gowen.

She remembered the shock that went through her. Was it possible Anson Beck had played a part at Congressional? She shook it off, wanting this chapter of her life to be over, knowing it wouldn't be until she and Beck met face-to-face a final time.

Late September in the U.S., capital was chilly. She snapped down the Hebridean summer cardigan. Though the invitation had said *'Coat and Tie,'* she refused to conform. Walking into the great hall, she despised the callousness of this gathering's location but, in a strange way, understood. Indeed, she was humored that it had been done specifically for her, as if to say, *Money is no longer the Party's problem.*

Surrounded by the teeming masses of pompous tuxedoed asses, she thought that soon would come the day … anywhere but Washington, D.C … she would once again pick up the microphone and speak into Wiggy's camera. In a strange way, she missed the gruff old bastard.

Hundreds of lemmings filled the hall, all paying homage to the shepherds who would lead them over the cliff. Be they male or female, of all races, hetero- or homosexual, they were dressed like their omnipotent leaders. Men and women, like those she exposed during a Congressional Suicide, who would do anything to be masters of their universe … and everyone else's. They had gathered to pay homage to America's oldest, slipperiest, and most powerful politician and to witness him taking his last stand at the lectern.

Dignitaries in uniforms, tuxedoes, and robes from all over the globe were in attendance. Party leaders, as well as the President and First Lady, assumed their rightful positions on the stage. Not surprisingly, few acknowledged their attendance.

Staring at Bridgewater with Dorothy Baldwin by his side once again … *until the end,* she thought. Kenna was glad the senator had taken her at her word. In her own way, though, Kenna had made a truce with Malcolm Bridgewater. The old man was a politician, something she would never understand. Indeed, Kenna was convinced that Bridgewater believed he was doing best for the country. Regardless, their friendship would never be the same. Indeed, it was over.

Kenna hadn't seen Charlie Sommer since that night at the 18th, though they talked often and promised to get together. She looked forward to that sooner rather than later. He had been too busy building his new career as a Washington Lobbyist. Remarkably, his first client was the Afghani government. Charlie brought out the worst and best in her. She admired that in a man.

Malcolm cut a swath through the crowd just as he had when Kenna was a girl, shaking hands with a politician's flawless expression. Though Kenna doubted many of them really listened to what was being said, the lemmings applauded every speech … the president was babbling now. It became more like a *'Dean Martin Roast'*. Sadly, the U.S.

now had Prime Time leadership. Center stage, Malcolm and Dorothy stood together as they had for over three decades.

Electricity shot through Kenna as a hand slid around her waist. She did not turn. The fresh, natural fragrance preceded the embrace by an instant.

"I've taken up private nursing as a second career and do house calls." Lips brushed her neck. "You owe me a drink."

Without turning, Kenna cradled his hand and lifted it to her mouth. His taste aroused her hormones ... as she remembered. She pulled him tight against her back, enjoying his arms around her body, the firmness of his perfect form fitting so well with hers.

"I know a quaint Thai place outside the city with cold beer," she said, squeezing his hand.

"You've been my only dream lately," he said, turned her, and kissed her flush on the lips.

She allowed a wry smile, then closed her eyes and enjoyed the dream, knowing it was real. She nodded to the podium where the president of the United States of America introduced the, "Retiring senator from the great Whiskey State of Tennessee, and ..."

An orchestra to the side of the stage drowned out the president's final words, undoubtedly by design. An array of balloons was unleashed from the ceiling and descended on the crowd. Popping like machinegun fire, they signaled the finale. Malcolm and Dorothy Bridgewater kissed at the podium and raised their hands together. Wedding rings sparkled in the spotlights and in public for the first time.

"Man and wife," Kenna said, as much to herself as to Charlie. "I was so wrong."

"What do you mean?" Charlie asked and broke the embrace to look at the podium.

'Born of youthful naiveté,' Gran Lockwood had once said. Or was it someone else? It didn't matter.

Kenna was no longer young and naïve. She knew The Chess Club wouldn't die with Malcolm Bridgewater's retirement or the death of Bernard Altmann. The pawn, all the pawns, assured it. Morningstar all but said so. The hard evidence of those events was but an unpleasant memory, lost in the archives of her country's past; shredded and cast into a landfill, buried for eternity by an army of bulldozers and earthmovers.

Charlie's grip tightened on her arm. "Married?"

"Since she came to Washington from—"

The orchestra played *The Tennessee Waltz*. Malcolm and Dorothy began the dance on the stage; everyone joined.

Kenna stared at the exit from the ballroom, once again wanting away from the Washington madhouse. At that moment, she knew she had to modify her article on the events at Congressional … she'd get to that later.

She shook her head, realizing, *Malcolm orchestrated only one thing: protection of The Chess Club member identities.*

"Malcolm was protecting her."

"Who?" Charlie asked.

"Dorothy Baldwin … she was the Queen of The Chess Club."

THE END